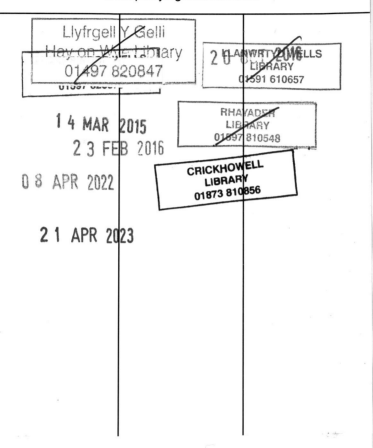

D1334869

37218 00540~~~

A SYMPHONY OF ECHOES

BOOK TWO OF
THE CHRONICLES OF ST MARY'S

JODI TAYLOR

**History is a symphony of echoes heard and unheard. It is a poem with events as verses.
Charles Angoff.**

Published by Accent Press Ltd 2013

ISBN 9781783751761

Printed and bound in the UK

This book is for Connie and Martin who had faith.
And for Dani who actually did it.
And for Christine.

Acknowledgments

My thanks to :

Everyone at Accent Press for their support and encouragement.

Ahmet for his technical support and explaining patiently that toast crumbs in your laptop are A Bad Thing.

Mike and Jan for their hospitality.

Peer Reviews for Just One Damned Thing After Another

Seriously?
L Farrell. Chief Technical Officer.

My office. Ten a.m. tomorrow morning, Dr Maxwell. Be there.
Dr E Bairstow. Director.

You really can't spell for tofee, can you?
T Peterson. Chief Training Officer.

You didn't put me in it.
Lydia Thighthruster. Housekeeping.

You made me a man?
M Markham. Security.

You made me a woman?
K Black. Liaison Officer.

In what universe can you actually sprint?
I Guthrie. Chief Security Officer.

I think there should have been more of me in it.
Professor A Rapson
Doctor O Dowson
Mrs T Mack
Mrs M Enderby
Et al.

Prologue

One of the best things about our job is that if you live long enough, you get to choose your last jump.

One of the worst things about our job is that, so far, no one has lived long enough to get to choose their last jump.

The last jump is supposed to be a quiet reward – the chance to enjoy a favourite moment in history – to visit Agincourt perhaps, or see Antony and Cleopatra floating down the Nile, or to hear Elizabeth I addressing the troops at Tilbury. To witness some epoch-making event of your choice. To fulfil a lifelong ambition.

In short, it's supposed to be enjoyable.

It is not supposed to be a whirling nightmare of blood and pain and terror.

It is not supposed to be about savage butchery, mutilation, beheading, and having half your face ripped off.

It is not supposed to be about dying in a blood-drenched pod, trapped with a monster and no way out.

It is not supposed to be about the paralysing horror of seeing your best friend ripped open to the bone and having to put her out of her pain.

It is not supposed to be about being abandoned and never seeing the sun again.

It's not supposed to be about any of that.

Chapter One

God only knew where we were, we couldn't see a thing. A real pea-souper. I said, 'Do you know where we are?'

'Well,' said Kal, 'we're in Whitechapel, in the right place at the right time. It's about eleven o'clock on the night of 8th November 1888. Not bad, eh? More accurate than I thought we would be. I suggest we tuck ourselves away in a pub somewhere and wait and see what happens. They say that tonight's is his last victim. Maybe that's because he gets to meet us in a dark alley.'

'We can't kill him,' I said, alarmed.

'No, but we could certainly scare the living crap out of him.'

I considered. That sounded good.

I'd read around the subject. Jack the Ripper famously terrorised London in the summer and autumn of 1888. There were eleven murders altogether, although only five are generally credited to the Ripper – Mary Nichols, Annie Chapman, Elizabeth White, Catherine Eddowes, and Mary Kelly. Kelly was murdered and horrifically mutilated in the very early hours of the 9th November, 1888 and although there were other killings afterwards, she was generally reckoned to be his last victim. She had lived in Miller's Court, off Dorset Road, and that was where we were headed.

Contrary to popular belief, we historians aren't completely stupid. We may have looked like a couple of poor but honest shop girls, but the amount of weaponry we had stashed around our persons was considerable. Although if the combined forces of H Division, the City of London police, and Scotland Yard themselves had failed to catch the Ripper, there was very little chance of us doing so. For Kal, this was a long-held ambition and her last jump. For me, it was just an adventure. I don't think either of us actually expected to see him.

We headed for the Ten Bells where Kelly was supposed to have spent her last evening. She left, late, to walk the streets, and she would take a man back to her tiny room. Her body would be discovered the next morning by Thomas Bowyer calling for the rent.

It was hopeless. The pub was heaving. There was no way we could pick her out. There could have been twenty Mary Kellys in there and we didn't want to draw any attention to ourselves by asking around.

Despite the November chill, the inside was hot, steamy, and smelled strongly of people and drink. We ordered a gin each and wedged ourselves in the corner where we got talking to a very jolly man, George Carter.

'Carter by name, carter for gain!' he said cheerfully, 'and my wife, Dolly.'

It turned out he knew the two men who'd discovered Mary Nichols.

'A shocking thing,' he said, draining his glass and wiping his mouth. 'Can I get you ladies anything?'

We declined politely, but he had plenty more to say about the 'Autumn of Terror' as it was dubbed by the newspapers and recited details with relish and at great length.

'Still, it's all finished now,' he said with authority, slapping huge hands on his fat knees. We did not look at each other. 'There are so many coppers around here you can't fart these days without at least three of them turning up. Carter the Farter, eh?' Our little party had greatly increased as others contributed their thoughts and reactions and we all laughed.

The hour was considerably advanced when we eventually got up to go. He was a decent man, was George Carter. His wife prodded him and he said, 'Now then, you ladies. Are you all right to get home? If not, there's Jabez here, or my son Albert,

4

or Jonas Allbright; they're all good lads. They all work for me and you can trust them to see you home safe and sound. I know we've had no more of it these last few weeks, but I have girls of my own and I don't let them walk the streets these days. Just say the word.'

'It's very kind of you, Mr Carter, said Kal, 'but we're not far away. Round the corner, just past ...' she cast round for a name, 'Castle Alley.'

'Well, if you're sure of it, we'll say goodnight to you.' With loud cries of goodnight and promises to meet again, we got away. Setting off at a brisk walk, we hardly weaved at all.

'Bloody hell,' said Kal, leaning against a wall and fanning herself. 'What was in that gin?'

'Lots more gin?' I said, helpfully. It had tasted like the landlord had made it in the bath and while he was still sitting in it, too.

'You didn't drink much, did you? You know what you're like.'

'Just a few sips. I stopped when my lips went numb.'

'Right,' she said, straightening up. 'Let's get –' and something came silently out of the fog, moving quickly, indistinguishable. I got a split-second impression of a long white face and black clothing. There was a nasty smell, but that was nothing unusual in this time and place. And then it was gone.

We looked at each other.

'Do you think ...?' I said. 'What's the time?'

'It's well after two. It could have been him, I suppose. I certainly didn't like the look of him, did you?'

'No,' I said slowly, staring into the swirling fog. 'No, I did not.'

'Come on, then.'

And we were off.

Except we weren't. You can't run on wet, slippery cobbles when you can't see your hand in front of your face, but we made the best speed we could down the rubbish-strewn street, peering down alleyways and into doorways. Looking for Jack

5

the Ripper.

And then we found him. Or rather, he found us.

We ran. My God, how we ran.

We ran until I thought my lungs would explode. We ran down dark, narrow, noisome alleyways, slipping and sliding on God knows what. We ran down deserted cobbled streets, their surfaces greasy with rain and heavy traffic. My stupid skirts kept wrapping themselves around my legs. My bonnet was falling off. And the bloody corset and bustle we'd had to wear for that authentic S-shaped silhouette were both likely to be the death of me.

Gas lighting had come to Whitechapel, but the lamps were few and far between, and we couldn't see clearly, each glow being just a faint nimbus in all this heavy fog. We blundered into piles of lumber, rubbish heaps, crates, and each other. We fell down unexpected steps. We fled, headlong, down empty streets that should, according to the newspapers of 1888, have been packed with policemen from H Division, but were not. My own frantic heartbeats pounded in my ears. It wasn't blind panic because we're historians, and therefore we don't do blind panic. But it wasn't far off.

It was our own fault. We'd brought this on ourselves. This was Kal's last jump. Her lifelong ambition – to see Jack the Ripper. Full of overwhelming confidence and conceit, and certain no 19th century monster could take on two modern historians armed with attitude, curiosity, and an overdeveloped sense of immortality – we'd gone looking for him.

And we'd found him. A figure rearing up suddenly out of the fog; right up close and more than personal; an ill-defined shape smelling of blood and decay and reaching out – for us. Suddenly, the chase was on and we were running. Running, although we didn't know it at the time, for more than our lives.

When we stopped being the hunters and became the hunted.

We flew through the maze of Whitechapel streets and alleyways, up and down steps, confident we would soon lose him in the choking, throat-rasping pea-souper. But we didn't. It seemed that wherever we went, he was there first. A shape in the fog from which we would wheel away and try another way out. We thought we had only to get back to our pod to be safe.

But we weren't anything like as clever as we thought we were. Because, in all that running, all that falling, all that headlong dash to get back to safety, it never occurred to us at all. We just thought we were running for our lives.

When actually, we were being herded.

As we ran, we looked and listened – every sense we possessed pinging off our surroundings. Alert for any sound, any movement, anything at all that would give us the slightest idea where he was. Because he was here. Somewhere, not far away, he was here. Possibly, even close enough to reach a hand out of the darkness and …

Kal skidded to a halt, I crashed into the back of her, and we both fell into a handy doorway. My chest heaved, trying to take in enough oxygen to fuel my screaming muscles. My legs trembled. I leaned forwards, put my hands on my knees, and fought for breath in my bloody corset.

'We can't stay,' panted Kal. 'We've got to keep moving. If he catches us – we're done.'

I nodded. However, we were still alive and that was something. More than could be said for Mary Kelly, anyway. I reached into my muff and looped my stun gun around my wrist. I had pepper spray as well and I was more than happy to use both.

'Come on,' said Kal, urgently. 'The pod's this way.'

Off we went again, but more carefully now, partly because we thought we had his measure and partly because we were exhausted. Kal led the way and I followed behind, watching our backs.

We stopped at a junction and took a few seconds to try to get our breath back, listening to the eerie, wet silence. We stood back to back. I screwed up my eyes in an effort to penetrate the thick tendrils of yellow-grey fog coiling around us.

Then, faintly, in the distance, we heard it again. A tiny

sound.

Behind us.

Moving as quietly as we could, we set off. Ignoring historical accuracy, Kal had a small torch. It was almost useless. The fog just swirled the light back at us. Thick and dirty-yellow, it tasted of cheap coal, stung my throat and made my eyes run. I'd read about these pea-soupers. Thousands of people in London died every year from lung complaints. And don't even get me started on The Great Stink.

'God knows what this is doing to our lungs,' said Kal.

'Thank God I can't breathe properly. Otherwise I might be dead by now.'

'Oh, stop moaning. I bring you for a nice night out and all you do is complain.'

'When I'm coughing up half a ton of black sputum tomorrow ...' and there was that sound again. Closer this time.

'Down here,' said Kal and we stood at the entrance to a long, narrow alleyway with high, windowless walls on each side. We'd have to go single file. I felt the hairs on my neck lift. The alley was very black and I really, really did not want to go down there.

'Do you think the fog is lifting?'

Actually, I thought it was. I thought I could make out a small, light patch ahead, which, if the god of historians was with us, might be the exit.

'OK, are you ready?

'Kal ...'

'Yeah, I know. But he's behind us and the pod is this way. We just have to get through this next bit and we're home and dry.'

We both took a deep breath. She went first, with the torch. I walked behind her with my hand on her shoulder, half-turned, so I could watch our backs. I had my stun gun and a deep sense of unease.

Only too aware of how sound could carry, I whispered, 'Are you armed?'

'Torch and gun.'

8

'You brought a gun?'

'You didn't?'

'No, I did not.'

'Don't panic. It's contemporary. Remington Derringer. They were known as muff pistols.'

'That does not make it all right.'

The fog shifted above us. We both looked up. I had the impression we had just missed seeing something. When I looked down again, I couldn't see the light at the entrance to the alleyway behind me. Something blocked the way. Something stood behind us. Something big. I felt a chill that had nothing to do with the weather. I always knew that one day we would bite off more than we could chew.

'Kal, something's behind us.'

Her arm appeared over my shoulder with the torch. Suddenly, shockingly close, I had the briefest glimpse of something wet and white, glistening in the flashlight. It moved with unnatural speed, knocking the torch out of her hand and brushing past us. It pushed me hard, but I managed to stay upright. I set my back against the wall, stun gun raised, covering us both.

'Kal,' I said, urgently. 'Are you all right?'

'I'm here,' she said faintly, close by. 'I think I've been stabbed. I'm bleeding.'

Every instinct I had told me to get out of that alley. To run. To flee blindly. Anywhere. Just get out. Get away. I took as deep a breath as I could manage in my stupid Victorian costume. Then another.

Historians don't panic.

Although we do.

I bent, found the torch, and switched it on. Contrary to all convention – it still worked. Flashing it up and down the alley, I could see nothing near us. For some reason I checked above as well. Looking ahead, I could see the exit. Closer than I thought. The fog *was* lifting.

'Can you run?'

'Oh yes. It's only my arm.'

We moved as fast as we could. Kal had hold of my arm and I relied on her to guide me because I was going backwards.

Again, I swallowed down my urge to run flat out. This narrow space was a death trap. We would be caught here. Crushed between these blind walls with no room to move. Nowhere to run. We were kicking aside litter and debris as we went.

'Nearly there,' whispered Kal and, with heart-stopping speed, the light at the end of our tunnel disappeared again.

I just had time to shout, 'Kal, he's back,' and a shape was upon us, looming above, smelling of blood and earth. I zapped him and he fell back with a hiss.

'Move,' I said, pushing her. 'Go, go, go.'

She took off and I followed, running crab-wise, watching her back as she was watching mine. Trying to cover all angles at once, heart pounding, desperate, *desperate* to get out of this enclosed space.

It was such an old movie cliché. To die on her last assignment. I wasn't going to let it happen to her. I was scared, and when I get scared, I get angry. Nothing would happen to Kal. I would get her back safely. I swore it to myself.

We erupted out of the alley into a wider street, skirts bunched high. Kal had her pistol. I had my pepper spray. We stood, back to back, staring into the night, ready to take on anything that followed us out.

Nothing happened. Nothing followed us out of the alleyway. The street was empty. A few dim lights showed in nearby houses, but all good citizens were in bed. It was just us on the streets. I stood panting, my ribs struggling in that bloody corset. Where did he go? How could he disappear? Had the jolt from the stun gun seen him off? He would not be used to women who fought back. We circled slowly, back to back. Nothing. We circled again. Still nothing. We were alone. Slowly, my breathing and heart rate returned to acceptable levels.

'Well,' said Kal, tucking her little pistol back into her muff. 'That was fun. Do you think it was him?'

I inspected her arm while she kept watch over my shoulder.

It wasn't deep but, as we say, it would sting in the morning.

'I don't know. I do know I didn't like the look of him. Or the smell. And what are the odds there would be two maniacs wandering the streets of Whitechapel tonight?'

'Other than us?'

Brave words aside, she was beginning to shiver. The sweat drying on my face and back was making me cold, too. We took a final look up and down the street. Whitechapel seemed strangely deserted. I suspected that pre-Ripper these streets were never quiet. Even after dark, all sorts of nocturnal transactions would have been taking place. But not tonight.

I was my usual directionally challenged self. 'Where's the pod from here?'

'Not far, actually. Just past that corner. On waste ground.'

Arm in arm, striding determinedly down the centre of the street, we set off. Our footsteps echoed off the buildings. An eerie sound. A small breeze stirred the ribbons of fog. I kept looking over my shoulder, unable to believe we had escaped that easily. Instead of being lost in the mazed streets of Whitechapel, we were exactly where we needed to be.

Because we'd been herded.

Chapter Two

Ages ago – when I was a kid – I was hiding. I remember crouching in the dark, eyes tight shut, not breathing, not thinking, fighting the overwhelming awareness of someone close by. I had exactly the same feeling now. Something was close by and –

'There!' said Kal. 'There's the pod. Over there.'

Good old Number Five was sitting exactly where we'd left it, which, when you've been to the Cretaceous Period and watched your pod sliding down a mountain without you, is always a relief.

We tripped and slipped our way over the rough ground, constantly turning, weapons raised. I could see dark blood running off Kal's fingers. She looked pale and was moving more slowly than usual. However, once I got her back inside the pod, dressed her wound, and got something alcoholic inside her, she'd be fine.

We were nearly there. We stopped about twenty feet from the pod. Kal called for the door to open and we did a slow 360-degree turn, just in case anything was still hanging around, but we could see nothing. Whatever it was had gone. And bloody good riddance too.

Half disappointed and half relieved, we backed slowly towards the pod. I darted the torch around. It seemed to take a very long time to get through that door. All the hair on my neck stood on end. I was physically fighting the urge just to drop everything and run.

'Keep going,' said Kal softly, patting my arm. 'We're nearly there.'

And then we were. The door closed behind us, shutting out the night and the monster. We were warm and safe at last and this was something to tell them back at St Mary's.

Number Five was Kal's favourite pod. They'd been through a lot together, but they'd both survived. Unlike my pod – Number Eight – still badly damaged after emergency extraction from the Cretaceous Period last year, and lying in pieces all over Hawking Hangar as Chief Farrell and his technical crew attempted to reassemble it.

The console and computer were to the right of the door in Number Five, with the two lumpy and uncomfortable crew seats bolted to the floor in front of it. The toilet was in a partitioned corner. Various lockers around the walls contained all the equipment any historian could possible require. Most importantly, a kettle, a couple of mugs, and a small chiller containing a bottle of something potent provided the essentials of life.

Pods are our centre of operations; solid, apparently stone-built shacks which jump us back to whichever period we've been assigned and from which we work, eat, and sleep. They are cramped, frequently squalid, and despite all the technical section's best efforts, the toilet never works properly. Number Five smelled as all pods do – hot historians, wet carpet, overloaded electrics, unreliable plumbing, and cabbage.

Bunches of thick cables ran up the walls and looped their way across the ceiling. Lights flashed amongst the mass of dials, gauges and read-outs on the console. The co-ordinates were all laid-in ready for the return jump. The effect was shabby hi-tec. Scruffy and battered. Just like us historians. Just like all of St Mary's, really.

We work for the Institute of Historical Research, based at St Mary's Priory just outside Rushford. We don't do time-travel. That's for amateurs. We're not time-travellers – we're historians. We *investigate major historical events in contemporary time*. So much more classy. We're fairly stand-alone, but we answer to the University of Thirsk for our funding. Sometimes, it's not a happy relationship, but we'd recently pulled off a huge coup, successfully rescuing books from the burning Library at Alexandria. At the moment, Thirsk loved us. That wouldn't last.

I helped Kal pull off her coat. As decreed by the fashion of the late 1880s, it was tight fitting, including the sleeves and this had helped prevent too much blood loss. I ripped the sleeve of her blouse (there would be a reproachful memo from Wardrobe in the morning) and slapped on a sterile dressing.

'There you go, as good as new. Sit down. I'll put everything away. Don't get cold. Put your coat back on.' She shrugged it on again. She wore navy blue. I had grey. Both outfits looked shabby but well cared-for. We had gone for the poor-but-honest-shop-girls look. Our bustles had caused much hilarity amongst our heathen colleagues. Our corsets had nearly bloody killed us.

I stuffed her pistol and torch back inside her muff and dropped it on her lap. She sat stroking the soft material. 'There's a bottle in the chiller. Shall we have a final drink for my final mission?'

I got the bottle and a couple of mugs and she did the honours. 'Cheers.'

'Cheers, Kal. All the best.'

We chugged back a mugful and I felt myself begin to relax a little. It had been a strenuous night, but it was over now. Time to unwind before going back. We leaned back and put our feet up on the console.

'My God,' said Kal, regarding me with a strange mix of euphoria, astonishment and sadness. 'That was my last jump. I've survived. I've actually survived. Do you know, there were times when I never thought I would? That night in Brussels after the Duchess of Richmond's ball – I lost Peterson in the chaos and thought I'd never find him or the pod again. The Corn Law Riots. That time with you at the Somme. Do you remember running through all that mud? Or Alexandria, when Professor Rapson nearly blew us all to kingdom come? I survived it all. And now, we may have seen the Ripper and lived. I've made it. I never thought I would.'

She shook her head in disbelief.

'Yep, the stories you won't be able to tell your kids.'

She laughed and drained her mug.

I leaned forward to refill.

'Will you miss it, do you think?'

'Oh God, yes. Yes, I'll miss it.'

'Then … why?'

She sighed. 'I want something more. This has been enormous fun. Still is. But I want something else. You may not understand, Max, but Dieter and I … well, maybe one day … maybe one day, I'll want a kid. I don't know. I'm not sure what I want, but I do know this isn't enough any more.' She smiled at me. 'And maybe, one day, you'll feel the same.'

'Unlikely.'

'Max, you never know.'

'We'll see.'

I didn't know else what to say. I couldn't allow myself to think about how much I would miss her. She was my rock, confidante, co-conspirator, drinking companion, and lifesaver. Whatever was required. The word 'friend' didn't even begin to cover it. I couldn't comprehend a world without her. And she was leaving St Mary's. This was her traditional last jump. She was going off to work as our liaison officer at the University of Thirsk. She'd been promoted.

As had all three of us.

Tim Peterson was now Chief Training Officer, and in a moment of inexplicable madness, Dr Bairstow had appointed me Chief Operations Officer. Since my responsibilities now included those loveable pyromaniacs in Research and Development, I still wasn't sure whether this was A Good Thing or not.

My name is Madeleine Maxwell. I shed the name Madeleine along with my childhood. Unlike Tim and Kal, I'm not tall, slender, and blonde. I'm short, ginger and, while not exactly fat, Leon Farrell, in a breathless and tangled moment, once described me as having *a great deal of barely-restrained exuberance in areas above and below the waist*. I did challenge

16

him on that, but since by then he'd lost the ability to speak, and seconds later, I lost the ability to hear, whatever he did mean remains unclear.

Back in the pod, Kal watched me as I sipped my wine.

'So, new challenges ahead for all of us. And you, Max, as Chief Operations Officer, you're going to have to start behaving yourself. No more getting drunk. Or sacked. Or stealing pods. Or seducing Chief Technical Officers. You'll be *Doctor* Maxwell, now. You'll have responsibilities.'

'Not a problem,' I said, taking off my stupid bonnet and dropping it on the floor beside my seat. 'According to the Boss, I've been pretty well responsible for everything that's happened at St Mary's since I walked through the door. Do you want a top-up?'

'And now, you have staff,' she said, laughing at me.

Yes, I had an assistant …

After a lively night celebrating our promotions, (during which we added to the list of things for which I was responsible), I was having a very careful late breakfast.

Mrs Partridge appeared at the table, soundlessly, as she always does. Perhaps it's in her job spec. *Wanted – PA to Director. Must be able to materialise at most inconvenient moments and look judgemental.*

'Dr Maxwell, I'd like to talk to you about your assistant.'

I'd never had one before. I tried to find some enthusiasm.

She said, 'I wonder if you remember David Sands.'

'Of course I do,' I said. 'He's the trainee who was involved in that road accident just outside Rushford. Is he out of hospital now?'

'He is, and has been for several months. He's ready to return to St Mary's – is keen to return, in fact. But he'll never be an historian now. He accepts this, not easily, but he's a boy of great intelligence and character. The final decision is yours, of course, but it occurred to me he would make a very suitable assistant. Would you like to meet him?'

'Certainly,' I said. 'When?'

'No time like the present.' She stepped aside.

David Sands was in a wheelchair. I turned in my seat and held out my hand. 'Mr Sands.'

'Dr Maxwell.'

'I'll leave you for a moment,' said Mrs Partridge and disappeared to wherever she goes.

The two of us looked at each other. His hair was shorter than usual for an historian because he wouldn't need the traditional '*one style fits all centuries*' look and his thin face showed lines of strain and pain.

I tried to remember how job interviews went.

'Tell me why you're exactly what I need.'

'I'm efficient and intelligent. I have my doctorate just like you. I know how this place works. I know who to go to for what. I can take a ton of work off your shoulders. I can perform tasks before you even know you need them done. I know how you like your tea and I've got an endless supply of knock-knock jokes.'

He had his doctorate. He could go and work at the University of Thirsk, at a job commensurate with his qualifications, but like the rest of us, St Mary's was in his blood and he'd rather be an assistant here than a higher paid something else somewhere else.

I was mystified. 'How do you get around the building?'

'Oh, that's not a problem. I go up and down in the heavy goods lift.'

I frowned. 'That doesn't seem right.'

'No, it's OK. Professor Rapson is usually in there with something interesting and we have some good chats. He's going to try and raise my speed limit.'

'You're going to let Professor Rapson tinker with your chair? You'll probably go into orbit. What sort of idiot are you?'

'I'm hoping I'm the idiot who works for you, Dr Maxwell.'

'So am I. You sound too good to be true. What's your position on chocolate?'

'You can never have enough,' he said, pulling a handful of miscellaneous chocolate bars from mysterious depths.

'You're hired,' I said. 'Starting now.'

Mrs Partridge appeared and raised her eyebrows.

'Don't say a word.'

She smirked and left.

So, that's what I had to go back to. Promotion, my own office, and an assistant with the world's biggest collection of knock-knock jokes. I'd need him. I had a big assignment to plan. Last year we had acquired a collection of Shakespeare sonnets and a perfectly genuine, previously-unknown Shakespeare play entitled *The Scottish Queen*. Unfortunately, in this play, a careless 16th century executed the wrong sovereign and Mary Stuart, the Tartan Trollop, went on to unite Scotland and England, and apparently change the course of History. As soon as I got back and washed the Whitechapel grime from my hair, I'd have to get to grips with that. My future was looking good.

Wrong.

'Are we all set?'

'Yes, let's get back.'

I dropped my muff on the console, smoothed my clothes, and patted my hair tidy. Historians never go back looking scruffy. Sometimes we go back dead, but even then, we always make sure we look good. Kal initiated the countdown, and the world went white.

Moments later, we were back at St Mary's. There were a few people around the hangar, but I guessed the majority were in the bar. We had a bit of a do planned for her. Kal operated the decontamination system to dispose of any nasty little Victorian germs, and we waited for the blue glow to subside. She was watching the screen and shutting things down.

With probably the only stroke of good luck we had that night, I was looking towards the door, directly at my muff, so I saw it happen. I thought afterwards, it would have been so easy to miss such a tiny thing. We would have blithely opened the door, and who knows what would have been unleashed upon the world, and it would all have been our fault.

The muff moved.

Just slightly.

All by itself – it moved.

I was looking directly at it. Kal, too, had spotted it from the corner of her eye. Just for a second, I couldn't think at all and then it hit me like a demolition ball. The only explanation possible. I felt my blood drain.

Something else was here. Something was in here with us. Unbelievably, something we couldn't see was in here with us. Something that was so eager to get out of the door that it had made the tiniest, clumsy mistake. We were not alone in this pod. We'd brought something back with us.

Casually, I turned my head to look at Kal. She was white to the lips. I'd never seen her look like that. She was deathly afraid. And if Kal was afraid, then so was I.

Something was in here with us and no one was getting out alive.

Chapter Three

People think we historians are lightweights. They think we whizz up and down the timeline, document a couple of battles or the odd revolution, swan back to St Mary's, and spend the night in the bar. To some extent, that's true. However, when it goes wrong for us, it really goes wrong. I remembered my friend and fellow-trainee, Kevin Grant, killed on his very first mission. Or Anne-Marie Lower sitting on the floor of her pod, blank-eyed and covered in blood, as her partner died in her arms. But this was the worst thing that could happen. Worse than death because our end was not going to be quick and it was not going to be easy.

We were contaminated.

It's not supposed to happen. Pods are not supposed to be able to jump with any foreign objects on board. If ever we inadvertently brought something into the pod then it just wouldn't jump. Simple as that. God knows how this had happened. However, happen it had and we were really in the shit. The rules were very clear. No one was getting out of this pod. Ever.

And we couldn't take him back. History states very clearly that Mary Kelly was his last victim. After tonight, he vanished. And now we knew why. So we couldn't jump back to Whitechapel and just kick him out to continue his reign of terror. Even if we could, we wouldn't.

I looked at Kal, who had obviously come to exactly the same conclusion as me. She gave me a small, sad smile, and after only the briefest pause, said lightly, 'Would you do the honours please, Max?' and slipped her hands into her muff.

I activated the external speaker together with the internal cameras so they could see what was going on. Whatever was in here with us mustn't know that we knew, so I said slowly and calmly, 'Attention, please. This is Pod Five. This is Pod Five. Code Blue. Code Blue. Code Blue. I say again, this is Pod Five declaring a Code Blue. Authorisation Maxwell, five zero alpha nine eight zero four bravo. This is not a drill.' I sat back leaving the mike open.

'Balls to the wall, Max,' said Kal softly and stood up. I got to my feet as well and we both moved casually, oh so casually, to the door, where we turned, to face back into the pod, backs protected, shoulder to shoulder. And much good it would do us.

She drew herself up and said commandingly, 'Show yourself. We know you're here. Show yourself.'

It wasn't invisible. But there are ways of not being seen. Something changed in our perception. Like staring at those 3D coloured dot pictures and suddenly you realise you're looking at a giraffe riding a bike. Nothing changes, but suddenly you can see it.

We saw it now.

It was tall and bony. Man-shaped. An unhealthy grey-white pallor. A bloodless thing. Damp skin glistened in the harsh light of the pod. I thought of a white slug, except slugs are fleshy. This thing had no flesh on it anywhere. Huge hands, big as shovels, with thick, yellow nails were caked with Mary Kelly's dried blood. Long arms hung loosely at his sides, reaching to his knees, palms turned backwards. The eyes were dark and hidden within creases of moist skin. They reflected nothing – light was captured, but not reflected. A one-way entrance to something unspeakable. The proportions of its face were all wrong. The too-big mouth was half way up its face. The chin was long, pointed, and not symmetrical. The nose was not central but set off to one side. There was no septum. This was something that had been put together wrong. I could smell bad earth. My stomach clenched. I clutched my stun gun in one hand and pepper spray in the other, but my defiance was only

22

for show. This was the thing known as Jack the Ripper and his record spoke for itself. There was no escape for us. This was going to be bad.

Kal spoke again, and her voice was firm and without fear. I never admired her more. 'Can you understand me?'

It dipped its chin.

'Then listen closely. I know who you are. I know what you've done. Look around. You are imprisoned in a pod. You will never leave it again. None of us will leave this pod alive. Do you understand?'

It dipped its chin.

'You heard my colleague. She declared Code Blue. That means we are contaminated. This pod is no longer under our control. We cannot open the door. We cannot get out. You cannot get out. We will all die in here. Do you understand?'

It hissed.

I gestured to the screen. 'Look.'

It leaned forward and I took the opportunity to move half a step closer. Outside, all the techies had disappeared. They'd dimmed the lights to a blue glow. A double ring of hazmat-dressed security guards surrounded the pod. Front row kneeling; back row standing. They all had some very serious weaponry pointed directly at us.

It dipped its chin.

'They cannot get in,' I lied. 'This pod is impregnable. They have only one purpose. To shoot dead anything and everything that might try to leave. They have firepower the like of which you cannot imagine. If you do somehow manage to get out, they will shoot you dead. And me. And my colleague. Everything in this pod is doomed. Do you understand?'

For the first time, it shook its head.

'I think not.'

Its voice was deep, thick and sibilant, with a slight accent. It had difficulty speaking. Its tongue was purple and far too big for its mouth. Yellow and brown saliva crusted the corners of its lips. The thought of them touching me was unbearable.

It spoke again. 'I think they will not be so happy to see such

23

pretty girls … suffer. I think when you have both screamed for a day, then they will be willing to open the door. Especially when they hear you beg.'

Kal shook her head. 'That will not happen. That door will never open again. There is no food or water here. After a week, we will be dead, either by your hand, or by ours. The guards will not move. They will stay until they see we cannot possibly be alive. On that day, they will take this pod and bury it for ever. It will be your tomb. I don't know what you are, or if you can die or not, but I hope for your sake you can, because otherwise you will sit here in this tiny box, alone in the cold and the dark, until the end of time. You should not have followed us here. You have made a big mistake. Do you understand?'

It dipped its chin. 'I understand but I do not agree. I propose to put it to the test.'

Suddenly it was in front of us. I never saw it move. I jerked up my stun gun but it was knocked from my hands before I could fire. The same blow knocked me sideways. I rolled as I heard Kal scream. Her gun went off. I saw its arm rise and fall, rise and fall, slashing and ripping. Kal screamed again. I grabbed the fire extinguisher off the wall and jabbed it into the side of its face. Something gave, but it had no real effect. Kal swung her arm and I heard the bottle break.

I reached behind my head and pulled out a long hairpin. I meant to shove it down its ear but it turned its head, and I sunk it into its eye instead. No credit to me, it did it to itself. It uttered a shrieking, wailing sort of cry and fell backwards, clawing with clumsy hands. I followed it up with a short blast of pepper spray, directly into its ruined eye.

It wailed again and threw itself at me. I saw nothing, but suddenly my face was on fire. I thought it had thrown the kettle at me. I could feel hot liquid running down my face and thought I'd been scalded. Its breath was in my face, its tongue falling from its mouth. I thought I was finished when, from the floor, Kal said hoarsely, 'Now,' and wrapped her arms around its legs, just below the knees. I shoved hard. It crashed to the floor. Hard. The impact caused a locker door to swing open, and hazily, I saw the fire axe.

I seized the extinguisher again and dropped it from waist height onto its face. It bellowed, its broken mouth opening and closing. Its arms flailed on Kal's back, ripping through fabric and flesh, through to the bone. She was still screaming, but she never let go. She wrapped herself around it, hampering its movements as best she could. She was my friend and she never let go.

I fumbled for the fire axe.

It's really not that easy to chop someone's head off. I swung the axe wildly. I couldn't see properly. I nearly took my own foot off twice. It took eleven strokes. I counted them. Every one. There was blood everywhere. Our blood. Kal's and mine. Kal was soaked in it. I couldn't make out the colour of her hair. I wasn't even sure she was still alive. My whole front was red with fresh, wet blood. I had no idea where it was all coming from. I didn't know half my face was hanging off.

On the eleventh stroke, the mangled head slowly rolled away from the body. A small amount of a thick, brownish-fluid oozed sluggishly from the torso, wrinkled almost immediately, and began to congeal. The smell made me heave.

Suddenly, there was silence.

A soft moan from Kal brought me back. Without letting go of the axe, I pulled out a pillow and got her to curl up around it.

'Press hard, Kal; try to stop the bleeding.' She was deathly white, but nodded slightly. She was still with me.

I stepped back, carefully avoiding that sticky pool of fluid. I leaned against the wall, chest heaving in that sodding corset and tried to get a grip. I had a vague idea of re-setting the co-ordinates to somewhere such as the Cretaceous, and just pitching it out of the pod. I really didn't want to spend what little time I had left with that thing rotting nearby. However, I no longer had any control over this pod. We were going to die in here. We couldn't get out.

I turned and looked at the screen. All the security team was still there – no one had moved. The Boss, Dieter, Peterson – they would all be watching this from the monitor room. I spared a thought for them. And Leon Farrell – what was he feeling at this moment? I couldn't afford to think about that now. I turned back into the pod.

And then, oh God, the worst moment of all.

Even as I looked, the head, a good eighteen inches from the torso and with one of my hairpins still sticking out of its eye, rolled back on itself. Back towards the body. The remaining eye opened, found me, and faintly, the lips smiled.

I've had some bad moments in my life and there were more to come, but this was one of the worst because I realised then that this was just part of the game. These were just the opening moves. I looked around at the blood-soaked pod, Kalinda, unconscious and possibly dying at my feet and then back again to this un-killable thing. This was it. This was hell. There was no escape. We were damned for all eternity. And this was just the first fifteen minutes.

The gun! Somewhere in this abattoir was Kal's gun. We had no hope of survival, but I could make our ending a great deal easier. I would shoot Kal and then myself. Then they could bury the pod, or drop it into the sea, and that would be the end of it.

I scrabbled one-handed, clumsy because I wouldn't take my eyes off whatever it was for more than a second, and I wasn't going to let go of the axe, either. I found the gun kicked under my seat. Only one shot fired.

I stood over Kal, emptied my head of all thoughts, and commended our souls to the god of historians.

Something crackled and I imagined that a voice said, 'Max, stand down. Put down the gun.'

I tightened my grip and blinked away the tears. Don't weaken now.

The door opened. Four masked and suited guards were there, two standing, two kneeling, weapons raised and swinging back and forth, covering every inch of the pod.

Major Guthrie said, 'Max, it's me, Ian. Put down the gun,' and stepping carefully through the blood, crossed to the toilet and pulled open the door. Another guard immediately took his place. Together, they formed an impenetrable barrier across the door. Nothing could get out.

He shouted, 'Clear!' and shouldering his weapon, bent over Kal, looking for a pulse. 'OK, let's get her out.'

Two men entered, picked up Kal, and carried her out.

I said, 'Make sure you don't stand in its blood,' but they told me afterwards it just came out as a series of meaningless sounds.

He came to stand in front of me. 'Max, it's Ian. Let go of the gun and the axe.'

I kept trying to look around him. I must not take my eyes off the head. I tried to tell him.

Finally, he said, 'What?' and I tried to signal with my eyes.

He turned round and said, 'He's very, very dead, Max. He's never going to do anyone any harm ever again,' and, then, thank God, just as he looked, the head moved again. Another small movement. Back towards the body.

He stood frozen for a minute and then said in a very different voice, 'Where's that axe?' He swung once, twice, three times, powerful blows with the full force of his body behind them. We both stared at the crushed, ruined head. Even then, I wasn't convinced. Neither was he.

'I'll see to all this, Max. Let's get you out. Leave all this to me.'

I tried to say something about contamination, but he said, 'Will you trust me to do this right?'

I nodded.

He carried me out of that stinking pod, through the plastic containment tunnel, into a small plastic treatment room and wonderful, glorious, fresh air.

I couldn't see Kal at all for the people bending over her. She was hooked up to all sorts of drips and stuff. They were calm but urgent. The bloody pillow lay on the floor with soiled dressings all around. They were cutting her clothes off her. Masked and suited figures appeared around me, cutting off my view. My turn.

Someone said, 'Close your eyes,' and I felt cool liquid

27

running across my face.

Someone else said, 'Keep irrigating. Don't stop.'

I recognised Nurse Hunter. Dr Foster must be with Kal.

Hunter bent over me. 'Hello, Max, what have you been up to now? Everything's fine. We're just going to have a look.'

They started to cut off my clothes, as well. Mrs Enderby, our wardrobe mistress, was not going to be pleased with us at all. I tried to tell them to bag everything, but no one was listening, and after all, we were in an isolation tent. It wasn't likely they would just carelessly toss it all away. Let them get on with it. I started to shiver.

'OK, let's have some heat pads here. Elevate the feet. Hang on, Max.' Voices came and went, the way they do when you doze off in front of the television.

'Cuts and abrasions on her forearms – probably defensive wounds, one is very deep indeed. Two deep gashes across her left ankle and some minor cuts to the abdomen. Nothing too serious, Max. You'll live to be grateful to that corset. In fact, we're ditching the Kevlar and replacing it with whalebone.'

I don't know why medical staff think they have a sense of humour. I went for a smear test last year and Helen swore there was an echo. How funny is that?

Stripping off her gloves, Helen replaced Hunter. 'She's still with us, Max. We're taking her upstairs now.' I saw her eyes shift to Hunter, who shook her head slightly. 'Don't be alarmed. You have a couple of bad cuts on your face. We're keeping them clean and Dr Bairstow wants you sent off to the big plastics unit at Wendover. Everything's under control here. You concentrate on you.'

Fog billowed and swirled like silk. A T-rex lowered its fearsome head, looked at me, decided it couldn't be bothered and wandered off, to be replaced by Major Guthrie saying, 'They're on their way – ten minutes,' and then my father said, 'Hello, Madeleine.' And I struggled to get away.

Mrs Partridge stepped into my view. She wore a white robe and her dark hair was caught up in a silver clasp. Everything

28

else was shadowed but I could see her very clearly. If Kleio, Muse of History was here, then things must be bad. I said, 'Am I dead?'

'Not this time. Stop fighting them. Let them do their job.' I relaxed and let my head fall back.

Helen had gone.

Someone said, 'Give her two gowns and plenty of blankets. She feels the cold.' Something warm and soft covered me. If there were heat pads, I couldn't feel them.

'Another blanket here.'

It made no difference. I was frozen, shivering violently and uncontrollably. Something pricked the back of my hand as I was hooked up to something else. Bright lights weaved and waved. Voices came and went. I could hear my teeth chattering.

I heard a loud and prolonged grinding of metal on metal. They were opening the hangar doors. Someone said, 'Keep her dry.'

They wheeled me to the edge of the hangar and we all peered out. Wind, rain – it was a hell of a night out there. It had been a hell of a night in here, as well.

Overhead suddenly, a rhythmical pounding cut through the sound of the storm. The outside lights blazed on. They hurt my eyes. Someone covered my face with a blanket. The rackety clatter got louder. People shouted.

Someone said, 'OK, here we go,' and I was wheeled at speed out into the storm.

'On three. One, two, three.' I was tilted, turned, tilted again.

Someone said, 'Is she dead?' and pulled the blanket down.

'In we go.'

I was tilted again and then bumped down. Someone's hands were setting up the drips and disentangling the tubes. I was still shivering. The noise was tremendous. I was scared. Someone said, 'Wait!' and Leon, his face grimmer than I could ever remember seeing before, touched my hand gently, said something that was lost in the noise of the night and disappeared.

A door slid and slammed, shutting out most of the noise. A figure in military flying gear leaned over me and said, 'Don't worry, pet, you're on your way.'

The engine note changed, the floor tilted, and we were away.

Chapter Four

I woke up stiff and sore. I was the only occupant in a four-bed room in a strange place. In the bad bed by the door. My forearms were heavily bandaged. My ankle throbbed. I had a clothes peg on one finger, attached to a chirping machine. Read-outs flashed blearily. Tubes dangled. I was piecing things together as best I could when a plump, smiling nurse came in.

'Hello again, Dr Maxwell, It's Tria.'

'Do I know you?'

'You've been in and out for a while, so you probably don't remember me. How are you feeling?'

'I'm fine. Why am I sitting up?'

My voice was hoarse and croaky but I felt no real pain. Thank God for major painkillers. My face felt stiff and strange, but my fingers touched only dressings.

'It helps keep the swelling down. The doctor will be with you soon. He said you had beautiful lacerations, and it was a pleasure to patch you up. He was quite enthusiastic.' She grinned. 'He doesn't get out much. Do you need anything?'

'My friend. How is she?'

'Would that be Kalinda Black?'

I nodded, very carefully. She rummaged through her file and pulled out sheets of torn-off paper. 'There have been a lot of telephone messages for you. Dr Foster …?' She looked at me enquiringly, and I nodded again. Carefully. 'Dr Foster says the surgery went well. If she can stay out of trouble long enough, she should make a full recovery. Apparently, you are to get well as soon as possible so she can tear you a new one. That doesn't seem right.'

I tried to smile. It seemed likely this bunch would nurse me back to health just in time for Helen to kill me.

'Dr Bairstow sends his regards and best wishes. One from Tim Peterson, asking where you put the Perkin Warbeck file and telling you to do as you're told. And a load from a Leon Farrell. One an hour in fact, asking how you are.' She paused. 'He sends his love.'

She put the notes on the bedside table and said, 'You can look through them later.'

'Thank you.'

I tried to smile at her and fell asleep.

Leon and Peterson turned up a few days later. I was busy.

Tim exploded. 'Bloody hell, Max, we drive day and night to visit you on your sick bed, and when we do get here you're – what *are* you doing?'

'Occupational therapy. I'm making a snake. If Dr Bairstow won't take me back then I'm considering a career as an exotic dancer. Pandora Pudenda and Pythagoras Python. What do you think?'

'You don't want to know what I think.' He looked from me to Farrell. 'He wants to yell at you, so I'm off for a coffee. See you later.'

He disappeared.

A couch by the window overlooked a small garden. We sat. He looked tired, his bright blue-grey eyes shadowed and heavy with strain.

The nurse, Tria, stuck her head in, glanced at him, said, 'I'll bring you some tea,' and left, sliding the door closed behind her.

He looked at me for a while.

'It's all right,' I said, hastily. 'You don't have to worry. The doc says I won't look like a gargoyle. It'll be almost as if it never happened.'

The storm broke. For a good ten minutes, I listened to a scathing denunciation of me, my life, my career, and my attitude. I just let him get on with it. He was due.

He was really beginning to pick up steam when Tria came back with the tea. He stood and turned abruptly to look out of the window. She raised her eyebrows at me. I grinned. She winked and went out. Silence fell.

'Come and sit down. Drink your tea and then you can start on Chapter Two – my beauty, my intelligence, and just how lucky you are to have me in your life.'

That went down about as well as you would expect. He sighed and came to sit beside me. I handed him his tea.

'You know, that would have been so much more impressive if you hadn't telephoned twenty times a day, driven a hundred miles to see me, and,' I craned my neck to look at my bed, 'brought chocolates, flowers, and what looks like a box full of goodies. If you wanted to thunder at me effectively, you really should have left them in the car.'

'If ever anyone on this planet deserved …' He stopped, gritting his teeth.

'I know. If ever anyone deserved a bloody good thundering, it's me.'

I got his crooked grin. 'I'm so pleased you survived, because now I can murder you myself.'

'Just don't tear my stitches. Some come out tomorrow and the rest the next day. After that, I'm available for murdering and general abuse.'

He gave a huge sigh. 'So, how are you?'

'Better than you, I suspect. Bet you didn't yell like that at Kal.'

'Do I look like I have death wish?'

'How is she?'

'Not as well as you, but recovering.'

Long silence. Here we go.

I took a deep breath and said quietly, 'Is it gone?'

'Yes. Completely, totally, utterly gone. Destroyed beyond recall. Trust me.'

I nodded. I did trust him.

Taking a small, careful breath, I said, 'So what was it? Any

33

ideas?'

'No, none at all. I'm sorry, love, but I don't have an answer for you. Dr Dowson has scoured the Archive. There are mysteries and rumours the length and breadth of the timeline, but nothing he could positively identify. I think maybe you're so used to getting out there and coming back with the answers that sometimes you forget – sometimes there's no explanation. Because some things we'll never know.'

'Why wouldn't it die?'

'I don't know. But it's certainly dead now.'

'Are you sure? I chopped its head off and it still didn't die.'

Once again, my mind played pictures of the two of us, trapped in that tiny space with an unkillable thing … as it took its time with us … until finally our tortured bodies could endure no more, and then …

'Stop that,' he said sharply. 'It has been destroyed. That's the important thing. Completely destroyed.'

I nodded and sipped my tea.

'I have to ask you this, Max. How did it manage to get into the pod? Did it force its way in?'

'We didn't see it. We couldn't see it. I think … I think it's like your pod. You know, your own pod. That's not always visible, either.'

'No, but you can't see my pod because of a sophisticated, computer-operated camouflage system. This was different.'

'What can I say? We didn't see it. I think we opened the door too early, and it somehow got in behind us. We didn't know it was there at all. And then, just as we were about to exit the pod, the muff moved and we realised …' my voice trailed away as I re-lived that moment. 'Didn't Kal tell you any of this?'

He shook his head. 'She did tell us a little but became – angry – and Helen threw us out.'

'Angry? What did you say to her?'

'Nothing. Nothing at all. I think she was angry with herself.' He paused. 'She's a little like you. When you're scared, you become angry. And she was very scared.'

I said quietly, 'So was I,' admitting it to myself for the first time. 'So was it Jack the Ripper? They called him a monster. Maybe he really was.'

'I don't know. Its lack of visibility would account for the ease by which it was able to evade pursuit. Why no one ever saw anything. And there were no more murders attributed to the Ripper after that date. Myself, I think it must have been. But, whatever it was – it's gone now. That's all any of us need to know.'

'Can you imagine what would have happened if it had got out of St Mary's? The death toll? The panic? The damage it could do?'

'But it didn't. It didn't get out of St Mary's. This is why we have contamination procedures. And they work. Don't waste time thinking about it. It's destroyed. Dr Bairstow gave very explicit instructions.'

'Why did he let us out? Why did he open the door? The regulations are very clear.'

'Well, partly because we all thought you'd killed it. Partly because you were about to take matters into your own hands with Kal's gun. Partly because the two of you were badly hurt and in need of urgent medical treatment, and partly, I think – well, you must know this, Max, he's quite fond of the pair of you. I don't think he could face …'

He stopped and then, not looking at me, said, 'I don't think he could face watching you die. And he would have, Max. He would have stayed with you to the end, talking to you, trying to help you, letting you know you weren't alone, watching you die by inches – loss of blood, shock, thirst, whatever. And so would I. And Dieter. And Peterson. Most of the unit was packed into the monitor room, cheering you on when you took its head off.'

'But it *wasn't* dead.'

'Well, we didn't know that at the time. But it is now. Dead and gone. Don't think about it any more. Later.'

'No, let's get it over with. I'll give you my verbal report now.'

He fished out a small recorder and I gave him the bare bones of the mission, ending with my declaring a Code Blue. He knew all the rest. I felt exhausted when I'd finished.

He put down his tea, took mine off me, and pulled me on to his lap. I made myself comfortable.

'Stop wriggling or I'll embarrass us both.'

I took a deep breath. There was more to be said. 'You do know it's not just my face, don't you?'

'Well, I watched you nearly hack off your own feet. Your technique needs work.'

'You saw that?'

'We saw everything.' Unconsciously, he tightened his grip. Without emotion he said, 'When all the screaming started and you went down, I thought you were being butchered.'

He took a deep breath. 'That was – not a good moment. Look, now is not the time, but when you're well again, there's something I want to talk over with you. Something important.'

'That sounds serious. What's the problem?'

'No problem at all. And it's not urgent.'

'You said it was important.'

'It is to me. You might have a different point of view.'

'No, tell me now. You know how things can be at St Mary's. How often do we get an opportunity to talk together? About something non pod-related, I mean.'

'All right. I wanted to say …'

The door slid open, Peterson walked in, the moment was lost and I forgot all about it.

Chapter Five

A week later, I was as free as a bird. I packed up my few belongings, which now included a ten-foot-long scarlet snake with black felt eyes and a big green forked tongue. I'd made it from red stockings, stuffed and sewn together. The only sewing I'd ever done in my entire life. The stitching was erratic and the eyes lopsided. I still have it, curled up on the top shelf in my office.

Leon drove me back to St Mary's. We drove slowly so we could have some time together.

He dropped me at the front door. 'Go and see the Boss. He's been a little – concerned.'

I bounced up the stairs. It was so good to be back.

Mrs Partridge sat at her desk. 'Go straight in. He's been at the window this last half hour.'

No, he wasn't. He was at his desk, buried under paperwork. I skipped across the carpet radiating health and beauty.

'Good afternoon, Dr Bairstow.'

He wrote on to the end of the line then looked up, his resemblance to a beaky bird of prey even more pronounced than usual.

'Dr Maxwell. Why are you wearing a red snake in my office?'

'Sorry, sir. Whose office should I be wearing it in?'

There was a bit of a silence.

'I understand the medical profession has washed its hands of you.'

'Yes indeed, sir. They've declared me perfect and there's no more they can do for me. I've been released.'

'I prefer the word *unleashed*.'

'If you like, sir. I wouldn't want to sully this happy moment by arguing with you.'

'Let me take advantage of your generosity. Light duties for a month.'

'Surely not, sir. They told me …'

'Are you sullying the moment, Dr Maxwell?'

'Perish the thought, sir. Just readjusting your perceptions.'

'And exactly which of my perceptions need readjusting?'

'So long as I don't lift anything heavy, bend over, or stand on my head, then I can work normally.'

'Really?'

'Yes, sir. Of course, it puts the mockers on my sex life.'

He became engrossed in a report – about light bulb consumption as far as I could see from reading upside down. After a while, he looked up. 'Still here, Dr Maxwell?'

'Not any longer, sir,' and whisked myself out. It was so good to be back.

It took me ages to get to Sick Bay. I stopped in the hall, greeted the members of my department working there, and caught up on recent jumps, who was where and when, and listened to all the 'face like a football' jokes. I looked in on Mrs Mack in the kitchen and took a couple of chocolate brownies for Kal and me. Various people stuck their heads out of various doors as I passed, and I could feel St Mary's opening up around me and welcoming me home.

The warmth and excitement stayed with me all the way down the corridor, but I found climbing Sick Bay stairs more of an effort than it should have been. My legs felt heavy. My heart felt heavy. Everything looked the same but there was something … The drive must have tired me more than I thought.

Dr Foster was waiting. She showed no signs of being pleased to see me. Patients ranked slightly below earwax in her scheme of things. I did get a hug from Hunter and some 'hamster face' jokes. If ever you have something life-threatening or embarrassing happen to you, you can always be sure St Mary's will treat you with sympathy, sensitivity, and support.

'Let's have a look at you,' they said, shoving me into a treatment room.

'Beautiful,' said Helen, her face about two inches from mine.

'Thank you,' I said, beaming.

'Not you, cloth-head. I was referring to the work. You, alas, look much the same as ever.'

'Well, it's not easy to improve on perfection. Certainly, no doctor could ever do so. Where's Kal?'

'In your usual room. We're renaming it The Black and Maxwell Wing. You'll be sleeping here tonight. In case your face drops off in the night.'

'OK,' I said, having expected that.

'A word, before you go.'

'What?'

She seemed unsure what to say. 'Kal has not – made the same progress as you.'

'Well, she was more seriously injured than me.'

'On the face of it, yes. I'm not saying her injuries were superficial – they certainly weren't, but her clothing and that corset did give her a certain amount of protection.'

I felt a sudden chill of unease. I looked around – for what, I'm not sure. She put her hand on my shoulder. 'It's all right, everything's fine. She's just not making her usual sparkling recovery. She'll probably be fine once she's seen you. She's been asking all day. The Chief dropped your bag off here. Let's go.'

It was a shock. I was glad she had warned me. Kal hunched against her pillows, grey-faced and heavy-eyed. Her fingers worked constantly at the covers and her eyes were never still.

'Hey, buggerlugs,' I said, sensitively. 'You look like shit.'

She made a huge effort. 'Well, shit is better than stupid. Why are you wearing a red snake?'

'Why, what colour should it be?'

She made no reply.

39

I tried again. 'You're in my bed. I always have the one by the door.'

'Well, I've got it now. You'll just have to slum it in the corner. Just keep the noise down and let me sleep.'

Helen interrupted. 'Max, stop annoying everyone and get into bed. Lunch will be along in a minute.'

'I'm starving.' I laid Pythagoras carefully across the window seat and said to Kal, 'If you're not hungry, can I have yours?'

'No. What's in the bag?'

'Brownies from Mrs Mack. For me.'

'Why you? What about me?'

'I'm recuperating. You're just lying around.'

I chucked the bag over and she took one. Helen watched her without seeming to. Kal looked at it, and then put it aside, untouched.

I climbed into bed just as lunch arrived. 'I see the service is improving. After all these years, Helen, you finally seem to be getting the hang of patient care. I'm so proud.'

'Eat, then sleep, or terrible things will happen to you.' She left.

I wasn't as hungry as I had thought and Kal ate virtually nothing. Farrell, Peterson, and Dieter turned up, but Kal's listlessness and depression was infectious and I wasn't good company either. I put it down to the long drive. They didn't stay long. We watched a little television. Neither of us ate our suppers. By mutual consent, we turned out the lights and tried to sleep.

I didn't think I would sleep, but I must have, because I dreamed. I dreamed I was wandering around St Mary's. I was in the long corridor leading to Hawking Hanger, which, in the way of dreams, seemed far longer than it actually was. I floated like a ghost. Walls were insubstantial and I could see people going about their normal business. No one saw me. No one ever saw me.

I drifted silently up the stairs, head turning, sniffing her out, and always looking. Across the hall at the top. All these doors. She was here.

I chose the first door on the left, opposite the nurse's station. The nurse didn't look up. They never did. I passed silently through the door. Now both beds were occupied. One was an old friend. I would see her later. The other – had come back. As I knew she would. I stood at the bottom of her bed.

See me …

She opened her eyes and saw me. And screamed …

… I screamed. Bloody hell, how I screamed. I wasn't alone. Kal screamed too. They must have heard us down in Hawking.

The door flew open and Hunter slapped the light switch. 'What's happening? What's going on?'

The room was empty. I mean, there were just the three of us. No one stood at the foot of my bed. I fell back on the pillows, panting in fright. With trembling hands, I reached for a glass of water. Bloody hell, that was a bad one. I looked over to Kal. 'Sorry I woke you. Bad dream.'

She said carefully, 'Me too,' and I remembered the simultaneous screaming.

Hunter said, 'You both had bad dreams and woke each other up. You scared the shit out of me. I'll go and make some tea.'

After she'd gone, I said to Kal, 'A long corridor. Looking for something. Invisible. Soundless. Standing, watching me sleep.'

'*Yes*! Thank God. Oh, thank God.' She lay back on her pillows. 'I thought I was going mad. Every day it gets worse. It's getting stronger and it's looking for me. It will find me and I'm helpless. And now you, too?'

'I asked Leon, over and over. Is it gone? Did you destroy it? Completely? And he said yes.'

'But they did. First thing I asked when I came round. Everything went. The pod was gutted. The remains themselves, our clothing, their clothing, medical waste – everything was incinerated.'

'We have an incinerator?'

'A big one. In the basement. Guthrie and Farrell oversaw the whole operation. They wouldn't botch it.'

No, they wouldn't. If there were two people in the world I

41

would trust to do this right, it was those two. But something was wrong. I climbed out of bed and started to get dressed.

'Where are you going?'

'To check it out. Something's wrong somewhere.'

'Not without me, you're not.'

I looked at her. She wasn't fit to be up. On the other hand, she had a little colour and her eyes were alive again. 'Can you walk?'

'Yes, but we'll steal a wheelchair so we can move faster.'

The old Kal was definitely coming back. I finished dressing, helped her out of bed, and found her dressing gown.

'Are you going to be all right? I don't want you falling down.'

'I'm fine. At least I haven't got a face like a balloon and eyes like two piss-holes in the snow.'

Yes, she was fine.

We were just oozing out of the door when Hunter came back.

'Where the hell do you two think you're going?'

'We're just popping downstairs to Hawking. Won't be a minute.'

'The fuck you are,' she snarled. That's Diane Hunter for you. Fluffy, blonde, and can out-swear a camel driver in the desert. 'Get back into bed. Now.'

'No, sorry, Di. Not going to happen. You can come too if you want, to keep an eye on us.'

'I'm not allowed to leave and neither are you. For God's sake, Max, you've been back less than twelve hours and the pair of you are already breaking every rule in the book. Get back into bed.'

We shook our heads.

'Can you find me a wheelchair?'

'Are you out of your mind?'

'Well, I'm going anyway,' said Kal. 'So if you don't want me falling flat on my face, it would be a good idea to get me a wheelchair.'

'And explain to Dr Foster how I aided and abetted? I don't

think so.'

'Di,' I said. 'She'll have no difficulty finding the right people to blame for this. You might get a token bollocking, but we're the ones who will be nailed to the door. Trust me.'

'If you think it would help, we could knock you unconscious and steal the chair anyway,' said Kal helpfully.

'Oh, good idea, Kal. Then she won't be in any trouble at all. Come here, Hunter, and stick out your chin.'

She looked at us, from one to the other. 'We'll compromise. There's a chair in that room there and I grass you up to Dr Foster as soon as you're out of the door.'

'Deal.'

We got out as quickly as possible. I could hear her voice behind us. We didn't have long before Helen would come sweeping down on us like the Mongol hordes.

We crashed through the doors to Hawking.

'Watch it!' said Kal.

'It's not easy, you know. I think it's got a wonky wheel.'

'The wheel's fine. It's the driver that's wonky.'

'Well push your bloody self if that's the way you feel.'

We looked up. Everyone was staring at us.

'What?' snapped Kal.

Dieter stepped forward, blonde, massive and puzzled. 'What's going on?' He cast Kal a quick, concerned look. 'Should you be up?'

'We've just come for a quick look at Number Five.'

He wiped his hands on his orange coveralls and nodded to his left.

'Where it usually is.'

We zigzagged across the hangar floor until we arrived at the pod. I put on the brake and Kal pulled herself up.

'I don't know why you're here,' he said. 'There's nothing left but the shell. We gutted it. See for yourself.'

We ignored him. Kal called for the door. As we stepped inside, we could hear him summoning reinforcements, too. Time was getting short.

But he was right. There was nothing here. The locker doors were off and stacked against the wall. All the lockers were empty and burnished clean. The ceiling was down, exposing the wiring. The floor covering had been ripped up. The seats were gone. The console panels were off and plastic taped over the innards to protect them. The door to the toilet was gone. The place stank of nostril-searing chemicals.

We split up in the doorway. Kal went left and I went right. We inspected every single inch. We met in the middle and passed each other, double-checking until we met at the door again, where Helen, Chief Farrell, Dieter, and a crowd of techies were waiting for us. No one looked very happy. Sighing, Kal lowered herself back into her chair, and I sat down on the plinth on which the pod stood.

The Chief said, 'What is it? What's the matter?'

Kal looked too tired to speak, so I said flatly, 'It's not gone. It's still here. There's something left.'

He didn't argue. He didn't laugh. He sat down beside me. 'What makes you say that?'

'It's here. We can sense it. I'm sorry, Chief, but somehow you missed something.'

He took it very well. He called up Major Guthrie. 'Ian. Yes, sorry to disturb you. Can you meet me in Hawking, please? Quick as you can. Yes, there's a problem. Thanks.' Then, to me, 'OK, well, let's go over everything, shall we?

'After you'd gone, Dieter and I, suitably clothed, ripped out and double-bagged everything. Nothing left the pod un-bagged. No one else was allowed in Hawking during this time. All clothing, ours, yours, the medical team's, was bagged. The pod was hosed clean and sterilised. After we'd finished – we did it all again. All run-off was collected. Helen herself bagged all medical waste, and the theatre was sterilised twice after Kal had been patched up.'

I looked up as he finished. Ian Guthrie had materialised, looking grumpy in sweats. He nodded. 'After it was all bagged up, the Chief and I transported it all downstairs. We fired up the incinerator to its highest temperatures and burned the whole lot.

Any ashes or residue were riddled out and incinerated again. Anything left was double-bagged. A friend of mine has a boat on the coast. We took it out on Sunday. We tipped the ashes into the sea. We came back, hosed down the boat, returned to St Mary's, showered, and burned our clothes. What did we miss?'

Put like that, what could they have missed? I looked at Kal and she shook her head stubbornly. 'It's here. I can feel it.'

Guthrie compressed his lips.

'Hang on, Ian,' said the Chief. 'If anyone would know, it would be these two.'

Helen was uncharacteristically silent, apparently deep in thought. Suddenly, she said, 'Come with me,' and we all set off again, Helen in the lead and the rest of us trailing behind like a dirty comet tail. Our weird little procession trundled back along the corridors.

It hit me as we stepped out of the lift. I felt as though I'd walked into something dirty. Whatever it was, it was here. Kal shivered and dropped her head.

Helen led us past a startled Hunter into one of the little labs at the back of Sick Bay. She shut the door and moved towards one of the storage units.

'All of you, keep back.' We stayed by the door. Donning mask and gloves, she tapped in a code and opened a cabinet. I stepped back with a hiss and Kal flinched.

Very carefully, she placed a glass case on the table. Inside lay another, much smaller Petrie dish, its lid forced off by something growing inside. It was vile and looked like a cross between a cauliflower and a scab.

I grabbed Farrell's arm for support as a wave of nausea rushed over me. We all stared in horror.

Helen said hoarsely, 'I took a tiny, a minute sample of the fluid, just in case any of your wounds became infected. It was no more than a smear. Look how it's grown!' Even as we stared, it pulsed strangely. I shut my eyes and when I looked back, I thought it was larger. I stepped behind the Chief, where I wouldn't have to see it.

'Get rid of it,' said Kal harshly, her voice rising. 'Get rid of it now.'

'All right,' said Guthrie. 'Try and stay calm.' He looked at the Chief. 'You and me, I think. I'll carry. You clear a path and open doors.'

'Agreed,' said Farrell.

He turned to me and said meaningfully, 'See you in ten minutes.' I nodded again. Guthrie carefully picked up the glass case. Farrell opened the door. They set off and the door closed behind them.

Nobody moved. Kal sat quiet, her eyes closed. I stared at my feet. Minutes ticked by. Oppression overwhelmed me. Would this thing haunt me all the days of my life? I would never be rid of it. And one day, inevitably, it would find me. I could feel the old panic rising. Kal stirred in her chair and I knew she felt the same. My heart pounded. I felt sick.

I was almost at screaming point when, imperceptibly, it began to fade. My mood lightened. I lifted my head. It was that wonderful moment when you've been prepared for a prolonged and unpleasant session of projectile vomiting and then, without warning, it subsides and you suddenly fancy a bacon sandwich.

Kal grinned at me. I grinned at Helen. 'It's gone.'

'You're sure?'

'Absolutely. It's gone. They've done it.'

Kal said, 'It's like Frodo at Mount Doom, isn't it?' She looked around. 'I'm starving. Any chance of some pancakes? With ice cream and maple syrup?'

Helen nodded. 'Oh, yes. Just like Frodo and Mount Doom. I remember now, the first thing he did was stuff his face.'

They hustled us off to bed. Kal got her pancakes.

I wandered into the bathroom, had a shower, and slowly dried myself. I took my time but when I emerged, there was no sign of Leon. Kal was sleeping like the dead. I looked at the clock. It had been nearly an hour and he'd said ten minutes. I dressed again, quietly, so as not to wake her and called him over my com. No response. I tried again. Still no reply. I called Hawking.

'Hey Max, how you doing?'

'Is the Chief with you, Polly?'

'Not any more. He left ages ago. More than forty-five minutes. Have you lost him?'

'Apparently. Do you know where he was headed?'

'He was meeting you, he told me.'

'OK, Poll. Thanks.'

Hunter was at the nurses' station, reading.

I said, 'Something's wrong.'

'Still?'

I nodded.

'Is it back?' She looked over her shoulder.

'No. Something else.'

I called him again. Again, nothing. Finally and very reluctantly, I called Major Guthrie.

'Good God, don't you people ever sleep?'

'Major, is the Chief with you?'

'Well, I hope not, I'm in bed.' A pause. 'Isn't he with you?'

'No.' I took a deep breath. 'And I can't raise him. What did he say when he left you?'

'He was going to Sick Bay. To see you.' I could hear him thinking. 'Stay where you are, Max. I'm on my way.' I sat at the station and tried to think. Where could he be? There was no way he wouldn't return to check on me. Something had happened. Guthrie turned up about twenty minutes later. In uniform, this time.

'No one has entered or left the building since quarter past seven this evening and that was a just couple of techies coming in. Did he say anything to you about feeling unwell?'

'No. Presumably there was no issue with disposing of – that thing?'

'No, none. We stayed and watched it burn away. On my instructions, Mr Strong kept the incinerator running for another thirty minutes. Farrell said he was going to see you and disappeared. I followed a couple of minutes later, so I didn't see which way he went.'

We traipsed down to the basement and found Mr Strong. 'Twice in one night, Major?'

'Can't stay away, Mr Strong. Is the Chief still here?'

'Good heavens, no. He left about an hour ago now.' Back up the stairs, I slipped into the paint store, just in case he'd felt the need to visit his hidden pod for some reason, but it was empty. We visited his room. Also empty. Now I really began to worry. Mrs Partridge wasn't in her office, but the Boss was in. Did he never stop working?

He looked up as we entered. 'There seems to be a lot of activity in my unit tonight, Major?'

How does he know these things? I sat while Major Guthrie reported on the evening's events. When he'd finished, the Boss sat silently for a while. 'No trace at all?'

'None, sir.'

'And he definitely intended to return to see you, Dr Maxwell?'

'He said he'd see me in ten minutes. That was over an hour ago.'

'That's not like him,' said the Boss. 'And there's no trace anywhere?'

'None, sir.' He stared at the papers on his desk and then came to a decision.

'All right. Major, turn out the unit.'

'Yes, sir.' He left the room.

'Stay here, Max.'

I sat in one of his armchairs and pulled my jacket around me. I was cold.

Three minutes later, every alarm in the building went off.

Chapter Six

I sat quietly as events raged around me. I had thought about returning to my room, but here in his office I could hear the reports as they came in, so I stayed quiet and hoped he had forgotten about me. Fat chance. During a momentary lull, he said, without turning his head, 'You checked the paint store?'

'Yes, sir.'

He nodded and carried on with whatever he was doing.

This was the elephant in the room. He and Chief Farrell were from the future. They'd been sent back to start St Mary's and keep it, us, and by extension, the future St Mary's, safe and secure. The Chief had his own pod that he kept, camouflaged, at the back of the paint store. Now he'd disappeared, but his pod was still here. He would never leave his pod. I had a bad feeling about this.

People came and went, reporting failure. After they'd drawn a blank with work areas, the search moved to staff rooms and private areas. They finished just before dawn, and as soon as it was light, they moved outside. By mid-morning, every square inch of St Mary's had been searched. I had long since fallen asleep and someone had tossed a blanket over me.

The sound of voices penetrated my light doze, I opened my eyes to see the Boss, Guthrie, Dieter, Peterson, and Professor Rapson seated around his briefing table. I could tell from their faces that they'd had no success. I struggled out from under the blanket.

'Sorry, sir. I'll make myself scarce.'

'No, please join us. We're just discussing our next move.' I sat down and someone passed me a mug of tea. I was cold, stiff, and a little scared.

Major Guthrie put down his tea and sat forward.

'I think,' he began, but we never did find out what he thought, because at that moment we heard running footsteps and voices raised in Mrs Partridge's office. The door crashed open. It was Polly Perkins, Head of IT, flushed with running.

'Sir, we've found something!'

'Where? What?'

'Gents' toilets down by Hawking. Writing. Maybe a message.'

The Boss stood up. 'Guthrie, Maxwell, and Peterson, with me.' We set off. 'How was this missed in our first search?'

Polly replied, 'You'll understand when you see it, sir.'

The toilets smelled the way men's toilets always do. Like a hundred wet tomcats had died in there. We looked around.

'Where?' said Guthrie.

'Watch.'

She put the plug in a basin and ran the hot water. Steam billowed, obscuring the mirror above. She turned off the tap and stepped back and there, plain as day, two rows of numbers.

We've all done it as children. You write on a mirror with a bar of soap, which remains invisible until the mirror steams up and reveals your secret writing. Peterson dragged his scratchpad from his knee pocket and typed them in.

I went to the door and looked out. On the left was the long corridor back to the main building. On the right was Hawking. Opposite was the door to the basement.

Interesting.

Guthrie was saying, 'Some kind of message?'

Polly said, 'The numbers are laid out like co-ordinates, although I don't recognise them. I'd need to check them out.'

'Not just at the moment, if you don't mind, Miss Perkins,' said the Boss. 'There are other avenues I want to explore first. Thank you for bringing this to my attention. I will contact you shortly.'

She said, 'Yes, sir,' threw us all a curious look and went out. We stood in silence.

'Major, your thoughts please.'

'Well, sir, unlikely as it seems, I think Chief Farrell has been taken – snatched – and somehow, someone managed to scribble these numbers as a clue. If indeed they are co-ordinates, then we know where to look. It seems a little – easy.'

Silence.

Peterson nodded.

I walked to the door again and looked out. If I was snatching someone then this was the place I would be. But what were the odds they'd turn up here, in this location, on one of the few nights of the year when the Chief was pottering around in the basement?

So, suppose it wasn't the Chief they were after. Then whom? Think about that later.

So, you have your man – a man, anyway – and this man, by some means, gets to write on the mirror. And no one notices? Or did they all politely give him some privacy so he could scribble these numbers? How likely is that?

Suppose the man is unconscious and requires medical attention? OK, so at a stretch of the imagination, they drag him back in here to mop up the blood. But in that case, he's in no condition to be writing anything anywhere. I inspected the basins. They were all clean and sparkling and there were no wet towels in the bin and certainly no bloodstains.

So they grab a man, who just happens to be the Chief. How did they get here? A pod. It had to be. I already knew from Guthrie that no one had entered or left the building. It had to be a pod.

Where had they landed? Apart from Hawking itself, only the basement was big enough and private enough. So how did they know that? That was easy. Someone who was familiar with the layout of St Mary's. And, if you followed that to its logical conclusion, then that someone may well have known the Chief would be here tonight as well. Someone from the future would have that knowledge. In which case, it *was* the Chief they wanted.

So, in – grab the Chief as soon as he's alone – and out again.

Minutes, maybe even seconds. And during that time, these co-ordinates were written on the mirror. Why? The answer to that was pretty obvious. Oh, God, we were in trouble again.

Last year, we'd come up against a renegade outfit from a future St Mary's. Led by an embittered fanatic named Clive Ronan, we'd engaged them in the Cretaceous Period and then again in Alexandria. He'd come off worse in both encounters. Very much worse. He had no reason to love us.

Peterson said, 'This isn't right. There's something wrong here.'

Guthrie nodded his agreement. 'True, but I'd like to investigate those co-ordinates before I commit myself to any course of action.'

The Boss shifted his weight on his stick. 'Dr Maxwell, your comments please.'

'Well, sir, in a nutshell, it's a set-up.' There were nods of agreement. Everyone had come to that conclusion.

I stared at the floor, a thousand thoughts whirling through my head. One was uppermost. Willingly or not, Chief Farrell had gone back to the future.

I might never see him again.

Three hours later, and I was exhausted. Nevertheless, I couldn't afford to show it. I could not afford to look in anything other than tip-top condition and fighting fit. I'd just repeated my plan for the second time and the storm of protest was, if anything, greater than the first time. Which was a shame. It was a good plan.

'It's a good plan,' I said, defensively and off they went again. Although not all of them. Dr Bairstow said nothing, just looking out of the window. I sat quiet. Best to let them get on with it.

Finally, the Boss raised his hand. 'Enough. Dr Maxwell, please remain behind. The rest of you, back here in one hour, if you would be so good.'

Great. I'd slept through breakfast and was now going to miss lunch. Last night's sandwiches seemed a long time ago.

Peterson was last out, fixing me with a look as he went. I grinned at him. The door closed. I turned back to the Boss, who moved a few things around on his desk and then said, 'I have a slight amendment to your plan.'

I listened carefully and at the end, I nodded. It was a much better idea.

'I won't leave this St Mary's unprotected,' he said; words I would remember later. 'I can't. No matter what else is going on, my first duty is always to this unit.'

I nodded.

'But I think this will re-adjust the odds a little more favourably. However, I have to say I am deeply unhappy with this – idea of yours.' He held up his hand to forestall any objections I might be thinking of making. 'I know. It is a good plan. It's logical. To some extent, it's playing into their hands, but it's what they will be expecting and you are exploiting that weakness. My concerns, Max, are for you.'

My concerns were for me too, but I didn't make the mistake of seeming dismissive. 'I understand, sir. It's not my most favourite idea, and trust me, I am fully aware of the risks. But it won't work with anyone else. They'll be expecting me. And that's their weakness.'

He sighed. I said nothing. There was no point in over-egging the pudding. He had weighed up the risks and the benefits. No one had come up with anything better. Guthrie's suggestion for a full-frontal attack had been vetoed. Anything that left St Mary's unprotected was off the table. This was all we had.

'Max …'

'I know, sir. Believe me, I'm not thrilled, either. But I can't see an alternative.'

'Nor I. But you'll be completely exposed.'

I nodded. 'That's the whole point, sir.'

'You're not fit yet.'

'I know, but I promise to keep my head down.'

'They can hurt you badly.'

I nodded. They could. 'Not if your idea works, sir.'

'They might just kill you on the spot.'

53

I nodded again. I was trying hard not to think of that.

He still looked unhappy.

'Sir, this is St Mary's. We don't leave our people behind. They won't be surprised to see me. Disobeying orders and mounting a rescue all on my own is exactly what I'm famous for.'

He nodded. 'Very well. Start putting things together. Liaise with Major Guthrie and Dr Peterson. Speak to Dr Foster about your face. There's no rush for this. We have the time and space co-ordinates. Take a day or so to make sure every contingency is taken into account. Keep me updated. I'll make sure everything is covered at this end.' He smiled. 'You'll want a secure St Mary's to come back to.'

I said, 'Yes, sir,' and slipped out of the room.

I had a bit of a job with Peterson. He really was not happy and, like many usually easy-going people, he was a bit of a bugger when he wasn't happy. In fact, it was the first time I had ever seen him really angry. Ten minutes later, he had barely drawn breath.

I interrupted him. 'Tim, this will work. We can't stage a full-frontal because it leaves us too exposed here, but this might work.'

Help came from an unexpected quarter. Guthrie said, 'She's right. I can see this working.' He looked at me. 'Whether you'll still be alive and kicking at the end of it ...'

'I'll be fine,' I said, careful not to sound boastful. Or defiant. Or scared. 'I'm aware of the risks. None better. I promise you both I won't do anything stupid.'

'The whole idea's stupid,' said Peterson. 'What am I going to say to Kal? Don't tell me she won't get it out of me in seconds. And what about Helen? It'll be all right for you – you'll already be dead. I'm the one who's really going to suffer.'

Guthrie patted his shoulder. 'Look on the bright side, Dr Peterson. You might not live that long, either.'

* * *

54

We don't jump forwards. It's not a good idea. Going back is easy because you know where and when you're going, but jumping forwards is a very different kettle of fish. You set your co-ordinates for say, London, one hundred years in the future; but in the meantime, if the earth is destroyed by a solar flare or a meteor strike, where do you land? Limbo? The place where London would have been? Empty space? A radiation hot spot? Or would the safety protocols engage, and the pod wouldn't jump at all? Despite the Cooper/Hofstadter papers on the subject, no one seems quite sure what would happen, and we certainly didn't want to find out the hard way. Therefore, we don't jump into an unknowable future.

Besides, we're historians. The past is much more interesting.

So this was a bit of a first for us. I still wasn't completely convinced the pod wouldn't implode on landing.

I drew two small, silenced handguns. I had no idea what I was walking into, but I was not the important one here. The Boss still wasn't happy with the plan. Peterson and Guthrie were definitely not happy with the plan. I didn't blame them. I wasn't happy with the plan either, but there really wasn't a lot of wiggle room.

I said encouragingly, 'It'll be fine. You just wait and see.'

Nobody replied.

When the Chief's pod landed, my initial reaction was one of huge relief. Our first jump into the future and the pod was not a smear of jelly on the timeline. With that anxiety out of the way, I could now focus on worrying about the next part of the plan. I checked all the visuals and proximity alerts very carefully, said, 'Well, it's now or never,' and activated the door.

I'm not sure to whom I was talking, and since I didn't get a reply, I suppose it didn't really matter.

The hangar was on emergency lighting and I could make out only two other pods. One sat on the plinth nearest me. I'd never seen that plinth occupied – ever. My heart began to thump. This must be the long lost Number Four. This was one of our two stolen pods. Clive Ronan had stolen Four and Seven years before I arrived at St Mary's and killed the crews. Five historians lost. If Four was here, then I was in the right place. There was no sign of Seven. The other pod was right down at the far end. Number Nine. Not one of ours.

My pod was camouflaged, but in this gloomy corner of a gloomy hangar, it would have been almost invisible anyway.

The hangar was deserted, everything shut down, and only the exit lights glowed faintly over the doors. I stood for a long, long time, watching and listening, but I really was alone. The overhead gantry was empty as were the offices at the other end.

I walked quietly along the wall. The floor felt gritty underfoot. Now that I was used to being here, I could smell stale air. This place hadn't been used for a while. I reached the doors and peered through the glass window. The blast doors were open. It was dark in the hangar and it was dark on the other side of the doors, as well. I wondered what time of day it was. In my St Mary's, even in the small hours there were lights on and people around. I'd half expected to exit the pod to a ring of armed guards, but there was no one. I wasn't sure if this was good or bad.

The security system was disabled and the door opened easily. The place seemed deserted. God, I hoped not. If Leon wasn't here, then I had no place else to look. I eased open the door and slipped through the narrowest possible gap. I felt the door close silently behind me. Now I had to make a choice. Did I go forward along the long corridor to the main building? Or turn right to the storerooms and the paint store? Or up the stairs to Sick Bay?

I decided to be methodical, rather than zigzagging around the building at random. Sick Bay first, then the storerooms, then the main building. I started up the stairs. Again, apart from the emergency lighting, everything was completely dark and deserted.

They'd fitted fire doors at the top of the stairs since my time. Trusting they weren't alarmed, I squeezed through. If they were then it was a silent alarm. I heard nothing, but someone was here. I could see a light shining dimly through the viewing window in a door on the left-hand side. They'd moved the nurse's station and had added more treatment rooms at the expense of the seating area, but otherwise the layout was very similar to my own Sick Bay.

I glided down the corridor. The nurse's station was deserted. Just opposite, was the door with the light. That didn't mean it was the only occupied room, however, and I listened carefully at every door. Nothing. No machinery on, no vents humming, no medical noises, not even the burnt paper smell of the medical waste disposal unit.

Returning to the lighted room, I lifted myself up and peered very cautiously through the window. It was the men's ward, dimly lit by a nightlight. A young nurse dozed in an armchair, wrapped in a blanket. Asleep on one bed, unshaven, bruised, and shadowed, lay Chief Farrell.

Well, that was easy.

I gently pushed down the handle and passed silently into the room. The nurse didn't even stir. I crossed to the Chief and touched his face. Cool, but he was alive.

Putting my gun to the nurse's head, I said softly, 'Wake up.'

She opened her eyes, gasped in shock, swallowed, got herself together and whispered, 'Go away. It's a trap.'

I stepped back, considering.

'So, Chief Farrell is in Sick Bay with just one nurse to guard him. What's to stop me waking him and taking him away now?'

'He's not asleep. He's in a coma. If you move him, you could kill him. Get away while you can.'

I shook my head. I had to get as much information as possible.

'What's going on? Where is everyone?'

She wasn't listening. 'Are you Maxwell?'

'Yes.'

'Then you must go. You're the one they're waiting for.'

'Me? Why?'

'Where are the others? You didn't come alone, did you? Where's the rest of your team?'

I took a deep breath. I had no idea how much time I had. I

57

wasn't at all happy with what I'd heard so far, and I guessed I wasn't going to like what I was about to hear either.

'Stop,' I said. 'Just calm down and help me with some info. Where is everyone?'

'Locked up downstairs in the basement. I'm allowed out to monitor him.' She nodded to the bed. 'He kept causing trouble, so they did this to him to keep him quiet. But they won't let me nurse him properly, and I don't really know what to do, and I'm afraid he's going to die, and it will be my fault.'

She was very young. In another time, she would be pretty, with dark eyes and curls, but her eyes were tired, and she was terrified, not least of me. I lowered the gun. 'What's your name?'

'Katie. Katie Carr.'

Oh, Katie. She really was new to this. You never tell people your surname. You don't want to meet your descendants. And you definitely don't want your descendants to meet you.

'You've got to help us.' She started to shake and her voice rose. 'They're shooting people. They want our pods. You must help us.'

She'd changed her tune now. She'd forgotten she wanted me to leave. Throwing aside the blanket, she moved to the bed, checking her patient. I found it easier to think of him as 'the patient'. The sight of him, lying on the bed, unconscious, dirty, and vulnerable was not easy. I moved to the door to watch the corridor.

'OK, Katie, start at the beginning. Who are 'they'? When did they arrive? What do they want?'

'They attacked about two weeks ago, in the night. Chief –' I made a warning gesture. 'Our Chief Tec and her crew got the pods away. Somehow. I don't know where they went. Only a few people know the location of the remote site. Every day they drag someone out and beat them up. Or worse. To make us tell them. But no one knows, so we can't. They shot our Chief Officers. Except for our Chief Tec and they're only keeping her alive because they think she'll tell them and she won't. No one knows what happened to our Director. You have to help us'

'Why do they want me?'

'I don't think they did, at the beginning. But no one would tell them. Then *she* said to get Chief Farrell because he'd know the remote site, and if they got him then you'd turn up sooner or later, and they could use you to get to him.'

Bloody hell! I was right! Me coming alone *was* part of their plan.

'Katie, how many are there? Do you know?'

'There seemed a lot at first, but actually, I don't think there's that many. Not more than ten or twelve, I think.'

'So, to sum up. A hostile force occupies St Mary's; its personnel are imprisoned in the basement; its pods sent away. Chief Farrell is in a coma in Sick Bay and they're all waiting for me to turn up so they can use me to pressure him to get the pods back.'

She nodded.

'Well, I'd better not keep them waiting then.' I gestured to the bed. 'Can you wake him?'

'No, I don't know how to do it.'

'Where's the doctor?'

'In the basement, treating the others. They won't let him bring them up here for treatment until we tell them.'

And that would be their undoing. If they'd shown a little common decency and compassion and brought the wounded up here, then they'd have caught me as soon as I walked through the door. If I did the next bit right, we really might have a chance.

I was silent so this could be thought over.

'OK, Katie, I'm going to leave you and have a look around.'

'No, you can't go. Not now.'

Poor Katie. She didn't want to be alone again.

'Yes, I must go, Katie, but I'll be back, I promise. Look after yourself and your patient for me, will you? I will come back.'

I opened the door, checked the corridor, waited a few minutes for my night vision to come back and set off again.

They were waiting for me at the end of the long corridor. I felt a bit silly – they'd watched me inch my way along in the dark, taking nearly five minutes to get from one end to the other, and then, just when I thought I'd made it, they switched the lights on.

Nobody shouted, 'Surprise!'

I blinked a bit, and then had a good look round. 'Only five of you? I'm disappointed. I thought I'd warrant a lot more.'

No response. They took my guns, vest, and helmet.

'You do know who I am, don't you?' I said, carrying on like some petulant celebrity. I got a rifle butt in the kidneys for my pains. The next hour or so wasn't going to be pleasant, but all things pass.

I straightened up and they pushed me along to the hall. I tried to move as slowly as possible, exaggerating my injury and using the time to have a good look around. There had certainly been a battle here. Scorch marks up the walls and bullet holes everywhere.

Waiting on the stairs was a familiar figure. Clive Ronan. Ex St Mary's historian. And murderer. He looked older than when I last saw him. Possibly the arse-kickings he'd had from us had aged him considerably. His dark hair was nearly gone, his thin face even more creased and lined. A nasty-looking burn puckered one side of his face, and it looked as if his ear had melted. So we hadn't been wasting our time when we took him down in Alexandria, then.

He stood in my face. No greeting. No gloating. He never did. I'd get no helpful information here. I knew he hated me and I knew he hated St Mary's. St Mary's because he held them responsible for the death of his partner and lifelong love, Annie Bessant; and me simply because whenever things went wrong for him, I was never far away.

'Where's your pod?'

I looked around me as if expecting to see it in the corner. 'Um …' and his backhander knocked me to the floor.

Now that *was* personal. Maybe there was a chance after all.

Get up, Maxwell. If you don't want a good kicking, get up. I staggered to my feet. He was already turning away.

'Start waking him up. I want him conscious and aware as soon as possible. Take her downstairs. Give her some special attention. I want them both to know what's going to happen to her if he doesn't cooperate.'

No, no, no. This was too quick. Bloody hell, Maxwell, think. Think, think, think.

Then, suddenly, I didn't have to.

I knew she wasn't dead. I'd told Leon she wasn't dead. I always knew she would be back one day. And just for once, I was pleased to see her.

Isabella Bitchface Barclay.

Another former member of St Mary's. Strolling down the stairs as if she owned the place. Which, actually, at the moment, she did. Deliberately parodying the way I did it on the day I broke her nose. The day I exposed her for the treacherous bitch she was.

All right, I disliked and feared Clive Ronan. He was a bastard. But Barclay I loathed. Loathed and detested. And she loathed me. And it was personal. When I thought of what she had cost me ... One day, it would be her or me. She'd already told me so. And if it was today – then all well and good.

I could see what was going to happen next – everyone could. I tried to tell myself this was good. It was drawing attention. She got close and drew back her fist. They were holding my arms, but I still had feet. I kicked her hard. It would have been more effective if she'd been a man, but it still hurts if you're female.

I tore myself free from the suddenly loosened grip of my guards and waded in.

When you really hate someone, judgement and good sense just fly straight out of the window. And I really hated Bitchface Barclay. I seized a handful of hair and swung her round. She came back, clawing and biting. I kicked and punched. She nutted me. I fell to the floor, dragging her down with me. We rolled about and then I was on top, banging her head against the floor. She tried to scratch my eyes out. Both of us were screaming and spitting. Someone yanked me off and pulled me away. I tossed my hair out of my eyes and snarled at her, chest heaving for breath. Two men were holding her as well.

'Enough,' said Ronan.

She was enraged. 'You promised me!'

He seemed genuinely disinterested. 'She'll beat you to a pulp, Isabella. Is that really what you want?'

She wiped the blood off her chin. 'Not necessarily.' She gestured with her head towards the library. 'You two, bring her in here.'

They looked at him first, which told me what I wanted to know about their dynamics. If I lived long enough to take advantage of the knowledge. He shrugged and walked off. He'd learned not to make it personal. Sadly, she had not. I was due some of their 'special attention'. But at least it wasn't in the basement.

They'd really trashed the library. Piles of books lay everywhere. Some were charred. On top of everything else, these bastards were book-burners! Shelving units had been pulled off the wall. To what end was not clear. Just mindless vandalism. The furniture was tumbled around the room. Dr Dowson would have had a broken heart.

I put everything I had into making things difficult for them. Desperation gave me strength. If they'd had the sense to knock me out then it could all have been over in minutes, but she wanted me conscious and suffering, so I fought. I kicked, bit, scratched, punched, tore myself free occasionally, ran about, threw books and furniture, and generally flailed around. It didn't buy me anything like as much time as I would have liked, and I got slapped more than once, but two men in here were two less out there. Barclay didn't count.

I was face down on one of the tables when the explosions went off – three of them in quick succession – and suddenly, the pressure was released.

I gave silent thanks to the god of historians.

Someone said, 'What the fuck …?'

She said, 'Give me your weapon.'

I could hear voices shouting outside. The other two ignored her and ran out of the door. Sadly, she went with them. I kicked out at her as she passed, but she hit me with something hard and my lights dimmed for a bit.

Vaguely, I could hear shouting and gunfire. I tried to sit up. I felt someone close by and kicked out again. Someone wrapped something warm around me and held me tight. I struggled and Tim said, 'It's me, you idiot. Learn to recognise your friends.'

'Tim?'

'The one and only. Do all these clothes belong to you? How do you ever manage to move? Lift your arms up.'

I said, 'No ... Tim ...'

'It's OK. Female apparel holds no fears for me. "Fearless Tim" they call me. And your other arm. That's it.'

'Tim ....'

'Which way round does this go? Oh yes, I see. And tuck this in here ... Don't try to fasten that, I'll do it. I said, I'll do it. Will you listen to me? Fine, do it yourself then.'

I looked up at him. He held out my vest and gun. He'd switched out most of the lights. I couldn't see his face clearly. I took them with trembling hands. Finally, I was back together again.

I said, 'It's OK, Tim, it's not as bad as you think. You got here in plenty of time.'

'I know,' he said. 'But it was a crap plan, Max.'

'It worked, didn't it?'

He shook his head. 'Can you move?'

'You bet.'

'No, your part is done. Get yourself up to Sick Bay and watch the Chief. That's an order from Guthrie. And me.'

'But what's happening?'

'Time to catch up later. Go and keep the Chief safe.'

I set off for Sick Bay. The hall was deserted. I could hear sporadic gunfire outside. No one was in the long corridor, either. I ran as fast as I could, which wasn't fast at all, aching and wheezing and took the Sick Bay stairs two at a time. Consequently, I was completely winded when I got to the top, and had to take two or three seconds to get my breath. I quietly squeezed through the doors and looked down the corridor.

Everything stopped dead.

Because this was the day I killed Izzie Barclay.

She stood with her back to me. She had a blaster. One of the big ones. On full charge. I could hear it whining.

She was past the treatment rooms and outside the female ward. She stood on tiptoe and looked through the window. She moved on to the next door. The men's ward. With Leon and Katie.

I watched her put her head to the door and listen. I watched her lift the blaster. I watched her put her hand on the door handle. She went to push down.

I stepped out, lifted my gun, and shot her twice.

In the back.

The shots sounded like harmless little pops in the silent corridor. Not loud enough to do any real damage. But they did. She fell sideways, slid down the wall, and lay still.

I ran forward, kicked the blaster away, and stood looking down at her. Her eyes were open. She was conscious. I wanted her to see it was me. To know who had killed her.

Endless seconds passed as I waited for her to die.

Her mouth was full of blood. Her eyes blazed hatred. She said, thickly, 'You … think you've … won. You're wrong.'

She struggled to lift her head. 'Let me … tell you how … you die …'

Enough. Every second she lingered in life was another opportunity for her to damage someone, somewhere.

I raised my gun and shot her again.

Now she was dead.

I leaned against the wall, took a couple of deep breaths, and with trembling hands, made my gun safe.

She was dead, but Katie and Leon would live. I tried not to think what would have happened if I had been five seconds later coming through the fire doors. Just five short seconds.

She would have been through the door. At that range, a blaster that size would have cut Katie Carr in half. The heat cauterises wounds so she might well have lived for a while. Maybe long enough to see Leon Farrell go up in flames. I know he was unconscious, but what was the possibility that his mind, at some level, would have been able to register that degree of pain? Paralysed. Unable even to scream ... It takes a considerable time for the human body to burn. For how long would he have had to endure the agony? In my mind, I saw a burned and blackened figure on the bed; arms drawn up in that distinctive boxer pose ...

I bent and put my hands on my knees, sucking in oxygen.

Some instinct made me look up and Katie Carr was watching me. I said nothing. What could I say?

She disappeared, returning seconds later with a wheelchair. I bent to lift the body but she pushed me aside, hauled Barclay to her feet in one professional movement, and let her fall naturally into the chair.

I went ahead and called up the lift. She tipped Barclay out of the chair and into the lift. I'll never forget the noise her body made as it hit the floor. Leaning inside, I pushed the basement button.

I watched the doors close on Isabella Barclay.

I said, uncertainly, 'Katie ...'

Her young face gave nothing away. 'I never saw a thing.'

She walked back to her patient.

Isabella Barclay was dead.

I couldn't even begin to think how I would tell Leon – if I ever got the chance.

Chapter Seven

Back in the men's ward, I struggled to get myself together again. Time to think about other stuff afterwards. Concentrate on the now. I looked around.

An empty bedpan lay to hand. I suspected it had been destined for the first person through the door. Bedpan versus blaster. No prizes for guessing how that would have ended. I began to feel a little better. I liked Katie Carr.

'What's happening out there?' she hissed.

'It's OK,' I said. 'The cavalry has arrived. Both of them.'

'What?'

'I didn't come alone. Everyone thought I would and I was going to, but my Boss had a better idea and sent two colleagues with me. They slipped down to the basement while I was distracting the bad guys by playing big-headed heroine. They brought weapons and explosives and took out the guards who were crouched over their monitors laughing at me being slapped around. They released your people and stood well back while they got on with it. I came back here to make sure you were safe.'

She said, 'But your face – it's all swollen.'

'Well, to be fair, it was fairly swollen when I got here, so I'm not entitled to too much sympathy.'

'So, we're safe?' she said, handing me an ice pack.

'Probably. As you said, there weren't that many of them.'

'And there were only three of you?'

'Yes, but each of us has the strength of ten. Except for me.

I've just got the appetite of ten.'

I switched off the light and eased the door open a crack. 'Come here, Katie. I'm going to shoot anyone coming up those stairs that we don't recognise.' I crouched and sighted on the stairs. 'Ronan gave orders the Chief was to be woken. Has anyone been up here?'

'No, I've seen no one at all.'

I sent thanks to the god of historians. Who was certainly on the ball today.

She started pulling things out of cupboards. 'Med kits for the wounded.'

There was silence everywhere now. The shouting had stopped. So had the gunfire.

The silence dragged on and on. The lift started up. Beside me, Katie stiffened. The doors slid open. I lifted my gun and shouted, 'Identify yourself.'

'Max, it's Ian. Stand down. I've got wounded.'

'Come on out, Ian. Go, Katie.'

She trotted off and I could hear her giving directions. I closed the door and went to sit in the armchair, pulling the blanket over me. A few minutes later, Guthrie appeared. 'It's OK, Max. You can put the gun down.'

I smiled, threw back the blanket, and replaced my weapon.

'Stand up,' he said. 'Let's have a look at you.'

'I'm fine,' I said, because that's what we always say, but did it anyway. 'See, nothing broken. Just a few bumps and bruises. No permanent damage.' Nothing visible, anyway. 'I told you it would work.'

'What about …?'

'I told you. It's fine. Tim got there in plenty of time. She really was as thick as a brick, you know. If she'd just knocked me on the head and tied me to the table I'd have been in dead trouble, but she was so busy gloating and prolonging the agony that you were out of the basement long before anything terrible happened to me. Why do super-villains never learn? Don't gloat – just shoot!'

A wave of nausea swept over me. I sat down heavily.

He didn't notice. He was looking down at the bed. 'The doctor will be here soon. There's wounded out there and he's treating them first.'

I nodded. 'What about Ronan's lot?'

'Mostly dead. They've not found Ronan yet. Number Nine has gone so it looks as if he's escaped again. There weren't actually that many of them – as you so helpfully pointed out in your running commentary along the way. Most seemed to have died, either back in Alexandria or the Cretaceous. You think they would have got the message, wouldn't you?'

He paused. 'Barclay's dead. We found her body in the lift. It looked as if she was trying to get away.'

I nodded. There was nothing to say.

He poured himself a glass of water. Combat makes you thirsty.

'We have a problem.'

'Of course we do,' I said. 'It wouldn't be us if we didn't. What heroic deeds do we have to perform now?'

He put the glass down. 'Conditions in the basements were unbelievable, Max. Most of their senior staff are dead. Those that are still here are so young. Just trainees and junior members of staff. It's hard to see how they can carry on. They just don't have the experience. Many of them may not have the will.'

'They must,' I said. 'They've got to get their pods back for one thing. Is their Chief still alive?'

'She is. She's nearly as tough as this one here. It must be the breed.'

Suddenly I thought I knew where he was going with this. This was a unit in trouble. Their Director was almost certainly dead – God knows what they had done with him or her. Their Chief Officers were almost all gone. Their historians and experienced staff were gone. Even their pods were gone. If they were to stand any chance of survival, they needed a leader; someone experienced, mature and competent – a rock on whom they could lean while they got themselves back together again. There was only one obvious candidate and he was unconscious on the bed in front of me.

It was so inevitable. He was perfect for the job. The only possible choice.

I was going to lose him.

Guthrie said nothing but looked closely at me. 'We'll talk about this later,' he said. 'You must be tired.'

At that moment, the doctor came in.

He looked in need of treatment himself. Battered and blood-stained and exhausted. He looked at me and his tired face lightened. God knows why.

'Hello,' he said. 'You must be Max. You've been in the wars a bit, by the look of you.'

'Don't worry about me. I looked like this when I got here. What about the Chief? Can you wake him up?'

'Yes, I'll start tonight. Come and see him tomorrow morning. Don't expect him to know you. He won't know who he is either, or even where he is, but that will pass. Now, will you go downstairs and show yourself? It would benefit them to see someone in charge.'

They were all grouped in the dining room. Stitched, bandaged, and worryingly quiet. I felt so helpless. I didn't know what to do for them. We sat down and someone found us some tea. I took another ice pack for my face.

'What's going to happen to us?' asked one.

'Nothing. It's all over now.'

'No, I mean what's going to happen to the unit?'

Well, this was encouraging. They were thinking of the future.

'Now,' I said, swallowing my fears about who would do it. 'Right now, the unit pulls itself together, gets its pods back, and moves on.'

'But how can that happen?'

'Not sure yet, but it will. Let's get ourselves something to eat.'

'Will they come back?'

'No, never. Your own people saw to that. Everyone here is safe now.'

'But there's hardly anyone left. And our Director's gone.

70

They could come back and do it all again.' They all looked over their shoulders.

'Look,' I said, suddenly feeling very tired. 'You can't let this be the defining event of your lives.'

They stared at me.

'This time last month, you were enjoying your lives, your jobs (I'm assuming), and everything was just fine. Now, it's not and that's understandable. But we can all get through this. Not now. Not tomorrow, either, but one day. We can't let this one thing finish St Mary's or we're doing their job for them. If we can't get past what's happened to us, then they've won, even if they are dead or locked away for the rest of their lives. Would you rather they were thinking, '*Hey, look at us! We're the people who finished St Mary's!*' Or, would you rather they knew that nothing they did had any impact at all and that you all went on to do great things? It's no good moaning about what evil bastards they were. Men like that would see that as a compliment. Far better to regard them as an insignificant pimple on the arse of your success, don't you think?'

A pause.

'The arse of success?'

I shrugged. 'It's been a long day. Best I could come up with, but you know what I mean. Now, come with me.'

'Where are we going?'

'To get something to eat and meet the people who will keep you safe until you can do it for yourselves.'

Peterson and Guthrie were scoffing coffee and sandwiches.

'People, I'd like you to meet Tim and Ian. They're the reason we're all safe today. You can trust them with your lives. I frequently do and they've never let me down. Tim, Ian, this is …'

I paused. They introduced themselves. I went off and came back with sandwiches. It had been hours. It was nearly morning. I was starving.

When I started listening again, Peterson was saying, 'Yes, but you can trust her with your lives as well. She rescued the two of us from the Cretaceous period. And the man upstairs, as

71

well. Single-handed, in a stolen pod. And she fought off a T-rex with just a pepper spray and bad language. You couldn't be in better hands.'

Their eyes were like saucers. 'What happened? Tell us.'

Tim leaned forward. 'Well, you need to know she'd had a bit to drink, of course ...' and began to tell the tale. He did embroider it a little, but he got some smiles and then a laugh. Others drew closer to listen. Tension eased. I was actually a bit embarrassed and tried to move away, but Guthrie was blocking my chair and I couldn't get out. I gave it up and finished my sandwiches. Then Tim's, as well. Serve him right for talking too much. However, it seemed to have done the trick. They all looked more cheerful when he'd finished. I was scowling at the pair of them when Tim looked over my shoulder and said, softly, 'Well, I'll be buggered.'

'Very probably,' said Guthrie, dryly and turned to look.

Mrs Partridge was standing in the doorway. Only not our Mrs Partridge. This version had ash blonde hair. Mrs Partridge 2.0. I felt a huge relief. If the Muse of History were still here then not everything was lost.

I looked at the pair of them. How much did they know? How much was I supposed to know? I took the easy way out and said nothing.

Guthrie said, 'Would you excuse us, please.' He and Tim crossed the room to her. They talked together and then looked over at me. I was trying to carry on a conversation and watch what was going on at the same time. Because something was going on here. They were talking about keeping the Chief. I just knew it. I was desperate to join them and find out what was happening, but St Mary's personnel crowded round, all of them seeking reassurance of some kind. I turned my back on the group by the door and concentrated on what was going on around me.

Their basic needs had been met. They were fed, warm, and safe. Now they needed a night's sleep. Ideally, tomorrow someone would emerge and start putting it all back together again. Not the Chief, obviously. Major Guthrie would be a good

72

choice. Tim could take charge of the trainees, and I could get the history department back on its feet again. I thought I might have a look at their assignment list and pick something simple and easy. Let them get a couple of assignments under their belt, so they could ease themselves back in. They'd need some sort of recruitment drive eventually, but not yet. It could be done. Maybe if we got things organised, they might not need a Director immediately. My heart sank. Yes, they would.

Around me, St Mary's were still discussing my adventures in the Cretaceous. There were a few laughs. Someone said, quite wistfully, 'That sounded like fun,' and I suddenly thought, *Fun. That's what they need. Something silly and enjoyable. Something to put the sparkle back in their days.*

I said, 'Get some sleep, guys. It always looks better in the morning,' and wandered off into the kitchen to check there were enough people and provisions for breakfast. When I came out, Tim and Ian were waiting for me.

Major Guthrie said, 'Max, have you got a minute?'

'Yes,' I said dismally, unable to think of an excuse. We sat down and I said, 'Hello, Mrs Partridge. How are you?'

'Very well, thank you, Miss Maxwell. Dr Maxwell, I should say.'

'Please, call me Max. So, what can I do for all of you?'

There was a pause. I wondered who had been elected spokesperson. Mrs Partridge stirred. 'Max, we've been talking and we have a course of action to which we hope you will agree. I'm not sure how you'll take this, but I'd like you to think about it very carefully.'

Yes, my track record for thinking carefully was so good.

'You might not like it, but I think you will see that it's the only way forward. In fact, you might even have thought of it yourself.'

Well, I had, but I wasn't going to make this easy for them. They were going to have to come right out and say it. She cleared her throat.

'We feel, after careful consideration, that given the current state of disarray it would be better if we were back on our feet before looking for a new Director for St Mary's. We want to keep this as quiet as possible. The last thing we need is someone seizing on this as an excuse to interfere. Obviously, there's no one here presently capable of assuming the role, so it has to be one of you. There really is only one person who has the right attitude to guide the unit through its difficulties and so, what I am trying to say, Max, is that we think you should take over as Caretaker Director; at least for the next few weeks. What do you think?'

It didn't go in at all. I was so fixated on them wanting the Chief that I didn't actually hear it the first time round. I made her say it all again before I could find my voice.

'But why me? Nearly everyone in this room is better qualified to do this. You can't spend my entire working life calling me feckless and irresponsible and then tell me I'm just what the unit needs in a time of crisis.'

Major Guthrie interrupted. 'Yes, but that's just it, Max. They don't need a normal Director. They need someone like you. They can identify with you. You're one of them. You sent them to bed in a happy frame of mind. You've just organised breakfast.'

'For God's sake, you make me sound like their mother.'

'Well, that's not so far off, is it? They're children; they're frightened, shocked, and hurt. They don't need a Dr Bairstow, they need a Max.'

I was gobsmacked. Director! Me!

It wasn't the responsibility. I'd headed missions where everything had turned to shit, we were isolated and alone, and I'd brought them back safely. It had never bothered me before. But this was different. This wasn't a group of people who knew and trusted me. These were just kids. Kids who had seen too much, as well.

Nobody spoke. I sat back in my chair and started to think it through. They waited for me in their own distinctive ways. Tim stretched his legs, dropped his chin on his chest, and went to sleep. Guthrie started checking over his weapons. Mrs Partridge produced a scratchpad – presumably from another dimension, since I was pretty sure that impeccably cut suit had no pockets – and waited expectantly. I zoned them out and started to think.

All around us, the building fell silent. We'd left all the lights on to stop the kids having nightmares, but everything was quiet.

I said to Mrs Partridge, 'Please advise everyone. Tomorrow after breakfast, say at 11 a.m., there will be an all-staff meeting in the hall. I'll tell people what's happening. Can you let me have an updated staff-list and the most recent schedule of pending assignments? While I think of it, do we actually have anyone out on assignment at the moment?'

She shook her head.

'I want to establish exactly who is still with us and what they do. The main job is keeping them here. Their first basic need – food – is taken care of. We can run the kitchens for a few days at least. Mrs Partridge, please speak with the kitchen staff and start ordering supplies. I want people to see stuff coming in. Show them this unit has a future. Are we likely to have any problems paying our bills?'

'Not for a month or so. After that …'

Shit! I hadn't thought of this. No wonder the Boss was always in such a bad mood.

'We'll cross that bridge later. Major, our second need is security. That will be your responsibility. We'll identify all remaining security staff at tomorrow's meeting. I want everyone to know they're safe now. Get security together and do whatever it takes.'

'Yes, Director.'

Bloody hell, that was me.

'Tim.' I knew he was awake. 'You'll take charge of the trainees and, I believe, our one remaining historian. Unless he or she is a complete idiot, promote him or her to Senior Historian. I want them to see a career path in front of them. If the trainees are within three months of their Finals, then abandon all that and qualify them immediately. They can pick up the rest as they go.

'Any technicians are to be cherished. I want them starting in Hawking immediately. We're going to bring back the pods as soon as we can. Major, you and I will supervise that between us until someone emerges from Sick Bay and can take over.'

OK, they had wanted this, now they got it. I picked up speed.

'Mrs Partridge, please open up the Director's office; leave the door open and the lights on. I want people to wake up tomorrow morning knowing there's a Director in place and St Mary's is functioning. Please find me a uniform. I'm an historian, so make it blue. And if you could find us some accommodation, please. You two get your heads down for an hour or so. I'm off to Sick Bay to check on the wounded and brief the doctor. Any questions?'

They shook their heads. I was getting up to go when I remembered the most important thing. 'Please remember the basic rules of any assignment. Don't contaminate the timeline. First names only. In addition, Mrs Partridge, as a matter of urgency, if they haven't been destroyed, please could you remove the Boards of Honour from the Chapel. I don't want to see the dates we die.'

'Of course, Director.'

'OK, I'll see you all at breakfast.' I got up and walked away, so I never saw their faces and their reaction to the monster they'd created.

Sick Bay was dimly lit. The nurse said something over her shoulder and the doctor appeared. He beckoned me into his office. I explained what was happening. He seemed pleased.

I asked him his name.

'Ben. Call me Ben.'

'OK, Ben, update me.'

It was grim. All the senior members of staff were dead or missing. Eight others seriously wounded, but all should recover. Another seven were walking wounded and would be released tomorrow, in time for the meeting. He had enough staff and supplies to cope. For the time being.

That was a relief. If necessary, I would have sent Peterson back to my St Mary's for medical aid, but I was unwilling to do so. Firstly, I didn't want to leave my unit short should any of the Boss's fears about a counter-attack at St Mary's materialise. Secondly, I wanted them to stand on their own feet as soon as possible. However, I could hear the 'but' …

'But …?'

'But, Max, unless this is carefully handled, there's a very real possibility they'll be bolting out the door right after breakfast. Do you have a plan?'

'Yes,' I said. 'Nothing fancy. I'm going to feed them, pay them, keep them safe, make them laugh, and work them to death. Not necessarily in that order.'

He smiled tiredly. 'That should do it.'

I said, 'I have one concern.'

'Yes?'

'How is this to be explained away to outside authorities?'

He shifted in his seat. 'Things have changed since your day. Our link with Thirsk is almost severed. We are no longer answerable to them for our funding. We are pretty much stand-alone these days, which you must have guessed since we've been inoperative for over a fortnight and no one seems to have noticed. But where the money is to come from while we recover …' He pulled himself up. 'We usually hold a small service of remembrance. If you could appear at that as Director and speak, I think it would be greatly appreciated.'

Thirteen people dead. We were about to bury thirteen members of St Mary's. It was unprecedented. That bastard Ronan …

I said, with a viciousness that surprised me, 'I hate these fucking people.'

'So do I,' he said. 'So do I.'

I have to say I was curious to meet their Chief Technical Officer. From what everyone had been telling me, she was the person who had held it all together in the basement, despite repeated and often brutal punishment. Stubborn as a mule, they said and as soon as I clapped eyes on her, I could see what they meant. Even lying in bed, bandaged, bruised, and woozy, she radiated pugnacious belligerence, arguing with the staff and refusing her medication until someone – anyone – would tell her what the fu … what was going on. I liked her immediately.

She glared at me with the one eye that was working properly.

'Who the f …?'

'It's OK,' I said to the nurse. 'Can you give us just a minute, please?' I thought it best not to give her the chance to get going again.

'Good morning, Chief. I'm Max. Caretaker Director, for my sins. Here's what's happening. St Mary's is secure. Tomorrow – no – later today, we start putting things back together again. My aim is to have the unit ready for you to get the pods back as soon as possible. I want you on your feet and functioning, so I'll do you a deal. You take your meds and do as you're told, and when you say you're fit, I'll authorise your discharge. You don't need me to tell you how stupid it would be to discharge yourself before you're ready, so I'm quite happy to leave this in your hands. Yours will be the decision.'

She stared at me suspiciously. 'Who the hell are you?'

I threw caution and protocol out the window. I needed her on my side.

'I'm Maxwell.'

'You're the one they wanted.'

'Yeah. They should have been more careful what they wished for.'

'How did you know what was happening?'

'We didn't. We came looking for our Chief and stumbled on all this.'

'Who's we?'

'Me and two others.'

'Just the three of you?'

She slumped back again. I knew what she was thinking. Just the three of us had achieved what her entire unit could not.

I shook my head. 'We were expecting trouble. We had the element of surprise. And if your people hadn't held out for so long then our efforts would have been useless. Don't sell yourself short and don't sell your unit short, either.'

She blinked in surprise, then nodded and took her meds like a battle-weary angel.

'Our missing Director. Did you find him?'

'No. No sign.'

From what I could see of her under all the bruising, she had a square face, with sandy hair worn in a long, thick braid over one shoulder, eyebrows to match, and a jaw on which you could crack nuts. I would have said she was as immoveable as the Great Pyramid. I could see why Ronan had tried to use others to induce her to part with the information. She hadn't budged an inch, and now all those people were dead. I knew it. She knew it. I could see it in the shadows in her eyes.

I sat down on the bed, said nothing, and waited.

Eventually, she said, 'Thirteen dead?'

I nodded.

She exhaled a long sigh. 'Oh my God.'

'Yes,' I said. 'Only thirteen.'

She looked at me angrily. 'That wasn't what I meant.'

'But it was what I meant. Only thirteen. If you'd told them what they wanted to know they'd have shoved the whole unit against a wall, shot you all, and taken the pods anyway. That would have been the end of more than just St Mary's. I know how you must have felt, seeing your people die one by one – I've seen that happen myself – but you did exactly the right thing, Chief. You did your duty. Grieve for your friends and colleagues by all means, but the blame for all this does not lie with you. I don't blame you. No one out there blames you. Don't you blame you, either.'

She lay back on the pillows, turned her head, and stared out of the dark window, blinking angrily. I thought it best to leave her. She wouldn't want to cry in front of me. I got to my feet.

'I'll leave you to rest. If you like, I can come back later.'

She nodded, still not looking at me.

As I reached the door, she said, 'There's a data cube. Buried in the sand bucket behind my office door. Could you bring it to me, please?'

'Yes, of course.'

'Thank you.'

'You're welcome …' I paused and waited.

She sighed again. 'They call me … Pinkie.' Her voice still wasn't strong, but I could hear the challenge.

I kept my face straight and nodded solemnly. 'Goodnight, Pinkie.'

Chapter Eight

I got an hour's sleep and woke to my first day as Director of St Mary's.

I breakfasted with Peterson and Guthrie, and then we went to the briefing. Standing in front of them that morning was worse than my presentation at Thirsk, when at least I'd had a supporting cast of dinosaurs and volcanoes and a conscious Chief Farrell. And car-crashing sex afterwards, but it was probably best not to think about that now.

I was accustomed to moderately hostile audiences – St Mary's could be a tough gig. I'd even had people hanging on my every word (not as often as I would like, obviously), but I'd never before had to deal with apathy. They sat huddled together, taking up far fewer seats than I would have liked. However, at least they were here. Some had made it down from Sick Bay, which was good. I don't know how their Director had handled his briefings but I stood in Dr Bairstow's accustomed spot on the half-landing in the hall. They could see me, I could see them, and not too far away.

'Good morning, everyone. For anyone who has just regained consciousness or hasn't seen me yet, my name is Max, and I've been appointed Caretaker Director for the next few weeks. I'm afraid I don't know many of you yet, so can you get yourselves a sticky label, write your first name on it, and stick it where I can see it. Please bear in mind that I'm not very tall.'

If I'd said that at my St Mary's, the buggers would be wearing them at groin height. Everyone solemnly pasted labels on their left-hand breast pockets. This unit had absolutely no sense of humour.

'I'd like to congratulate you all on your performance these last weeks. You have survived. You won back your unit and soon you will have your pods back, as well. This is a huge achievement and you should be very proud of yourselves. St Mary's thanks you for your service.'

There was a slight murmur. Of what, I wasn't sure.

'I would now like to call for a two-minute silence to remember the friends and colleagues who aren't here with us today.'

They stood, and for two minutes, you could have heard a mouse breathe. It is a sad fact of life that the only time St Mary's is really silent is when something awful has happened.

I proceeded briskly. 'Now then, to business. Our priority is to get our unit up and running so we can get our pods back. I'm going to run through the details now, and I'll answer your questions at the end.'

I said this to forestall any awkward questions. I certainly wasn't going to ask if anyone wanted to leave. I didn't want to give anyone the slightest opportunity to bolt out of the door. I was going to proceed on the assumption they were all going to stay. I hoped that by the time I got to the end, they would all want to stay. Fingers crossed.

'Right. First on the list is the most important department in the building.' They all sat up in expectation. 'Where's the kitchen crew?'

There was a gasp and then, thank God, someone laughed. Three or four people stood up. 'Firstly, thank you for breakfast.'

They smiled.

'Are we OK for lunch?'

They looked at each other, but a leader usually emerges.

'Yes,' she said. 'I'm Christine.'

'OK, Christine. And this evening?'

She looked around. 'We can do soup and sandwiches for lunch. This evening ...' she paused. 'Toad in the Hole. Vegetable Lasagne. Apple Crumble.'

Good to know the menu hadn't changed much over the

years. Except the introduction of a vegetarian option. They had vegetarians here?

'Thank you, Christine. Put me down for a large portion of everything, please. Next ...' and they all sat up again. 'Could the admin staff stand up please?'

This time there was a more than a murmur. I looked down my nose at them. 'What? You don't want to be paid?'

Silence.

There were a quite a few admin staff present. Obviously they weren't considered important enough to kill. 'Your priorities are the payroll and re-establishing contact with the outside world in such a way that no one knows we've been gone. Mrs Partridge, if you could liaise with me on that, please.'

I looked at them all and they all looked back at me. Rather in the manner of the abyss.

'Could the security staff stand up, please?'

There were more than I thought there would be, but on the downside, they were all pretty battered. Two of them couldn't stand straight.

'I'd like you all to meet the current Head of Security. Ian, could you make yourself known, please.'

He stood slowly and turned so they could all see him, competence and confidence radiating from every orifice.

'Ian will help you run through your systems and get your equipment working again. Never mind the grounds for the time being, just concentrate on these buildings and Hawking. One step at a time, people. I leave you in Ian's capable hands.

'OK. Technicians. I know you're out there – I can hear you breathing.'

That got a laugh. The technical section was nearly intact. Of course, they'd keep them alive to service the pods.

'I've seen your Chief this morning and she continues to recover. She'll be back in a few days and God help you if everything's not up and running for her to bring the pods back. Please check everything thoroughly. Report any problems to me and we'll find the answer together. Let's just give her a day or two, shall we?

'IT, that goes for you too. Any difficulties, tell me, so I can stare at you, baffled and confused.

'This leaves, yes, R&D. Where are you?'

A bunch of uncoordinated people shambled untidily to their feet.

'Do we have a Librarian?'

No, was the answer to that one.

'Deputy?'

Same answer.

'Anyone?'

After some *go on* gestures, a young woman timidly raised her hand. 'I'm Alicia.'

'Good morning, Alicia. I've seen the library.' I didn't say how and I certainly didn't tell them that I'd done some of the damage. 'You have a huge task ahead of you, but it has to be done. People, the Archive is our heart and we have to restore it as quickly as possible. If anyone has finished in their own areas, or is unable to continue for some reason, please report to Alicia to see if she can use you.'

Some security and technical people stirred. To nip that in the bud, I said, 'I'll be along myself, later on, to do a bit.'

She nodded and said clearly, 'Thank you, Director.'

That was when the responsibility and the enormity of what I was doing actually hit me. A moment when I seriously wondered what the hell I thought I was playing at. I took another deep breath and stared at the expectant faces in front of me.

'And finally, historians and trainees. Where are you, guys?'

There were six trainees and just one historian. A young lad, only recently qualified, I guessed. He put his hands on his hips and glared defiantly around him. And at me. I asked him his name.

'Evan.' He stared suspiciously at me. 'And you are?'

I saw Tim hide a smile. I put my hands on my hips and mirrored his pugnacious stance.

'Max.'

'Should that mean something to us?'

84

Oh God, I thought it had all been too easy. I was going to have to do the Director thing. I'd seen Dr Bairstow do this when we all went that bit too far. I stared long and hard. The silence went on. And on. I began to see the first flickering of uncertainty in his eyes. Now.

Then, thank God, I had second thoughts. I smiled down at him.

'Were you anything like this stroppy in the basement?'

'A bit.' One eye was nearly closed and he had a big bruise over his cheekbone. Otherwise, he seemed intact. He had got off lightly.

'Well, good for you, Evan. But direct it towards rebuilding your unit. In honour of your friends.'

He said nothing, but he didn't back down either.

I said, 'Tim, would you stand up please. Ladies and gentlemen, this is Tim.' He stood, tall, relaxed, confident, good-natured, and non-threatening. They were going to love him. 'He will be taking charge of your department until you are able to look after yourselves. On his recommendation, I am promoting you, Evan, to Senior Historian and you trainees can now regard yourselves as fully qualified. Draw your blues as soon as possible. The pods will be back soon. I have here a list of assignments. Each mission will consist of three newly qualified historians, together with Tim and Evan in a supervisory category. Tim, please have mission plans on my desk in three days' time.'

I wanted them out there as soon as possible. Sending them in groups of three would give them confidence. Sending Evan to supervise would give him confidence, and sending Tim with all of them would give me confidence. I hoped to God I knew what I was doing.

I passed Tim the list. The Seven Wonders of the Ancient World. I'd chosen them because they were not event specific. They could be visited at almost any time in their existence. It was a kind of historical Sunday afternoon out. Easy but worthwhile. It was important they felt they were making a real contribution.

85

I continued. 'On your return, you will work up your findings in the usual manner and present them to St Mary's, prior to filing them in the Archive.' Many of us found the presentations more nerve-racking than the assignment itself, so it would give them something to take their minds off the present. Worrying about the future has that effect.

'So, to sum up. Business as usual, as soon as possible. I'd like to thank all of you in advance for the truly enormous amounts of work you are about to embark upon. Anyone still alive at 1900 hours tonight – the first drink is on St Mary's.'

Well, it wasn't my money!

I swept off to my office, conveniently forgetting to ask if there were any questions.

Mrs Partridge brought me a cup of tea. In a delicate flower-patterned cup and saucer. With two chocolate digestives.

Oh, yes!

I have never done so much paperwork. Where does it all come from? Who needs to know this stuff? Why don't they get lives? I fled to see Leon.

'He's awake,' said Ben. 'Don't be upset if he doesn't know you. He doesn't always know who he is at the moment and when he does, he keeps forgetting. Don't be alarmed if he drops off in mid-sentence. Especially don't worry if he starts talking strangely. He's not mad – well, no more than anyone is who works at St Mary's, but he doesn't always know if he's awake or dreaming.'

'All right,' I said slowly, trying to sound calm and confident.

He patted my shoulder. 'He'll be fine. And so will you. Go on in.'

'I'll come and see you afterwards.'

'I'm in my office.'

Leon was asleep when I went in. But now, at least, he was clean, shaved, and gowned. I stood at the bottom of the bed, unsure, but even as I thought about coming back later, he jerked awake, fixed me with eyes that saw something else, and said hoarsely, 'You need to take care. It's the same name.'

I said nothing and waited for him to re-focus. Gradually, he returned to the here and now. His eyes slid over me, wandered around the room, came back to me, and then closed again. I waited another few minutes, but that seemed to be it. I closed the door quietly behind me and went to find the doc.

'It's all right,' he said, as soon as he saw me. 'It takes a while. Please don't worry.'

I nodded and tried not to worry. 'How are your other patients?'

'Pinkie had a better night and ate a little this morning. I'm not sure what you said, but well done. In fact, everyone continues to improve.'

'How about you?'

'Me? Oh, a bit tired but things are easier now. I'll give you back your unit and then take a day or two for myself. Has anyone left yet?'

'Not as far as I know. I'm going walkabout. I'm hoping that, if I keep moving, then no one will be able to catch me long enough to resign.'

He laughed. 'Come back this afternoon.'

Actually, it was all going quite well. I saw the kitchen taking in supplies, and no one was shouting about unpaid bills. Christine brought me a sheet of paper.

'What's this?'

'The week's menus, Director. For your approval.'

What? Seriously? Their Director approved the weekly menus? What sort of control freak was he? Anyone trying that with our Mrs Mack would soon find themselves on the business end of her battle-ladle.

I handed it back. 'It's your kitchen, Christine. I have every confidence in you. Whatever you decide will be just fine.'

She seemed surprised. 'Are you sure, Director?'

'Absolutely,' I said firmly. 'See me or Mrs Partridge if you have any problems, but you're the one in charge now.'

Ian had everyone stripping down weapons. The techies had begun checking systems prior to initiating the return procedures.

In the training wing, Peterson flourished a schedule at me, looked at me more closely and then sent his people off to help in the library.

'What do you need?' he said.

'I need Helen to know how wonderful you are,' I said, perching on the corner of his table.

'She knows,' he said smugly, 'I demonstrate my wonderfulness daily. Twice on Sundays and Bank Holidays. What do you want me to do?'

'Can you go back to our St Mary's? Will anyone miss you for a couple of hours?'

'No. We can leave them in the library for the rest of the day if necessary.'

'With luck, you'll be back by this evening.'

'Sure. Is anything wrong?'

I looked around at the shattered unit and traumatised personnel.

'You know what I mean.'

'I need you to do something for me.'

He smiled. 'Consider it done.'

He was as good as his word, re-appearing just before knocking-off time. As far as I could see, no one had even missed him. I caught his eye. He wandered casually past, muttered, 'Under the fourth step again,' and then went off to see his people. I felt as if the weight of the world had lifted.

I found Ian Guthrie. 'Have you got a minute?'

'Of course, Director.'

I scowled at him. We went outside and stood on the steps, ostensibly getting some fresh air, while I explained what I wanted.

'Dr Bairstow has reburied the sonnets under the fourth step for us to "discover" again.' I did the hooked fingers thing. 'So we'll need an independent authority as a witness. I'll get the SPOHB people round.'

The Society for the Preservation of Historical Buildings

people were old enemies. Over the years, St Mary's has had a long and exciting relationship with the ancient building in which it was housed. The Clock Tower had inadvertently participated in an experiment based on the guns at the charge of the Light Brigade and was never quite the same again, and various fires, explosions, collisions, and catastrophes had taken their toll on the fabric. On one memorable occasion, swans had occupied the library for two days. SPOHB inspectors arrived nearly every month. Sometimes, they got a bit tight-lipped.

'I'm going to hold a small competition. Each department can design and build a flying machine. It is important that at least one machine will not fly. There will be a small accident, resulting in damage to the steps. The subsequent inspection will reveal the sonnets. SPOHB will verify the discovery. St Mary's sells them on for a fortune. Any questions?'

He goggled a bit.

Before he could recover, I said, 'There's one other thing. I need some of your people for a small building project.'

I explained again.

He groaned.

'Can you do it?'

'Probably.'

'This needs to be done with flair and panache.'

'I haven't got to know all my team yet. Who are they?'

'I made you,' I said darkly. 'I can break you.'

He snorted.

And back to Leon. I had no idea being the boss was such hard work.

I entered his room warily, expecting God knows what, and he was awake and sitting up.

'Hey,' he said, as I walked in.

'Hello, you,' I said. 'Any chance of any –?' and Katie appeared with a mug of tea. I really liked being Director.

He smiled at me, still heavy-eyed with drugs. 'You always come for me, don't you?' And fell asleep again.

I went to see Pinkie and she definitely seemed better. I

fished out the data cube she had asked for, handed it over, and asked no questions. As usual, that tactic paid off.

She balanced it on the palm of her hand and looked up at me.

'This is what I thought they had come for. It seems I worried for nothing. If they knew what this was, they wouldn't have wasted their time trying for our pods.'

She fell silent again.

I still said nothing. I knew she'd been making enquiries about me. About all three of us. She was making up her mind ... The silence went on so long that I guessed we hadn't made the cut and got up to go.

'Max, I've had an idea. I'm sure I can get it to work and if I do, believe me, it will change everything. For everyone. I haven't written much down, but there are some preliminary – thoughts – on this cube. I was terrified they'd stumble across it while looking for the location of the remote site. Please tell me they're all dead.'

'Most of them, yes. One or two got away, including Ronan, but he has other things on his mind at the moment. Who else knows about this? What about your Director?'

'No. Nor any of the other senior staff. To be honest, it sounds so crazy on the face of it, that I'm reluctant to mention it to anyone until I've got a better handle on things.'

'Well, no one will hear about it from me.' I was intrigued, but knew better than to ask. This was future stuff and nothing to do with me. 'So, when may we expect the honour of your company?'

'Maybe the day after tomorrow,' she said.

'Excellent. You just lie there and heal and I'll see you the day after tomorrow.'

I announced the deadline at the next morning's meeting.

'She's healing as fast as she can,' I said, 'and I don't want to be the one telling her we're not ready, so let's get cracking.'

We pretty well made it. She limped from Sick Bay after lunch on her designated day to a round of applause from everyone in Hawking. They immediately formed some sort of techie huddle and after that, no one's feet touched the ground. We scheduled the pods to return in two days. IT protested and Pinkie told them to move it up a gear. Words were exchanged and I experienced the novelty of peace-making. The kitchen worked overtime to keep us all fed and watered, and the rest of the unit pitched in. Barely in time, we were ready for our pods.

I had wanted flags and bunting to mark their return, but the remembrance service was that afternoon. It wouldn't have been appropriate, and I wanted the service held as soon as possible, so everyone could say their personal goodbyes to friends and colleagues, and move on.

Mrs Partridge gave me brief personal details of those who had died and somewhat nervously, I spoke. I paid a small tribute from us all, which seemed to go reasonably well. There were tears and tissues were passed and hands were held but we all got through it together. Now, we looked to the future.

I chose Number Three for the first assignment – the pyramids at Giza. Techies swarmed all over it like orange ants and it was pronounced fit for purpose. The jump was scheduled for the next morning, and now we really could make a fuss.

Everyone crowded on to the gallery and gave them a round of applause – Tim, Evan, and three very apprehensive, newly qualified historians. I walked with them to Number Three. We stopped at the door.

'Right,' said Peterson. 'Has everyone been to the toilet and got their lunch money?'

Evan snorted, but the three trainees found a small chuckle from somewhere. I shook hands and retreated behind the line. Pinkie looked knackered but fairly relaxed, so I wasn't going to worry either.

They seemed to hang around for a very long time. Certainly long enough for me to panic and imagine three terrified trainees clawing at the door to get out. Just as I was about to use my com link, they jumped, and the collective sigh of relief nearly blew me over.

I made sure the whole unit assembled for the return. I dragged everyone out of offices, kitchens, toilets, everywhere. There were too many for the gantry, so some of us gathered behind the line, ready to cheer. Peterson and I had a pre-arranged signal should disaster have occurred, but everything seemed OK, which didn't stop me shifting from foot to foot, imagining the worst, muttering under my breath, and generally annoying Guthrie.

The door opened, and Evan led them out, smiling and waving. I will never forget the great roar that echoed around Hawking, and my heart swelled in response. Some people jumped up and down, cheering. Others hugged or shook hands, depending on their people skills. R&D staff unfurled a huge banner reading: 'One Down. Six To Go'. It seemed to be made of bed sheets stapled together and I could see I would have Housekeeping talking at me for an hour or so later on. I began to feel a certain sympathy for Dr Bairstow.

Peterson followed them out, quietly effacing himself, which I appreciated. He looked for me in the crowd, then made his way over.

I said, 'Nice one, Tim. Any problems?'

'No, none at all.'

'What was the delay setting off?'

'Oh, someone farted and the nervous tension set them all off. It took ages for them to stop giggling, pull themselves together, and make the jump.'

I looked at him. 'So who farted then?'

He grinned evilly. 'That would have been me.'

Guthrie said, 'Can't speak for Max, of course, but when we go home, mate, you go alone.'

After that, it was easy. The second jump, the Colossus of Rhodes, went really well. The third, the Hanging Gardens less so, because they couldn't find them. Which was interesting. I added it to the pile of things to think about.

St Mary's got noisier. People ran up and down the stairs shouting at each other and doors slammed everywhere. R&D

blew the cistern off the wall in the third trap of the gents' toilet on the second floor. Actually, we never really got to the bottom of that.

We removed the more obvious signs of battle and strife and I asked Mrs Partridge to get the SPOHB people in to oversee the repairs so they could witness our 'discovery' of the sonnets.

'Actually, Director, they're not the Society for the Preservation of Historical Buildings any longer. Some time ago, they merged with a similar organisation and are now the Society for the Preservation of English Regalia and Monuments.'

'You're kidding,' I said, astounded and remembered, too late, that this was Mrs Partridge. The room temperature plummeted.

'Sorry,' I said, hastily. 'I was just – a bit surprised.'

'As were we all,' she said, dryly. 'However, they are the people who should supervise our repairs, so I'll contact them immediately. When would be convenient?'

'Two weeks. We'll get our flying machines built – please emphasise they are to be unmanned – and then we're ready for anything.'

'Surely there must be a simpler way.'

'Yes, probably, but there's a certain symmetry to this. And, it's more fun, I think. Don't you?'

One lovely sunny afternoon, Guthrie took teams from each section up on to the roof, for our Flying Machine Competition. He was there to ensure fair play. And that no one fell off the roof. Peterson was with me on the ground to ensure things went according to plan. Wings of various shapes and sizes had been cobbled together by the different sections, including a monstrosity from R&D, which looked to be about as aerodynamic as the Isle of Wight.

'That'll never fly,' said Evan scathingly, stroking the history department's offering, lovingly constructed and painted in shades of blue and purple.

'It had better not bloody fly,' muttered Peterson. 'If it does, you're in trouble, Max.'

It didn't. Accompanied by cheers from R&D and jeers from everyone else, it slid down the roof like public confidence in the banking system and crashed heavily onto the steps below. St Mary's personnel scattered. Large lumps of stone and wooden shrapnel shot in all directions, and two of the steps were badly damaged.

'You're up, Max,' murmured Peterson.

I moved smoothly into Irate Director Mode, shouting up at the roof.

'What is the point of me knocking myself out putting this bloody unit back together if you lot are wrecking it even before the bloody glue's dry? Someone get down here and check out the damage. Now, please.'

Members of R&D hung over the edge of the roof. Laughing historians inspected the steps. Someone pointed. Others bent over and peered. Someone else shouted and waved an arm. The doctor strolled over.

'Oh! My goodness! Has something occurred?'

'Jesus,' muttered Tim.

'Good heavens, whatever could it be?'

'Kill me now,' said Tim. 'Max, stop laughing and get going.'

I joined the crowd on the steps. 'How bad is it?'

'Never mind that, Director,' said someone. 'There's something under there.'

I stepped back and made way for the Regalia and Monuments lady, who was actually very sweet and certainly deserved better than she got from us.

'Perhaps, Miss … um … you would like to see …'

She knelt, tilted her head and peered. 'Yes, there's certainly something there. This is most exciting. This won't be the first time something remarkable has been found here at St Mary's.'

'Goodness gracious,' said Peterson. 'How remarkable. I had no idea.'

'Yes, yes and I believe a member of our organisation was present on that day too. We were SPOHB then, of course, the

94

Society for the Protection of Historical Buildings. I think it only fair to say that then, as now, the Institute of Historical Research was not always as careful with the fabric of this wonderful old building as it might have been.'

'Wouldn't it be exciting,' said Peterson, clasping his hands to his chest like a Victorian heroine, 'if something similar occurred on this occasion? Although now, you are in your … Regalia and Monuments … incarnation, rather than SPOHB, of course.'

I shot him a look.

'Well, yes, it would,' she said, wistfully, polishing her glasses. 'It would certainly be one in the eye for our critics. It's hard to believe, but there are many who question our relevance and importance.'

I suddenly felt quite sorry for her. It can't have been much of a job, arriving regularly at St Mary's to view the results of our latest careless … incident.

'Well,' I said, 'we certainly hope you'll stay around for this one. Imagine the additional prestige if this artefact can be witnessed and verified by such a reputable organisation as …' my voice wobbled.

Peterson moved smoothly up a gear. 'Yes, indeed. An important body such as SP … yours … can only enhance the reputation of this artefact, whatever it is. I am hoping very much that you will supervise its removal and assist in conveying the artefact to a safe place, pending inspection and verification.' He smiled down at her and she blushed.

Guthrie turned up. 'Oh! Goodness me! It would appear the apparatus slipped from their grasp, Director, and rolled down the roof, generating enough velocity and mass to shatter the third and fourth steps thusly. Oh! Is that a hole? Could something perhaps be concealed beneath?'

'It would appear so,' said Peterson, quickly, before I could take Guthrie away and shoot him. 'Fortunately for us, the lady from … the monument society is present and has agreed to supervise the extraction, so we really have no need to keep any of you from the rest of your day. I believe you may safely leave this to us. We will report as soon as we can.'

He took her arm, she blushed again, and we were home and dry.

I went to see Mrs Partridge.

'That seemed to go well,' she said.

'Yes, it was quite plain sailing really, although I've seen less ham on a pig. Are the press releases all prepared?'

She passed them over. 'On behalf of this unit, Director, may I thank you?'

'Not me,' I said, skimming through them. 'Dr Bairstow is the one to thank. He's the one who actually reburied the sonnets for you to find. I just had the idea.'

'Nevertheless, it's a very generous gesture which will certainly solve our financial problems for more than the foreseeable future.'

'Well, my St Mary's still has The Play.'

Yes, we still had a more-than-dodgy Shakespeare play based on the life of Mary, Queen of Scots – or the Tartan Trollop, as I always thought of her – in which they executed Elizabeth by mistake. Something else I was going to have to sort out when I got back.

Busy, busy.

Chapter Nine

We were off. On a proper team-building exercise, no less. Just like a real organisation.

St Mary's on the move is a terrifying sight.

'I'm not sure the world's ready for this,' said Guthrie, watching as they piled into the big transport pod, TB2. The cages were stacked along one side, with a pile of nets by the door and several sacks full of fruit that should have been eaten last week. It was a bit whiffy, but, with luck, not for long. Wisely, he, Tim, and Leon had elected to remain behind. Now it was my turn. I had Mrs Partridge to lend moral guidance and support.

We landed gently and they assembled in their teams. Historians in their blues, techies in orange, security in green and R&D in what they fondly imagined was woodland camouflage.

I had no idea how this was going to turn out. I'd considered (briefly) a paintball day. That's what normal organisations do to promote team building. In reality, of course, it's just an excuse to stick it to the bastards in Management. There was no way I was going to give this lot that opportunity, hence – The Great Dodo Hunt. We had arrived at Mauritius in 1666. In London, the Great Fire was raging and the Lord Mayor was saying dismissively that the blaze was so small a woman might piss it out. He probably wasn't re-elected. Bet he got an earful from the missus as well.

I had sent Tim back to St Mary's to accomplish two tasks. The first, burying the sonnets for us to find in this time, had gone remarkably well, considering it was St Mary's. The second part was to bring Dieter's Dodo House designs back with him. He, Ian and an increasingly mobile Leon had supervised the building of our rather nifty looking Dodo Research Centre, which had been knocked up alongside the stables, out of main view. Consisting of indoor and outdoor quarters and a sizeable run, complete with running water, we were confident it would appeal to even the most discerning dodo.

A quite accidental discovery last year had shown us that objects facing imminent destruction could be removed from their own timeline and relocated elsewhere. That was how we'd managed to save some of the Great Library of Alexandria. Now, we were going to have a shot at saving a few dodos. I had no idea how this would pan out – standard St Mary's methodology – but the presence of Mrs Partridge, part-time PA and full-time Muse of History, was reassuring. We would not be jiggering the time continuum. Not this afternoon, anyway.

Since we'd been unable to complete the Flying Machine competition and to spice things up a bit, I had a small cup to award to the most successful team, and a huge wooden spoon and unit-wide ridicule for the losers. In the normal St Mary's spirit of free and fair competition, all teams were now regarding each other balefully, waiting for the off. There would be tears before bedtime.

We'd decided on twelve birds, altogether. Any twelve. No one had any idea how to tell the sexes apart so we'd take anything we could get. The optimum male to female ratio was unimportant. Twelve neat cages stood ready. It was time.

I read them the guidelines again, making sure I included the long list of disqualifying acts. Deep down, I had no real expectation of seeing any dodos, let alone capturing any. Their date of extinction was around 1681 and, even by this date, they were very scarce. They might even be gone already. If we did catch a glimpse, we might be the last humans ever to do so.

Still, it kept the children out of mischief. Team building at its most bizarre.

'Remember,' I said, wondering when I'd turned into such a nag, 'no harm is to come to any of these birds on pain of instant death and disqualification. They're scarce, they're stupid, and I don't want the last one dying because someone even more stupid has sat on it. All right? Ladies and gentlemen, start your engines.'

They seized their nets and whatever dodo-capturing equipment they'd come up with and stood at the top of the ramp.

'You have two hours,' I said, pretty confident that: a) they'd never see a dodo; and b) they'd certainly never catch a dodo. 'Three – two – one – go, go, go.'

And off they went, went, went.

I turned around to Mrs Partridge, impeccably attired in holiday gear, cream chinos, and a crisp white shirt, making Mauritius look scruffy by comparison.

We stepped outside. The day was warm and muggy and to some extent reminded me a little of the Cretaceous. Without the giant carnivorous lizards, obviously. I stood listening to the sounds of the forest and watching the sun filtering through the foliage, making golden patches on the forest floor. It was astonishingly peaceful.

'Tea, Director?'

She'd procured a table – with a cloth – and laid for afternoon tea.

'Mrs Partridge,' I said, laughing.

She smiled. 'It's been a busy time for all of us and I know how fond you are of afternoon tea.'

I sat and she produced a plate of tiny triangular sandwiches. 'Let me see, ham, egg, and salmon and cucumber. Please help yourself.' She passed me a pretty, floral plate and a napkin. When Mrs Partridge does afternoon tea, she really doesn't mess about. The sandwiches were delicious.

I sat back in my chair and sighed. 'This is very pleasant, Mrs Partridge. Thank you.'

'Your tea, Director, with lemon and three sugars.'

'Thank you.'

In the distance, I could hear raised voices growing closer. Team History erupted out of the undergrowth and with substantial amounts of Mauritius in their hair.

Evan was gently rebuking his team.

'I told you, stay left, you pillock. You let it get away.'

'I was left.'

'My left.'

'You didn't say.'

'It should have been obvious, you moron. How could you not see it?'

'Well, I can see it now. It's behind you. Tally-ho!'

The clearing grew silent again.

'So, how are you, Mrs Partridge?'

'Very well, thank you.'

'And your sister, Mrs de Winter?'

There was a slight chill to her voice. 'Bolivia.'

'Bolivia?'

'Bolivia.'

'But …' I said, bewildered, although it doesn't take much.

Mrs de Winter was my former teacher, recruitment officer for St Mary's and Sibylline Oracle. What was she doing in Bolivia?

'This happens – occasionally,' said Mrs Partridge.

'What does?'

'Bolivia.'

I wasn't getting any clues at all. Bolivia could be a country, an event, a person, a cat …

I opened my mouth to frame a careful question and had another sandwich passed to me. I took the hint. Even so – Bolivia?

'Well,' I said carefully. 'Please pass on my best wishes when she returns from – Bolivia.'

She inclined her head graciously. 'I shall certainly do so. She will be sorry to have missed you.'

I was conscious of a low drumming sound. Teacups rattled. Were we having an earthquake? The drumming drew closer. Hoof beats?

Nearly right. From around the corner galloped Team Security, going flat out, muddy faces set with determination.

'Don't let it get away.'

'I'm not. Get the nets ready.'

'We're ready. Just tell us when. We can't see from back here.'

'Now! Quick!'

Three tablecloth-sized nets sailed gracefully through the air, floating slowly but surely over the entire team who, suddenly, were using the sort of language you would expect from a bunch of people who had gone from a flat-out gallop to a dead stop in less than a second. There was an enormous amount of flailing. Eventually, words were discernible.

'Get off me. Bloody get off, will you?'

'I can't. You're on my arm.'

'Ow. Bloody hell. Watch your elbow.'

'I swear, Russell, if you touch me there again …'

'I can't help it. And you can talk. Get your face out of my …'

'Oh my God, is that your …? Oh, gross!'

Someone got an arm free. 'I've got an arm free. Just keep still, the rest of you.'

'Get me out of here.'

'I'm trying. Just bloody keep still, for God's sake.'

There was the sound of a ringing slap.

'Ow! What the hell was that for?'

'I warned you.'

'Not my fault!'

'Look. Look, over there. It's by that tree.'

'We're in a forest, for crying out loud. Which tree?'

They heaved themselves to their feet, more or less extricated themselves from their own nets and set off in pursuit of something apparently only they could see.

Silence fell.

'Would you like a scone, Director?'

'Oh, how lovely. Do we have jam and cream as well?'

'Of course.'

I spooned copious amounts of jam over my scone, being careful to snag a strawberry and finished it off with a small

101

mountain of cream. Cholesterol holds no fears for me. I should live so long.

'I've been meaning to ask,' she said. 'How is Dr Bairstow these days?'

'He's very well. Completely on top of his game. There's a rumour he laughed last month.'

She smiled to herself and her eyes softened.

'Do you miss him?'

She didn't answer immediately. Whoops. However, it was she who had raised the subject. She picked up her tea and stared into the cup.

'Yes. Yes, I do. I miss him very much.'

I watched her, sitting quietly in the shadow of the forest, staring into her cup, remembering …

'Sometimes, it's not easy,' she said, not looking at me. 'I try to remember people are a renewable resource, but sometimes … sometimes there is someone special. Sometimes, it nearly breaks my heart.'

There was a scream, a noise of tearing branches, and Team Technical dropped suddenly from above. To give her time, I strode over and said in tones of enormous restraint, 'What *are* you doing?'

'We thought we'd look for a nest.'

'They're flightless, you imbeciles! Have you never heard the word *research*?'

Sheepishly, they took themselves off and I threw myself into my seat. 'I'm worn out. Can I have another scone, please?'

'Of course.'

It was as she was leaning forward for the plate that I saw them over her shoulder.

'Mrs Partridge, please could you keep very still?'

'What is it?'

'Dodos. Over there. Just at the edge of the clearing.'

She leaned back slowly in her chair and turned her head. There they were. We'd found them.

Well, they'd found us.

The first thing that struck me was that they were absolutely enormous. If I stood up, they would reach well past my waist. The second thing was that they were really bloody ugly. One of their names had been Dodaar – knot arse, probably because of the knot of plumage on their backsides. At the other end, their heads were completely naked. Being dodos, they'd probably been facing the wrong way when feathers were being allocated. They weren't even a pretty colour. On an island filled with jewel-like bird life, they were a kind of grey-brown. Some were a kind of brown-grey. Their most colourful feature was their great nine-inch green, yellow, and black beaks. They looked like a cross between a turkey and a compost heap. And they were fat. I may be unjust; it was possible they stocked up on fruit in the wet season to get them through the dry season. But all the same, these puppies were fat.

Nobody had moved. It dawned on me that it wasn't us they were eyeing – it was our afternoon tea. The same thought had obviously occurred to Mrs Partridge. She picked up a slice of Victoria Sponge, broke it into large pieces and tossed them in their direction. I hadn't had any yet, and could not suppress a small whimper.

'It's for science, Director,' she said. 'We must all make sacrifices.'

Two or three of them bundled over and inspected the cake, heads on one side. One nibbled with its beak, let out a cry of 'Grockle,' and made a grab for another. Immediately there was a free for all as they milled around, hoovering up Victoria Sponge as fast as they could go.

'Quick,' I said, struck with inspiration. 'Lay a trail.'

We began to break up the remaining sandwiches, cake and scones and backed towards the pod. The phalanx of dodos watched us silently – just like that scene from *The Birds*. Suddenly, with no signal given that I could see, the whole flock attacked, stubby wings and necks outstretched, grockling away for dear life. We turned and fled.

'Never mind the cages,' I said, 'I'll lure them inside and you get the door. We'll sort out the cages later.'

God, they were dim. They raced around in excited circles,

gobbling up afternoon tea. None of them looked where they were going. They collided with each other. They tripped over roots and brought down their neighbours, and those behind fell over them. If I had a gun then the world would already be down twenty or so dodos. Short of pulling the trigger themselves, they couldn't have had less sense of self-preservation. They squabbled over the food, tried to clamber over the table for more, knocked over the teapot, grockled indignantly at each other, spotted more food nearer the pod, and launched another airborne attack. Of course, they all tried to stand at the same end of the table, which at once tipped over. They landed slightly less gracefully than the dancing hippos in *Fantasia*.

If ever a species was marked for extinction by suicide ... I felt quite sorry for them. It's not as if they were beautiful or intelligent and opinions varied greatly as to whether they were good eating. The only recipe I'd found had not been helpful.

First, catch your dodo. Marinade in lemon juice, or something equally acidic for as long as possible. Preferably overnight. Stuff with breadcrumbs, roughly chopped onions, sage, rosemary, and thyme. Season robustly, lay on a wide plank or something similar, and cook over an open fire or BBQ until the juices run clear. Carefully separate the light meat from the dark. Throw the whole lot away and eat the plank.

I waited until they were marginally calmer and looking round for more food. Slowly and ostentatiously, I began to lay a trail up the ramp. They followed, bundling together, grockling to each other and squabbling over the food. It wasn't so very different from managing St Mary's. They followed me into the pod, looked around with loud exclamations of grockle, took one look at the cages and made a mad, feathery dash. In seconds, each cage had a dodo or two inside, lowering its undercarriage and making itself comfortable. Those who couldn't be inside clambered heavily onto the top of the cages and sat, grockling contentedly to their neighbours.

I backed out quietly and Mrs Partridge shut the door. We picked up the table, threw the food away, wrapped everything else in the tablecloth Dick Whittington style and sat down to await the return of our failed expeditionary force.

Team Techies were the first back, proudly displaying a small collection box, which they opened with a flourish. We peered inside.

'It's a pigeon,' I said.

'It's a young dodo,' they said.

'It's a pigeon.'

'Are you sure? It could be a new strain of dodo.'

'It's a pigeon.'

They let it go.

Next back was Team History, clutching a wriggling bundle.

It was a monkey. It stuck an out an indignant head, bit someone, and shot up a tree.

'Get a tetanus shot,' I said.

Team Security weren't speaking to each other. Russell had a black eye.

Team R&D brought back a small rock on which they had attempted to glue a few feathers. Someone had drawn a face on it in pencil.

I stared at it in disbelief.

'What?' they said.

I sighed loudly, trying very hard not to laugh.

They were, all of them, covered in mud, shit from various forest-dwelling species, leaves, crushed fruit, and something viscous that should always remain nameless.

'So,' they said. 'What now?'

'Well,' I said. 'I present the trophy to the winner, and we all go home, and many of us have a really good bath before presenting ourselves for the party this evening.'

Hearing there was a winner perked them all up. The teams jostled for position. I picked up the cup.

'For successfully accomplishing our mission – which was to locate and collect twelve dodos; in fact, for more than accomplishing our mission and for providing a very excellent tea, I am pleased to award this cup to – Mrs Partridge.'

I thoroughly enjoyed the looks on all their faces.

'But …' they said, looking around the dodo-less clearing.

Then it dawned on someone; the ramp was up.

Evan got it first. 'How many?'

'Seventeen.'

You'd have thought they'd caught all seventeen themselves.

We jumped back and decanted seventeen dodos into their beautiful new home. They rushed around, bouncing off walls and each other, grockling ear-splittingly. One cage already had an egg in it, which we gently placed in a nesting box. One of the parents immediately nudged it back out again. It bounced heavily onto the floor. We winced, but it survived. An anonymous dodo sat on it and all the others milled around, pushing and shoving. I was rapidly concluding that their extinction might not have been completely man's fault. Dodos – our dodos anyway –displayed the parenting skills of a brick.

With Mrs Partridge proudly clutching her trophy and the others bickering about who got custody of the Losers' Ladle, we made our way back to the main building.

I caught Tim counting heads.

'No need for that. They're all present and correct.'

He grinned. 'Just checking. How did it go?'

'Well. Very well.'

'In that case …'

In that case – the time had come for the final test. The real deal.

'Do you have the details for me?'

'On your desk.'

'What did you go for in the end?'

'Thomas Becket.'

I said nothing for a while.

'Too much too soon?'

I shook my head. 'No, It's perfect. They're going to have to face violent death sooner or later. Let's make it sooner. Find out what sort of job we've done.'

'OK. I'll set it up.'

England's not very warm at the best of times, and on the 29th

December 1170, it was very cold indeed. A glittering frost ripped straight through my thermals, thick woollen dress, surcoat, and two cloaks. I had gloves and boots as well and they were of no use whatsoever. So I started the evening cold and rapidly became even colder as we entered the huge, echoing, very dark, but above all, really, really cold Canterbury Cathedral.

I'm not especially religious. The odd blasphemous curse or a hasty appeal to the god of historians is about as far as I'm prepared to go so I'm not that familiar with the inside of churches. Plus, of course there's always the fear that I'll burst into flames as I cross the threshold. And I know churches aren't supposed to be comfortable. Most gods seem to like their followers to suffer. Very few religious ceremonies take place on a tropical beach with the congregation benefiting from warm breezes and a continual supply of Long Island Tea. But until now, however, I'd had no idea how much of a difference Victorian pews and modern heating and lighting made towards actually surviving the service long enough to worship another day.

For a start, the interior was very, very dark. Churches are, anyway, but this was real Stygian gloom. Flickering candles and the odd lamp threw out small pools of wavering light. We stumbled in the murk, moving from one insubstantial puddle of light to the next, following the press of people as they assembled to hear the Archbishop celebrate vespers.

And it was so cold. Worse than cold. The damp stones gave off a chill that penetrated my very bones. I could feel it striking up through the flagstones and numbing my feet. The chill radiated out from the walls, effortlessly penetrating my clothes. I began to shiver.

Peterson glanced down. 'It's not that cold.'

Sometimes I think he inhabits his own universe.

Around us, people shifted and muttered, their echoes bouncing around this giant stone cavern, the height and width of it lost in the leaping dark shadow. Peterson and I moved towards a pillar. Evan and Theresa were opposite – their view was better than ours, but it was Evan's assignment. He was in charge. He'd allocated positions.

He'd stationed two more people outside to cover the knights' entrance and exit and the rest were scattered around the congregation to record reactions.

I got some establishing shots, while Peterson shielded me, although my hand shook so much that IT were going to have their work cut out to refocus this footage.

As far as I could see, the Archbishop had not yet arrived. People waited patiently, as soft chanting echoed gently around the building. Slowly, everything grew still. There was silence, apart from the odd cough or shuffle.

'A few minutes yet,' whispered Peterson and I nodded. Thomas Becket would make his entrance, resplendent in the magnificent regalia of the church and escorted by a full complement of clergy.

In the Middle Ages, the Church was the most powerful institution in the western world. In England, the struggle between church and kings would take centuries to resolve. Interestingly, in the end, neither institution came out on top. Today, each is as powerless as the other. As people power emerged, we invented politicians. We're not bright.

Tonight, however, would be a major episode in that struggle. We were about to witness the event of the century.

With the power to appoint England's leading cleric, the Archbishop of Canterbury, Henry II, whose realm stretched from Hadrian's Wall to the Pyrenees, was determined to exert himself against the power of the Pope and so appointed his good friend, drinking companion and fellow bad-boy, Thomas Becket to the post, confidently expecting Thomas would assist in undermining the power of the church and generally playing the game according to Henry's rules.

It didn't happen.

No one seems quite sure why, but Becket embraced his new job with enthusiasm and devoted his considerable talents and abilities to the benefit of the Catholic church and the service of God.

Henry was not impressed and when Becket went so far as to excommunicate the Bishops of London and Salisbury – the message being that anyone who supported the king against the church would go to hell – Henry lost his famous temper. Furious at what he saw as Becket's betrayal and realising he himself had provided his enemy with a powerful weapon, he uttered the immortal words: 'Will no one rid me of this turbulent priest?'

Four knights caught each other's eye and slipped out of the room.

To do Henry justice, he regretted his hasty words and sent after them almost immediately. Too late. They'd already sailed for England.

And now they were on their way here. In fact, they had already arrived. Faintly, in my ear, I heard James. 'They're here. Four of them. Heading towards the cloister door.'

Away, out of sight in the gloom, the congregation stirred. A brighter light approached. The rhythm of the chanting changed.

The Archbishop was on his way.

He had only minutes to live.

'Heads up, everyone,' said Evan in my ear. 'We only get one chance.'

He sounded nervous but calm. As he should be. As they all should be.

Becket was a very tall man – a good head taller than most of those around him. His face, austere but serene, glowed in the candlelight. Although many of the paintings of the scene have depicted him dressed in red robes, in fact he wore an outer robe of shimmering emerald green, with a white cross on its front, formed by bands of white from shoulder to shoulder and from neck to hem. He was bare-headed. I took a deep breath and tried not to remember that in a few minutes this man would be dead. And there was nothing we could do. Or should do. St Mary's job is to observe and record. The trainees would observe events as they unfolded. Tim and I would observe them. This was their last test. A violent death was about to occur. How would they react?

The procession passed us, gently chanting and disposed themselves for vespers. A slight pause of expectation before the service began – and then, in the silence, a door boomed back against a stone wall, disturbingly loud in the darkness. Hasty footsteps sounded.

The singing faltered, but Becket appeared unmoved and unworried. Had he any idea what was about to happen? None of the eyewitness accounts, including that of Edward Grim, himself wounded, make any mention of Becket attempting to flee or defend himself in any way. I've often wondered if he took a deliberate decision to sacrifice himself, assure himself of martyrdom, and deal Henry a blow from which he would never recover.

We were about to find out.

The four knights emerged out of the darkness, like something from a bad dream. They had not, at this stage, drawn their weapons. One strode forwards and faced the congregation, hand suggestively on his sword hilt. Crowd control.

Two of them laid hands on Becket, attempting to drag him away from the altar. He clung to something – the altar, a pillar – I couldn't see clearly. He shouted defiantly, his words lost in the echoes.

The third knight, clad in a red cloak, whom I took to be Reginald FitzUrse from the bear on his badge, roared an order and again they tried to dislodge the Archbishop's grasp. At this point, it was unclear whether they simply wanted to remonstrate with him or remove him from consecrated ground and away from witnesses. They were in a difficult position and they knew it. For all they knew, the congregation would rally to Becket's defence. Someone might already have gone for help. They were running out of time.

I saw FitzUrse draw his sword, as it glinted dully in the candlelight. He paused, possibly to gather his courage, and then struck.

The blow caught the monk, Edward Grim on the arm as he threw himself protectively at his archbishop.

With the courage of one who has not struck the first blow,

William de Tracey closed in and struck harder. This time the archbishop staggered. De Tracey stepped back, I could hear his breath coming out in gasps. He waited, sword raised.

The crowd gasped in disbelief, but no one moved.

There was no going back now. Blood had been shed. And on consecrated ground. Another blow drove Becket to his hands and knees but he still would not give in. Bleeding heavily, he twisted his head and tried to speak, but I couldn't make out what he said.

The fourth knight, Richard le Breton, who had chain mail under his brown cloak, probably wanting to get it over with, impatiently shoved his fellows aside, lifted his sword high and struck with all his might. The fearsome blow passed straight through Becket's skull, completely severing the top of his head. The sword shattered on the flags beneath. Blood and brain matter exploded into the air.

Now the crowd shouted and tried to surge forwards. The fourth knight, who must have been Hugh de Morville, stepped into the light and drew his sword. The ring of metal on metal rang around the dark cathedral. The message was clear. They'd killed the Archbishop. No one had anything to lose now.

The scene was appalling. Three knights stood over the body, motionless, swords dripping blood. Their breath puffed in the icy air, forming a cruelly ironic halo around their heads. Edward Grim, that brave man, still tried to protect his Archbishop. His bloody arm hung uselessly as he weakly called for aid.

The Archbishop of Canterbury lay face down in his own cathedral. Blood, red and wet and bright in the candlelight spilled out across the reddish-brown flagstones in a dark, widening pool, the only movement in this frozen tableau.

And then, to pile horror upon horror, another man, a clerk, dressed all in brown, known everlastingly as Hugh the Evil, appeared from the shadows. He put his foot on Becket's neck and grinding the remains of his face down into the flags, scattered brain tissue and blood even further across the stones. His voice carried clearly. 'Let us away, knights. He will rise no more.'

Still with swords drawn, they wheeled about and were gone, back into the darkness whence they came. The door boomed closed behind them.

The spell broke.

Panic and confusion reigned. People screamed and wailed. Some ran from the cathedral, whether in pursuit or to spread the news was not clear. Others ran to help Grim rise to his feet. Tears ran down his face. He was covered in blood. His own and his archbishop's.

I could hear a voice in my ear, dutifully reporting the knights' departure. I saw Evan nod and speak. They'd all kept their heads. Tim exhaled with relief. I rubbed his shoulder and said, softly, 'Good job, Tim.' He nodded but before he could speak, people ran forward and began to tear off pieces of the archbishop's robes. At first I thought they were attempting to staunch the flow of blood, but they dipped the rags carefully in the red pool and stowed them away.

Already the legends had begun.

Tim went off to speak to Evan while I stood still, collecting my thoughts, letting others mill around me.

When they came to prepare his body for burial, they would find he wore both a hair shirt and hair breeches, both garments stained with blood as they irritated and chafed his skin. They would also find his body riddled with worms. He must have been in constant pain. I could not help comparing this emaciated man, suffering gladly for his faith, with the hard-drinking, hard-riding playboy companion of the king. He hadn't played at being Archbishop of Canterbury. He hadn't used his office as an excuse for high living as so many did and would do in the future. He had found a purpose in his life. I felt a slight sadness at my own lack of faith.

Tim and I stood back as Evan collected his team together, checked them off, and we made our way softly through the crying people, outside into the brilliant, star-studded night and back to St Mary's.

They were ready.

And so to our Last Night Fancy Dress Party.

I knew Peterson would go as Robin Hood. He always did. Guthrie usually went as a Viking, complete with historically inaccurate horns on his helmet. I'd been so busy organising my departure I'd forgotten to sort out my own costume until Mrs Partridge brought in the most gorgeous golden gown and hung it on the back of the door.

I gasped. 'Where did you get that?'

'Wardrobe,' she said, smugly. 'It was commissioned for a series about the Borgias. They didn't like this one.'

'Why ever not? It's wonderful.'

'The actress playing Lucretia Borgia claimed it made her look sallow.'

'And did it?'

'Oh, yes. But her bad complexion is your gain, Director.'

'Well, thank you, Mrs Partridge. I confess I'd forgotten all about it.'

She nodded. 'I thought you had.'

I wondered briefly if she had ever performed similar services for Dr Bairstow. It seemed unlikely. Firstly, Dr Bairstow never forgot anything and, secondly, at similar events in our time, Dr Bairstow always went as the Director of St Mary's. He'd found his look and he stuck with it.

'And you? What's your costume?'

She just raised an eyebrow and I kicked myself. Of course, she'd be going Greek.

I never gave a thought to what Leon might wear.

The first thing I discovered was that the dress was so low-cut that the wearing of any underwear at all – anomalous or otherwise – was not even to be considered. Theoretically, the dress was boned and so tightly laced that any additional load-bearing garments should be superfluous. That's all well and good, but even after I'd defied the laws of physics and fastened it all up there was still a horrifying amount pushed up and out, apparently defying gravity. Modest ladies could insert little lace or muslin fichus, to prevent early-onset blindness in their male escorts. I did my best, but even a tablecloth the size of the plain at Marathon wasn't going to cut it. I bundled my hair up in a jewelled net, slapped on some make-up, and made an entrance.

I had two energetic dances with Evan and instructed him, as Senior Historian, to dance with every member of his department.

'Even the girls,' I said, nastily and left him spluttering. He was such a product of the previous regime.

I saw Leon across the hall. I don't know who he'd come as. He was wearing a loose linen shirt, unlaced at the throat, tight breeches, and leather boots. He looked like every 19th century hero come to life – Mr Darcy, Heathcliff, Mr Rochester … all distilled and poured into a pair of skin-tight breeches. They were cream and very, very tight. I had always thought he had a nice bum anyway, but it wasn't just … they fitted him well … really well … he had good, strong legs … they really were quite tight … things were … outlined …

I walked into a table.

'Good evening, Director,' he said, calmly and I knew he was laughing at me.

'Good evening, Leon,' I said, vowing future vengeance.

'How did Thomas Becket go?'

'Without a hitch,' I said, proudly.

'Well done,' he said, failing to make eye contact.

'Hey. I'm up here.'

'Yes, but we're all down here. Care to join us?'

'What sort of example is this to be setting?'

He laughed and went to talk to Pinkie.

I circulated. I had another Margarita. The corners of the room blurred comfortably. Things began to pick up. The volume of music increased considerably. People had to shout now to make themselves heard. Somewhere, someone dropped a glass. There was a shout of laughter. I recognised this moment.

I'd seen The Boss do this. He would stay for maybe an hour or so, showing his face and then things would start to get rowdy. He knew, none better, that steam needs to be let off occasionally. You never actually saw him go, but you'd look up and he'd be gone. His senior staff would melt away shortly afterwards and then the party would kick up a gear.

Of course, being Dr Bairstow, he always got his own back the next morning with an unpleasant combination of a prolonged and complicated all-staff briefing and widespread distribution of the 'Deduction from Wages for Damages Incurred' paperwork. However, the point was that somehow, he knew when to make himself scarce and now, so did I.

I put down my glass and oozed backwards out of the door. As I left, they cranked the music up again.

It took a while to negotiate the stairs; heels, long dress, alcohol, and an inability to see my own feet being the main problems. I started down the corridor and an arm shot out from a curtained window alcove and dragged me inside.

I knew his smell. I knew his touch. Most of all, I knew those breeches. I fell gracelessly into his arms and found his mouth. Things got a little hectic for a while until a couple of people ran past, shouting, and we remembered where we were.

'My room is just around the corner,' I said, trying to adjust my clothing. 'You couldn't have waited?'

'You're lucky I didn't throw you across the sausage-rolls and take you there and then.'

I had a sudden mind-picture and sagged against the wall, struggling a little for breath, but that would have been because it was a small space and the curtains made it stuffy. Not because of the sausage-roll thing at all.

'What are you doing?' he said.

'I'm trying to get *these* back in *there*.'

'Why would you want to?'

'So I can decently walk around the building.'

He surveyed the problem with an engineer's eye. 'No, I don't think it's going to happen.'

'It must. I got them in there.'

'Barely.'

'You're not helping.'

'Why would I want to?'

'Well, I'm obviously going to have to spend the rest of my life in here, then. Good night, Chief Farrell.'

He pulled his shirt over his head and dropped it over mine. 'Here, borrow this.'

I looked at his broad chest and had to lean against the wall again. 'Tell me how that is supposed to help.'

He stuck his head out of the curtains. 'Come on.'

We sprinted out of the alcove and along the corridor, crashing through my door. The shirt came off again and sailed over his shoulder.

'I should get out of this dress.'

'You're already out of that dress.'

Having been made for a TV programme rather than for an actual assignment there was an anomalous concealed zip. He fell to with enthusiasm and slowly the dress began to slither to the floor in a whisper of silk. I reached out an arm and switched off the lights.

He stopped what he was doing and said, 'You really don't have to do that, you know.'

'I know,' I said, 'it's just … next time, maybe.'

'Next time, definitely,' he said, resuming normal service.

'Yes,' I said, lost in him and what he was doing and not really paying attention. 'Next time,' and pushed him hard against the door.

'Don't think I'm not very appreciative, but are you on some kind of medication?'

'It's the breeches,' I said, channelling Sarah, Duchess of Marlborough, whose husband was well known for pleasuring her with his boots on.

The darkness was thick and warm and curled around us. Small breezes wafted through the open window, cooling my skin but nothing else. Two floors down I could still hear the music, throbbing, deeply insistent, finding an echo in this hot, dark room. I could feel my heart pounding. And his. We were slick with sweat. I could feel his need, as great as my own.

'Whoa,' he said, lifting his head. 'Is there a time limit? Are we trying to set a record?'

116

'I want you,' I said simply. 'I'm hot and full of desire for you and I want you now, before I lose that feeling. I want to feel real, raw, red-hot passion.'

He pulled away again, looking down with shadowed eyes.

'Then you shall.' He pulled me down onto the floor. My pulse rate kicked up even higher. This was going to be good.

He dropped off to sleep like the Great Pyramid trying to hang glide. I lay for a while, reliving some moments and then abandoned the pursuit of sleep in favour of something more practical. Slipping his shirt over my head, I picked up the poor, misused dress and hung it carefully on a hanger. Either they'd turned the music down or the party was over at last. The building seemed silent. This was my last night here. This time tomorrow, I would be back in my St Mary's.

I went through into my office – the Director's office rather, and sorted and tidied the paperwork there. Nothing important. Mrs Partridge would be easing the handover. I made sure nothing personal was hanging around and went back into the bedroom. I checked the wardrobe, making sure I was going back in the clothes I came in with. Everything was there except for my weapons. Ian had taken charge of those. There really was nothing left to do.

I heard Leon stir and went to sit beside him on the floor. 'You fell asleep unflatteringly quickly. Were you bored?'

'Yes, but good manners prevented me from leaving early.' He sat up and kissed my hand. 'I must go.'

'Why?'

'Well, I'm not doing the boots and breeches walk of shame at 8.00 a.m. tomorrow, just as everyone's going in to breakfast.'

'No need. Your Director has everything covered. Your going-away outfit is in the wardrobe over there.'

'My Director always has everything covered. I live for the day she doesn't. You made me a promise. I'm going to hold you to it.'

'You can hold me to anything you like.'

'All right then, how about this? Not tomorrow night – I'm

certainly going to be in Sick Bay and you might be too. But the night after – shall we do something special?'

'Not like tonight, then?'

'Better.'

'Oh, good. I didn't want to complain, but I definitely felt there was some room for improvement there.'

'Yes, you need to work on your scream. I want a full-throated roar next time, not that little girlie squeak. Or two, maybe.'

'Says the man who can barely keep his eyes open.'

He lay back, looking absolutely wrecked. I was worried I'd done some damage. 'Are you all right?'

He whispered something I didn't catch. Alarmed, I said, 'Leon?' and leaned forwards.

I really should have known better.

'So,' he said, after a while. 'It's a date then. You, me, the day after tomorrow. I love you, Max. You don't have to hide yourself from me.'

'You shall see me,' I said, softly.

He closed his eyes and I curled up alongside him, still on the floor, warm and safe. It was one of the happiest nights of my life. I believed every word he said.

Some forty-eight hours later, I would happily have torn out his heart with my bare hands and made him eat it.

The next morning, I assembled them all together for the last time. They had dignified the occasion with formal uniforms. I was a little moved. And sad. This had been my unit – albeit temporarily. True, my work here was done, but I was going to miss them. It was impossible not to compare the bright-eyed, slightly hung-over individuals before me with the damaged children they'd been all those weeks ago. It was just faintly possible I'd done a good job here. I wondered if the Boss would agree. Of course, he might feel that actually commanding St Mary's myself would give me insight and wisdom, and make me more amenable to the day-to-day rules and regulations pertaining to the smooth running of his unit. I looked forward to correcting this unreasonable assumption.

They were all looking at me. I'd better get started.

'Extraordinary people achieve extraordinary things. Your achievements over the past six weeks have been more than extraordinary. I am full of admiration for this unit. I have watched you face your enemies and your own fears, and give them both the kicking they deserved.

'I count it an enormous privilege to have been able to make a contribution to what is, already, an exceptional unit and will go on, I'm sure, to truly spectacular achievements.'

I couldn't help glancing at Pinkie, wondering again, just what it was she was up to. What was on that cube? Her face, as always, gave nothing away.

I continued. 'There is nothing now for me to do. You are a fully functioning unit. Your new Director must now decide in which direction you are to move, and appoint the right people to achieve these goals.

'Before that, however, I would ask you, please, to join with me in thanking Leon, Tim, and Ian for their invaluable help and hard work. They are far too modest about this, but I would like to state publicly, that without them, none of us would be standing here today. Tim, Ian, and Leon, St Mary's thanks you for your service.'

The room erupted with cheers and applause. I joined in. Ian actually blushed. And me without any sort of recording device. They rose slowly to their feet and made those awkward bobbing movements with their heads. As the senior officer, Leon said, 'An honour and a privilege, Director,' and they all sat down again.

Those were the last words that anyone spoke to me as Director.

I swallowed and continued.

'In this business, I'm never sure whether to wish people a successful future or a successful past, so I shall wish you both. It has been an honour and a privilege to serve with you. I hope to get around later and say a personal goodbye and thank you to everyone, but my final duty is to announce the name of your new Director.

'I've consulted widely on this, but at the end of the day, there could only be one choice. One person here, above all others, held things together in the basement. One person never gave in. One person's determination will lead you all in to the future. Madam Director, would you step up, please.'

It was better received than I thought it would be. There was some surprise because she wasn't an historian, and Evan had a sour face, but he surely could never have considered himself eligible.

She stood, to enthusiastic applause and slowly mounted the stairs to stand beside me. She looked very smart, extremely serious, and more than a little nervous. I winked at her and we stood facing each other.

The hall grew very silent.

'Director, you are relieved.'

'Director, I stand relieved.'

We shook hands. I made a move to join Tim in the front row, but she put a hand on my arm. 'One moment please.' She faced the hall. I stood, hot and embarrassed as she made a small speech.

'I'm sure this unit would like me to take this opportunity to thank you personally, for everything you have done for us. I know you don't like to be thanked, but just for once, you must endure the embarrassment of receiving our gratitude. Without you, we would not have survived. You have been our Director and we have been proud to have you so. Director, St Mary's thanks you for your service.'

I swallowed and turned to face the still hall. 'St Mary's, it's been an honour and a privilege.'

The applause did not die away and when I could see clearly, they were on their feet and I suddenly realised I was going to miss them more than a little.

Pinkie spoke for a few minutes. Evan was confirmed as Senior Historian. Christine got her beloved kitchen to run. Alicia was made Librarian. I was glad she was promoting from within. She kept it short, however. I guessed that, in the nicest possible way, she wanted us gone so she could get cracking. I didn't blame her. I would have too.

Guthrie, Peterson, and Leon extricated themselves from the throng. Leon still looked a touch wobbly. I tried not to feel guilty.

'We're off now,' said Ian. 'We've said our goodbyes and we'll just slope off while no one's looking.'

'I'm holding on for an hour or so,' I said, 'then coming back in Number Four as agreed. Is no one coming back with me?

No, seemed to be the answer to that. Leon wanted his own pod. Tim was going with him in case he fell asleep in the middle of something important and Ian was just going with them, anyway.

'OK,' I said. 'I'll tie up the loose ends here and see you in a couple of hours.' I watched them go. I spent an hour with Pinkie and then half an hour just chatting to Mrs Partridge, which I think we both enjoyed. Although I still lacked the balls to ask about Bolivia.

That done, I set off for Hawking. It took a very long time, not least because I did make an effort to speak to everyone.

Finally, I found myself outside Number Four.

'The co-ordinates are all laid in,' said Pinkie, unconsciously echoing Chief Farrell's own words on my first solo jump, all those years ago.

We stepped inside and she ran a professional eye over the console. 'Everything's fine. Just press the button and go.'

'Thank you,' I said, meaning a lot more than that.

'You're welcome,' she said, meaning a lot more than that.

'Good luck with everything,' I said. 'Especially the new project.'

'You too. Take care, Max.' She stepped outside. Then stepped back in again.

'What the hell am I going to do with seventeen dodos?'

I laughed. Not my problem!

The door closed. I sat on an unfamiliar seat and started the countdown.

'Jump initiated.'

And the world went white.

Chapter Ten

The next day, I reported to the Boss directly after breakfast. Mrs Partridge was in her office and nodded me through.

To my surprise and dismay, we sat in the armchairs. It was going to be one of *those* interviews. Rumour had it that he'd once attended a seminar on caring management, and these two armchairs were the unnerving result. Personally, I was always more comfortable with his desk between us – like the Romulan neutral zone.

We sat and contemplated each other for a while.

'So,' he said, '*Director* Maxwell.'

I grinned.

'Dare I hope this has given you a unique insight into the daily problems of running this unit?'

'Indeed it has, sir. Many things have now been revealed to me. But there is just one thing about being Director that does still bother me.'

'And that would be?'

'What do you do *after* lunch?'

Holding my gaze, he said, 'Disciplinary issues, mostly. Recently, not so much. Although I am expecting that to change any time now.'

I thought it wisest not to push my luck any further.

He picked up my file and flicked through. I could hear his old clock ticking in the corner.

Finally, he said, 'I am becoming increasingly concerned at the toll this job is taking on you. I would like you to take a fortnight's leave.' Well, that didn't sound too bad. I could happily do that.

'These last twelve months have been interesting.' I couldn't argue with that. 'Mrs Partridge informs me that apart from some sick leave, you've had no real time off since before your assignment to the Cretaceous.'

Well, good for Mrs Partridge.

'I would, therefore, like you to spend today tying up any loose ends in your department, writing a report on your recent experiences, with particular reference to your tenure as Director, and making all necessary arrangements for fourteen days leave. You and Chief Farrell will present yourselves at The Redhouse Centre at 11.00 a.m. tomorrow morning. You don't need to take anything with you. In fact, they prefer it if you don't. They will provide everything you need. I will speak to Chief Farrell separately. That will be all, Dr Maxwell.'

Bloody hell! The Redhouse Centre, or just The Red House as it was usually known, was the place where they shoved royalty, high-ranking politicians, and captains of industry who had gone off the rails a bit. Rumour had it Princess Alice had spent some time there after her month-old marriage to that rock star had broken up so spectacularly, and the Defence Secretary had been taken there after he raced naked through the corridors of power, shouting, 'I'm Titania, Queen of the Fairies!' Given the balls-up he and the government had made of everything, that might have been the most accurate statement he ever made in his entire life.

Anyway, this was where the rich and powerful went when feeling 'tired and emotional'. They were opulent, effective, discreet, and utterly trustworthy. The man in charge, Dr Knox, reportedly held the secrets of the nation in his hands.

But, mostly, it was incredibly, horribly, enormously, expensive. About a year's wages for just an overnight stay. Of course, that said more about our levels of pay than Dr Knox's prices.

I gaped at him. 'You're sending both of us to the Red House? For fourteen days?'

'Yes, I believe that was what I said. Which part was

unclear?'

'Can we afford it?'

He smiled. 'I've known Alexander Knox for some time. He's interested in Chief Farrell's condition and is happy to take you both at short notice.'

'But do we have a cover story?'

'Dr Knox is aware of St Mary's. He knows what we do here. You can speak freely to him. Dr Foster has informed me she does not have the necessary expertise to be sure of the best treatment for Chief Farrell. You are going, ostensibly, as his carer. In reality, you are going for a spot of R&R. I believe the facilities at The Red House are among the finest in the country and I expect you to avail yourselves of them. Make sure you get my money's worth. On your return I intend to work you to death, so make the most of it.'

He stood up. The caring manager was back in the box. I left before he started talking about making deductions from my pay. Always one of his favourite subjects.

I spent the rest of the day briefing and being briefed. I dictated my reports to my assistant, David, for onward transmission to the Boss after I'd gone. The place had ticked over pretty well without me, which was gratifying. I have no time for people who ensure their departments can't function without them. I've always had a sneaking suspicion mine functions slightly better when I'm not around. Still, they seemed pleased to see me back.

Best of all, Kal was still there. She was leaving the next day but I hadn't missed her. I was so glad. She, Tim, and I had a last lunch together. Tim shot off to terrorise his trainees, Kal went to finish her packing and I went back to work. David had set up a series of meetings for me. First off were Miss Schiller and Miss Van Owen. I was setting them to work on The Play.

Our genuine Shakespeare play. From the hand of Shakespeare himself, as attested by Dr Bairstow who stood over him while he wrote it, and then buried it here. Under our fourth step, actually, where it had been discovered along with the collection of sonnets which were now being used for the benefit of the future St Mary's. We owned a manuscript beyond price. Except we couldn't use it because, for some reason, in this play, they executed Elizabeth, not Mary Stuart.

I said, 'We need to get this sorted. This is your immediate priority. I want an in-depth study. Somewhere in this play, there must be a point where the histories diverge. A kind of tipping point, if you like. I want you to find it. Somewhere, our history goes one way and the play goes another. Cross-reference every event in the play against actual events. Find me a starting point. Let's ascertain what we're dealing with and when. It's going to be detailed and painstaking – you'll have to check everything against reputable sources and there's always the possibility that Shakespeare has been flexible with actual events, so keep that in mind as well.'

They nodded, heads bent over scratchpads. Although I had the Tudors as one of my secondary areas, Schiller's main specialty was Tudor and Stuart England and Van Owen was the go-to person for detailed work.

'Is there a deadline?' she muttered, still tapping her scratchpad.

'No,' I said. 'I'm off on leave for fourteen days. Accuracy is more important than speed. We have to get this absolutely right. Requisition whatever you need. See Dr Dowson if you have any problems. Any questions?'

'No,' they said calmly and disappeared with no fuss. When I came back, I was going to make them Senior Historians.

David updated me on who was where and when. Clerk and Spencer were in Regency Bath.

Yilmaz and Travis had gone off to see Drake singe the King of Spain's beard at Cadiz and Roberts and Morgan were writing up their last assignment.

'Anything else I need to know?'

'No, everything here is fine. Professor Rapson has completed his catapult and called for volunteers.'

'What?' I was suddenly wary.

'He plans to see how accurately he can fling plague-ridden bodies over the walls of a besieged city.'

'Not this time,' I said. 'Mannequins, sacks of flour, car tyres – yes. People – no.'

'But the entire department has volunteered,' he said, tragically. 'They'll be very disappointed. It's quite safe – he was only going to toss them into the lake, and many of them planned to make themselves up with pustules and bleeding sores.'

Not so very long ago I would have been one of the volunteers. In fact, Tim and I would probably have been top of the list. Suddenly, I felt very old. I definitely needed a holiday.

'I'd rather they lived with disappointment than multiple fractures. Definitely not. Any problems from them, see Major Guthrie. Tell him if he can't sort them out then he has my permission to shoot them.'

'Yes, Max,' he said, grinning.

'Anything else?'

'Knock, knock.'

'Shut up.'

I was up at dawn the next morning to see Kal leave.

In defiance of regulations, Dieter had brought her car round to the front door. We reckoned it was so early that no one would ever know. He was just opening the boot for her last bits and pieces when the front door opened and Dr Bairstow emerged.

Whoops.

Kal walked up the steps to meet him. They talked quietly for a few minutes. I don't know what he said, but if you knew her you could see she was moved. He put out his hand. She ignored it, stepped forward, hugged him, and kissed his cheek. And lived.

She stepped back. He swept us with a look that promised later retribution and disappeared back into the building.

She sniffed and rejoined us. I watched her say goodbye to Helen and Leon. She wasn't finding this easy. I myself was conscious of a horrible cold feeling inside. She was going. She was actually going. Then she turned to me. I had nothing to say.

There were no words. We hugged for a long time. Neither of us was going to let go. Behind me, Leon said gently, 'Max …'

I couldn't watch her say goodbye to Tim. They'd been partners for so long. They were both in tears. Dieter had to push her into the car. Slowly, she drove away. I looked at Tim. He wasn't going to have a good day. Leon and I were away after breakfast, and he would be alone. I looked at Helen. Her people skills were minimal and I wasn't sure she would realise what this meant to him, but she was already talking gently to him. Well, what do you know? Personal growth.

Farrell took my arm and we climbed the steps. When I looked back, Kal was just pulling out through the gates. There was a solitary pip from the horn, an arm waved out of the window and she was gone.

Two hours later, so were we. We were in Farrell's car and I was driving because he wasn't allowed. It was a beautiful car, sleek and black and handled like a dream. I drove very, very carefully. The deal was that I would drive and he would navigate. This would give us at least a fighting chance of arriving at our destination intact.

I said, 'Shouldn't we be arguing about directions or something?'

'No, I looked at the route last night. I know the way.'

'You take all the fun out of life, you know that?'

'Well, I aim to put it back again as soon as possible, so try and stay out of trouble till then.'

I did manage to keep the car on the road. He tutted.

'Hey, I'm not the one who hits trees.'

I was referring to the famous occasion when he crashed the Boss's Bentley and I finished up across the bonnet and never saw my knickers again. Happy days.

We pitched up just a little before eleven. We're a time-travelling organisation. Punctuality is written into our contracts.

A young woman in a white coat met us on the steps. Her short, dark hair emphasised her beautifully shaped skull. She had eyebrows and cheekbones to which lesser mortals could only aspire. I tried not to sigh.

'I'm Dr Joanna Trent. Dr Knox is still with a patient, so he's asked me to show you around and make you welcome. So – Mr Farrell, Dr Maxwell – welcome to The Red House. If you can let John here have your keys, he can park your car for you.'

I handed the over the keys. Obviously Red House inmates never did anything as mundane as parking their own cars. I felt rather than heard Farrell's sigh of relief. He had obviously been picturing his beloved car bouncing around a packed car park like an impala on a trampoline.

She was speaking again. 'I'll leave you to explore the grounds yourselves. We're very proud of our gardens and they're here to be enjoyed. Now …' We walked up the steps and through the main doors. You could tell this wasn't the British National Health Service. They had carpet on the floor. Obviously the inmates never did anything as low-class as bleed or puke on it. Comfortable chairs and low tables were scattered around. Another young man sat behind a polished mahogany reception desk.

'This is Paul. He'll be along later to do the paperwork. Now, we're standing at a kind of crossroads here. To the left is the library; a lovely room, well stocked and with a wide range of daily papers for the benefit of our guests.'

Guests! Not inmates. Get the terminology right, Maxwell.

'Which reminds me, no electronic devices and definitely no mobiles.' She held out a hand.

Farrell dug his out and handed it over. She looked at me.

'I don't have one.'

She raised one disbelieving, beautifully shaped eyebrow.

'No, it's true,' said Farrell. 'She really doesn't.'

I shook my head in agreement. She still didn't look happy, but it's a look I've been familiar with all my life. I was beginning to feel my old dislike of authority stirring inside.

'Next to the library is the Guests' Lounge and, at the very end, the Guests' Dining Room. Should you have any special dietary requirements, please be sure to speak to Paul about them. He's here to help, as are we all.'

She turned and gestured gracefully to her right. 'Down this corridor, we have a series of consulting and treatment rooms and Dr Knox's office at the end.

'Straight ahead and through the big doors is our Annexe, consisting of the Arts and Crafts Centre, our gym, swimming pool, and spa facilities. Please make full use of them whenever you can.'

I tuned her out and looked around. It was sumptuous. The colour scheme was cream and pale blue with occasional touches of a deep rose pink. It smelled of lemons. Everything was spotless. Everything looked very expensive.

At the top of the stairs was a nurses' station and corridors branched off in spokes.

'Your rooms are down here. This is normally the Ladies' Side,' she said, 'but we were asked to house you together, so you have the two adjacent rooms here.' She fixed Chief Farrell with a severe frown. 'Please be discreet.' Behind her back, I laughed at him.

He murmured, 'Of course, Doctor,' but she had opened the first door and swept inside.

'Dr Maxwell, this is your room.'

I'd never seen anything like it. The curtains matched the bedcovers, which matched the cushions – always the sign of a diseased mind. There was a big double bed piled high with pillows, two deep armchairs, a dressing-table-cum-desk, a wardrobe, a carpet, *and* rugs. The floor was level. No pockmarks marred the smooth perfection of the walls. Both curtains were the same colour. This was a whole new world to me.

There was a connecting door to Chief Farrell's room, which was blue and cream to my cream and blue. We walked between the two rooms a couple of times, trying to look as though we were accustomed to this sort of thing, and probably failing wildly.

'I'll leave you to settle in,' she said, opening the door. 'You'll find clothes in the wardrobe, toiletries in the bathroom, a selection of books on the bedside table, and water in the chiller. The telephone connects with the nurses' station. Just press zero.

'Just the one rule you need to know now. Between 2.00 and 4.00 p.m. in the afternoon, all guests must return to their rooms. It's OK if you want to doze, and equally all right if you don't. We call it Quiet Time. Actually, the whole thing is not so much for our guests' benefit as ours. It gives us a chance to put our feet up, have a cup of tea, write up our notes, and generally catch up. The chimes will sound at 2.00 p.m., so you'll know. Dr Knox will see you in his office at 12.00 noon. Can you remember the way?'

We nodded. Well, Leon could remember the way. I'd probably find myself on the outskirts of Aberystwyth.

She disappeared and we looked at each other.

'I do like a place where you have to go to bed at two o'clock,' he said. 'I wonder if we could get Edward to introduce the same thing at St Mary's?'

'Yes, just what St Mary's needs – another excuse to climb into bed with each other.'

'I don't need an excuse,' he said, backing me towards the bed.

'It's ten to twelve,' I said, trying to wriggle free.

'No problem.'

'Seriously? Less than ten minutes? You think that's something to be proud of?'

'Later then,' he said, reluctantly removing his hand.

'Yes, right in the middle of Quiet Time – you practising your famous Rebel Yell, I'm going to take my clothes off now. You need to leave.'

He laughed. 'You really thought that one through, didn't you?'

'Later,' I said, resting my forehead on his chest and feeling his heartbeat.

'Yes,' he whispered. 'You promised.'

'I did, didn't I?'

'Yes, you did and I'm holding you to it. Don't make me come looking for you.'

Well, that could be fun, but probably not here.

'OK,' I said. 'Two o'clock. I'll see you then,'

'No,' he said, bending to kiss me. 'I'll see you. That's the whole point.' I closed the door behind him, opened the wardrobe and yanked out a set of sweats that probably cost a week's pay.

The end of my world was here and I never saw it coming.

Chapter Eleven

I don't know what I'd been expecting. A tall, skinny, wild-eyed man with a shock of electric hair and an Austrian accent? In reality, Dr Knox was only just average height, very slight, with dark hair just beginning to be threaded with grey, brown eyes, and an over-tailored pinstriped suit.

He came to greet us and smiled at me as if he knew exactly what I had been thinking. I resolved to be more careful. We shook hands and he ushered us in.

His carefully designed office felt relaxing and reassuring. There was no modern chrome or glass here. A good but shabby, slightly threadbare carpet lay on the polished floor. The furniture was dark and slightly battered, with a couple of carefully distressed sofas. As opposed to my own sofa at St Mary's, which was not so much distressed as distraught. Open French windows looked out into a small walled garden, and light muslin curtains billowed gently into the room. Nothing bad could ever happen here.

He invited us to sit. Farrell dropped heavily onto a sofa. He was more tired than he knew. I curled up at the other end. Dr Knox began.

'Firstly, let me say, I've known Edward Bairstow for some years now and I know who you are and what you do. We have all sorts of – guests – here. I've been told all sorts of things I probably shouldn't know, by all sorts of people I wouldn't normally meet. I don't take notes and there are no recording devices anywhere. After you've gone, I'll scribble a few lines, but that's only so I can remember for our next session and not waste any time going over old ground again. So, shall we get started?

'Mr Farrell, I'd like to start with you. Just a quick session today, mostly just admin stuff, a quick history, and a few other things.'

I sat back as he went over names and carefully prepared dates.

'Yes, that all seems to be correct.' He tossed the folder on to the floor. That was apparently supposed to be a symbolic gesture. It looked rehearsed to me. I didn't like this man …

'So, a medical coma, I understand. What can you tell me?'

'What would you like to know?'

'Well, how do you feel?'

'I'm fine. I still get a little tired occasionally.'

'I'm sure you do. How are you sleeping?'

'Mostly, very well. Occasionally …' He paused.

'Let me guess. You dream.'

'Yes, not all the time. It's not happening anything like as frequently now.'

'Yes, I understand that vivid dreams are a side-effect, both during and after the coma.'

'Very vivid.'

'Did you ever feel the dreams were more real than reality itself? That the dreams were real and reality was a dream?'

'Yes, very much so. It's unnerving.'

'I imagine it must be. If it's any consolation, firstly, it's normal for this experience and secondly, they will slowly cease, if they haven't already begun to do so.'

'Yes, it's nowhere near as bad as it was.'

'Tell me, you're the first patient I've ever had with this particular condition, were they narrative dreams? Was there a story? Or a connected theme? Or just the usual jumbled collection of thoughts and experiences?'

'Oh, definitely narrative. I'm not saying each one carried on from the previous dream, but there was certainly a common theme.'

'Really? That's most interesting. How much of them can you remember?'

'Less and less as time passes, but there are some highlights – if that's the word I want – that I'm never going to forget.'

'Can you give me an idea?'

Leon stared into the middle distance, eyes unfocused and his voice as far away as his thoughts. 'Lights. Voices. Rain. A shouting crowd. But not hostile. My clothes are stiff and heavy. People around me. I know them. Glittering fabric. Mist. Waiting.' He frowned. 'Buildings. A town.'

'Do you know where you are?'

'Scotland.'

Dr Knox sat back thoughtfully. 'How very interesting. Do you know when?'

Old training dies hard. 'I don't think so.'

'Well, this is fascinating. We'll leave it for now, Mr Farrell, but I hope to pick this up again, soon.'

I was a little surprised he let it drop, but Leon nodded, leaned back and closed his eyes. A few seconds later, he was asleep. I looked at Dr Knox, who laughed ruefully and said, 'Am I that boring?'

'He does this sometimes. He'll be back in about twenty minutes, and he just picks up where he left off.'

He smiled. 'He's lucky to have you.'

'Finally! A doctor I can agree with.'

'Shall we step outside? It's lovely in the garden and then we won't disturb him.'

He was right. The little walled garden was lovely. Thickly planted with roses, lavender, geraniums, and others I couldn't name. A little gravel path led to a small fountain. The tinkle of water and a lazily droning bee were the only sounds I could hear.

We sat at a small table.

'Yes, I love my garden and thought it would be nicer for us both if we fenced out here.'

'Fenced?'

'I've had a telephone conversation with Dr Foster, who says under no circumstances am I to allow myself to be intimidated by you, and, I warn you now, if you start to get out of hand, I

135

will hit you with a chair. Just so you know.'

'Duly noted.'

'I gather he's not the only one who's had a tough time recently.'

Not hearing a question, I didn't reply.

'What happened to your face?'

'I was attacked. All healed up now.'

'Yes, you can barely see the scars any more.'

'And soon, you won't be able to see them at all.'

'Is that what they told you?'

I was certain my expression didn't change for even a fraction of a second, but I felt the skin tighten around my eyes. I did not like this man. The smiling charm had disappeared and something else had taken its place.

Forcing myself to smile, I said, 'Oh, I never make the mistake of believing anything doctors tell me.'

'How wise,' he said lightly and now the gloves were off. I felt a bit like David and Goliath and unfortunately, this time, Goliath just rolled right over the top of me.

'So, tell me about your family.'

'I'm afraid I haven't seen them for some time.'

'Why would you be afraid? Do you regret you haven't seen them for some time, or do you fear your family?'

'Neither.'

'Then why say you're afraid?'

'A figure of speech I utilised to soften the blow.'

'The blow?'

'You make your living by restoring people to what you consider to be normal behaviour, an occupation I consider to be irrelevant at best and dangerous at worst. Naturally, I'm far too polite to say so and was simply attempting to convey my – lack of faith – in your profession without hurting your feelings.'

'I'm not sure you achieved your objective, but you must be accustomed to failure.'

'Oddly enough, making a practice of avoiding the medical profession, politicians, bankers, and similar people has given me a healthy relationship with success.'

'You have a strange definition of success. You have no contact with your family, were nearly expelled from school on several occasions, there are multiple disciplinary sheets on your file, you are unable to form close relationships, no husband, no children – no living children, I should say – and yet you consider yourself successful. Do you think others share this view? Dr Bairstow for instance?'

'I have no idea. Perhaps you should ask him.'

'Perhaps you should consider who sent you here.'

I felt the ground fall away beneath my feet. Surely, Dr Bairstow wouldn't … If I trusted anyone in this world … Everything I'd ever known … Everything I'd built my life around … Old insecurities never go away. They just lurk in the background ready to jump out when you least expect them … And when you least need them …

We stared at each other for a while. The bee staggered groggily past.

And then, having goaded me into unwise speech and undermined the foundations of my entire world, he switched again, and the smiling charmer was back.

'Well, you do give as good as you get, don't you? I wouldn't want to cross your path on a dark night,' he said cheerfully. 'Don't worry. All done.'

Slowly, I let myself relax, leaning back in my seat. I could feel sweat in the small of my back. I closed my eyes and felt the sun on my face. It was all very peaceful.

'Does he know you're a cold-blooded, murdering bitch?'

My eyes flew open. I lurched forwards. He was scribbling in a file, a small smile on his face. He looked up. 'What?'

'What …? What did you say?'

'I said, "*Don't worry. All done.*"' His eyes slid past me. 'Ah, Mr Farrell, you're with us again.'

Shit, shit, shit …

My innards turned to ice. I stood up. He was standing just inside the French windows. He looked shocked and disoriented. I hoped to God that it was only because he'd woken up suddenly in a strange place.

I needed to get away. Averting my face, I said, 'Will you be OK here, on your own?'

He didn't speak, but nodded.

'I'll see you later, then.'

He made no reply and I made a huge mistake. I turned and walked away. I should have stayed and toughed it out, but everyone's wise with hindsight.

I nodded to Dr Knox, who was looking at me in a way I didn't much care for, and left as quickly as I could. I spent about twenty minutes wandering around the gardens until I felt a little calmer and returned to the main building.

Back in my luxurious room, and mindful of Dr Bairstow's instructions, I decided to try out the bathroom facilities. I had a long, hot shower, anointing myself liberally with all the expensive unguents I could find, a few of which I subsequently discovered to have been mouthwash. I took my time, basking in the unexpected luxury of it all, and pushing the events of the afternoon to the back of my mind.

Relaxed and tranquil once more, I wafted back into the bedroom in a cloud of fragrant steam, let down my hair, and brushed it out with long, slow strokes. I took my time, remembering some things, anticipating others, thinking thoughts. Occasionally, I grinned to myself.

I caught one last glimpse in the mirror. Even I had to admit I didn't look too bad – flushed cheeks (from the shower, obviously), bright-eyed and ready to go.

I heard movements in the next room. He was back. Carefully arranging the towel so it would easily fall away, I took a deep breath, lifted my chin and stepped through the connecting door.

He was on the bed reading, propped up on pillows. We looked at each other.

I let the towel fall.

The silence went on for far too long.

After a while, it dawned on me that I wasn't being fallen upon. Doubt and uncertainty crashed down upon me. He didn't move at all. I felt a cold that had nothing to do with being naked. What had he heard? Or worse, what was he seeing?

Suddenly, I saw myself through his eyes. Not young any more. Not old, but definitely not young. Scars everywhere, thickening waist and hips, cellulite, stretch marks.

For God's sake. What had I been thinking?

He spoke.

He said, 'I don't think so, Dr Maxwell, do you?' and returned to his book.

I was still standing like a pillar of salt. I hadn't moved. I couldn't move. I had to move. Move, you stupid pillock, Maxwell. Are you waiting for him to change his mind? Move!

No power on earth could have made me bend and pick up that towel. Holding tight to the doorknob, I stepped back and closed the door behind me. After a moment, I locked it. After another moment, I remembered to breathe in.

Hanging off the back of the door was a towelling dressing-gown. Soft and fluffy, like the towels. I put it on and buried myself in its warm depths. There was water in a small chiller and with shaking hands I poured myself a glass. I sat on the bed and leaned back against the headboard. Somewhere in the building, something chimed. Two o'clock. Nap time for the kiddies! I started to think again, but before I could do anything, I heard Dr Knox's voice in the corridor. I grabbed a paperback and lay back.

He knocked. I didn't answer. He knocked again. I called sleepily, 'Come in.'

He stuck his head round the door. 'I'm sorry. Did I wake you?'

There's something inside me that responds to an emotional crisis. I smiled guilelessly. 'No, just dropping off.' My voice was perfectly calm and my hands quite steady.

'Well, I'll leave you in peace. Have you seen Mr Farrell at all?'

'I think I heard him moving around next door about ten minutes ago.'

'Ah, he's back safely then. I'll leave you both in peace and see you at dinner this evening.' He closed the door quietly behind him.

I sprang off the bed, opened the door a crack and watched him stride off and round the corner, talking on his phone. Shutting the door, I thought for a moment. I was out of here! My first thought was to do the thing with the pillows so it would look as if I was still in bed, but that never looks real. Besides, this was a loony-bin. Admittedly, their clientele only consisted of the industrial, religious, and political leaders of our nation so they wouldn't be expecting too much in the way of brains, but I was sure they'd be a bit more rigorous than that with their checks.

I scattered stuff around the room, pulled the bedclothes back and laid the dressing gown untidily across the bed. I hid the Red House sweats in the wardrobe and dressed in my own clothes. The car keys were on the dressing table. Of course, they'd given them back to the driver, not the owner. Good for them.

At the door, I turned and checked the room. It really did look as if I'd just got up, but not gone far. They'd waste a few minutes thinking I was in the bathroom, then maybe some more time looking around the building – I might have gone to explore. They might even search the grounds before thinking to check the gate. I know, voluntary patient and all that, but I didn't mind betting that, when the chips were down, Knox would find some way of keeping me here, and it was a nice place – I really didn't want to have to torch it.

The corridors were deserted, patients in bed, staff putting their feet up and having a cuppa. I tripped lightly down the stairs, car keys swinging from one finger and stopped at the desk. The orderly, Paul, wasn't there and I was sorely tempted to keep on going, but I didn't. He came back with a file.

'Can I help you, Dr Maxwell?'

'Yes, do I need to sign out?'

'You're leaving us so soon?'

'Well, I stayed until he fell asleep. While I think of it, can you tell me what the visiting hours are, please?'

He handed me a small brochure. 'Visiting details on the back.'

'Thanks, this is just what I need.'

'If you give me your keys, I'll get the car brought round for you, miss.'

No, no, no, no …

'Thank you, that's very kind.'

He disappeared. I heard voices.

Come on, come on. I was sick with anxiety.

He reappeared. 'If you could sign here, please.'

I signed out and put the time. 'Are there contact details in this brochure?'

'Yes, on the back. You can telephone at any time; someone will always be available. You can't call him directly, of course, no mobiles allowed to our guests, but there are patient telephones, so he'll be able to telephone you.'

'Excellent.'

'Anything else, miss?'

'No, I think that covers just about everything.'

Come on, come on. All it would take would be for any member of the medical staff to walk across the hall.

'Here's your car, miss. Safe journey.'

'Thank you. See you tomorrow.'

The hell they would.

As I turned away, he pressed a button on his call set. I guessed it was to tell the gate to let me through. I was so glad I hadn't just walked out. I'd never have got through the gate. I walked slowly down the steps. An orderly handed me the keys.

'Thank you. See you soon.'

I climbed in. The car started easily and I trundled slowly down the drive. My heart was thumping a little, but the gates opened for me. No one prevented my leaving. I eased the car out into the road and was away.

Now, I could allow the hot, bitter humiliation to roll over me in waves.

I don't think so, Dr Maxwell, do you?

I swallowed bitter bile and fled back to St Mary's. I wanted to be home, to pull the comforting routine around me like an old blanket and bury my head and cry.

I was roused from this unpleasant state of self-pity by a big bump. I'd drifted too far to the side of the road and hit something on the verge. It made me start thinking properly. I wasn't going to slink, pitiful and sobbing back to St Mary's. I was going to do what I always did in a catastrophe. I was going to do some damage.

I took the next turning to Rushford and pulled into the multi-storey car park. There was a hairdresser's just over the road and yes, they could do me now. I told them what I wanted and settled back while they got on with it. I left the salon with a tiny, chic little ponytail bouncing and swinging as I walked. I loved it. Female historians have yards of hair. It's in the rules and regs. This was about as radical as I could get and still not be handed my P45. I got out of Rushford without much mishap and headed for St Mary's.

Now for Stage Two. I waited until I was off the main road – I didn't want to be arrested until I'd finished. For starters, I ran the car up onto the grass verge. There were several bangs as it connected with boulders and branches, but there didn't seem to be a great deal of damage. Curse this superb German engineering!

I changed down to second, put my foot down, and watched the rev counter climb. By now, even I could hear the engine complain. However, it was whingeing in German and I was listening in English, so much good it did.

I don't think so, Dr Maxwell, do you?

Two very large boulders blocked the entrance to a forest track. I pulled up and reversed back into them a couple of times. That felt good. There were tinkly noises. There were some very satisfying graunchy noises. I turned around and drove into them front first. More noises. I pulled alongside the poor abused boulders and slammed the driver's door into them a couple of times. By now, I was getting hot and tired. It took several goes to inflict any sort of damage at all to the door panel. Bloody Germans!

I got out and looked at the results so far. Lights gone on one side, boot caved in. Ditto the front. Water dripped down into a puddle, so the radiator was shot. The driver's door – finally –

was nicely dented.

I frowned. Not a lot to show for all that effort. I picked up a rock and chucked it at the back windscreen. It just bounced off. Unbelievable! In a spurt of temper, I raised it above my head and hurled it with all my might. The glass crazed. That would have to do.

I had another idea. Pulling the travel rug off the back seat. I tugged on the bonnet catch. Using the rug, I got the oil cap off. The engine did start, but it definitely wasn't as enthusiastic as it had been. I shoved it into gear and we clanked our way down the road. Lights on the dashboard winked and flashed. Not my problem. I think I'd lost a part of the exhaust somewhere along the way, because by now we sounded like a tank, and something was dragging along the road behind me. There was the odd spark. Steam hissed from under the bonnet. Black smoke billowed from somewhere and there was a bit of a funny smell. Probably because I was still in second gear.

People came out to stare as I drove through the village. I drove nonchalantly up the road and through the gates, waving cheerfully at Mr Strong's worried face. The engine was really straining as we crawled up the drive. The noise was tremendous. Still, not much further now.

I don't think so, Dr Maxwell, do you?

Over to my right I could see the Friday afternoon football match had halted through lack of interest. Everyone was watching me instead. Even the Boss was out on his balcony. I suspected there had been telephone calls. I couldn't see the expression on his face. At the end of the drive, I should turn left and go round the side of the building to the car park. I turned right.

The car was now making legitimate complaints in a language even I could understand. We banged along the terrace. There were a few people sitting at the tables watching the game and enjoying the sunshine. They stared, mouths open.

I shouted, 'Get out of the way, you morons.' At the last moment, they leaped for their lives.

I clattered through the garden tables and chairs, got

something caught in a wheel arch and felt the steering wheel jump in my hands. The car bounced heavily off a large stone urn full of geraniums.

We clonked across the grass, shedding garden furniture faster than election promises the day after the results are announced. I had hardly any speed at all, but it was downhill now. I clipped a silver birch, to the detriment of the wing mirror, but that was going to be the least of his problems.

I don't think so, Dr Maxwell, do you?

Nearly there.

I floored the accelerator to build up the revs. We surged sluggishly forward. With the engine screaming and trailing clouds of smoke, steam, and glory, I drove Chief Farrell's car straight into the lake.

The engine died and everything was suddenly very quiet. Smoke drifted serenely across the surface. There was a little bubbling and hissing but otherwise everything was surprisingly peaceful.

If I hadn't been getting wet, I could have sat there all afternoon. With some difficulty, I forced the door open and fell out. The water was nearly up to my waist. I struggled to the bank. What seemed like the entire unit lined up on the bank, faces blank with shock. Guthrie, still in his mud- and blood-stained football kit said, 'What the ...? What happened? Are you hurt? Where's the Chief?'

I was tempted to say he was in the boot. 'Still in the hospital.'

'But why ...? What ...?'

I walked past him and strode, alternately whistling and squelching, back along the terrace and through the front door. Faces appeared at all the windows. Without slowing, I took the stairs two at a time, and preceded by the smell of stagnant water and leaving a trail of pond scum, I dripped into Mrs Partridge's office. She looked up with absolutely no expression whatsoever.

'Dr Maxwell.'

'What ho, Mrs Partridge! Do you have some of those

'Deduction from Wages to Pay for Damages Incurred' form-thingies?'

She reached up behind her and pulled one off a shelf.

'On second thoughts, better make that two. It's carnage out there.'

Silently, she handed me another. I signed both and cheerfully handed them back to her. 'There you go. Save you a bit of work later on.'

As I turned to go, the Boss called from his office. 'Ten o'clock tomorrow morning, Dr Maxwell. My office.' I was too angry to care.

'Already looking forward to it, Dr Bairstow.'

I did not slam the door on my way out.

Peterson turned up. I suppose I'd been expecting him. We climbed out of the window and sat on the flat roof outside my room. It was sunny and warm in the evening sun and a million years from the trauma of the afternoon. He cracked a beer.

'Want one?'

'God, no.'

I wasn't going to break the silence, which stretched on and on.

He finished his beer, crushed the can and said, 'So, it didn't go well, then?'

I didn't know whether to nod or shake my head, so did neither.

'Hey, this is me. Remember last year, when it was you and me against the world?'

I didn't know what to say, but I didn't want him to go away, so I reached out and clutched at the material in his sleeve. He leaned back against the wall, eyes closed. To all intents and purposes, he was asleep.

I made a huge effort to get on top of the hot rock of betrayal sitting on my heart. Blue sky, white fluffy clouds, birds twittering, distant voices; everyone else's world was carrying on while mine had fallen apart. There was no movement from Peterson. I went to get up but without opening his eyes, he pulled me back again.

'Do you want me to kill him for you? I can do it slowly and painfully. He will suffer.'

'That's very sweet of you, but I can kill him myself. I've already made a start with his car.'

'Yes, that was awesome, Max. You never disappoint.'

I smiled bitterly, but said nothing.

'What are you going to do now?'

'My job. As well as I can. As hard as I can.'

'Can I do anything?'

I controlled a quivering lip. 'Well, I have to see the Boss tomorrow at ten. I think we can guess what that will be about. I might need you. Afterwards.'

'Is Farrell coming back?'

'Don't know. Don't care.'

I leaned back and closed my eyes as well. The sun went down behind the roof parapet and all the shadows inched their way towards us.

Chapter Twelve

Yesterday's bravado had subsided, leaving a nasty, cold, empty feeling. I really wasn't looking forward to my interview with Dr Bairstow.

There was no hint of the cosy armchair chat this time. He'd cleared his desk – never a good sign – and stared bleakly at me over the empty expanse. I wasn't asked to sit. I stood before him, slightly tidier than usual and with a dawning realisation of what I'd done.

He contemplated me silently for what seemed like a very long time. Dimly, in the background, I could hear the rest of St Mary's crashing through their working day. Up here, in his office, it was very quiet indeed.

After an age, he spoke.

'When I promoted you to Chief Operations Officer, Dr Maxwell, I confess I did not think it necessary to apprise you of the sort of behaviour I would find unacceptable in a member of my senior staff. That I obviously did need to make this plain to you, leads me to believe I may have made a serious error in promoting you.'

He paused. I gritted my teeth and stared over his shoulder.

'You appear to have committed a felony, and should Chief Farrell wish to proceed against you, I shall not interfere. Am I making myself clear?'

I nodded, waiting for him to ask that all-important question – why? Because I couldn't tell him why. I could never tell anyone why.

'The only thing at present staying my hand is that Chief Farrell telephoned me last night to inform me of your precipitate departure and expressing concern for your welfare.'

I wondered what Farrell had told him. How much did he know?

'I advised him of the situation here and he is to return either later today or tomorrow, to assess the matter and proceed accordingly.'

I nodded again, waiting for him to demand my resignation. As usual, he read my mind.

'I will tell you what I told him. I would not accept his resignation, and I will not accept yours, either. I neither know nor care what is happening between you, but you will find a way to work together. That is an order. Am I still making myself clear, Dr Maxwell?'

I nodded again, praying for this to be over soon. I'd had many bollockings over the years but his words were searing my soul with shame. True, I'd annoyed him once or twice, but I'd never disappointed him before.

I focused hard on the wall behind him.

'Do you have anything to say?'

I lifted my chin.

'I'm not sorry I did it. I'll take whatever punishment comes my way, but I'm not sorry I did it. However, I am sorry to have disappointed you, sir.'

'I will not tolerate such behaviour in my unit.'

'I understand, sir.'

'I suggest, Dr Maxwell, that you review your financial resources. The events of yesterday are going to cost you dearly.'

'Yes, sir.'

'Dismissed.'

I fled, and by a devious route, avoiding people wherever possible, made my way back to my room where Peterson was waiting with a mug of tea and a packet of tissues. Twenty minutes later, I blew my nose and was ready, although with no great enthusiasm, to face the world.

* * *

The next day, I was in the dining-room, nose down in my lunch and wondering why personal catastrophe never affected my appetite, when a ripple ran around the room and everyone suddenly stampeded out the door.

I knew what this was. Chief Farrell was back.

Peterson and I continued a somewhat dogged conversation concerning upcoming assignments. Through the window, I saw the taxi drive away. Chief Farrell walked up the drive, looked over to the lake, paused for a moment, and then started off across the grass.

I knew Dieter had winched his car out of the lake, because David had persisted with a blow-by-blow account, despite my loudly expressed lack of interest.

The Chief disappeared from view and Peterson and I continued to eat. People slowly filtered back again. I hoped their gravy had congealed.

Neither of us attempted to seek out the other. We communicated by email, our com links, or by proxy. I was, therefore, quite surprised when he paused by my table one lunchtime and handed me a piece of paper.

I took it without looking at him. Around the room, everyone fell silent, presumably waiting for me to fall senseless to the ground, which I nearly did when I saw the total. I could have bought a house for the same amount. Or two houses. Or possibly a small village. How could it cost so much to repair just one car?

I took it between two fingers and handed it back to him.

'Please give that to my assistant.'

He handed it back.

'Please do not use St Mary's resources for personal matters.'

'Mr Sands will deliver it to my in-tray for my attention later on. The matter will be attended to when I have a moment.'

I pushed it back to him.

He left without a word.

* * *

149

That night, I fired up my laptop and emptied every bank account I had. I still had the compensation from my unfair dismissal and, having been alerted the hard way to the stupidity of not having any savings, I had been putting a bit by. If I added everything together, I could just cover it.

Just.

The remaining balance was in double figures and followed the decimal point. I had barely pennies to my name.

I shunted the whole lot into his bank account, told myself I regretted nothing, and settled down to watch the latest Bond movie with Peterson and Helen.

The next day, the whole lot pinged back into my account again.

I thought it was some electronic cock-up and whizzed it back to whence it came. Barely an hour later, it came back again.

What the hell did he think he was playing at?

I stormed back to my office and David.

'Knock-knock.'

'Shut up.'

I sat, seething, at my desk and then spent twenty minutes rummaging in unexplored drawers for my rarely-used chequebook.

'What are you doing?' said David, as I banged another drawer shut.

'Chequebook.'

'Bottom left-hand drawer in an envelope marked "STD clinic – test results".'

It was, too.

I scribbled out a cheque, shoved it in an envelope, and gave it to David with instructions to put it in Farrell's pigeonhole.

The next morning there was an envelope addressed to me in familiar jagged handwriting. I opened it up and a hundred tiny pieces of cheque fell out.

I drew out the money in cash and spent the evening pulling the bank wrappers off the bundles, shoving it all in a carrier bag, and mixing it up. The next day I entered the dining room, marched up to the table he was sharing with Dieter and Polly and upended the bag. Loose banknotes floated everywhere. They fell into his lap, his gravy, his water glass, on the floor, in Dieter's custard, and Polly's coffee.

I dropped the bag on the top and left the room.

When I returned to my office an hour later, my desk was heaped high with dirty, sticky banknotes. They were stuck to each other and my desk. Many had fallen on the floor and had dirty footprints. I identified gravy, custard, ketchup, mayonnaise, coffee, butter, and what smelled like motor oil.

'This is ridiculous,' I said. 'What the hell is he playing at?'

'Don't you know?' said David.

'Apparently not. If he doesn't want the bloody money then why stick me with the bill?'

'Put the money back in your account,' said Peterson, coming in behind me.

So I tried and that wasn't easy. Hot with embarrassment, I explained it was exactly the same money I'd drawn out a few days ago. Remarks were made about abnormal wear and tear. I was sick of the whole bloody business by now. If he wanted reimbursing, he could come and ask for it. Otherwise – forget it.

'It worked then,' said Peterson.

I stared at him blankly.

'Well, look at you. You're hot, cross, you've wasted a whole afternoon at the bank, and they think you're an idiot. You're frustrated because you can't ease your conscience by just giving him money. He wanted to wind you up and he certainly succeeded. It's his way of revenge. I know this is not possible for you, but the best response is to remain calm and dignified and rise above it.'

'I'm not a bloody hot-air balloon.'

He remained silent.

'Oh, all right then.'

It was fear and loathing at St Mary's, or annual staff appraisal, as it was sometimes known. I had files spread all over my desk

151

and was not in the best mood. David was banging industriously at his keyboard – he never usually worked that hard. I suspected he was looking up new knock-knock jokes. On the plus side, he hadn't tried to tell me one all day. It was warm and snug inside, cold and wet outside. I was about to mention tea when something made me look up and Chief Farrell stood in the open doorway.

'Can I come in?'

'Yes, of course, Chief. How can we help you?'

'I'd like a word. Mr Sands, could you excuse us a moment, please?'

Bless him, David didn't move but turned his chair to look at me, raising his eyebrows.

'If you could, please, David…'

He grinned. 'I have to see Professor Rapson anyway. He says he can fit blades to my wheels. You know – Ben Hur? How cool will that be?' He disappeared before I had time to veto the blades.

'Please sit down, Chief. What can the History Department do for you today?'

Keep it polite and distant. It was vitally important not to be angry. Hate and love are pretty much the same thing. Someone you hate is as much the centre of your world as someone you love. Indifference is the killer.

He sat for a while, looking at his feet. Rain lashed against the windows. He looked up.

'For how long are you going to keep punishing me?'

I finished stacking the files, taking my time, then picked the whole lot up and dumped them on David's desk. That would keep him quiet for a bit. Ben Hur!

Finally, I sat back down, clasped my hands on the desk and said, polite and distant, 'Oh dear, I think I owe you an apology, Chief Farrell. I'm so sorry if you thought I was just indulging in some sort of grand sulk or having a snit. I thought I had made things perfectly clear and if I haven't then that's my fault. I had no idea you felt there was still something to be salvaged from the wreckage. Obviously, I was in error and I'm sorry if this is painful for you, but it must be said. I'm not punishing you. I'm not doing anything at all to you. As far as I'm concerned, it's all over. I'm sorry, but I've moved on.'

'Well, I haven't. I'd like to apologise.'

'I'm really not interested.'

'And explain.'

'Still not interested.'

'You need to hear this.'

'I doubt it.'

He banged the desk. 'Listen to me!'

I sighed, threw myself back in my chair and looked out of the window. 'Whatever.'

The wind hurled more rain against the glass and the window rattled. It sounded very loud in the silence. There was no expression on his face. Endless moments passed.

Suddenly, he pushed himself up from his chair and walked out, leaving the door open behind him. I sat back in my chair, feeling suddenly cold. David came back in. He ignored his own desk and plonked himself in front of mine.

'What?'

He banged the arms of his chair in frustration.

'For God's sake, Max, are you insane?'

I said, 'What?' in a completely different tone of voice.

He took a deep, shuddering breath.

'I work for an organisation that manipulates time. Do you think that every day I don't try to think of a way I could go back and warn myself, leave a note, disable my car, do anything, anything at all to change the thing that ruined my life? But I can't and there's nothing I can do about it. It's too bloody late. But for you, this can be fixed. All one of you needs do is swallow your stupid pride and find a way. Because this is not unchangeable and one of you has to do something before it's too late. Suppose one of you dies – there's nothing at all you can do then. It's too bloody late. But it's not now. This can still be fixed. So I'm saying, Max, don't you spend the rest of your life regretting ...'

His voice cracked and he wheeled himself off, crashing

153

heavily into the corner of his desk and having a coughing fit.

I stood up, although whether I meant to help him or go after the Chief, I'm not sure and was never resolved, because, at that moment, Schiller and Van Owen arrived in the open doorway and in their excitement and impatience tried to get through together. I used the time it took for them to sort themselves out to pull myself together.

'Max, we've done it. We've found it. You need to come and see this. We've found the tipping point.'

For a minute, they'd lost me. Then I remembered. Our play. The one where Bill the Bard had obviously in some sort of wonky moment immortalised the death of the wrong queen.

I said, 'That was quick guys, well done. Show me,' and we all clattered out together. I turned in the doorway and said, 'Whenever you're ready, David. I'd appreciate your input.'

Face still averted, he said, 'Two minutes, Max,' so I left him.

The hall was buzzing. It looked like everyone who wasn't actually out on assignment was there. Whiteboards and walls were lined with pieces of paper. Two horizontal rows of paper, one pink and one yellow, ran round the walls. Things were circled or highlighted and arrows led from one page to another and back again. Table tops were littered with maps, photos, reference material, disks, cubes, and sticks. There were piles of paper on the floor with the skull and crossbones motif – the traditional St Mary's sign for *Do Not Touch*. Housekeeping had been having a fit for a week. It looked like chaos, but it wasn't.

I found the corner of a table, perched, and Van Owen yelled for quiet.

I said, 'OK, let's hear it.'

'It's a belter, Max. There are some powerful scenes. If it ever gets performed it's going to be a sensation.' She walked to the start.

'The play begins with the Queen Mum, Mary de Guise, receiving the news that the English king, good old Fat Harry, is planning to marry his son, the future Edward VI, to her daughter.

She's an astute woman and realises Mary will be a key player in the years to come. So Mary gets shunted off to France for safety. By marrying her to the sickly Dauphin, Mary's uncles hope to rule France through her. It's a fairly wordy scene, where everyone obligingly outlines their past histories and future motives. The Queen, Catherine de Medici, glides menacingly through everyone's lives like a well-fed snake and battle lines are drawn up.

'The next scene is the wedding. Everyone's over the moon, except the Queen of course, and everything looks set for a happy ending.

'Except that, as we know, the French King dies prematurely in a jousting accident and the young couple become King and Queen rather sooner than everyone intended. Then, of course, the Dauphin upsets everyone's apple cart by dying himself, apparently of an ear infection. There's a fantastic scene when uncontrollable hostility rises to the surface, Mary and Catherine are hissing venomously at each other over his deathbed, and the upshot is that Catherine forces Mary to return to Scotland. Her reluctance to do so is somewhat played down for the Scottish audience. But from our point of view, so far so good, everything's pretty well spot on.'

She paused for a glug of water.

'Mary returns to Scotland. In the traditional thick Scottish fog. Standing on the shore, she makes a stirring speech about how happy she is to return to her native land, how she will rule justly and fairly, and everything's going to be rainbows and bunny-rabbits from now on. I suspect she actually said, "Shit, I'm soaked. Doesn't the sun ever shine in this God-forsaken dump? Someone find me some dry shoes and give me a drink," and in French too, but there you go.

'In the light of subsequent events, her marriage to Darnley is somewhat played down and we move straight into what is the climax of the first part. The whole tone of the play darkens. Mary, heavily pregnant and attended only by two or three women is complaining bitterly about her new husband. She hates him. Everyone hates him. He's a waster. He's a loser.

He's a tosser, etc. etc. Rizzio arrives for an intimate supper as, apparently, is his wont. As we all know, Darnley and his friends rudely interrupt this little idyll. He restrains the Queen while they stab Rizzio. Many, many times. They counted fifty-six wounds, afterwards. That's a lot. He's clutching her skirts and screaming for her to save him. She's screaming and cursing her husband. Her women are screaming for help, which doesn't come. It's actually a very disturbing scene, ending with the pregnant Queen collapsing in a pool of Rizzio's blood.

She stopped and looked at me. 'Now we come to it. According to the play she does not leave Holyrood. She stays put and Shakespeare gets round this by giving Mary a *"Will no one rid me of this turbulent husband?"* moment and a besotted and unbalanced Bothwell races off to do the deed. In other words, Mary is completely innocent.'

Someone snorted.

'The news of Darnley's death is brought to her and she is properly horrified and appalled.

In the play, she immediately distances herself from Bothwell. As far as we can tell, she never sees him again. So, there's no rape, no disgrace, no fatal third marriage, no uprisings against her, no long imprisonment in England.'

I drew a deep breath.

'Bloody hell! So, that's it, then. That's what's different. No Bothwell.'

'It would seem so, yes.'

'What next?'

'Well, of course, we're well down the wrong path now and picking up speed as we go. Encouraged by Mary, the north rises against Elizabeth, aided by Scottish and French troops. Philip of Spain, alarmed by French ascension in Europe, overcomes his religious scruples and secretly aids Elizabeth. An unlikely scenario but contemporary sources always reckoned he fancied her a bit. Holland falls, of course, because Elizabeth is in no position to send it aid. Vast numbers of Protestants flee England for the safety of America. The Armada sails, only this time to save England, rather than invade, but the result is the same. The ships are scattered by the weather. French and Scottish troops – The Auld Alliance – pour down across the border. Elizabeth flees but is captured and imprisoned. She plots with Spain to return to power and is betrayed.

'In the climactic scene, Mary visits her secretly on the eve of her execution and as one queen to another, begs and implores her to renounce her claim to the English throne. If she publicly acknowledges her illegitimacy, she will be allowed to live out her life quietly under house arrest. Elizabeth rejects this offer with scorn, obviously remembering she spent her childhood in a similar situation, and the two redheads spit unqueenlike insults at each other before a brief moment at the end, when we see them, women in a man's world, tearful and regretting the past. It's a moving and emotional finale. Except …'

'Except what?'

'Except it's all bollocks.'

She opened a file and paused dramatically. Considering it was full of historians, the hall was abnormally silent.

'From the murder of Darnley onwards, everything is a fake. This is Dr Dowson's report. Paper, ink, style – all different. Definitely not Shakespeare.'

'A modern forgery?'

'That's the weird bit, Max. The second part is contemporary with the first. It was written at the same time but just not by the man himself.'

'But it was buried at the same time as the first part?'

'Oh yes. Someone – God knows who – wrote the second part, substituted their version, and it was all buried by Dr Bairstow in good faith.'

I struggled to make sense of this.

'So the play is early 17th century. All of it. But was written by two different people, only one of whom was Shakespeare?'

'Yep. Here's a summary for you.' She passed it over. I took it blindly, while various thoughts ran through my head. Everyone was very quiet. I could hear people's brains working.

I said slowly, 'Very nice work, you two. Well done. I'm off to see Mrs Partridge to make an appointment with the Boss.

Work all that up and you can present it to him tomorrow sometime.'

They backed off and started to gather material. I looked around. David was at the back, still coughing slightly. I raised my eyebrows and he nodded and smiled.

It was only now that I became aware of a rhythmic thumping noise in the background. No one else seemed to notice, so I said nothing.

It grew louder as I climbed the stairs and walked around the gallery to Mrs Partridge's office. She wasn't there. I stuck my head into Admin and they told me she was down the corridor. The thumping noise got louder as I approached the door. I felt my scalp prickle.

Something was happening.

I found her in the printing room. Our nice, sleek, up-to-the-minute digital printer was ominously quiet in the corner and some old clanking thing with moving parts was crashing and thumping away to itself. Papers spewed from an orifice and were being gathered and stapled by Mrs Partridge and her team. I pulled one off the pile. It was nothing, just the annual archive update.

But something was happening.

I turned my head slowly, trying to locate ... something.

With one final, dying clatter, the machine ceased. The silence that fell only emphasised the noise that had gone before. Everyone sighed with relief. Mrs Partridge's team loaded everything onto a trolley and disappeared. Mrs Partridge herself walked quietly around the room, switching things off. That done, she turned to face me.

'Can I see the Boss sometime tomorrow? To report on The Play.'

Without a blink, she said, 'Ten o'clock, tomorrow morning.'

'Thank you.'

I wasn't really listening. I looked up and she was standing quietly and watching. Every time something important happens at St Mary's, Mrs Partridge is always there. Somewhere. Always.

I started to walk around the room. Taped to the wall was a big black plastic bag, half-full of rejected sheets. Without knowing why, I reached in and pulled out a few.

'Be careful,' she warned. 'Some of those will still be wet.'

'What happened?'

'Our usual printer is broken, so we had to use the old machine and we over-inked it. The first few hundred sheets were useless.'

This was important and I didn't know why. I looked at the sheets I'd pulled out. Ink still glistened wetly in places. The printing was blobby. I turned it over. It had leaked through the paper to the back.

Bleed-through.

A hundred thoughts crashed through my mind.

I looked out at the rain. Rain. Dreams. Dreams that were real.

I looked over at Mrs Partridge, who was gathering her equipment and regarding me with the sort of expression usually reserved for a kitten who has just successfully used the litter tray. She stood expectantly by the door. I took the hint.

'Don't forget. 10.00 a.m. tomorrow.'

'No,' I mumbled. 'I won't forget,' and wandered blindly down the corridor. I found myself at the top of the stairs more by good luck than good judgement. David was looking up at me. I went down to join him.

'Can you get back to the office? Clear my desk. I don't care where you hide it. Set up a recorder. Can you do that in twenty minutes?'

'Yes.'

'OK. I'll be along in a minute.'

He set off and I wandered into the library, where it was quiet. This was going to be awkward, but I couldn't help that. I activated my com.

'Chief Farrell?'

'Dr Maxwell?' Puzzled but neutral.

'Yes. I wonder, if you're not too busy, could you spare me half an hour in my office? If it's a problem, I can come to you, but I think it's quieter in my office.'

There was a pause. I shifted from foot to foot, but said nothing.

'Do I get a clue?'

'We're doing some work on Mary Stuart and I think you may have the answers to some questions.'

Another pause.

'Me?'

'Yes. Is it possible for you to come at once?'

And another pause.

'Can you give me ten minutes?'

'Yes,' I said, and closing the link before he could change his mind, I sprinted to my office.

I don't know what David had done with everything. For all I know he'd just opened the window and flung it all out into the rain. I didn't care. I was conscious only of a burning sense of urgency.

I was waiting for him when he stood, somewhat warily, in the doorway. David had put up the red light outside the door. It made us look like a brothel, but it meant no one would come in. I stood up politely, but formally. Our earlier conversation might never have happened.

'Chief Farrell, thank you for coming so quickly. I do apologise if I've disrupted your afternoon. There are some things I'd like to ask you, if you don't mind. Please come in and sit down.'

We sat in the armchairs. I made sure I got the one near the radiator. Just listening to the rain outside made me feel cold. He regarded the little recorder with suspicion.

'It's nothing sinister, Chief. I just want to concentrate on what you have to say, rather than keep trying to remember things. If you have no objection, that is.'

He looked a little dubious. 'This sounds important.'

'Actually, I think it is. And, before you ask, I'm not sure why. I can only ask you to bear with me while I bumble around in the dark until I find what it is I don't know I'm looking for.'

160

'Sounds like typical History Department methodology to me. Very well, Dr Maxwell, do your worst.'

'I'd like to ask you some questions about recent events. I'll happily tell you what it's about when it's over, but not until then, if you don't mind, because I don't want to influence anything you say.'

He nodded, face closed. I knew that look.

'When you were unconscious, you dreamed, right?'

He nodded again, arms folded, chin on chest.

'Can you tell me what you dreamed?'

'I'm not really sure. I can't remember much of it now.'

'But it was very vivid at the time, you said?'

He nodded.

'Very real. More real than reality when you woke up?'

He nodded again, obviously unwilling to commit himself. This wasn't going anywhere. I decided to revise my strategy. I dragged out a sheet of Mrs Partridge's rejected printing and laid it on the table in front of him. He picked it up.

'The new Archive list?'

'Look on the back.'

He turned it over.

'Messy.'

'It's called "bleed-through".'

'And?'

'And I think that's not the only example of bleed-through I've recently seen. I think … I think while you were in a state of altered consciousness, you yourself were subject to – bleed through. I think your dreams may not necessarily be dreams after all. I think the reason it seemed so real to you, is that it was real. I think something bled though and that's what you remember now. Imperfect blobby bits like the reverse side of this printing. You said …'

I took a deep breath and he tensed slightly.

'You said – *Scotland, long skirts, lights, glittering cloth.* That's quite a vivid description. I think you know more than you realise. I'd like you to relax, stop, think and tell me what you remember. If it turns out I'm wrong, then we'll give you a cup of tea, our grateful thanks, and you can go on your way; no harm done.'

He stared at his feet for a while then said, 'I'm not sure I remember very much any more.'

I wasn't going to let this go. 'Well, shall we give it a try?'

He sighed. 'You're like a terrier, aren't you?'

I ignored this. 'OK, just cast your mind back. Try and actually be in your dreams. What can you smell?'

The answer came immediately.

'Horses. Wood smoke. Damp. Musty.'

'What's the weather doing?'

'Rain. It's chilly. Getting dark.'

'Are you outside?'

'Yes. I'm going home.'

That was interesting.

'Where's home?'

'Just round the corner. Through the gates. The house with the gable. There are stone eagles over the door. One has a broken wing.'

That wasn't what I expected. I'd been waiting for a location but I'd got something else. I tried to chuck all pre-conceived ideas out of my head and follow where he led.

'What happens next?'

'Across a small courtyard. Up the steps. Three steps. A wooden door. It's warm inside. There's a big fire.'

'Who's there with you?'

'I see Guthrie. He's wet and shaking out his coat. No, his cloak. Shaking his cloak. I see Peterson as well, sitting at a table. A long table. You and someone else are by the fire. Flickering shadows. Opening the door blows out a candle. Talking. You said … It's gone.' He shook his head.

'No, that's very good. See how much you knew. Is it always that room?'

'No, there's another. With beautiful panelling. Opulent. Many people. Glittering. There's noise. Music. It's hot. I can't see faces, but there's someone. It's like a performance. Applause. Laughter. I'm …. Uneasy. You're standing with your

162

back to the window. You're tense. Everyone is looking at me.'

He stopped. 'There's no more.'

'Do you know why you're so uneasy?'

'No.'

'Anything else? A phrase? A picture in your mind? A feeling?'

He stirred again.

'There's one thing. This was a recurring dream. I'm waiting. In the dark. It's black. I can't see a thing. Rain is lashing down. I can't see. I can't hear. Something is really wrong. I'm waiting for … something. Someone. They're not coming. Something's wrong …' He trailed off. 'That's it, I think.'

I switched off the machine. 'Any thoughts?'

He sighed heavily, staring back into the past. 'No, I've made a good job of forgetting it.'

I got up and switched on the kettle. 'Do you want some tea and I'll tell you what it's all about?'

'No, thank you. I'm rather busy at the moment.'

He didn't want to talk about it. He just wanted to be gone. I didn't blame him.

I sighed. 'Well, thanks anyway, Chief.'

He left. I switched off the red light and sat back to think. There was nothing there at all. Nothing tangible. Nothing I could point to and say, '*There.*' I was stumbling round in the dark. The only thing I had was a feeling. And Mrs Partridge and her bleed-through. I was convinced it was important, but was I reading too much into a sheet of messed-up print? I sat and scowled at my desk. The person I usually talked things over with had just left. I needed some perspective.

I called Peterson. 'Hi. I can't work, so I thought I'd stop you working too.'

'I'm not working. I'm staring in dismay at the answers to this week's exam, wondering whether to cut my losses and expel the whole bloody lot right now. Prentiss describes a closed timelike curve as a …'

'Do you want some tea?'

'Oh God, so much. I'm on my way.'

Arriving precipitately through the door, he flung himself into an armchair. 'So, what's up, Shorty?'

'Where do I begin?'

'At the beginning. Go on to the end and then stop.'

I sat back and told him everything, including assumptions, feelings, guesses, intuition, the lot.

'So you see,' I said, 'in reality, I've got nothing. Certainly nothing tangible to take to the Boss.'

'Oh, I don't know. Let's listen to this before we succumb to despair and despondency.' He activated the recorder, listened for a while, then pulled out his scratchpad and got busy.

'OK, listen. Keywords. Horses. House. Gates. Eagles. Guthrie. Me. You. A grand room elsewhere. A performance of some kind that's important. We could use this. We could work this up into a scenario for an assignment.' He switched on the recorder again and we listened. I saw little pictures in my mind.

If the Chief's recollections were not just dreams then this was an absolute gift. This was a scenario. The personnel would be right. These were the people I'd take, plus a few more, maybe. It was cold and rainy – that would be Scotland in early summer. And we already had Edinburgh in the 16th century. If you followed that logically, you got summer 1567. After Darnley's murder but before Bothwell. Peterson was right, if you looked at it in those terms then it was easy.

On the other hand, they might be just dreams and my Mary Stuart-soaked mind was reading too much into this. In the old days, the old, confident me would have built a house on these rocky foundations. I was still missing something. But, it was a starting point.

I fired up my data table and started working up a scenario. He moved to David's and did the same. After thirty minutes he said, 'I'm done.'

'Me too, just about.'

'I'll show you mine if you show me yours.'

We swapped – the two were reasonably similar. We merged the two, combined the common points, and picked and mixed the rest. There were several vigorous exchanges of views and a free and frank discussion at the end, but, hours and hours later, we finally had something. We worked it through again until at last we were satisfied and then went for a late supper.

I was up bright and early the next morning, too wound-up to stay in bed.

Early though I was, others were up before me. There were a number of historians milling around the hall, examining the displays, pointing and arguing. Standard historian behaviour. I stood at the back, watching. Arranged along the back wall were piles of working papers, secondary source stuff, background details, and a few maps. I picked one up at random. The 1852 Ordnance Survey map. The familiar landmarks were there, Holyrood House, Princes Street, John Knox House, Greyfriars, the castle. I looked at it for a moment and then knew, with absolute, total, complete, unqualified certainty that I was right. The knowledge made my head swim.

I took a moment to try and think clearly. The human brain is programmed to find patterns in a random world. Was that what I was doing? The unending human struggle to bring order into chaos? I leaned back against the table, feeling my heart pound while I tried to pull myself together and think this through calmly. I breathed deeply and found a point on which to focus. Now was not the time to go all wobbly.

I saw Dr Dowson enter the library and followed him in.

'Good morning, Max, you're an early bird this morning.'

'Good morning, Doctor. I need some information urgently, please. Now, if possible.'

He looked at me over his half-moon spectacles. Possibly I still looked a little shell-shocked because he nodded.

'I'll get it for you myself. What do you want to know?'

I told him.

'Well, that seems straightforward enough.'

He bashed a few keys and waited, frowned, bashed a few more, frowned again, went to a data table and fiddled there for a while.

I felt my heart pick up. I was right. I knew it.

'Well, that's a little odd ... Just a minute, Max ...' He consulted an old-fashioned card index. At the end of the table, a printer hummed and spat out a sheet of paper. He brought it over. We surveyed it together.

'Is that all you've got?'

'I'm afraid so.'

'Can't you get any more?'

'There isn't any more. What you see is all there is.'

'What, anywhere?'

'So it would seem.'

'But how could that be? There must be more somewhere, surely?'

'No, Max, that's it. My only explanation is that it's classed as sensitive information and restricted under the 30 Year Rule, or something similar. Although why is a bit of a mystery. It seems a perfectly innocuous request to me.'

I gave him back the paper.

'Yes, I expect that's it. Oh well, never mind. Thanks very much anyway, Dr Dowson.'

He wasn't fooled for a minute.

'If you say so, Max.'

I shot out of the library and ran headlong into Chief Farrell. He steadied me, realised who it was, and quickly dropped his hands.

'Dr Maxwell?'

I decided to push my luck.

'I'm not sure whether to be pleased to see you or not, Chief Farrell. I was just on my way to steal your pod. Do you want to come too?'

'To steal my own pod?'

'Only if you want to, of course. I'll quite understand if you have other plans for the morning.' I tried to get past him. He caught my arm.

'Why?'

'I need to make an unauthorised jump. Now. And I'm sorry but I don't have time for this. Come or not, I really don't mind. I think I'd prefer it if you do come, because this concerns you too, but if you are coming it has to be now.'

'You're stealing my pod and offering me the option of accompanying you?'

'Yes,' I said, impatient at his slowness. 'Are you coming or not?'

He stared at me for what seemed a considerable time, his face unreadable.

'Very well. But don't race through the hall attracting so much attention. Stroll casually.'

'OK,' I said, strolling casually.

I couldn't help speeding up down the long corridor, but by exercising huge, huge self-control, managed to keep it down to a casual canter.

Once inside his pod, however, he slapped my hands away from the controls.

'No, that's enough. What's this about?'

I took a deep breath.

'You may not remember this, but when you woke after your coma, the first words you said to me were, "*Be careful, the names are the same.*"'

'No, I don't remember that.'

'Well, you did. It was the most lucid moment you had for ages.'

'I'll take your word for it but I don't see the significance. Whose names are the same?'

'Knox. Dr Alexander Knox and John Knox. They have the same names. Well, the same surname anyway.'

He stared at me. I suspected Alexander Knox was a bit of a taboo subject.

'John Knox. You know, the famous Scottish clergyman. Led the Protestant Reformation in Scotland. Met John Calvin. Instrumental in the removal of the Queen Regent. Wanted Mary Stuart executed for murder.'

'I know who he is,' he said, impatiently. 'What's that got to do with Alexander Knox? And do not answer that question by saying – *Their names are the same.*'

'Well, they are,' I said stubbornly. 'And you're the one who

167

warned me about it.'

'I was in a coma!'

'No, you weren't.'

'As good as.'

'Maybe that's when you do your best work. Maybe you had a moment of clarity. Let's face it, you're about due. Look, I'm trying to find some information about Alexander Knox and all Dr Dowson can dig up is a few lines about him opening The Red House, seven years ago. There's nothing on his background or education. Not even his qualifications, which you have to admit is a bit dodgy.'

'Given what he does, it's probably restricted information.'

'Precisely. That's why I'm going back to the future to see what they've got. The 30 Year Rule won't apply any more. Now, can we go?'

'Why are you always in such a hurry?'

'I'm seeing the Boss at ten this morning with the iffiest proposals you ever heard in your life and I really would like to have something more solid to give him. Can we go now, please?'

We went.

We materialised on the pan in front of Hawking and sat quietly while all the bells and whistles sounded. A double half-circle of armed guards surrounded the entrance to the pod. They'd learned their lessons well. I was proud.

'I'll go first,' said Farrell. 'Exit slowly and carefully.' In the old days, he would have said, 'Don't bounce out like an excited wombat and get yourself shot,' but we weren't on those terms any more.

We walked slowly out of the pod, hands up.

A voice called, 'Identify yourselves.'

'Good morning. Farrell and Maxwell. To see the Director.'

'This way, please.'

Some few months had passed since we left and renovations were still proceeding. The walls were still pitted and scorched, but the place was clean and tidy and people were going noisily about their business. There were familiar faces around and some waved.

Someone must already have contacted her. She was waiting for us on the half landing. I was impressed. Exactly the spot I would have chosen. She'd done us the courtesy of coming to greet us, but the half landing, while friendly and informal, still meant we had to walk up to her. I liked her style.

'It's good to see you both again. How can St Mary's be of assistance?'

I smiled. 'A very simple request to use the library, if I may, Director. I urgently need some information that's not yet available under our 30 Year Rule. I'm hoping you can help.'

'Of course. If you can be specific, I'll have my people bring it to us in my office. I hope you have time for coffee.'

'That's very kind and, actually, I did miss breakfast.'

'So, what exactly are you looking for?'

'I'd like anything you can dig up on a Doctor Knox.'

Any doubts I might have had about whether or not I was wasting everybody's time were immediately dispelled. She grabbed my arm and said in a fierce undertone, 'What do you know about Alexander Knox?'

Two could play at that game.

I said, 'What do *you* know about Alexander Knox?'

She looked around for a moment and then back at me again, plainly undecided.

I caught Farrell's eye and he had the grace to nod.

I opened my mouth to speak, but she said, 'Not here,' and we set off for her office where I repeated my request to be allowed to check his background, credentials, anything they had on him.

'You don't have to,' she said bitterly. 'I can tell you everything you need to know about Alexander Knox.'

Having said that, she fell silent again, staring at her desk. We sat quietly. You couldn't rush her. After a while, she looked up and said with a half-smile. 'If you want this chronologically, it's hard to know where to begin.'

'We're the guests,' I said. 'We'll start if you like.'

I gave her almost everything. Knox. The Red House. His lack of background. The coincidence of the surnames. She listened in complete silence, her face was expressionless.

Eventually, silence fell again. We waited. I made myself be patient. There was more here than I knew.

She pushed herself back from her desk a little and clasped her hands in her lap. In a voice carefully devoid of any emotion whatsoever, she said, 'Dr Alexander Knox is our missing Director.'

Chapter Thirteen

At first, I couldn't grasp it at all. I had wild ideas of him being cast adrift in time, making a home and a life for himself with The Red House. But no, St Mary's was only just up the road. He only had to bang on our door. Was he suffering from amnesia perhaps? Being propelled precipitately through time can sometimes do funny things to the human brain – and it's not as if the brains at St Mary's were particularly normal to begin with. Then, because the mind assigns strange priorities, I thought – *I didn't escape from The Red House at all. He let me go.* Oddly, this made me hate him more than ever.

Everyone was looking at me, obviously having reached the correct conclusion long before I did.

'He ran away,' I said slowly, trying to imagine how the unit would feel if Dr Bairstow had abandoned us when we fought Ronan at Alexandria. I remembered how, when we were planning the mission to rescue the Chief, he had said he wouldn't abandon St Mary's; how his first duty was always to his unit.

Still no one spoke. I stopped talking and did a little more thinking.

'No,' I said eventually. 'He sold you out. Ronan had so few men your kitchen staff could have dealt with them. Knox gave them information; entry codes, security protocols – everything they needed to get in, grab the pods, and get out. But Knox underestimated his own unit, though. Hawking was defended almost to the last man, buying you the time to get the pods out of his reach. Seeing it all go wrong, Knox disappeared with… Number Seven … and the wherewithal to start a new life. In our time. What a bastard.'

Chief Farrell stirred. 'Actually, I think it's worse even than that. It's maybe no coincidence he's not far from St Mary's. I've often wondered about Sussman. He loved you. He hated you as well, at the end, but in his own way, he loved you. There never seemed any good reason why Sussman did what he did, but suppose Knox got to him. Suppose Knox got to Barclay. Not to destroy St Mary's, but Barclay did an awful lot of damage in the four months she was Director.'

This just got worse and worse. Davey Sussman, my one time partner, had pushed me off a cliff in the Cretaceous Period. He'd subsequently come to a bad end. A very bad end. Maybe he had been working for Alexander Knox. And Barclay, who had left four men to die; who had sacked me and whose performance as Caretaker Director had nearly finished St Mary's. Had she been working for Alexander Knox? With Ronan? Suddenly, it was all coming together.

Dr Bairstow had sent us to The Red House in all good faith. Knox could probably hardly believe his luck when we turned up. I felt hot with shame when I realised how easily he'd manipulated me. In less than one hour he'd thrown me off balance and caused me to question the fundamentals of my own life. He'd gone straight for my weak spots. That I was still at St Mary's was a miracle. That the Chief was still there was only because the Boss refused to accept his resignation. Knox wasn't Ronan – he didn't kill – what he did was even worse. How much damage had he quietly done to St Mary's over the years? And I bet he'd provided a base for Ronan and his crew whenever required. In fact, that was an interesting point. Who worked for whom? Knox was clever – Ronan was ruthless and driven. Which of them called the shots? I remembered the ravine outside Alexandria and the good people who had died there. A slow burn started deep inside.

I looked up. Everyone's faces said the same.

I said, 'What do you need?'

She said, 'Co-ordinates. An idea of The Red House layout. As much information as you can give me. And a date when the two of you have unbreakable alibis.'

'Why?'

'You two were among his last patients. He's an important and influential man who almost certainly knows more than he should about nearly everything. When he disappears – as he shortly will – the authorities will look very closely at anyone with whom he has had dealings. I need a date, so you won't be implicated. We'll get him and bring him back here to answer for his actions. Don't worry – your St Mary's will be represented and you'll have your say. Just leave the rest to us, please.'

She swept out.

I said hopefully, 'Is it too early for lunch?'

Of course it wasn't. You can eat any time you like at St Mary's and I frequently did. Mrs Partridge wasn't in her office. I hoped I'd see her before I left. I felt strongly that she should be represented as well.

Farrell went off to see Katie Carr and I slipped quietly out of the building and trotted off to see the dodos. They hadn't changed – as fat and clueless as ever. I watched them milling around, grockling in astonishment at a sinister twig or a threatening rock and smiled, remembering that happy day. And night. Life had been a lot simpler then.

I met Farrell in the dining room, where the kitchen staff rushed out clutching ladles, oven gloves and other implements of mass destruction and we submitted to having a fuss made of us. It wasn't unpleasant.

There wasn't a lot of talk over lunch. I was hungry and Farrell was distracted. Very distracted.

'What?' I said, finally.

'I've been thinking about Knox.'

'I think we all have,' I said.

'No. I mean, I think we might have another problem.'

'Which is?'

'I told him about Scotland.'

I stopped eating. A bit of a first.

173

'Yes, you did, didn't you.'

I put down my fork and started to think. He'd mentioned Scotland and Knox had changed the subject immediately afterwards. He'd been so keen to talk about the Chief's condition and as soon as Scotland came up, he moved the conversation in a completely different direction. An hour later, I was on my way back to St Mary's with our relationship beyond repair, and we'd barely spoken since.

'Have a think about this,' he interrupted. 'History goes wrong in the 16th century – we suspect. Something else happened in the 16th century that seemed – not trivial – but fairly minor in the scheme of things.' He paused for me to catch up.

I shook my head.

'Can I have a clue?'

'Close to home.'

I got it.

'Annie died. Oh, my God, Annie died.'

My mind flew back. Again, I heard Farrell telling me the story. 16th-century Scotland. James VI. Three young historians, Edward Bairstow, Clive Ronan, and Annie Bessant are on assignment. Annie catches some disease. Quarantine is not declared. Protocols are ignored. Ronan shoots Edward Bairstow, leaves him to die and brings her back to St Mary's. But, Edward is rescued. Ronan is arrested, breaks free, steals Number Nine, causes Annie's death (to the everlasting and unspoken grief of Dr Bairstow) and disappears before anyone can stop him.

I moved cutlery and condiments aimlessly around the table while I worked it all out in my head. He reached out and stilled my movements. I had forgotten how warm his hands were.

'Say it out loud,' he said.

'I haven't had a chance to tell you this, but the second half of the play, although contemporary with the first part, was written by someone else.'

'A forgery?'

'Or a fake. I never know the difference.'

174

It was his turn to stop and think.

'Someone in the 17th century substituted a different ending? Why?'

I shook my head. 'A message, maybe. I don't know.'

'From another historian? Trying to tell us something?'

I'd been thinking about that. One person above all others would have known of Dr Bairstow's intention. One person was always around when something important happened ...

'I don't know. I don't know anything. I thought, when I saw the OS map with the John Knox House that I was on to something, and now, the plot is not just thickening but solidifying. What's going on?'

'There's two separate issues here. The mystery author. And the altered ending. Who? And why? Speculate.'

I ignored the *who* and concentrated on the *why*. 'I think ... I think something is happening in 1567 and someone is trying to tell us that. The altered ending is a warning. Suppose the Play comes true. Mary lives and Elizabeth dies. Mary is Queen of Scotland and England. She moves to England – the seat of power. Her son, James, remains behind as nominal king of Scotland. Mary dislikes him – he's Darnley's son, after all. His power is minimal – he doesn't have the freedom to pursue witches. And if James isn't pursuing witches, Annie may not be arrested. She doesn't become sick. The whole thing never happens. That's the reason for all this. Clive Ronan is deliberately trying to change the course of History. For Annie.' I paused. 'Except that ... why hasn't History intervened? We all know what happens to historians who even think about interfering. Why is History holding back now?'

He said quietly, 'I think you haven't thought this through.'

'Really, what did I miss?'

'You didn't miss anything; you just didn't go far enough.'

'Tell me.'

'If Annie doesn't get sick then Ronan doesn't shoot Edward. Or steal Number Nine. Or kill anyone. Edward doesn't need to travel back to found St Mary's. I don't join St Mary's. Maybe St Mary's isn't founded at all. In which case ...'

I caught my breath.

'Paradox.'

He nodded.

I said urgently, 'So I ask again. Why hasn't History laminated him across the landscape?'

He looked thoughtful. 'I don't know ... But I may have an idea ...'

I was angry. 'This is ridiculous. This guy is ripping a hole in the timeline and History does nothing. I only *think* about intervening in a possible robbery and history nearly drops a ten-ton rock on me. Kevin Grant tried to save a woman and child at Peterloo and had his head split open. And these were trivial events. Comparatively. This bastard Ronan is interfering with major events and History does nothing. Why? What's going on here?'

'I don't know at the moment,' he said again, looking even more unhappy. 'I really don't. Don't press me. There's something I must check when we get back.'

'Is Ronan mad to take such a risk?'

'Yes, I think he's mad.'

'Do you think he's in Scotland?'

Yes.'

'We should go,' I said, getting up.

'No. We should finish this first. We need to neutralise Knox before we go off to deal with Ronan, otherwise one day they'll catch us in a pincer movement and crush us. One thing at a time, Max.'

I sat down again and thought about the series of events that had led to this moment.

Dr Bairstow, motivated by economic reasons, had had what probably seemed at the time to be an excellent idea and jumped back in time to commission The Play. Which gave someone an opportunity to warn us of events we would otherwise know nothing about. Four centuries later, investigating that had led us to the discovery of that treacherous bastard Knox and the damage he had done.

No incident, however seemingly trivial, is unimportant in the scheme of things.

One event leads to another, which triggers something else and before you know where you are, the ramifications spread far and wide throughout History. Echoing down the ages. Getting fainter and fainter, but never completely dying away. They talk of The Harmony of the Spheres, but History is A Symphony of Echoes. Every little action has huge consequences. They're not always apparent, and sometimes, in our game, sometimes effect comes before cause, not after.

It makes your head ache.

We took our tea and coffee outside, and that was where Pinkie found us. We were politely invited to join the briefing being held in her office.

I recognised familiar faces, especially from Security, but there were new ones as well. They were getting themselves back on their feet, and if they could nail the bastard who had sold them out, then they would be able to draw a final line under what had happened to them.

It was a snatch squad, pure and simple. Touch down, locate and apprehend; then straight back home again. No messing. They were aiming for three in the afternoon. Quiet time – when he should be working in his office.

We watched them go from Hawking. They all seemed confident, if grim. I wasn't so sure. He was a slippery son of a bitch and it sometimes seemed that he and Ronan had people everywhere. Everyone has a price and it's not always money. I could see him slipping through their fingers, as Ronan always seemed to slip through ours.

As soon as Number Five disappeared, techies moved forwards and began to put out chairs; three chairs in a line behind a table and then a mass of seats behind them in a semi-circle. All facing one solitary chair set a little distance away. A very familiar adversarial layout. What seemed the entire unit was filing into the hangar. Some arranged themselves along the gantry. We took seats in the front row alongside the other Chief Officers. I picked out familiar faces, but this wasn't a social occasion. It was necessary, but no one was going to enjoy this.

The hum of conversation slowly died away as the minutes passed. Tension built. I sat quietly and looked at the floor.

They were only gone about half an hour. The lights flashed above the plinth and a heartbeat later, Number Five was back. Ten seconds later, Number Seven materialised. They had him. And his pod. Our pod, rather.

Immediately, the blast doors came down, sealing Hawking from the outside world. I felt the building shake. Armed guards took up positions around the hangar. All the lights came on, bathing the entire hangar in a harsh and unforgiving glare. As harsh and unforgiving as the next hour was likely to be.

At last, the pod door opened and the Director led the way out. Behind her, walked a heavily guarded Alexander Knox. He seemed in pristine condition. I admired their restraint. If it had been me, he'd have fallen down every flight of stairs between my time and theirs. Still, most people are much nicer than me.

It was so quiet I could hear the electronic hum of lights and equipment.

They pushed Knox forward. The Director sat in the middle chair. Ben, the doctor, was to her right and Evan, the Senior Historian, to her left.

I watched Knox settle himself and look confidently around at his former unit. I thought of Dr Bairstow and couldn't help making the inevitable comparison.

The Director stood.

'This is not a trial according to the laws of this land. St Mary's deals with its own problems. Your crimes are against St Mary's. St Mary's will judge you. Does anyone here have any objections?'

The obvious answer to that was Knox himself, but he said nothing, just blinking in the bright light. At a gesture from the Director, some of the lights were lowered. The rest of us were in shadow but he was still alone and exposed in the harsh glare. Vain as ever, he tried to straighten his clothing, but maintained his silence. No bluster or hasty denials. This was a clever man and he was holding his fire. I remembered again how effortlessly I'd been manipulated and wondered if he might actually talk his way out of this one.

Mrs Partridge slipped into the seat next to me and gave me a brief smile.

The charges were read. They were straightforward. They listed everything Ronan had done and charged Knox as an accomplice. It was a very long and comprehensive list.

Still he said nothing. I stirred uneasily.

The Director asked him to plead.

He said nothing.

She said, 'If you do not speak, we will assume you are admitting your guilt and proceed accordingly.'

He said nothing.

Around me, people were restless. This was bad. All right, they hated him. They wanted him dead, but they would have been more comfortable with outright denial, or pleading for his life, or even any sort of response at all. This behaviour made them uneasy. The Director had wanted this done in front of everyone because everyone had been affected. Everyone should see justice done, and I could see why, but I was wondering if this was going to backfire on her. He'd only been here a few minutes and already resolve was wavering. He really was a master manipulator.

Perhaps he thought Ronan would descend and pull him out of this. Or no, maybe he still had people here. People he hoped could get him out. I watched him closely. His eyes flickered around the hangar. He could only clearly see the three judges in front of him. The rest of us must be just a blur in the shadows.

Around me, dust fell and the building ticked in the silence. Everyone waited in vain. He still said nothing.

She conferred briefly with her fellow judges.

'Dr Knox, your failure to respond to the charges laid against you leads us to assume you believe you have no defence and are, therefore, pleading guilty. This is your last chance to answer the charges before you. Do you have anything to say?'

He spoke.

Finally, he spoke.

'I ran. I admit it. I ran. Not in fear for my life as you are so quick to assume, but in a last, desperate effort to save my unit and induce the invaders to follow me. By leaving St Mary's, I hoped enough of them would chase after me, thus enabling you to overcome the rest. That my efforts were unsuccessful is not my fault.'

Evan said, 'And why would they follow you, Dr Knox?'

He smiled slightly. Evan had asked exactly the right question. I began to feel the whole thing sliding away.

'Because, *Director,*' he paused very subtly after the word, 'members of St Mary's, I knew the location of the remote site. If – as you are all so keen to believe – I am a renegade and a traitor, tell me why didn't I just give him the details immediately and save the lives of what – thirteen people? If I am indeed as bad as you think me, all I had to do was tell them. After all, according to you, I'd already given them everything else – codes, protocols, etc. So why didn't I give them what they came for; the location of the remote site, as well?'

Shit! Shit, shit, shit, shit.

All around me, I could hear whispering. Suddenly, it was so obvious. Why hadn't he told them?

Because he wasn't one of them.

But he ran, the other half of my brain argued.

Yes, he had, but to draw them away. It could have worked.

No, hang on. St Mary's – my St Mary's – was only half an hour up the road from The Red House. He could have got help any time. Instead, he'd started a new life – a very successful new life – influencing the great and the good. Politicians, royalty, church leaders, business people, top-ranking police, and military personnel – they all passed through his hands. Forget St Mary's. What damage had he been doing to the country over the years? And the arrogant bastard hadn't even bothered to change his name.

Was he going to get away with this?

And then Mrs Partridge stood up.

'I wonder if I might speak?'

I don't know about other organisations – I expect it's the

same pretty much anywhere. People think power lies with the Director, or the CEO, or the General, or whoever. No, it doesn't. The most powerful person in any organisation is the PA to the boss. The keeper of secrets. The only person who understands the filing system. The key holder. The gatekeeper. The one who takes the minutes. And in St Mary's case, Kleio, Daughter of Zeus and immortal Muse of History, as well.

It was a dramatic moment and not surprisingly, given the Ancient Greeks' love of drama, she made the most of it. Murmurs swelled and faded again as she walked slowly forwards, her heels clicking on the hard floor. She took her time and when she eventually arrived to stand in front of the three judges, complete silence had fallen.

But, most importantly, and for the first time, Alexander Knox had started to sweat. On the surface, he was as relaxed and casual as before, but under the glare of those harsh lights, I could see a tiny pulse throb under his jaw.

Evan pushed his chair back slightly and the legs grated on the concrete floor. He raised a hand in apology.

The Director said, 'Please, Mrs Partridge, go ahead.'

She half-turned to include the judges and Alexander Knox together.

'Dr Knox is correct. He did not give away the information regarding the location of the remote site.'

Whispers echoed around the hangar. I had the strangest sensation that everything was sliding away. We were losing control. He was going to get away with it.

She walked forwards until she was so close to the judges she could have touched them. They gazed up at her. Her voice carried around the hangar, loud, clear and firm.

'I took the co-ordinates from the safe and hid them before the attack occurred. Dr Knox could not possibly have given them away to our enemies.'

'You see,' shouted Knox. 'Didn't I just say that very thing?' He made a huge effort to regain his composure. 'I mean, thank you, Mrs Partridge. Thank you for telling the truth today.' He moved towards her and she drew back behind the table to stand alongside Evan. The guards pulled him back to his seat.

He was gabbling now.

'I told you, I told you. It's all a mistake. I know how it looks but that's not how it was. I thought if I ran, then they'd think I was trying to hide the co-ordinates and come after me. I was trying to draw them away. This is my unit. I would never do anything …'

He was pushed abruptly into his chair and subsided.

'May I continue?' asked Mrs Partridge, apparently unruffled. The Director nodded.

From behind the table, she turned to face Knox. 'You did give them the co-ordinates, but not the right co-ordinates. You passed on the ones I had substituted some time previously. You, Director,' she nodded at Pinkie, 'in your capacity as Chief Technical Officer had the correct ones, of course, as did the then Head of Security, both of you being, in my opinion, loyal and dependable members of this unit. You –' and she fixed Knox with a look somewhat similar to the harpoon Captain Ahab used to pursue Moby Dick, 'in my opinion, were not. Therefore, I removed them and substituted – something else. As I had anticipated, you did indeed attempt to betray your colleagues. You were, however, unsuccessful.'

Knox found a voice. 'You can't prove any of that.'

She smiled thinly and her voice sliced through the hushed hangar.

'Acting on information provided by you, Dr Knox, Ronan sent twelve of his people to those co-ordinates to locate and bring back the pods. They never returned. They couldn't – not from where I'd sent them.'

She paused and I shivered, wondering just where and when they were. It wouldn't be good and if Mrs Partridge said they wouldn't be coming back, then they wouldn't. I remembered Katie Carr saying there seemed to be fewer of them after a while.

Knox was staring at her, his mouth open. He wasn't the only one.

She continued.

'I imagine that, at this point in your relationship, you and Mr Ronan decided to part company. Your usefulness to him as Director was ended. You were allowed to take Number Seven and depart for a new life. In return, you agreed to provide a base for him and his people whenever required. And that, Director is what I wanted to say.'

I could only see her profile as she stood slightly behind Evan, already merging slowly back into the darkness.

You could have heard a thistledown drop.

The Director stirred and cleared her throat.

'Does anyone else have anything to add? Not you,' she said, as Knox opened his mouth.

Complete silence all around the hangar.

'Very well. Alexander Knox, you have …'

And that was as far as she got, because Evan leaped to his feet beside her, stuck a gun in her temple and said, 'Shut up. Dr Knox. Quickly. Go to Number Seven. Get the door open and I'll …'

And that was as far as he got because Mrs Partridge stepped back out of the darkness, walloped him hard round the back of the head with her scratchpad, which shattered on impact and he fell face forward across the table.

At the same time, Knox got a rifle butt in the kidneys, so that was both of them out of the game for a bit.

Long seconds passed. Farrell poked my knee.

'Breathe.'

I took a couple of deep breaths to get my lungs working again and waited to see if anything else would happen, but that seemed to be it for the time being.

Knox was replaced, not gently, on his chair and Evan, bleeding and dazed, dropped beside him.

Mrs Partridge made no move to pick up the pieces of her scratchpad. Obviously feeling that *finally* the children could be left to handle things by themselves, she said politely, 'Do you require me for anything further, Director?'

Pinkie dragged her eyes away from the scene in front of her.

'No, not at this moment, thank you, Mrs Partridge.'

'Thank you, Director,' and she undulated back into the darkness.

Now they had him, they had to decide what to do with him. And Evan too. I stared at the man I had made Senior Historian and wondered if I should be locked up somewhere where I couldn't do any harm. This was why his injuries had been comparatively light. And why he'd been so bolshie afterwards. Of course, Ronan would leave one of his own people in with the prisoners. He had been one of them the whole time. Saying nothing as his colleagues were shot, beaten up, raped – maybe, in some way, he even helped to select the victims. I was not the only one gazing shocked and bewildered as he struggled to sit up. He got no help from Knox.

The Director stood up and waved us over. Together with her senior officers, we crowded into a huddle.

'My recommendation,' the doctor was saying, 'is that we take the pair of them to somewhere remote in time and place, and leave them to survive as best they can. If they can. It's certainly more mercy than they've shown anyone here.'

I stared at my feet, waiting for someone to object, but no one did. Finally, I looked up and caught Farrell's eye. He nodded grimly.

I said, 'With respect, Director, I disagree,' and found everyone staring at me. I hated this. Gritting my teeth, I went on. 'I think we must remember that Ronan is still out there. They may not be best friends, but they're all each other has. Knox has provided a sanctuary for him over the years. We must ensure he can never do so again. There's no guarantee they don't have some form of communication and Ronan won't swoop down and scoop him up again as soon as our backs are turned. And then neither St Mary's will be safe.'

Alongside me, the Chief nodded.

I continued. 'I don't think we can take the chance of that happening. Dr Bairstow is about to consider an assignment in which we hope to engage our Mr Ronan. You may safely leave him to us, Director. However, I think we should deal with Knox

184

now. And permanently.'

Instinctively, everyone glanced over at them. Evan had pulled himself into a sitting position and was holding his head. Knox was staring intently at his hands. I wondered if, even now, he expected Fate to intervene on his behalf. I remembered all the people, good people, who had died defending St Mary's – present and future – and hardened my heart.

Pinkie stepped aside with her Head of Security and they talked for a while. Orders were issued. Knox and Evan were bundled back into the pod. The Director returned. 'You are invited to attend – as witnesses. Everyone must know what happens today.'

Silently, we nodded. I really wasn't looking forward to this, but you can't condemn someone to death and then disown the consequences. I stood beside Farrell as we jumped. No one looked at anyone else.

The door opened onto a bleak, empty landscape. It was cold, but not Arctic. I stepped outside, my breath puffing ahead of me. There was a light dusting of snow, like talcum powder. The other pod was a few yards away. Evan and Knox were already standing alone, looking around. The sun was rising on a day neither of them would get to see.

It was only as the six security guards lined up that they realised what was going to happen to them. Incredibly, they must have thought we would just release them into the wild. For future rescue, they hoped. Now that last hope had been dashed and they panicked. Both stared frantically around, seeking a hiding place; any sort of hiding place, but the windblown grass was the tallest thing around. There was nowhere to run.

'You can't do this,' screamed Knox into the wind. 'It's not legal!'

Neither he nor Evan seemed able to comprehend what was happening. People sometimes think St Mary's is just a charmingly eccentric bunch of amiable history nuts. And we are. But make no mistake, St Mary's has teeth. And when we have to – we bite.

The Director was saying something. It was hard to hear over

the wind and the screams. I moved closer. She was reciting a list of names. Tears stood on her cheeks. In my head, I added my own list.

They were both screaming themselves hoarse by now. I heard the order given and made myself look. I was part of this – part of the responsibility was mine.

I've seen death before, but this was an execution. Another one. The nightmare came back. I saw Barclay lying at my feet, wasting the last precious seconds of her life in hatred. I had to get through this. And live with the consequences afterwards. I stood next to Farrell. He grasped my cold hand, squeezing tightly. I squeezed gratefully back.

A very quick succession of short sharp cracks – so quick they almost sounded like one single, ragged shot – and it was done. The Head of Security walked toward them.

Farrell said quickly, 'Wait for me in the pod.'

For once, I didn't argue.

I heard two more shots and then it was finished.

Chapter Fourteen

We didn't hang around. We wanted to get back to our St Mary's as quickly as possible. Pinkie escorted us to our pod. All around us, the mood was sombre. No one had taken any pleasure from the day's events, but they would recover. It was finally over. Time to go home.

Farrell took his pod and went first. I entered an unfamiliar Number Seven and took it home.

Farrell had alerted Hawking to the return of our final lost pod. A token security force awaited my return. I was out of the pod as soon as the decon light was finished and raced to the exit. At the door, I stood and looked back down the hangar. For the first time I could remember, every plinth was occupied. We had our pods back. It was a moment that demanded more respect than I was giving it.

I set off for the main building. There was no sign of Chief Farrell.

I looked at my watch. I had twenty minutes before my appointment with the Boss. Just time to wash my face, comb my hair, grab a mug of something hot and sweet, and get to his office.

I got all that done and scooped up Schiller and Van Owen on the way. I was stressed, breathless, and disoriented. My boots and the legs of my jumpsuit were still wet from the snow. I could still see two dark shapes on the ground and those patches of crimson snow. I could still hear the shots, crisp in the frosty air ...

I took a deep breath outside Mrs Partridge's door and entered quietly. The Boss was waiting in his office doorway. His face was grave. Over his shoulder, I could see Chief Farrell sitting in one of the two chairs put ready, a pool of print-out at his feet.

The Boss said, 'Dr Maxwell, would you go straight in, please. Miss Van Owen, Miss Schiller, thank you for coming. We won't keep you a moment.'

I followed him in. Chief Farrell turned his head as I entered. He didn't look good at all and I suspected I looked worse. The Boss seated himself.

'Which one of you will begin?'

Chief Farrell had seniority and I was happy to leave it to him.

He made a better job of it than I could have, and at the end, the Boss got up and looked out of the window.

'Definitely dead?' he asked.

'Definitely dead,' confirmed the Chief. 'I checked myself. They were both dead.'

I nodded, even though the Boss couldn't see me. He was quiet for a very long time.

I waited.

For the first time ever, I saw him at a loss. Finally, he turned back into the room, saying, 'It seems I owe you both an apology. I really had no idea of Knox's identity and purpose when I sent you to The Red House. I understand it wasn't a pleasant experience for either of you, and I'm more pleased than I can say to see that you emerged from it mostly unscathed.'

This was unexpected and unfamiliar, but he soon reverted to normal. 'Max, that your instincts are so sound is, I believe, a tribute to your training and development and St Mary's takes full credit. Your urge to remove yourself as quickly as possible was, under the circumstances, absolutely the correct thing to do. Subsequent events – less so, of course, but we have already discussed that.

'His disappearance will cause more than a stir. I don't think

St Mary's will be implicated in any way. We should receive nothing more than a cursory interview, but you can rely on me to provide any alibis you both may need.'

Farrell said, 'Thank you, sir.'

He sighed once more and then seated himself at his desk, folded his hands and looked expectantly at me.

'Well, Dr Maxwell, what do you have for me today?'

He knew perfectly well why I was there, but I think it helped us all to pull ourselves back into the here and now. Assembling people and files, I took him through everything, step by step. Schiller and Van Owen walked him through The Play. His office filled up with papers, diagrams, cubes, and disks. They'd worked it up very nicely. We booted up his data table and they brought up their data stacks. He peered closely, firing questions at them, but they'd done their work well and had their answers ready. I was proud of them.

When they'd finished, he thanked them politely and escorted them to the door. They escaped.

He returned to the rotating data stack and regarded it silently.

'I assume you have more.'

I told him about Chief Farrell's dreams and the bleed-through. He listened attentively and Farrell rounded it all off with his theory about changing History to save Annie. Both their faces were expressionless, so I made sure mine was as well.

At the end, I said, 'I agree that individually, it's not that strong, but if it's all put together sir, I hope you'll agree it is at least worth investigating.'

'I do agree. However, while you were concentrating on this particular problem, Chief Farrell has been studying the records from Number Four. Chief, I believe you have something to add.'

'I think so, sir. By downloading and analysing the jump history of Number Four, I've managed to trace most of its movements since it was stolen from us. He did indeed make a jump to Edinburgh, 1567.'

'Well,' I said to him, 'surely that's good. We know where to find him. We yank him out before he can do any further damage and neutralise him. With extreme prejudice.'

He said slowly, 'No, it's not good at all. Mr Ronan was still a comparatively young man when he escaped from St Mary's. He appears to have arrived in Scotland only a few months after Annie Bessant's death, obviously still hell-bent on changing History and not caring for the consequences.'

I turned to Dr Bairstow. 'I don't understand this, sir. Why didn't History intervene? Why didn't History kill him there and then and spare us all of this?'

They looked at each other and then Dr Bairstow said, 'You have answered your own question, Dr Maxwell. We must not be "spared all of this." If he is killed as a young man then he will not be alive to interfere with us in the Cretaceous or Alexandria or anywhere else. Our past will change. St Mary's might not exist and again – paradox. We are on the horns of a dilemma. Either inadvertently or not, Mr Ronan has rendered himself untouchable. Neither we nor History can do anything. We must investigate and rectify this anomaly, yet we cannot kill or interfere in any way with the cause of it – our Mr Ronan.'

'So what can we do?'

'Last year, we undertook to police the timeline and make ourselves responsible for any and all irregularities. Therefore we investigate. We identify the problem, and attempt to repair the timeline before it gets any worse. As they say – a stitch in time …

'Dr Maxwell, start putting things together, please. I want a …'

'Actually, sir,' I said, bringing up another data stack, 'Dr Peterson and I already have.'

He read through it once.

Then he read it through again. Chief Farrell was still working his way down the stack, eyebrows climbing as he did so. I had to say I agreed with him. But there was no alternative – Peterson and I had run through all the files several times and in the end the choice had been between Farrell,

190

Peterson himself, and Major Guthrie – an unlikely third. Farrell had the edge.

He was looking bemused.

'Why me?' said he said. 'Why not …?' he paused, rummaging for someone else, anyone else – and coming up with no one. 'Why me?'

'It's your own fault,' I told him, with a certain malice. 'You speak perfect French. She's going to love you.'

Afterwards, I found David in my office having another coughing fit.

I passed him some water. He looked flushed and hot.

'Everything all right?'

It took him some time to get his breath back and I could hear his chest straining.

'Surely … I should be asking you that. You're the one just back from the …very dodgy mission you … 'won't tell anyone … about.'

'Stop changing the subject,' I said, recognising the signs. 'Are you taking anything for that?'

'Not … at the moment.'

'Well, go along to Dr Foster and get yourself sorted out. I don't want an office full of phlegm.'

'Nice … to see you too. How did it go?'

'Mission accomplished,' I said, not really wanting to talk about it.

'Congratulations,' he said, obviously recognising the signs too. 'You'll be delighted … but not surprised to hear that your … staggeringly brilliant assistant is completely on top of things here, and absolutely nothing is outstanding. You may as well go back … to bed.'

'When you next see this staggeringly brilliant young assistant please thank her for me and ask her if she'd like your job full-time?'

'Very funny. Speaking of which, knock-knock …'

'Shut up.'

Muttering and coughing, he brought over a pile of post.

191

'Nothing here is urgent. I've drafted replies to everything…
Just say the word and I'll send it all off. Tea?'

'Mm … yes, please,' I said, thinking, in my innocence, we
were about to do some work.

'So how are you?' he said.

'I'm fine,' I said, not really listening.

'You look like crap.'

'I'm fine,' I said again, in my 'change the subject' voice.

He did. I wished he hadn't.

'So … how's Chief Farrell?'

'Fine.'

The silence made me look up.

'That wasn't what I meant.'

'I know.'

More silence.

'Have you looked at him recently?'

'David, I've just spent the entire morning with him. Of
course I've looked at him.'

'No … really looked at him.'

'You can't go around peering closely at senior officers. It's
probably a chargeable offence.'

'I'll do you a deal.'

'If it involves no more knock-knock jokes then I'll take it.'

'I'll … go to Dr Foster if you'll talk to Chief Farrell. You
don't have to have a mad reconciliation on the … spot. Just sit
down and talk a little. You'll feel better, trust me …'

I sighed, channelling hard-done-by Chief Operations Officer
as hard as I could.

He started to cough again. Deliberately, I was sure.

'OK, I will. I don't know when, but I will. Do you want me
to sign something to that effect? Now, get yourself to Sick Bay
before I pick up the phone and make Sick Bay come to you.
And that's never pleasant.'

He backed out of the door, scraping the paint as he went.
There was barely any left now and the whole jamb became even
more gouged and gashed every time he passed through. It
looked terrible. It still does. I've never let them paint over it. He

disappeared and his coughing Dopplered down the corridor. There was a distant cry as he collided with someone.

I ran through the post – everything he'd done was spot-on – so I dropped it all back on his desk for onward dispatch. I made my own tea – again – and started on the Mary Stuart assignment.

I was soon engrossed. Hours passed and I never noticed. I never noticed that David didn't come back.

Then the phone rang.

It was Helen and she wasted no time.

'Max, get yourself down to Sick Bay. Now.'

I don't think I even bothered replacing the receiver. I was out of the office and sprinting around the gallery at a speed I hadn't achieved since I was a trainee. I went down the stairs three at a time. Astonished historians stood frozen as I raced past them. I crashed through the doors into the long corridor, shouting, 'Get out of the way', to anyone who didn't move quickly enough. Someone had the sense to open the doors at the other end. I lifted my chin and sprinted. They'd sent the lift down, thank God. I don't think I could have made the stairs. All the time I was thinking, *Who? Who is it this time?*

I stepped sideways through the lift doors when they were barely inches apart and ran to the nurses' station. There was no one there.

I called, 'Helen? Doctor Foster?' and she appeared round the corner.

'This way, Max.' She strode off. To my surprise, we bypassed the wards and headed for the isolation room at the end. I'd been in there once when I'd come back from Nabataean Petra with what turned out to be nothing more than a cold. It was a small room, rather more nicely furnished than the wards since inmates tended to stay longer.

Dr Bairstow and Mrs Partridge stood quietly outside. His head was bowed and the distress on her face stopped me in my tracks.

I said to Helen, 'Who? Who is it? What's happened?'

'It's David. Take a deep breath, Max. You must be calm. He doesn't have very long.'

No. This could not be happening. We'd just been talking. How could this be happening?

I stood in the doorway, took several breaths and lowered my shoulders. When I had achieved a level of calm, I stepped into the room. They'd made it warm and quiet. The lights were on low. He lay on his back, hands across his stomach, chest rising and falling with every painful breath. I looked in vain for machines, drips, oxygen even. There was nothing. He might as well have been in his own bedroom.

I stepped back out again and said in a fierce undertone, 'Where's the oxygen? Where's the equipment? Why aren't you treating him?'

She sighed and looked sadder than I could ever remember.

'He's refused treatment, Max. No,' she said as I tried to speak, 'it's not a spur of the moment thing, he signed the papers months ago.'

'Helen …'

'Max, not everyone takes it all the way to the wire like you do. Now go and see him. Time is precious.'

I couldn't believe it. I thought he was happy. I thought he enjoyed his job. That he'd come to terms with his life. How could I have missed this?

I dashed an angry sleeve across my eyes, sniffed and walked quietly into the room. Helen followed me in.

'It's difficult for him to speak.'

I nodded, sat carefully on the bed and leaned forward so he could see me.

'Hey.'

He tried to smile. He looked ghastly: his face was grey, his lips bloodless and he had dark shadows under his eyes. His breath rasped in and out, as he struggled to breathe. I'd always known he was vulnerable to infections; this looked like pneumonia. How could it be so quick? For how long had he been ill and I hadn't noticed?

I gently took his hands and leaned into his face.

'David.' His eyelids flickered. 'You have to come back to the office right now. I can't find the Pericles file.' He caught his breath, which I guessed was a kind of laugh.

I said, 'Stop that. You know Dr Foster doesn't like patients laughing.'

He smiled and gripped my hands feebly.

I lowered my voice. 'You were right about me and Leon, David. I'm going to fix it. Now you have to get better, so you can tell me you told me so. Let Helen treat you. Please. I can't do without you.'

His eyes never left me.

I kept whispering, 'Don't die. Don't die. David, don't die,' as if I could talk him back to health. As if by sheer force of will, I could prevent him leaving us. Leaving me.

'David. You're my friend. Please don't die.'

His lips moved and I leaned close to hear him. Faintly, oh so faintly, he said, 'Knock … knock.'

I swallowed and said, 'Who's there?'

But he never spoke again.

I sat and held his hands, unable to comprehend what was happening, as he quietly faded away.

After an age, Helen touched my shoulder. 'Let me see to him, Max. Come on, up you get.'

I got stiffly to my feet as Helen and Hunter moved around the bed. I walked slowly out of the room. The Boss and Mrs Partridge were still there.

I said, 'I'd like his name to go up on the Boards.' They nodded. 'He should be buried in his blues as well. He was an historian and a good one.'

Dr Bairstow said, 'Of course.'

I walked off down the corridor, down the stairs, through the doors, along the corridor, through the hall, up the stairs, around the gallery, turned right instead of left, up a different set of attic stairs, tapped at a door and went straight in.

He was sitting in an armchair, open files spread on his lap and around his feet. We looked at each other. He scooped up the whole lot and tossed them on the floor. I kicked the door shut behind me, walked across the room, climbed onto his lap, curled into a tight ball, and wept the tears of a lifetime.

I woke the next morning feeling absolutely dreadful. My eyes felt gummy, my throat raw, and I appeared to have slept in my clothes. I tried to sit up and found I was cocooned in blankets, which had somehow wound themselves around me. Then I discovered I wasn't in the right bed. Or the right bedroom. Then I remembered why.

David ...

I thrashed around a bit, got my arms free and dragged myself into a sitting position. Pushing my hair behind my ears, I looked around. There was a note propped up on the bedside table.

No one expects to see you today. I won't be back before noon, so take your time. LF.

There was a flask of tea next to the clock. It was only just gone nine. I had plenty of time. So long as I was gone before he got back. I poured a cup, thumped the pillows a bit, sat back, and sipped. It was hot and sweet and just what I needed. I was just taking another gulp when, after a brief tap on the door, Chief Farrell walked in.

We looked at each other for a while and then I picked up the note and read aloud, '*I won't be back before noon.*'

'I lied,' he said calmly and sat down in the armchair. We looked at each other some more.

'I'm sorry about David,' he said at last.

I felt tears prick my eyes and blinked them away. I wasn't doing that again, but I knew what he meant, so I nodded.

I sipped a little more and he looked at his feet.

'You'll miss him.'

My lip quivered and I buried my face in my mug. I don't know why I was so bothered about crying in front of the man whose T-shirt had been stiff with snot by the time I'd finished last night.

'Max, you gave him dignity and self-respect. You gave him a purpose. He loved working with you. He was always talking about you.'

'Not enough to put up a fight at the end.'

'He always knew it would come to this. He just chose sooner rather than later.'

I finished my tea, shook the flask to see if there was anything left, and poured myself another.

'I'll be gone in a minute. I'm just very thirsty.'

'No, stay. I wanted to talk to you.'

Well, it had to be done. I had promised David. I leaned back. 'Go on then.'

'This is not an excuse. I just wanted to tell you what happened and why. And to apologise, which I've tried to do, but ... Max, you must know how sorry I am.'

I made a gesture to stop, but he ignored me.

'When I walked out into that little garden at The Red House, I honestly thought Knox had hit you. Your face was – I hadn't seen that look since Sussman died. I was still a little groggy and bewildered, but I could see something had happened. But before I could pull myself together and ask, you were gone. I sat down and Knox got me a glass of water. He seemed rather concerned about you. He said having seen the both of us, he was of the opinion that you were in greater need of help than I was. He said there were some – issues – and you were putting up barriers. He said in the normal course of events this would not be a problem; in time, these could be overcome. But since he had only two weeks in which to work, he needed to take action that I might consider somewhat drastic. He asked if I would be willing to assist and I said yes, of course.'

He paused, drew a deep breath, and still looking at his feet, went on.

'He said he wanted to give you a huge jolt, then kick down your defences, get straight to the heart of the matter and spend the rest of your time there more or less putting you back together again. He said it would be brutal, but it could be very effective, especially in cases where time was an issue and was I still willing? I said maybe and what would it entail? He told me and I said no. I want you to know this, Max; it's important that you know. I did say no. I kept saying no. He said he'd expected that response and went on to explain how it would work. Why it had to come from me. Why it had to be swift and shocking. The more he spoke, the more reasonable and logical it sounded. He assured me, repeatedly that it needed to be done because he had concerns about your mental state. I kept saying no. He went on and on. He had an answer for every objection and in the end he made it seem a necessary course of action.'

He sighed. 'As we now know, it was all lies and I still can't believe I agreed to it. I can't believe I said yes.'

I suddenly remembered Ben, the doctor, saying, '*You will need to be careful for a while. He will be very suggestible.*' I could easily picture the scene – that warm, peaceful, drowsy garden and Knox's voice droning on and on ...

He started up again. 'Well, you know what happened next. When I discovered you'd gone I ... well ... He was very soothing, apologised, and said if I wanted to leave too then that was fine with him. He said it was important that I spoke to you as soon as possible. To force you to listen, if necessary. And I would have, but Guthrie got hold of me first and said that was rubbish, to leave it for God's sake, because at the moment it was only my car that was floating face down in the lake ...'

Guthrie had saved his life. The mood I'd been in, crushed between the twin rocks of humiliation and rejection, if he'd approached me I would have killed him. Knox would have known that. Bastard!

He smiled, tired and sad.

'I thought you'd calm down, that one day I'd be able to explain, but you became very – impregnable – and I couldn't think of any way to make things better. I tried to talk to you. I've tried to write, but I can't find the words, because really there aren't any, are there? And things have just limped on, until here we are.'

And here we were indeed.

I said, 'Before you go any further there's something you need to know. You won't like it but you need to hear this. Knox wasn't completely wrong. Something bad had happened and obviously I wasn't doing as good a job at dealing with it as I thought I was.'

I put the mug down, pulled the blanket around me like a barrier and punched the words at him.

'It was me who killed Isabella Barclay. I shot her in the back. I gave her no chance. Then I shot her in the head. I killed her without hesitation, hid the body in the lift, and sent it down to the basement.'

'Yes, I know.' His voice was very neutral.

They say the ground opens before you …

'How do you know?'

'We worked it out. Me, Guthrie, Peterson. It was fairly obvious.'

I stopped, stricken. 'Does everyone know?'

'No.'

I didn't know what to say. 'I …'

'Max, you saved our lives. On behalf of both of us, me and Katie, I thank you.'

'I …'

No words would come.

He moved to the window seat and sat down. This brought him closer to me, but meant he was just a dark shape against the window. Behind him, raindrops dribbled down the windowpanes. He said and I could hear the hurt in his voice, 'Why didn't you talk to me about this?'

Because you rejected me.

'It was too raw. And then we got overtaken by events.'

'I didn't mean any blame. If anyone is to blame, it's me. I should have seen … This was what I wanted to say to you Max. If we knew each other better …'

I thought of some of the things we'd been through together.

'I think we know each other very well.'

'No, I don't mean that. I don't mean it that way.'

I went to pick up my tea and then had second thoughts and fought my way out of the blankets again.

'Where are you going?' he said, alarmed.

It's all very well having these emotional moments, but eventually after two cups of tea, someone has to go to the bathroom. I washed my face and hands as well and stared in

199

dismay at my hair.

When I came out, he was waiting for me.

I sat on the bed and started to pull on my boots.

'Where are you going?'

'Shower. Breakfast. Office. In that order.'

'Is that it? You're going? Why do you do this? Why can't you talk to me?'

'I don't know what you mean. I've been talking solidly for the last hour. What do you want from me?'

Suddenly, he was angry.

'More. I want much more. I was afraid of what you would say and now, suddenly, you're not saying anything at all. Why are you leaving now?'

'I'm tired. I have a lot to do. People to talk to. About David, I mean.'

'No! No, you don't do that. You don't drag David Sands into this because you don't want to talk.'

Now I was angry too. Time to go before something was said that couldn't be unsaid.

'You don't get to call the shots. I make the decisions in my life. No one else.'

'Really? How's that worked out for you so far?'

'I'm doing OK.'

'Liar!'

Now I was beginning to get really angry. I could feel the blood pulsing in my head. I had to get out fast before I lost control.

He continued. 'You're a sad and lonely woman, Maxwell. You always will be.'

'Takes one to know one.'

'What's that supposed to mean?'

This was getting ugly. It was time for one of us to take a step back.

'I'm leaving now.'

'No, you're not.' He caught my arm as I tried to brush past him. I raised the threat level to Defcon 3.

'What do you think you're doing?'

'Trying to stop you running away again.'

'And from what am I running away?'

'Everything. Yourself. Your past. Your emotions. Your regrets.'

'I don't have any regrets. My life is fine. I love my life. Let go of me or lose your arm.'

'Your life is not fine. It's not fine now and it certainly wasn't when you were young.'

'I'll say it again. I have no problems with my life now and the past is over and finished. All right, I'll grant you my childhood wasn't the best, but it was part of the path that brought me here. It was the price I had to pay for my life now and I'm happy to pay it. Understand?'

He shook me slightly.

'No, you're wrong.'

'I assure you I am not.'

'No, I mean you didn't actually pay the price, at all, did you?'

'What? Let go of me right now. I'm warning you, Chief Farrell, senior officer or not, I will deck you if you don't get out of my way.'

Far from letting go, he grabbed the other arm. I kicked out viciously and it had to have hurt him, but he didn't let go.

'You're very fond of saying that because it distances you from your childhood, Max, but you didn't actually pay the price, did you? You're strong, noisy, grown-up, over-achieving Maxwell. You're the Maxwell who was born at the University of Thirsk and went on to have the life of her dreams. The person who paid the price wasn't you – it was little Maddy. Do you ever remember her at all? Little Maddy, sitting alone in the dark, hiding in her wardrobe with no one to turn to.'

How did he know that? How did he know about the wardrobe?

I opened my mouth, but he hadn't finished.

'It's poor, forgotten, little Maddy who paid the price for your success today and you just left her behind without a backward glance, didn't you?'

It took everything I had not to rip his head off his shoulders. I drew a deep breath, made myself relax and stood still, eyes on the floor. For a long time, nothing happened. The only sound was our breathing.

It came to me suddenly. He knew about the wardrobe. The wardrobe where, long ago, I'd found a book about the Battle of Agincourt. The book that set my feet on the path to St Mary's. Now I knew how it had got there. He'd left it. Somehow, he'd left it for me to find all those years ago.

I couldn't look at him. It was taking everything I had to deal with the maelstrom of guilt, remorse, grief, rage, and hurt I was experiencing. For someone whose proud boast was that she'd never had more than two emotions in her entire life and those not for very long – this was mind-shattering. I concentrated on keeping myself together. Walking and talking could come later.

I became aware of him speaking in a low, dull voice.

'I don't understand you. I'm beginning to think I never will. That worthless piece of shit Sussman throws you off a cliff and you forgive him. Your father makes your childhood a living hell and you pretty well take that in your stride. But not me. I'm trying to make this right and you won't even look at me, let alone talk to me. Why can you forgive them and not me?'

I hadn't meant to answer him, so initially I had no idea where the voice came from. It ripped out from my clenched teeth, harsh with rejection and betrayal.

'Because Davey Sussman and John Maxwell – they don't matter. They're not important. But you – you were supposed to be different. You were the centre of my world. I adored you and you hurt me, Leon Farrell. You hurt me more than anyone in my entire life. You taught me to love you and trust you and when my last barrier went down, you just killed me. You worse than killed me. I wish you'd killed me so I didn't have to be alive and feel this pain every moment for the rest of my life.'

I stood stock-still and listened to words which should never have been spoken reverberate around the room. Neither of us moved. Neither of us knew what to do next. We listened to the rain outside for quite a long time.

He dropped his arms and let me go.

'So,' he said heavily, 'where do we go from here, Max? What now? Is there any way we can make this right again?'

I found a voice. 'I don't think there's any way this can be salvaged. I think the best thing to do now is draw a line underneath it and move on.'

From the way his shoulders slumped, I could see he had misunderstood me, so I added, 'Together. Perhaps, somehow, we could start again. Maybe we could do it better next time.'

'Yes,' he said quietly. 'Yes, that would be good. Perhaps, in a day or so, after David's service?'

I nodded, and because he looked so – broken – I touched his forearm gently before I left the room.

Chapter Fifteen

David's service was very simple. Everyone attended. The Boss spoke. Outside, afterwards, I looked at all the headstones. I saw Kevin Grant, my fellow trainee who died on his first assignment. Tom Baverstock, who died on the floor of his own pod. Just their names, we never did dates. Their stones were beginning to weather. David was in front of Big Dave Murdoch and Jamie Cameron, who both died at Alexandria. It occurred to me I knew nearly as many people dead in the churchyard as I did living at St Mary's. Peterson glanced at me, and I could see he was thinking the same thing.

The next day we got on with things again. Slowly at first, but with my office door open I could hear the increasing buzz in the hall downstairs.

It was very quiet in my office. I was not looking at the empty desk by the door.

I was dealing with my post – one of the many things David had done for me when Mrs Partridge marched in. She had 'new assistant' written all over her. I wasn't sure I wanted another one.

'Good morning, Dr Maxwell.'

'Good morning, Mrs Partridge. What can the History Department do for you today?'

'Well, as you've guessed, I'm here about your new assistant.'

I interrupted. 'I'm not sure …'

'Please hear me out.' She was unstoppable. I really should know that by now. I put down my letter-opener lest I became tempted to use it and sat back to listen to her sales pitch this time.

'There are busy times ahead as I'm sure you're aware, and I've given careful consideration to your needs. You need someone efficient, dedicated, effective, organised, adaptable to a changing workload, personable, and amenable. After a lot of thought, I've allocated you Miss Lee.'

I sat forward abruptly. I needed efficient, dedicated, organised, adaptable, amenable, whatever, and she saddled me with Rosie Lee? She was rude, unhelpful, stubborn, and argumentative – the list just went on. I strongly suspected Mrs Partridge of taking the opportunity to dump an unpopular member of staff on me.

I had a vague memory of Miss Lee – small, dark, and vicious. I needed to think fast.

'What about …?' I said, cunningly. 'What about Miss Lee going to work for Peterson? Everyone likes Peterson – even she will, and I'll have his Mrs Shaw instead.'

This was a brilliant move. Mrs Shaw was lovely – and she brought him biscuits. Mrs Shaw I could live with. 'I'm sure Miss Lee would benefit from being Peterson's assistant.'

She looked at me pityingly.

'Actually, Dr Maxwell, I'm giving you Miss Lee for your benefit – not hers.'

I wasn't sure how that would work at all.

'Thank you,' I said sarcastically, but it just bounced off her.

Deliberately misinterpreting me, she inclined her head, smiled smugly, said, 'You're welcome,' and departed. I'd lost another one. The score so far, Partridge 33 – Maxwell 0.

I sighed and began to sort through the chaos that was my in-tray. A small sound in the doorway made me look up. It was Medusa, dark hair curling around her head like so many snakes, giving me the evil eye. She had no little cardboard box full of plants, photos, personal possessions – just herself. She was neatly dressed but there was a quiet shabbiness about her. Her hair hadn't been styled in months. She lifted a chin and radiated defiance. We stared at each other.

I remembered this was the girl whom nobody wanted. Shunted from department to department, lasting no longer than the initial month's trial. No wonder she hadn't brought anything with her – she wasn't expecting to stay. She stood in the doorway, attitude oozing from every pore. I wondered if I was her last chance.

I kicked what I had been going to say into touch and said instead, 'Miss Lee, you are very welcome. I'm glad to see you. Your desk is over here. Perhaps you'd like to take some time to have a look around the office and get your bearings. I believe Mr Sands was a methodical worker – it should all be quite straightforward. When you've got yourself sorted out, please could you look through my in-tray? I'd like you to prioritise this lot: stuff I need to do now, stuff that can wait, and stuff I can pass on to other people. I'll leave you in peace, now. I'm down in the hall if you want me.'

Not bad, eh? I was impressed. She wasn't. She stared long enough for me to register that entering the room was her choice and nothing to do with me in any way whatsoever and crossed to the desk.

'There's no chair.'

'Well, there wouldn't be, would there? David was in a wheelchair. He brought his own,' was what I hadn't meant to say. God, she did have a real knack for rubbing people up the wrong way. 'Give Mr Strong a call and he'll bring one up for you,' and left the room before she ended up wearing the filing cabinet.

Mrs Partridge was pretending not to lurk near the stairs.

'The body's under the desk,' I said as I passed, just to give her something to worry about.

Down in the hall, I ran into Peterson.

'I was just coming to find you,' he said. 'Do you fancy a trip out?'

'Maybe … What did you have in mind?'

'Pathfinders,' he said. 'They've completed their last simulation. Time for the real deal. Would you care to join us?'

The Pathfinders are recently qualified trainees. They do what it says on the tin. They find the path. Sometimes, when we're not sure of our dates, they don't so much jump as hop, looking for the event in question, narrowing down the co-ordinates until we find what we're looking for. They also maintain the Time Map. They don't usually get involved in the more lively aspects of the job until they have a bit of experience under their belt.

I pushed thoughts of my Mary Stuart-covered desk to the back of my mind. 'Anywhere in particular?'

'Yes, actually. Do you remember, when we were at the other St Mary's, we couldn't find The Hanging Gardens of Babylon?'

'No one's ever found them. Or any trace of them.'

'I think everyone's been looking in the wrong place at the wrong time. There's very strong evidence they may have actually been The Hanging Gardens of Nineveh. Fancy checking it out?'

'Yes,' I said, enthusiastic at the opportunity. And even more enthusiastic at the thought of leaving my emotionally tangled life behind me for a while, and enjoying something as simple and straightforward as running for my life while being pursued by a blood-crazed mob, or succumbing to some deadly plague in the dim and distant past.

We assembled in Hawking, outside Number Three. Peterson in his role as trainer and mentor; Messrs Hopwood and Dewar and Miss Prentiss on their final training jump. And me. Ostensibly along to help supervise, but, in reality, just running away.

Peterson and I made ourselves scarce in the corner as they laid in their carefully calculated co-ordinates and, under Dieter's watchful eye, carried out their pre-flight checks. I smoothed the folds in my tunic and arranged my shawl over my headdress. Eventually they were finished.

Dieter withdrew.

Peterson said, 'In your own time, lady and gentlemen,' and the world went white.

'Bloody hell,' said Hopwood, unprofessionally, and I had to agree. Nineveh in 680BC was mind blowing.

We stood quietly under a small tree, just inside the Mashki Gate on the north-west side of the city, and tried to take it all in. The last king, Sennacherib, had extensively remodelled Nineveh, laying out new, wide streets and squares, and building 'The Palace Without Rival'. He'd brought water to the city by building canals and aqueducts. He'd planted gardens and erected hundreds of statues. I was looking at a giant man-bull a few yards away and it was looking right back at me.

Nineveh was a huge city – about seven hundred and fifty hectares – and built on a scale to match. The gates – all fifteen of them – were colossal. The stone and mud brick walls were sixty feet high and fifty feet thick. And as if that wasn't enough to deter invaders, stone towers had been cut into the walls every sixty feet or so.

Inside the walls, the city was dominated by the royal palace. Built for Sennacherib's beloved wife, Tashmetu-sharrat, it soared above the city.

We'd been standing for about ten minutes or so and, as far as I could see, no one was paying us the slightest attention. As usual, we didn't quite blend in, but Nineveh straddled the important trade routes of the time, so the streets were already full of other strange-looking folk who spoke funny.

This part of the assignment was under Mr Hopwood's control.

'This way,' he said, confidently. 'Miss Prentiss and Dr Maxwell, if you would be kind enough to bring up the rear, please.'

This was a polite way of saying, 'Women at the back where you belong.' Still, at least they hadn't brought anything heavy for us to carry. In ancient times – and modern, now I come to think of it – it's always women who do the heavy lifting.

We set off for the palace. Even I could have found it. Sennacherib had been a fully paid up member of the 'in your face' school of architecture. Built of huge white limestone blocks, it dazzled in the hot sunshine. A pair of magnificent copper lions guarded the main entrance. I saw terraces, pillars, and walkways, all heavily planted and cascading with running water. You could have been forgiven for thinking that here, indeed, were the famous hanging gardens, but you would have been wrong. Because the gardens were next door, connected to the palace by a canal and a royal avenue.

I caught my breath. We all caught our breath. The Hanging Gardens of Nineveh were beautiful. A green jewel in a dusty desert. Built in concentric squares, the largest, the outer square, was laid out as a public park. I could see small groves of trees. Shady paths invited further exploration. Entrance, to this part at least, seemed to be open to all.

Inside this park was a wide, lily-covered, square moat and inside this, another, smaller square park, more thickly planted and obviously private. But the centrepiece was the huge, three-storey ziggurat towering above its surroundings. Each terrace was lush and beautiful, landscaped with statues and planted with ornamental bushes, trees and the hanging foliage that gave the gardens their name. The summit was crowned with a copse of full-grown trees. Water cascaded wastefully from one terrace down to another, making the statement – *We are Nineveh and we are rich and powerful and we can afford to chuck it around.*

'Bloody hell,' said Mr Hopwood again. Again, no one argued.

'Right,' said Mr Dewar, pulling us all together. Historians do tend to get lost in the moment. On some assignments we really could do with a couple of well-trained sheepdogs and a cattle prod.

His was the next part of the mission. We'd all been allocated tasks. He made us check our com links – he was going by the book – and we all scattered. Peterson and I, who knew as much about horticulture as the average politician knew about effective and efficient government, were allocated the north side of the park.

We walked slowly, not drawing attention to ourselves – we hoped. The park was full of families enjoying a respite from the late afternoon sun. Heatproof children ran around, shouting. Water sellers lined the paths. Stone benches invited rest under the shady trees and everywhere was the sound of running water.

'I want to see how they get the water up there,' said Tim, gazing up at the ziggurat. 'Sennacherib – never unduly modest about his achievements – claimed to have used something that sounds suspiciously like the Archimedes screw – four centuries before Archimedes got round to inventing it.'

'Interesting. Lead on.'

The sun was far too hot to move quickly, so we strolled along happily, politely stepping aside with a smile whenever we encountered anyone else. It was easily the most peaceful assignment I'd ever had.

Miss Prentiss spoke in my ear.

'Dr Peterson. We have a problem.'

Tim sighed.

'Go ahead.'

'Mr Hopwood's been stung. By a scorpion.'

'Did you see it? How big?'

Believe it or not, the smaller they are, the more dangerous they can be. So if you are ever stung by one the size of a small truck, you should be fine. Size matters. Never mind whether it's women, chocolate, or scorpions – big is always beautiful.

'Smallish. But that's not the problem. He seems to be having some sort of allergic reaction.'

'Symptoms?'

'Rising temperature. Erratic pulse. Tingling in his extremities.' There was a pause and an unpleasant noise. 'And severe vomiting.'

'Where are you?'

'The three of us are already in the pod.'

'Get him back at once. You can return for us later. We're right at the northern end and it would take us a good twenty minutes to get to you. Go now.'

'Sir, are you sure?'

'Yes. Medevac. Get him out now. My authorisation.'

'Yes, sir. We'll be back as soon as we can.'

'No rush. Take your time.'

In the background, I could hear the computer counting down. '... Three, two, one ...'

And they were gone.

'Well,' said Tim, briskly, to cover the sudden feelings of unease we were both experiencing at being left here with no means of getting back. 'Shall we continue?'

I'd never actually been left behind before. With no means of escape should I need one. On the other hand ...

I looked around. Lush green growth rioted all around us. Beautiful birds flitted from tree to tree. I could hear gently trickling water somewhere to my left. A path twisted enticingly deeper into the gardens. A peacock called. The whole scene breathed peace and serenity. When you consider our usual setting was some bloody battlefield, or rat-filled slum, or viewing a spectacular but hazardous natural catastrophe, it could have been a lot worse. We were in a garden. What could go wrong?

We ambled slowly around the park, pausing every now and then to admire a particular flower, peer into the dark depths of an ornamental pool, or just inhale the cool, green, garden fragrance. Occasionally, through the trees, we caught glimpses of the giant central ziggurat with its green crown.

We still had no way of knowing whether these were *the* hanging gardens, but if they weren't, then Babylon was really going to have to get its green wellies on to go one better than this.

Slowly, we left the more popular areas behind us, drawing near to the moat to get a good view of the ziggurat.

I was entranced.

'Tim, this is wonderful.'

'Isn't it?' he said. 'I could stay here for ever.'

We never learn.

As he spoke the words, we stepped out from under the trees and found ourselves looking across the moat to the ziggurat and a flight of steps leading to the first terrace. Even though this was the least visited part of the park, Sennacherib had still paid attention to detail, and two winged leopards guarded the stairway.

We ascended a small, grassy hump for a better view.

And then, as we watched, three sumptuously dressed figures emerged and stood directly opposite us on the other side of the moat. One, several steps above the others wore a tall, golden conical hat. The other two were bareheaded. They talked among themselves. They were obviously high-ranking noblemen, their beards curled and oiled in the fashion of the day. The two younger men wore robes of gold with scarlet shawls. The older wore purple. Royal purple.

Tim stiffened. 'Is that who I think it is?

I nodded. Something was wrong. Really wrong. I had a very nasty feeling we were looking at the mighty Sennacherib himself. And with the lack of guards and personal retinue, the two younger men must be family members. Sons, probably. Two of them.

My happy feelings evaporated.

'Tim, we may need to move pretty sharpish.'

'Why?'

Too late.

Even as we watched, one of the younger men laughed and pointed upwards, drawing attention to a bird passing overhead. The older man looked up and as he did so, both younger men fell upon him with swords. Taken completely unawares, he went down at once. It was over in seconds. He lay, head down on the staircase, not moving. Scarlet trickles of blood ran down the steps in a dreadful parody of the cascading water around us.

We stood frozen.

They'd killed the king. Right in front of us, they'd killed the king. The mighty Sennacherib. The Assyrian who came down like the wolf on the fold was dead. Killed in his own back garden. By his own sons. And we'd witnessed it.

This was bad. This was very, very bad.

My next thought was even worse. We'd got the date wrong. We thought we were in 680BC and we weren't. If the records were right – and they were – we were in 681BC, instead. Which meant …

No time to think about that now. Both men straightened up from examining the body. One of them casually wiping his sword on his father's robe, glanced across the water and saw us watching.

I saw it all in slow motion. He stared for a second, then turned his head and shouted.

They weren't alone at all. Some dozen or so heavily armed men emerged from the trees and bushes.

He pointed directly at us. I don't speak Akkadian. I didn't need to. Standing on a small, grassy knoll at the site of an assassination is never good in any language.

'Shit!' said Tim, encapsulating the situation nicely.

They began to run towards one of the delicate bridges spanning the moat.

'Run,' I said. 'Come on.'

We fled.

'We have to get out,' said Tim.

We certainly did. Once they closed the gates to the gardens, we would be trapped. They'd beat the grounds and it would be only a matter of time. But not if we could get to the gates first.

So we ran.

I shed my shawl – an action I would later regret, and pulled down my hair. From a distance, I was now a red-haired girl in a tunic rather than a mature woman in a traditional shawl.

We flew down the path, emerging near the gate with the stone stele. We're old hands at avoiding pursuit. We slowed down and walked behind and then alongside a family group on their way out.

The little boy dropped a small, carved toy and Peterson picked it up and began to play with him. At the same time, I relieved one of the women of her heavy basket. I'm not sure how happy she was to relinquish it, but I didn't give her a lot of choice and we all walked out together. From the corner of my eye, I could see movement. Voices were raised behind us.

Once outside, I handed her back her basket. She snatched it from me, but we were out and I was past caring. We hurried away, back towards the Mashki Gate.

'What just happened?' said Peterson.

'Assassination of Sennacherib in 681BC, by two of his sons in revenge for his desecration of Babylon. Another son, Esarhaddon succeeds, but not yet because he's not here. Probably there will now follow a period of turmoil and lawlessness while everyone sorts themselves out and new players emerge. A bit like after a general election.'

'You mean there isn't turmoil and lawlessness *before* general elections?'

Joking apart, we were not in a good position. There would be soldiers on the streets soon and almost certainly a curfew. And until Number Three turned up, we had nowhere to go.

And we'd witnessed the murder. And they'd seen us witnessing the murder.

Number Three didn't come.

We were right about the soldiers. And the curfew. And having nowhere to go.

'Look,' said Tim. 'We can't hang around here waiting for St Mary's. God knows when they'll get here. It'll be dark soon and we have to find somewhere to hole up for the night. Just in case.'

He was right. St Mary's would come, but they might not come in time. We needed to find somewhere safe and we needed to find it soon. Before it got dark.

We stepped off the main thoroughfare and lost ourselves in the maze between the Mashki and Nergal Gates, choosing narrower and narrower streets until we finished in a tiny alley behind blind walls. It was a dead end, which wasn't ideal, but the wall was low enough for us to scramble over should we need to. And from there we could nip through someone's back yard, over another wall into a similar alley and away.

It wasn't a comfortable night. We were tired and thirsty and became more so as the night progressed. The sky was clear and full of stars. We sat with our backs to the cooling wall and quietly discussed our predicament.

The first thing, obviously, was that something had gone wrong when the co-ordinates were laid in. The date of Sennacherib's death was widely and extensively documented. The date was right. We were wrong. And if this mistake wasn't somehow picked up, they'd look for us in the wrong time. We were in 681BC. They'd be looking for us next year.

Peterson was confident. 'Chief Farrell, Dieter, Polly Perkins,' – Polly was head of IT – 'one of them is bound to pick it up. And if not immediately, they'll recheck when they can't find us. They'll jump about and eventually they'll get to us.'

Beside him, I nodded in the dark.

'In the meantime, we need to stay safe. The soldiers are probably looking for us, but the population is around a hundred thousand and so long as we keep our heads down, we'll be OK.'

He wasn't being over-optimistic. It wasn't the soldiers we needed to worry about too much. If we weren't rescued within a day or so, then life for us was going to get very tough. Very tough indeed.

Everyone has their own place in time. Almost everyone is part of a family unit, or a tribe, or a guild, and even those who aren't – those who live outside of normal society – usually have the knowledge to survive. Where to go – where not to go. Where they're likely to pick up free food. Who to watch out for. We had none of that knowledge. We didn't speak the language. We weren't prepped for a long assignment. We had no money – or the equivalent. We had nothing tradable. Nothing to barter. If we wanted to eat then we'd have to steal it – with all the dangers of being caught. Hanged. Hands chopped off. Impaled. Not all at the same time, obviously, but none of it was good.

Water was not so much a problem. There were public wells. But we had nothing in which to carry it. We'd have to persuade someone to draw it for us. Or we could go down to the riverbank. The Khosr flowed through the city and the mighty Tigris itself was only a mile away.

But we couldn't go too far away from the Mashki Gate because that's where they'd look for us. Except they'd be here next year. Because we were in the wrong time. We would never survive for a whole year.

Neither of us got any sleep that night. Soldiers were everywhere. Whether they were searching for us, or simply enforcing the curfew during the current power vacuum, we had no way of knowing. Twice loud voices sounded at the end of our little alley, but no one ventured near us.

Night in the desert is very cold. We both shivered in our thin tunics. We huddled closely together, tucking Tim's shawl around us.

He said, 'Do you remember our first jump together?'

'I certainly do. You peed on me.'

'Do you want me to do it again? For old times' sake?'

'Save it. If we have to go into hiding, we may have to drink our own urine.'

'That's something I've often thought about. Do you drink your own – or the other person's?'

'When you say *often* thought about' …'

'Well, you know, every now and then. Just out of idle curiosity.'

'You're not drinking my urine.'

'That's a little selfish. Surely, in our current crisis, we should be working together. I'm rather disappointed in this "me first" attitude.'

'Fine. Half a pint of Maxwell's Old Peculiar coming right up. Get it while it's still warm.'

I felt him chuckle. 'This time tomorrow we'll be back at St Mary's.'

We weren't.

We had a shit day. Even by St Mary's standards, it was a shit day.

We snuck out of our alley at first light and walked to the well at the end of the street. Early though we were, a couple of old crones were there before us. Peterson heaved up a couple of buckets of water for them and they gave us a drink in return. We chugged back as much as we could handle, nodded our thanks, and set off for the Gate again.

We hung around all day, moving on when we started getting suspicious looks. We would walk around in the hot sun for a while and then return.

The result was always the same. No St Mary's.

Soldiers were everywhere. Troops marched purposefully from A to B and then, presumably, back to A again. Groups of them stood on street corners, and large contingents had been drafted to the Gates. We couldn't have got out even if we'd wanted to.

The sun rose and the heat intensified. I had no shawl to protect my head. Without a comb, I twisted my hair up as best I could. Peterson said I looked like someone's mad granny.

The city seemed calm but tense. People knew something had happened, but not what. Nineveh under Sennacherib had enjoyed a period of stability. What would happen when the news got out was anyone's guess. Widespread panic, probably. People don't like change.

Their plan was obviously to keep a lid on things until a peaceful succession could be achieved. But Esarhaddon was a long way off. He would undertake a series of forced marches. He would get here. But he wasn't here yet.

I wondered what had happened to the murderers. Did they sit tight and ride out the storm? Or were they out of the gates before the body cooled? And speaking of the body …

'Let's go and look,' said Peterson. So we did.

The site was pristine. Gazing across the moat, we could see no traces of violence at all. That was what all the guards had been for – they were the clean-up squad. Not a trace remained of yesterday's drama.

We returned slowly back to the Mashki Gate. Still no sign of St Mary's.

'Typical,' said Peterson. 'Without you or me to show them the way they probably can't even find Hawking by themselves, let alone Nineveh.'

There was quite a crowd at the public well by now, and we had to wait a long time for our turn. We were hungry, too. The time for the mid-day meal was approaching. Succulent smells drifted around. My stomach rumbled.

We returned to our little alley, stifling between the high walls. The citizens of Nineveh employed the time-honoured method of rubbish disposal. They chucked it over the back wall into the alley. Problem solved.

We poked around, found some odd bits of wood, one sandal (why is there ever only one?) some strange bits of shrivelled vegetables that presumably even the goats wouldn't touch, a certain amount of night soil, a dead rat, and some broken pots.

We're St Mary's. We can make anything out of anything. We could probably build a nuclear reactor out of this little lot. However, we settled for propping the wood against the wall and draping Peterson's shawl over the top, which gave us shade and cover. Crawling underneath, I picked over the pottery and we found a broken piece that could hold several inches of water.

We slept for a while, roused only by the family on the other side of the wall all of whom seemed to have all traipsed outside for the sole purpose of yelling at each other for half an hour, and then traipsed back inside again.

It was still stifling in our alley, so we set off to the well again. Using our precious piece of pot, we were able to rinse off some of the dust and drink our fill.

The sun was going down. We'd been in Nineveh for twenty-four hours. With that thought, my stomach rumbled again. The street markets were packing up for the day and we wandered slowly along, keeping an eye out for discarded fruit and vegetables. No such luck. The street urchins had long since done all that. We really needed to get our act together. I started to think.

Peterson, turning to speak to me, brushed against a pile of figs and knocked some half-dozen to the ground. He stopped, picked them up and replaced them, contriving to keep two back. And the stallholder kindly gave him another two – one each – by way of thanks.

A feast!

We sat on a low wall and ate them slowly. Two figs seemed very inadequate. Over the way, a man was stirring a huge

219

cauldron of something savoury and dispensing ladlesful to people who turned up with bowls. And money.

We moved on.

The smell of piss told us we were in the dyeing and laundry area.

I had an idea.

The secret is not to run. Running draws attention. Move slowly and with confidence. I walked to the nearest vat full of reddish-coloured water, picked up a nearby bowl, filled it and walked slowly out again. I don't think anyone even noticed me. Peterson waited outside.

'What on earth ...?'

'We're going to break curfew tonight.'

'We are?'

'Yes. We need to be more proactive. St Mary's are all over this city even as we speak. But they're looking in the wrong time. And I'm getting fed up with waiting. So we leave them a message. As big as we can. On the side of that big white building near the gate. Where even St Mary's can't miss it.'

We crept out after curfew, just as the last light died away. I kept watch while Peterson did the deed.

He did his best in the dark. We could only cross our dye-stained fingers.

Stumbling out of our alleyway the next morning, we paused to admire our handiwork. Scrawled hugely across the wall in brownish-red stain, was the date:

681BC

You couldn't miss it. Even St Mary's couldn't miss it. And the beauty of it was that no one here would have a clue what it meant. They might even think it was building decoration. And the BC was the clincher. The message could only be from us.

Search parties would be looking for us. They would start in 680BC. When they couldn't find us, they would start to fan out across time. We had to leave them some sort of message. Show them where to look. Sooner or later, if no one wiped it off, or the building didn't fall down, or it didn't just fade away, next year someone would see it. Then they'd concentrate all their resources on 681BC. We were tagged. Once they had the right time, they'd find us.

They had to. Because something was happening. I could hear marching feet. Trumpets sounded. Orders shouted. Soldiers were on the streets.

The secret was out. You could see it. You could see the news fly from one group of people to the next. Shock and fear were written across people's faces. Women covered their faces and cried aloud. Men shouted, vainly demanding more details. Even the children stopped running and stood still, unsure what was happening, but aware that something was very wrong.

Soldiers started pushing people around, trying to restore order. Traders hastily shut up their stalls. Trouble was brewing. People vanished off the streets. Children were yanked inside. Doors and shutters slammed shut. Those far from their houses ran along the streets, desperate to be home and safe. Livestock mutinied in the panic and refused to move. Soldiers pushed and shoved, shouting incomprehensibly, but the message was clear enough.

Get off the streets.

People milled around in all directions. I managed to grab a couple of apricots and when we returned *chez nous*, Peterson had a flat loaf tucked under his armpit.

'What do you think's going on?' said Peterson.

'The news is out. They're clearing the streets to prevent trouble. It might only be for today. If not, we could have a problem.'

'We should eat all this bread now,' said Peterson. 'It'll be uneatable tomorrow.'

True. Never, ever underestimate the wonderful properties of food preservatives. In this dry climate, bread was as hard as nails after only an hour or so. Bakeries produced small batches all day non-stop. Loaves were snapped up and often eaten warm and on the spot. So we ate the bread and kept the apricots for later.

I was so thirsty. My tongue seemed too big for my mouth. I

had the beginnings of a dehydration headache. And it was hot. And getting hotter.

'Keep your mouth closed,' advised Peterson. 'Don't breathe through it.'

For the first time ever, I entertained the possibility that St Mary's might not find us in time. That they would find us, I was sure, but they might be too late.

Years ago, we lost five historians in two separate incidents. It was before my time, but I know they searched and searched for months afterwards. Not a trace of any of them was ever found. And that was our worry. Not whether we would be rescued, but whether we would still be alive to be rescued. Which we wouldn't be if we didn't get some water soon.

The long, hot day wore on.

The well was only a hundred yards away. The question was whether to break curfew and go at night, when the dark would be both friend and enemy, or try it during the day when we could see but as easily be seen. If soldiers were stopping everyone on the street then, as all foreigners are in times of unrest, we could be in trouble. And they might still be looking for their witnesses as well.

We both plumped for breaking curfew. It was like being back at school. If you're going to break the rules – go for it big-time. There are only so many detentions you can possibly attend in one term. Sadly, the penalty for being caught on the streets was probably slightly harsher than detention, but the need for water was becoming imperative. And we now had a bowl. A bit brown, but we didn't care. We could bring water back to the alley at night and wait out the day. It seemed a good plan.

We left it as late as we could, partly to give the heat time to dissipate and partly to let the moon rise. Finally, we set off.

We slunk out of the alley like a couple of street cats up to no good. Hugging the walls, we groped our way down the streets, flitting from shadow to shadow. Three soldiers lounged at the corner. One leaned against a wall, one squatted on his heels, and one was staring vaguely in the other direction. They'd have to wait more than twenty centuries before they could pass round a cigarette.

We slipped past them and out on to the main road.

Peering anxiously up and down, we could see no one. The entire area was deserted. I could see the darker shadow, which would be the top of the steps leading down to the well. Already I could picture the cool damp cistern, the wet slap of water against the stone walls … taste the ice-cold water … And there was no one in sight. Surely we couldn't be that lucky.

Of course we couldn't.

We were just easing our way cautiously along the front wall of someone's house, when I heard Guthrie's voice in my ear.

'Max?'

I jumped a mile and knocked over something that fell with a clatter. A dog barked. Inside the house, a nervous voice called out.

'Shit,' said Peterson.

We'd have been all right if it hadn't been for that bloody dog. It just wouldn't shut up. A shutter was thrown back and a light appeared.

We ran. No choice.

'We're in trouble, Major,' I said to Guthrie. 'You're going to have to get us out. And quickly.'

A voice shouted behind us. The dog was having hysterics.

I followed Peterson.

In the surrounding houses, other, flickering lights appeared. Doors opened. Men stuck out their heads, presumably demanding to know what was happening. We pressed back hard into a patch of darker shadow.

And then someone let the bloody dog loose.

'Go up,' directed Guthrie.

We went up, scrambling up on to the low roof.

Not the best idea he'd ever had. In the summer heat, half the city was sleeping on their roof.

All around us, people sat up, heads appeared, children started to cry, women shrieked.

'For crying out loud …' muttered Peterson and we dropped off the roof again, abandoned any attempt at silence and just ran for it.

'No go, Major,' I panted. 'And no time to chat. Just find us.'

We had no idea where we were going. Getting away from all this racket was our main aim. We could work out the details later.

I could see a light bobbing ahead of us. Soldiers. We swerved to the left, but they saw us. They shouted. I could hear a strange metallic clatter. They must be bashing their swords against their shields to alert others nearby. I could hear the clatter taken up in the distance.

More shouting now, closer at hand. What to do? To stay on the main road, or risk one of these narrower streets with the possibility of being trapped?

The decision was taken out of our hands.

Four men stepped out of a doorway. One swung a shield and Peterson went down like a tree. He didn't move.

I should have run. I should have left him. At least one of us would escape. But this was Tim. My friend Tim.

I stood over him and snarled defiance. They laughed at me and someone grabbed me from behind. He stank of onions, leather, sweat, and dust. I didn't struggle. I didn't want to give them any excuse to rough us up. Maybe I could tell them we were only looking for water and they'd let us go. Maybe a pig would fly past with a nice cup of tea.

I'd dropped the bowl, but I cupped my hands together, mimed drinking and pointed back down the street to the well.

They held up the light and stared at me.

As well they might. My hair had come down. I was covered in dust and grime. My hands were still stained brownish-red from the dye and there were splashes of the same colour all over my tunic. It looked like blood.

I knew exactly what they were thinking.

Looters.

People out after dark, taking advantage of the prevailing confusion to help themselves to anything of value. To steal. Maybe even to kill.

There's never any mercy for looters in any age. Throats cut.

Dropped back into the dirt for the cart to collect the next morning. They'd think no more about it. We would lie, dying, watching the lifeblood pour out of our bodies to soak into the ever-thirsty desert dust.

The most peaceful assignment I'd ever had was not going to end well.

'Major, where are you?'

No reply. Were we in a dead spot?

I struggled but I might as well not have bothered. I don't think my captor even noticed.

'Water,' I said, desperately. 'We were looking for water.' If they realised I was foreign they might think we hadn't understood the curfew and let us off.

They weren't even listening.

Peterson stirred. They glanced at each other and nodded.

One crouched alongside him, grasped his hair and pulled his head back. Dimly realising what was happening, he tried to struggle.

I said urgently, 'Major, now would be a really good time.'

One of them said something that even I realised was, 'Get on with it.'

I heard the rasp of steel as a dagger was drawn.

My own head was pulled back so hard it hurt.

I looked up at the beautiful, uncaring stars.

I felt the cold touch of metal.

A voice that was both in my ear and above me said, 'Max, hold on,' and Major Guthrie dropped from a nearby roof at the same time as Markham and Evans stepped out from the shadows.

With their usual disdain for historical accuracy, the security section was wearing full body armour and visored black helmets. Our captors must have thought the desert demons had risen against them. But not for long. Seconds later, all four guards were lying in the dust.

'Good evening, historians. Can I be of any assistance?'

I glanced down at the four unconscious soldiers.

'Why did you do that? We were winning.'

They helped Peterson to his feet.

Guthrie spoke into his com. 'Mr Clerk – we've got them. Send everyone else home and await our arrival.'

Along the street, someone shouted. We weren't out of the woods yet.

'This way.'

Following Guthrie, we set off. Weller and Evans supported the still-not-firing-on-all-cylinders Peterson.

'Pod Five. Two streets down. On the left. Can you walk?'

'Of course I can.'

More shouting. Even closer.

'Can you run?'

'Can you keep up?'

I took off like a rocket.

The whole city was waking now. Shouts and clanging metal echoed off the buildings. Every dog in the city was yelling his head off. You could tell St Mary's was in town.

'Good job this is a stealth operation, Major. Imagine if people knew we were here.'

'Just shut up and run.'

The pod was just ahead of us. Clerk had the door open. Ritter covered our approach.

We hurtled into the pod in the traditional St Mary's manner with everyone yelling for the door.

We were safe.

I braced my hands on my knees and tried to get my breath back.

'Well,' said Guthrie, stowing his weapons, 'you made a complete dog's breakfast of this one, didn't you?'

I slid gratefully down the wall to sit on the floor. 'Don't know what you mean. We saw Sennacherib die.'

'You must be thrilled. Because that worked out so well for you, didn't it?'

'And did you notice,' said Peterson groggily as they lowered him to the floor, 'they were infantry – not archers.'

I glugged some water.

'Yes – no ear flaps on their helmets.'

226

'And we discovered The Hanging Gardens of Nineveh. Not Babylon.'

Guthrie took my water off me. 'Not too much.'

He began to feel my arms and legs.

I took the water back. 'What are you doing?'

'Trying to see where all this blood is coming from.'

'It's not blood – it's dye. Can't you tell the difference?'

'How's Mr Hopwood?' said Tim.

'Completely recovered. Why are you both covered in dye?'

'Didn't you see our message?'

'What message?'

'We left a message for you. On the wall. For God's sake – it was in big writing. Even the security section couldn't have missed it.'

'We didn't need a message. We just followed the riot. And surprise, surprise – there you were.'

'You cut it a bit fine, didn't you?'

'We'd been with you for a good five minutes. We were just waiting for an opportunity to get you out quietly. Which never came.'

'You could have given us a clue you were so close.'

'You seemed to be managing perfectly well in your mission to wake the entire city. You didn't need us.'

'How long have we been missing?'

'Six weeks.'

'What?'

For us, it had been two, no, three days.

Reaction set in. I closed my eyes and felt again that cold touch of metal.

Guthrie laid a gentle hand on my arm and I clutched at it for a moment and nodded my thanks to him.

He stood up. 'All right, Mr Clerk. Has everyone else jumped?'

'Confirmed, Major.'

'Let's get them home.'

The world went white.

* * *

The whole world was waiting for us in Hawking. Armed and armoured people milled around, shouting and cheering. Miss Prentiss, Mr Dewar, and Mr Hopwood stepped forward.

Peterson, supported by Markham and Evans, drew himself up and reverted to full Training Officer Mode.

'Right. Can anyone tell me where we went wrong?'

When I opened my eyes in Sick Bay, the room was very quiet. I was in my usual bed by the door.

Dr Bairstow sat beside the bed, his face turned away. One hand rested lightly on mine.

I closed my eyes again, sighed, and fluttered my eyelids a little. When I opened my eyes, he had both hands resting on his walking stick.

'Good morning, Dr Maxwell.'

'Good morning, sir.'

I always appreciated that he never asked how I was. In his book, if you weren't actually dead then you were fit to work.

'An eventful assignment.'

'Yes, indeed, sir.'

I struggled to sit up and he passed me a rehydration drink.

'So,' I said, sipping. 'Six weeks.'

'Or three days.'

This was an old argument. I would argue that we'd been missing for six weeks and our pay packets should reflect that fact. He would respond that according to my personal timeline, only three days had passed and therefore I was only entitled to three days' pay. I never won, but I never wearied of the argument, either. It's our responsibility to keep senior managers on their toes. I was doing him a kindness, really. He was never the slightest bit appreciative but we should never let management ingratitude deflect us from our duty.

Dr Foster wandered in an hour later, peered at me, lit a cigarette, typed into her scratchpad, and began to mutter apocalyptically about liver flukes.

I beamed at her because I knew it would annoy her. If there

was one thing she hated more than a patient – it was a happy patient.

And the next visitor, of course, was Leon, who stood uncertainly by the door.

I'd been doing some thinking. There's something about being adrift in time that rearranges some priorities and perceptions.

Looking up at the stars while waiting to have your throat cut rearranges the rest.

I climbed out of bed and wobbled towards him.

Nobody said anything for a very long time. I think we both felt that more than enough had been said already. Eventually though, I had to speak.

'Leon. Need to breathe.'

He slackened his grip slightly. But not much.

So there we were. All set for a romantic reconciliation. I gazed into his eyes. Rainbows blossomed. Bluebirds sang. The music swelled to a crescendo.

The bloody fire alarms went off.

He uttered a paint-blistering curse. 'I don't believe it.'

Neither did I. Normally, there wasn't a smoke detector in the building that had a battery in it.

He strode from the room. There was a lot of shouting in the corridor. An awful lot of shouting. I could hear Leon. And Peterson. And Mr Markham – of course he *would* be here somewhere, wouldn't he?

Since Dr Bairstow wouldn't let us have a goat, Mr Markham was the nearest thing we had to a mascot. Small, spiky-haired, and perpetually grubby, he had acquired unit-wide respect by running into a horse's bottom and laying himself out cold. And that was just the beginning of his adventures here at St Mary's. Invincibly cheerful, he had been badly injured on several occasions. He always bounced back. We reckoned he was indestructible. He was coming with me to Edinburgh.

I could also hear Helen's voice cutting effortlessly through the racket. And Major Guthrie's. Everyone seemed to have a lot to say. It was tempting to go out there and make things worse, but I resisted.

The ear-splitting shriek of the alarms just went on and on. Then, suddenly, there was blessed silence.

The shouting, however, continued for some considerable time afterwards.

Eventually, Leon returned, closing the door firmly behind him.

'What was that all about?'

'While visiting Mr Peterson, Mr Markham contrived to set fire to the curtains in the men's ward. Everyone's blaming you. Come here.'

'What? Why?'

'Because I want to hold you again. Come here.'

'I mean, why are they blaming me?'

'You instructed him to practice his conjuring tricks. The curtains ignited. All over now. Come here.'

'The trick involves producing silk scarves, for crying out loud. How the hell could he possibly manage to set fire to the curtains?'

'How should I know? I'm only grateful he's not sawing a woman in half out there. Please, come here.'

We sat in the window seat and he talked quietly to me. His words were simple, but came from his heart. They reached out and touched my very core. And the whole black, ugly, gunky mess that had been inside me for so long just cracked apart and flowed away, like the tears on my cheeks.

Chapter Sixteen

My Mary Stuart briefing was set for two days after I left Sick Bay.

Not without a great deal of trepidation, I assembled everyone in my office to divvy up the mission responsibilities. This would be our first mission with such high levels of interaction. This went against all our training, all our instincts. We would not be melting into the background this time.

Present were Chief Farrell, the world's most reluctant volunteer; Mr Dieter from the technical section; Major Guthrie, and Tim Peterson. Mrs Enderby, representing Wardrobe, separated Professor Rapson from Dr Dowson. Miss Schiller, Miss Van Owen, and Miss Lee squeezed themselves together at the foot of the table.

I looked at them. They looked at me. And off we went.

I said, 'Has everyone read through their background notes?' and they all nodded. 'I'm going to run through this from beginning to end because some of you know more than others. After the briefing, I'll be happy to answer questions and listen to any suggestions you may have. I don't pretend to have all the answers, and if there's anything you think I've missed, please speak up.

'Initially, we thought this mission would be fairly straightforward, but things have moved on and we now have two mission objectives. The first, as you know, is to ascertain whether Mary Stuart, Queen of Scotland is married to, or about to marry, James Hepburn, Earl of Bothwell. If not, one of our objectives is to insinuate ourselves into her court and – nudge –

events back into line. This is high-profile stuff. There will be no question of us working quietly in the background. For the first time ever we'll be looking to interact with the major players of their age. And we don't have long. Darnley is murdered on 10th February 1567 and Mary is supposed to marry Bothwell on 15th May. This gives us a window of only about 90 days to find out what's gone wrong and to put it right. So we're going to have to move fast. Make no mistake about this, people – we will be in harm's way.

'The second objective is to locate and neutralise the probable cause of all this. I present to you the villain of the piece, Clive Ronan, already known to most of us here, I believe.'

I brought up the best image we could find.

'Not content with getting his arse kicked in the Cretaceous Period and in the Alexandrian desert last year, we believe he's attempting to manipulate events for his own personal benefit. You've read your notes; I don't have to tell you the consequences if we don't act.'

A damaged timeline. Altered History. Personal consequences. Paradox. Nothing good for anyone.

'So, let's make a start. We're jumping to 16th-century Edinburgh and far from keeping our heads down and staying out of trouble, we're going to be walking right into it. Dr Peterson and I have put together a scenario, approved by the Boss, as follows:

'Scotland is a trading nation. So is England. English wool is the backbone of their economy. Scotland exports wool too; Melrose wool is a quality product but, when it comes to wool, it's England that the world looks to. We intend to come at this in an unusual way. The deal is that we offer Mary exotic goods and fabrics from the east, in exchange for Melrose wool. To establish Scotland on the important trade routes of the time. To raise its profile and give it the opportunity to get in with the big boys. If, and we emphasise this, *only if* she will substantially undercut Elizabeth's prices. We don't want to raise suspicions by making the offer too good to be true. However, given the rivalry between the two of them, we think she'll jump at the opportunity to gain such a lucrative advantage over her cousin.

'To this end, we will be posing as a delegation from Istanbul. And be careful here. Constantinople fell in 1453, and officially became Istanbul. You will find the city referred to by either name. Be aware of this. We are representing a guild of international merchants eager to open a trading relationship with Scotland. This should not have too great an impact on the timeline. We're simply anticipating the formation of the Levant Company by a few years. We will be rich, grand, ostentatious, and very, very visible. We will obtain an audience with the Queen, present our credentials, letters of introduction and recommendations, and bring gifts – precious gifts.

'This should give us the entrée and, from this grand opening, somehow, we will be seeking to influence events and get things back on track. And before you all look too dismayed, remember this. Just for once, it might be that History is on our side. We're the good guys in all this – this time she might just bat for our team, so keep your fingers crossed.

'Now, how do we achieve all this? If I could refer you to your cast of characters, please. The delegation will be headed by the French speaking Sir Richard Hampton, representing the merchants of Istanbul. Or Chief Farrell as he prefers to be known. Accompanying him are his brother Christopher, that's Dr Peterson and his aide de campe, Robert Morton. Major Guthrie, that's you. Major, Mr Markham is already signed up, but please can you select two or three more people from your team to accompany us. Please emphasise their main objective will be to safeguard a bunch of historians hell-bent on disaster, and therefore some sort of death-wish and a complete disregard for personal safety will be an advantage on this assignment.'

Guthrie grinned.

'They're queuing up.'

'Really?'

He grinned again.

'Are you kidding?'

'OK. Well, setting aside the lemming-like behaviour of the security section for one moment, I'm going as the sister, Mary

Hampton. A female presence may be useful since we're dealing with a queen. Miss Schiller, our Tudor specialist, will accompany me as Janet, maid and chaperone.'

'Good luck with that,' said Peterson and she laughed.

'Moving on,' I said, glaring at the two of them. Water off a duck's back. 'Equipment required:

'We'll be using Pods Five and Six. The big ones. However, they're not big enough for this number of personnel, so ...' I took a deep breath. This was the biggie. 'We won't be using them as our base. They are transport only. We'll leave them outside town. We're actually going to be living amongst 16th century contemporaries.'

Complete silence.

OK, it could have been worse. They were all still here. I ploughed on.

'We could be there for up to three months. There will be at least eight of us, coming and going. With all the gear we're taking, we'd need at least four pods. Too many. Besides, we'll be high profile. We may need to entertain. So, we'll be hiring a house. Right slap bang in the most fashionable area – Canongate, where the top people live.

'Firstly, however, I want to send Mrs Enderby, properly escorted of course,' I said to reassure her, and wasting my time because her whole face lit up with excitement, 'to 16th-century Istanbul to organise the purchase of carpets, silks, lace, velvets, all kinds of fabrics – gifts with which to tempt a Scottish queen to sign a trade agreement.'

'Can we not use contemporary fabrics?' she asked.

'We could, but if we have to leave in a hurry – and past experience suggests we will – we can't leave them behind and we can hardly present her Scottish Majesty with fabulous gifts then ask for them all back again, can we?'

'We could show them to her and then take them away afterwards,' suggested Guthrie.

'They're gifts, Ian,' said Peterson, crushingly, 'You're not supposed to ask for them back. Jeez, I bet Christmas is fun in your house.'

234

I continued. 'From a security point of view and given the nature of the assignment, I am not in favour of anything that could delay our getaway. However, it does seem quicker and simpler to present her with stuff from our time. It would certainly make a greater impact.'

'Yes,' said Mrs Enderby, joining the discussion. 'Modern fabrics, modern colours, modern techniques. That would certainly stop her in her tracks. I could put together something really sumptuous. After all, the whole point is to impress her. If we don't gain access to her court, then the whole mission is over before we even start.'

'Mrs Enderby makes a very valid point,' said Peterson. 'But then what?'

'But then nothing,' said Guthrie. 'We leave it there. If we're successful then she only has a very short time left in Scotland anyway and she's going to be much too busy to worry about frocks. It's all biodegradable. It'll probably just be shoved in a cupboard somewhere and forgotten. We leave it there.'

'It would certainly simplify things,' I said, trying to overcome instincts and training and failing.

Lovely Mrs Enderby came to the rescue. 'We can do both, Max. I'll use modern fabrics for your own costumes. That will make her eyes pop, and then we can use the contemporary stuff for the presentations. Best of both worlds. Trust me; I'll put together a collection that will rock her world. We'll start with colour. The Ottomans used metallic thread to make their silks shimmer in the light. I know she likes white and we can use that to set against their rich, deep colours. I think maybe Bursa, rather than Istanbul. Then there's Italian velvet, of course, we can pick some up easily enough. Plus taffeta, satin, damask. And accessories, of course, braiding, ribbons, lace. Oh, lace ruffs, too. And she likes her caps. And slashing,' she said excitedly and for one moment I thought we were back to Jack the Ripper again. 'You just leave all this to me, Max.'

'Wonderful idea,' I said. 'Thank you. Now, Dr Dowson and the archive staff will forge our papers, which are important and need to be able to withstand close scrutiny. Professor Rapson, can your R&D people assist, please?

They nodded, temporarily united. That wouldn't last long, but with luck long enough to get the job done. Just so long as they didn't actually blow anything up. On the other hand, we wouldn't be St Mary's if something wasn't on fire somewhere.

'The next step – Dr Peterson and Major Guthrie's team jump to Edinburgh. They rent a house – a big one – and prepare the way. Gentlemen, I want lots of glitz and glamour. Throw your money around. We only have 90 days at the most. Less, if we don't get the co-ordinates quite right, so we can't afford to be shrinking violets. Forget blending into the background on this mission.

'When everything is ready for their big entrance, Sir Richard and his party arrive, gain access to the Queen, present their papers – and gifts, Major – insinuate themselves into her good graces and …' I stopped.

And that was where everything stopped, of course. It looked so simple on paper. *Get the Queen and Bothwell married.*

'The truth is,' I said, 'from that moment on we're just going to have to wing it.'

Silence.

'We'll think of something,' said Peterson. 'We're St Mary's.'

The magic words. Everyone cheered up.

'The second part of the assignment is less easy to define. Somewhere, amongst all this is the cause of all the trouble, our old friend, Clive Ronan. Whether he is working alone or with contemporaries is unknown. We have no information on his whereabouts. We think we know his objective but we might be wrong. In short – we have nothing. The only thing we do know is that something is very wrong in 1567 and we have to sort it out.'

I waited, but apart from the sound of people bashing away at their scratchpads, there was no other sound.

'It gets worse,' I continued. 'Having located Mr Ronan, we have no idea what to do with him. I'm not singling out the security section, Major, but we all need to be very clear about this. No harm must come to Mr Ronan. We've all read the notes. If he's dead then he's not in the Cretaceous. Or at Alexandria. Or anywhere. And by extension, we might not be, either. I don't often lay down the law but I'm doing so in this case. Everyone on this assignment needs to be very clear about this. *No harm must come to Mr Ronan.*'

Guthrie nodded, tight lipped.

'Question,' said Schiller. 'Where's History in all this? How have things got this bad? Clerk got his arm broken last year when he reached out to help a woman down some steps.'

'We think, in this case, that it is very possible that History is employing more – subtle – methods, by using St Mary's.'

'St Mary's is the subtle option?'

'As opposed to exterminating Ronan, damaging the timeline, and causing the end of all things as we've known them – yes. St Mary's may be the only option.'

'We're doomed,' said Guthrie and everyone cheered up.

'Next stage.' I said. 'Having achieved our objective, we implement what is always the most important part of any assignment – the safe return. Major, one of your team will remain at the house at all times to ensure we can go at a moment's notice. Their priority, should anything go wrong, is to strip the house of anything anomalous and get it back to the pods. Please make that clear to them. Everyone will need to pack their personal gear in grab-bags and keep them available at all times. We will almost certainly be looking for a speedy exit. There will be no time to pack. It's a chore, but it must be done.'

He nodded. I paused and sipped some water. Everyone bent over their scratchpads. I waited until they'd finished.

'So, your individual responsibilities are as follows:

'Chief, please get the pods prepped and start work on the Richard Hampton character.

'Major Guthrie, select your team, brief them up, and start work on your character.

'Mrs Enderby, please choose the members of your team who will accompany you. You know the brief. You'll be in Pod Six with Mr Dieter. Major Guthrie and his security team will escort you in Pod Five. Buy whatever you need; Dr Bairstow has persuaded the history department at Thirsk to supply us with contemporary currency. Load your goods into Number Six for Major Guthrie to take to Edinburgh.

'Mr Dieter will bring you back here in Number Five.

'Using Number Five again, Dr Peterson will jump back to Edinburgh and rendezvous with Major Guthrie. You will hire a house and get things ready. Send someone back in Five when you're all set.

'Chief Farrell, Miss Schiller, and I will join you.

'And then, we ride into Edinburgh, making as much noise as possible.

'Miss Van Owen, you will have responsibility for the History Department until we return, but I'd like you to keep attending these meetings as first reserve.

'Dr Peterson, can your Pathfinders narrow down the co-ordinates? We don't have a lot of wiggle room and we don't want to arrive with less than 24 hours to the deadline. And we'll need them to locate a secure site outside the city where the pods won't be noticed.

'Everyone get themselves off to Wardrobe to start getting kitted out. Those wishing to grow a beard should note they are fashionable for men only.

'In addition to our forged papers, Dr Dowson has produced detailed briefing notes for 16th-century Scotland, together with a simple vocabulary. Study this carefully. Many words have changed their meaning over time. For instance, apprehensive pertains to the word apprehend – to understand – rather than our current understanding of the word. Geek means to look at, and does not refer to any member of R&D. There are many words for whore, including guinea hen, harlot, and drab. Nicked and knackered mean exactly what you think they do. Don't say *thee* and *thou* unless you want to be laughed at as old-fashioned and anyone uttering the word 'forsooth' in my hearing will be consigned to Professor Rapson to play the lead role in his "How many times could the Druids actually wind a person's entrails around a sacred oak tree?" experiment. Also included are words or gestures that should *not* be used. There's enough conflict in our lives without inadvertently insulting anyone's mother.

'In addition, we have notes on royal protocol, forms of address, polite manners, etc. And an Istanbul background as well, in case some smart-arse starts asking questions. Speaking of which, does anyone have any?'

'Not at this stage,' said Peterson, speaking for everyone. 'Maybe later.'

'OK then,' I said. 'We'll meet here at 0930, the day after tomorrow for updates and briefings. Miss Lee will distribute the minutes this afternoon. Thank you everyone.'

Chapter Seventeen

What an entrance we made; months of hard work finally paying off. Beautifully attired and mounted on the best horses Peterson could find, we entered Edinburgh in triumph.

Markham led the way on foot, banging a drum for reasons known only to himself and shouting, 'Make way, make way,' in English, French, Latin, and some incomprehensible dialect he said was Geordie.

People did scatter, but any ill-will caused by his multi-lingual high-handedness was easily assuaged by the handfuls of coins he carelessly tossed around him. Small fights broke out.

Farrell came next, with Peterson beside him, both doffing their caps and waving to passers-by, who, despite having no clue what was going on, cheered with enthusiasm. We had 'money' written all over us. I could imagine the local merchants' eyes glistening with anticipation.

Schiller and I followed on. I rode a dainty cream mare, spirited, but easy to control. She arched her neck and pranced, showing off like the rest of us. I pushed back my hood and made sure to smile.

Behind us rode a surprisingly dashing Major Guthrie, and Randall and Weller brought up the rear, driving a heavily laden wagon bearing the fruits of Mrs Enderby's labours.

People shouted – for various reasons – my little mare neighed, dogs barked, Markham banged his drum. Oh yes, we had arrived.

* * *

There was the house and there were the two eagles over the door. The one on the right had a broken wing, just as Leon had described to me that rainy afternoon in my office. I caught Peterson's eye and he smirked. He had found exactly the right house.

Leon stared up at it for a brief moment. He was seeing his nightmares come true. I smiled reassuringly as he helped me dismount. He formally offered me his arm and we mounted the steps to the front door. Markham flung one last fistful of money – Thirsk was going to have a fit – gave us one final dramatic drum roll and followed us up the steps and into the house. The door closed on all the clamour.

Now everyone knew where we lived.

Like most houses at the time, the front door opened directly into the main parlour. A screen protected us from draughts. Two large oak settles either side of the fireplace had to be more comfortable than they looked. A battered chest stood under the windows and a big, ornate cabinet affair loomed in a corner. All were of oak and beautifully made. A number of stools stood against the walls. Every room was panelled. The wooden floors glowed gently in the light of two very whiffy oil lamps. Some of the windowpanes were glazed, but others contained an opaque substance Schiller said was horn.

At the back, the kitchen was nearly as large and dominated by a big scrubbed table in the middle. Two benches stood against the wall and a series of mismatched wooden cupboards containing earthenware crockery ran down one side. I yanked open a badly fitting drawer containing spoons and knives. No forks. Another settle was pulled in front of the huge hearth, which bristled with irons, spits, stands, cauldrons, and other items of a dubious and culinary nature. I was reminded of the Spanish Inquisition.

The stairs were really not something you wanted to gallop up and down in a long dress bearing only a flickering candle.

Schiller and I shared the bedroom at the back and I saw my first tester bed – a four-poster with a red canopy overhead. It was small for two people and lacked matching hangings, but the feather mattress was unstained and looked quite comfortable. We dropped the sleeping bags we'd brought with us and looked around. Another chest stood at the foot of the bed. There was no wardrobe, but pegs hung around the walls for our clothes. Farrell and Peterson were in the front room, similarly furnished, and a small room leading off that would be where we stored the Queen's gifts until required.

We had truckle beds, but Guthrie and his people preferred to sleep downstairs.

'Just in case,' he said.

We started to unpack, bustling about, feet clattering on the wooden floors until we laid down some carpets. We hung two or three on the walls where they could impress any visitors. Peterson had fires going in all the rooms and the place smelled of wood smoke, cloves, and warm wood, with not so pleasant undertones of tallow and burned fat.

I made a mental note never, *ever* to set foot in the backyard privy. Or even the backyard itself. I could feel my colon assuming a defensive posture.

'It's not so bad,' said Peterson, cheerfully. 'At least it's in our own backyard. Most people have to trudge down to the midden by the stables.'

I made a mental note never, *ever* to trudge down to the midden by the stables.

He became aware of the silence.

'Fine. There are buckets in the bedrooms. Just empty them into the privy as and when.'

Rampant constipation is not always a bad thing.

'And then,' he continued, 'we can just empty the ashes from the fire over the top and it's all nice and neat and there's no smell. Cutting-edge hygiene, eh?'

'Dear God,' said Guthrie. 'How are you people still alive? Did our last misadventure in Alexandria teach you nothing about methane?'

We stared at him.

He sighed.

'I'll keep it simple for the historians. There's a pit, full of … effluent. Things build up. Some idiot tosses in a bucket of hot ash and maybe a glowing ember or two. No prizes for working out what happens next. I've been showered with shit once. It's not happening again.'

We stared at him.

'OK,' said Peterson. 'Scrub round the ash thing. Just chuck in your bucketful and retire immediately.'

Oh, the romance and glamour of time travel.

We established the date – mid April. We had just under a month. Less time than I would have liked, but it could have been worse.

Two days after our arrival, Chief Farrell, Major Guthrie, and Peterson went to the palace. Weller and Randall went with them. Markham stayed behind with us, practising his conjuring tricks. The curtains remained unignited. There was nothing more we could do except wait for their return, so we decided to keep busy. Not that we had much choice. Just keeping the house going took up all of our time. No wonder everyone had so many bloody servants.

For a start, water had to be brought in and lugged up the stairs. After a particularly wet incident involving an ascending Mr Markham and a descending Mr Randall, we decided to wash in the kitchen. Schiller and I went first, then the boys. Then a water carrier turned up at the door looking for business and Markham nearly married him on the spot.

After washing, we donned what seemed an enormous number of garments. A shift, hooped underskirt, petticoat, another velvet underskirt, an overdress, sleeves, hose, shoes and headgear. Schiller got away with a bum roll, but I was cursed with what Mrs Enderby had assured me was a very moderate farthingale. I had four dresses: two court dresses, a travelling outfit, and a supposedly more comfortable woollen dress to wear around the house.

Once we'd eased each other into our clothing, there was

breakfast to sort out. We'd brought some food with us, but that was kept for emergencies. Weller and Randall would return from the market with bread, cheese, and baskets full of mud-covered objects that apparently were vegetables. Turnips figured prominently. However, Weller's father had been a butcher and therefore, he knew one end of a rabbit from the other. Farrell assumed charge of the cooking and I was relegated to unskilled labour – chopping, peeling and, occasionally, stuffing. It all took hours. As did the clearing away afterwards.

Then there was the house to tidy, fires to lay, buckets (!) to empty – it just went on and on. How the hell did these people ever find the time for war, adultery, cattle-rustling, sheep-shagging, and all the other traditional pastimes of a bygone age?

The three of them arrived back in the early evening, having been gone for hours. They parked the horses, came quietly through the back door, and dropped, exhausted onto the benches. Markham passed them some beer, although how that would help was a bit of a mystery to me.

Farrell was last man in. He stood just inside the doorway, a strange expression on his face. I looked around. Guthrie was wet and shaking out his cloak. Peterson, sitting at the table, turned to greet him. Schiller sat with me by the fire. The sudden draught from the door blew out one of the candles. Smelly smoke drifted across the room. I knew what this was. He was seeing the scene he had described to me in my office.

I said, 'It's fine. Come on in.' My voice broke the spell and the moment passed.

I was desperate to know what had happened, but made myself give them a minute first. Guthrie drained his cup, peered dubiously into the bottom, and pushed it away from him.

I couldn't stay quiet any longer.

'How did it go? Did you see her? What did she say?'

The correct procedure is to say, 'Report'. However, you can't always remember everything.

Farrell sighed. 'We never saw her.'

'What? All that time and you never saw her?'

This had been a fear of mine. That we would turn up, day after day after day and she couldn't or wouldn't see us and we'd never get access and time would roll on and soon it would be too late …

'It's not all bad,' he said, wearily. 'They did take our papers. We were well treated. They knew who we were.'

'And?'

'They'll get back to us.'

This was awful. I'd envisaged (and planned for) death, disaster, or discovery, but never that they would just ignore us.

'The place is packed,' he said, sensibly not quite draining his cup. 'There are queues of people seeking an audience. She couldn't possibly see them all. This is just some sort of weeding process. They'll get back to us.'

Time to take the initiative.

'Right,' I said. 'Tomorrow, we're out on the streets. We're going shopping. We'll buy everything in sight. Don't worry about payment. We're gentry. No one ever expects them to pay for anything. We'll have to leave it all behind when we go, so no one's really losing by it. Mr Markham, you can do the money-slinging thing. And your conjuring tricks. Play with the kids. Tim – smile at the ladies. I'm going to flirt with everyone. Even their horses if I have to. Chief, you'll be decisive, commanding, and radiate wealth. Major …'

'I know,' he said, resigned. 'We'll be making sure none of you get mugged, murdered, or molested.'

We strode out around noon, leaving Weller behind to mind the shop.

Farrell and I led the way through the muddy streets. Small boys and dogs followed on behind us. Markham swung into action. Peterson, a little apart from us, bowed and smiled his way through the crowds.

We stopped at a trinket stall. Farrell bought every item I admired. I don't think the stallholder could quite believe his luck.

Following the smell of cooking, we entered a small inn. The

landlord made a private room available. We enjoyed a roast bird and a pastry stuffed with dried fruit. Drink flowed. Farrell ruthlessly over-tipped everyone.

A small crowd waited in the street, all with invitations to visit their brother's inn/shop/stall/whatever and possibly buy their sisters.

Markham and Randall were slowly weighed down with our purchases, which included several pairs of soft gloves, ribbons, a length of lace ('Oh good, more lace!'), some honey cakes, a couple of small and very shrivelled lemons, a birdcage complete with songbird occupant (who was released around the very next corner), a packet of needles (which would be very useful should any of us ever learn to sew), a small pillow stuffed with herbs (to ensure my ladyship's peaceful repose), a copper bracelet (to ward off painful joints), and a pot of honey.

Farrell was measured for a pair of boots he was assured would be ready on the morrow and even Guthrie was sorely tempted by a small Italian dagger, complete with worn leather sheath.

Peterson divided his time between young girls (who giggled and blushed) and old women (who made him giggle and blush).

It felt as though half the town was following us from stall to stall and I suspected a good number of them were from Holyrood. Eventually, as it began to get dark, Guthrie called a halt.

We returned home, tired, muddy, and hungry. We could do no more. It was all in the lap of the gods now. Or History herself.

I went out the next day, walking around town with Schiller and Markham, getting our bearings and planning possible escape routes back to the pods which were located about a mile outside town, and so we missed it. When we got back to the house, everyone was upstairs, frantically lugging down bolts of cloth and all the other bits and pieces. While we were out, the Queen's messengers had called. We were summoned to the palace the next day. To present ourselves to the Queen. All of us.

My restlessness that night was not completely due to the fleas in the mattress. I hardly slept at all, running over everything in my mind. Beside me, Schiller tossed and turned as well.

We were downstairs early, sitting around the table, drinking tea (our one luxury – we're St Mary's – we run on tea) and eating bread and cheese. There wasn't a great deal of conversation. We all knew what we had to do; there was no point in banging on about it.

Schiller and I disappeared upstairs to start dressing. We had decided that, for our first appearance, I'd go for something a little different. I had two court dresses. One was magnificent but conventional, in black and gold. However, the second was of a glorious turquoise, a colour that would not be widely known in this country until around 1573. For the purposes of this assignment, we were calling the colour Celeste. We'd chosen it specifically because it looked spectacular with red hair and Mary Stuart had red hair.

In common with the English court, fashion here followed the Spanish tradition, with dark, heavy colours and wide sleeves. Mrs Enderby had dressed us in the lighter Italian and French styles, hoping they would appeal to an exile from the French court. Schiller fastened my exquisite lace ruff and we bundled my hair into a jewelled net.

Farrell and Peterson looked magnificent, in similar outfits of black and silver. Guthrie wore dark red and even the security team looked good. We'd dressed them in the richest fabrics allowed in an age where your rank clearly defined the clothes you wore.

By the time we got downstairs, the wagon was loaded, the horses were ready, and this was it.

Once again, Markham and his drum preceded us. You could argue it was all a bit over the top for so short a journey, but we were too important to visit the palace on foot or without an entourage.

Reassuringly, we were received with the greatest courtesy. Guthrie and his team remained behind to supervise unloading the wagon and the rest of us were escorted inside at once, relieved of our outdoor clothes by an army of servants, shown into a large, chilly, crowded room, and just when I was beginning to think it might be easy after all, they left us there.

We clustered together for security and, in my case, warmth.

Time passed.

Then some more time passed.

'Come on,' grumbled Peterson. 'We've only got three weeks, you know.'

It was unlike him to complain. He was nervous. We were all nervous.

To relieve the tension, I placed my hand on Farrell's arm and we began to walk slowly around the room. See and be seen. This chamber was full of second-tier courtiers – those not quite important enough to be in the same room as royalty. Just as we had hoped, our attire attracted a certain amount of attention. Heads turned to watch us pass. I caught sidelong glances and people whispered behind their hands.

Even more time passed.

'This is normal,' I said, hoping it was. 'If we didn't have to wait, then how would we know how important she is?'

Farrell nodded, then stiffened and stared over my shoulder. 'Something's happening.'

I could hear a bustle behind me, but refused to turn around. We stood, apparently oblivious, discussing the weather in light, social tones.

Someone cleared their throat. Farrell turned slowly. A man bowed low and murmured something I never caught. He turned away and set off down the room. Farrell and Peterson fell in behind him. I, of course, brought up the rear. Silent courtiers watched us go. I could hear my dress swishing as I walked.

Ahead of us, a door was flung open. Someone announced us.

I caught a vague impression of light – a lot of light – warmth and colour.

We stepped over the threshold.

This was it.

Chapter Eighteen

Years ago, I'd waited outside another door, not knowing what was on the other side. On that occasion, it turned out to be Mrs Partridge's sister, the Sibylline Oracle, with an offer that changed my life. But what I remember most from that day was the sensation of stepping blindly into the unknown.

This was no different.

To begin with, I couldn't see a thing past Farrell's broad back. A sudden silence fell as we were announced. As carefully instructed, the men bowed and we curtseyed. We straightened, walked slowly down the room, paused and bowed again. We all stayed put as Leon advanced alone, bowed before her for a third time and waited for royal acknowledgement.

I shifted my weight slightly so I could see past Peterson. Being women, of course Schiller and I were at the back.

The queen sat at the far end. She wore black, as did many of her court, but there's black and then there's black. This was the second kind. Her famous cap nestled amongst flaming red hair dressed with pearls. I know she wore a red wig to her execution and I suspected she wore one now, as well. But that wasn't unusual; many women in this age wore wigs. Her skin was good – she had no need to whiten her face with the lead-based cosmetics that probably did for Elizabeth in the end. And she was beautiful. Classically beautiful, with large, well-opened eyes and a short straight nose. I never saw Elizabeth Tudor, but I doubted the Queen of England could match the Queen of Scotland. It was fortunate perhaps, that they never met.

Her ladies in waiting clustered at her feet, sitting on cushions, their skirts billowing out around them and looking like opulent mushrooms. No one else was seated. The room was very hot and very crowded. Still, if I fainted, my clothes would probably hold me up.

I saw her smile graciously, then take a second glance and smile again, more warmly this time. Her taste in husbands notwithstanding, she knew quality when she saw it. She said something. The room was silent and watching, waiting to take its cue from the queen, no doubt. Farrell had his back to us so no clues there. I made myself stand quietly and wait. There was nothing I could do. Slightly behind me, Schiller's gaze would be raking the room trying to identify those present, to put names to faces. Behind me, Guthrie had waited at the door as instructed. Randall and Markham were getting things ready outside.

Farrell turned and caught our eye. Peterson offered me his arm, Schiller fell in behind and we slowly approached the queen.

My God, I was going to meet Mary, Queen of Scots! I was actually going to meet Mary Stuart! My heart hammered away and when I curtseyed for the third time, I wasn't sure I could get up again.

She wasn't an unkind woman. Unlike Elizabeth, who famously didn't like other women at all, she seemed charmed to meet me, allowing me to rise almost at once. Farrell introduced Peterson first. He murmured politely and then it was my turn.

I heard Farrell say, 'My sister, Your Grace.' I kept my eyes on the floor until she spoke. Don't stare, Maxwell. You're a professional historian.

She greeted me. Her voice was very quiet and she had an accent. I obviously wasn't expected to reply. In charge of this mission I might have been, but I was still as nothing in the scheme of things. She cast an appraising glance at my dress and nodded. I was dismissed, but kindly.

With relief, I curtseyed, stepped back carefully and found a place off to one side with my back to a window. This suited me.

I could see what was going on.

Now Peterson joined in the conversation, smiling and gesturing. It all seemed to be going quite well.

I left them to get on with it and gazed around the room. It was panelled, as most rooms were, in some old, dark wood, darkened further by fire and candlelight. The room smelled of candles, smoke, perfume, and bodies.

Behind me, Schiller whispered, 'Beside the window, there, in black, with red sleeves – that's the French Ambassador, de Castelnau.'

And then, even as I stared, Clive Ronan slipped quietly through the door, past Major Guthrie, who kept his head and politely stepped aside for him, and made his way to Michel de Castelnau's side. They exchanged looks but said nothing.

For a moment, I think we were all paralysed. Was it really going to be that easy?

Guthrie looked directly at me. I pulled myself together and made a tiny negative gesture. Now was not the time or the place. Concentrate on one thing at a time. If we got this afternoon wrong, we could lose our heads. Concentrate on the now.

Guthrie casually turned away so his back was to Ronan. Behind me, Schiller grasped my sleeve and gently drew me back a pace or two so we were sheltered by two very young women, who seemed, in some way, to be attached to the queen's famous ladies – the Four Marys. Beaton, Seton, Fleming, and Livingston. Only two of them were here today and which two was anyone's guess. However, they were important women in their own right and these two younger women were, I guessed, ladies-in-waiting to the ladies-in-waiting.

There was so much to watch and think about, I hardly knew where to start. In front of me, Farrell and Peterson were doing a good job. Schiller was safe with me. Randall and Markham were outside if anything went wrong and Guthrie would hold the door until we could get away. All of which left me free to consider Clive Ronan, standing a discreet half pace behind the

French ambassador.

The first thing that struck me was how young he was. How very, very young he was. He had hair. And two ears. And no scars. The second thing, to my huge relief, was that he didn't know us at all. He hadn't met us yet. His future was our past. I glanced at the oblivious Farrell and Peterson. They were doing their job. Guthrie was watching Ronan without seeming to. I turned my head to Schiller and cut my eyes to Ronan. She nodded and slipped quietly away. Other people were moving around too and chatter was springing up again as it became apparent the queen was occupied for a while. This seemed a very informal court. An approachable and affable queen set the tone.

I turned back and inadvertently brushed someone's arm. One of the young ladies in waiting said, 'Oh,' and dropped a piece of embroidery. Quickly, I picked it up and handed it back to her.

'Your pardon, mistress.'

She smiled nervously, considerably flustered. I put her age at around fifteen or sixteen.

'Your stitching is exquisite.' Which it was. Don't underestimate our ancestors because they can't drive cars or build a data stack. They had their own skills. She spread it out so I could see it properly. Beautiful birds swooped and danced in a variety of brilliant colours and complex stitching. It was lovely.

She blushed a little. 'Thank you.'

We both shot a glance back to the queen who was still occupied with my boys. They all seemed to be getting along really well. So long as neither of them married her!

I had no idea of the protocol here and hoped for the best.

'I am Mary.'

She smiled again, nodded and whispered, 'Margaret.' Either she was very shy or we were breaking some sort of rule and not wanting to push any further, I turned to watch the room, straining to hear the conversation with the queen. Within the last few minutes, the noise levels had risen considerably, not helped by two or three musicians playing softly in the corner. Well, they say the watcher sees most of the game, so I'd better watch.

Now the queen was openly laughing and Farrell gave the signal. The doors opened and heads turned in surprise. Markham and Randall entered, bearing a large carpet, and we were off.

With a flourish, they threw it down and its momentum propelled it down the room, unrolling as it went. It was a beauty, the biggest and best we had, in shimmering shades of red and gold and woven with intricate symbols, the meaning of which I could see Farrell explaining to the queen. She nodded vaguely, unimpressed. She had her own carpets. However, that was just the beginning.

I saw Markham speak to the musicians and coins changed hands. They broke immediately into something loud and lively.

The atmosphere changed and before people had a chance to take in what was happening, the show began.

We'd agreed that speed was the key. Surprise piled upon surprise. Keep it coming. Don't give them time to keep up. The ancient Persians demonstrated not only their wealth, but also their contempt for it by casually flinging around their priceless carpets as if they were nothing. Exquisite kilims dropped carelessly one on top of the other, the visible top layer only hinting at the treasures buried beneath. We intended something similar.

Before anyone had time for more than a startled exclamation, Randall hurled a bolt of white velvet. Shot with metallic thread, it unrolled across the crimson carpet, glinting softly in the light. The queen leaned forward, but before she could take it in, it was gone, buried beneath an undulating ruby red silk, and then that was gone, covered by a black and gold brocade and then another silk, green, shot with blue. Great bolts of material tumbled down the room. We barely gave her time to assimilate one marvel before partially burying it under the next.

The musicians, who knew their trade, picked up the beat. The pace quickened. Purple and blue taffetas rolled across the carpet.

Peterson was laying out beautifully carved cedar wood boxes, inlaid with mother of pearl and redolent with the scents of the east.

Leaving Randall to hurl fabric around as if his life depended up it – which it did – Markham was working the room. He produced, apparently from nowhere, a number of flimsy, silken scarves, one of which he flung artistically into the air. It hung, weightless, glittering in the candlelight before he laughingly snatched it down, drew it through a ring seemingly plucked from behind a lady's ear and presented both to her with a sweeping bow. She clapped her hands with delight and he made his way around the court, generating a vortex of colour and movement, presenting rings and scarves to every woman he encountered.

Randall tumbled bolts of lace in a heap and topped them with muslins and linens so sheer they were almost transparent. I could hear cries of astonishment from around the room.

I stole a look at the queen who sat quite still, her face expressionless.

With a final flourish, Randall threw his last bolt of velvet; Markham let his scarves flutter and rest where they fell. The musicians drew one final chord and to cries of appreciation and regret, it was over.

Everyone turned to see the queen's reaction.

She sat back and regarded Farrell steadily.

'A pretty show.'

He bowed.

'You think to win me over with this display?'

'Oh no, Your Grace.'

She looked at him.

'These poor things are just today's offerings.'

'What else do you have for me?'

No pretence, no politely leading up to it – just straight out with it – what else do you have for me?

'Spices, Your Grace, every flavour known to the east.'

She shrugged. 'Nutmeg, cinnamon, I have all this.'

'And yellow saffron, more precious than gold.'

She raised an eyebrow.

'And perfumes. All the scents of the Orient for your pleasure alone.' He smiled at her.

She smiled back.

This seemed to be going quite well.

And then, all of a sudden, it wasn't.

A flustered chamberlain appeared at her elbow.

'By Your Grace's leave, the Earl of Bothwell desires admittance.'

I had a sudden flare of hope. He was here. Would she see him? Was our intervention unnecessary? Was History working alongside us to put this right?

Apparently not. All the progress we had made flew straight out of the window.

The French Ambassador stepped forward with Ronan a pace behind.

'Your Grace, if you remember, it was decided you would not receive my Lord ...'

She didn't even bother to look at him. Her eyes flashed with something. Anger? Fear? Guilt? Her voice effortlessly carried around the suddenly silent room.

'I gave explicit instructions that Lord Bothwell is not to be admitted and yet, here he is. Again. God's Blood, I would know why I am so ill served in this. Send him hence. With all speed.'

A man Schiller later identified as Lord Seton, stepped forward. 'Your Grace, I beseech you ...'

She said through clenched teeth, 'I will not see him.'

'But Your Grace,' he murmured, placating, 'the Earl of Bothwell was acquitted. Lord Lennox accused the Earl of murdering your hus – his son, but subsequently failed to appear at the hearing, and therefore ...'

He was a brave man, but sadly, she was having none of it.

'Enough!'

Her voice rang round the room like a pistol shot. Seton stepped back immediately and took good care to be lost in the crowd. There was a very careful silence. No one even moved until de Castelnau said quietly, 'If Your Grace will give me leave, I will gladly convey Your Grace's message to the Earl. Again.'

Bloody hell, this could be nasty. I had a very good idea of how that message might be conveyed. Especially with Ronan behind him whispering in his ear. Somehow, we had to get this back on track.

She nodded curtly, not looking at him. He bowed and backed from the room. Ronan went with him. So, he was working through the French Ambassador. This was going to be tougher than I thought. But at least Bothwell was here, somewhere. And under the protection of the powerful Lord Seton, who would be one of the few supporters of Bothwell's marriage to the queen. Should that ever occur.

Back in this chamber, still no one had moved. Had all our good work gone for nothing? She was in a shitty mood and we had nothing left. Yes, we had spices and perfumes but the fabrics were our star turn. If they didn't impress her, she was unlikely to be excited by a bunch of dried sticks and leaves. There was nothing I could do. Stuck on the fringe of things, I fretted inwardly and tried to think.

However, I didn't have to. Farrell already had the situation well in hand.

She was saying pettishly, 'So, my masters, spices and perfumes? How easily did you think I could be bought?'

'I expressed myself badly,' he said calmly and it might have been a good idea to bow and scrape a little, not look her in the eye, grinning as if he knew something and she didn't. This was my first royal personage and certainly my first case of royal mood-swing. I had felt the blast of it standing all the way back here and I suspected this one was comparatively mild in the scheme of things. Over the border, Elizabeth's courtiers had been known to wet themselves in fright under her vicious tongue.

I resurfaced from that mental picture to find her in no way returning his smile.

'How so?'

'All this –' he gestured dismissively around the room. 'These are gifts from my masters in Istanbul. Tokens of goodwill and respect.' He paused. 'What will come tomorrow …' he paused again, 'is something quite different.'

He stopped speaking.

She waited, but he said nothing.

She tapped a foot.

He said nothing.

She played with a pomander hanging from her waist.

He said nothing.

At last, she said quietly and with beautifully understated menace, 'I'm waiting.'

'Your Grace would like me to spoil the surprise?'

She hunched a shoulder and said flatly, 'I don't like surprises. Tell me.'

It was a command.

'What will come tomorrow is a personal gift. From me to the Queen of Scotland.'

'You could not have brought it today?'

'But Your Grace, if I present you with everything all at once then there will be no reason for Your Grace to grant me further audiences – and that would be a great sadness.'

'How so?'

'Your Grace has only to look in the mirror to answer that question.'

I was gobsmacked. He was leaning in very close, smiling directly into her eyes, his voice low and intimate. He was flirting. She was lapping it up. I'd had to work my way through years of his stifled inarticulacy and here he was now, practically sitting on her lap.

A long moment passed and then she laughed and slapped his hand. A long exhalation of relief ran around the room.

Her good humour apparently restored, she said, 'Tell me of this gift.'

There was no doubt that was a command.

'Jade, Your Grace. Carved and shaped especially for you.'

She raised her heavily plucked eyebrows.

'A chess set, Your Grace. One set of players fashioned from exquisite green jade, the most expensive there is, and the other from lavender jade, rare and precious. The board is black and white, set with gold and mother of pearl and most cunningly hinged. The only example of its kind in the whole of the Christendom and beyond. Carried by caravan across mountains, deserts and oceans, to delight the most beautiful queen in the world.'

He paused and eyed her challengingly. 'It will be my pleasure to instruct Your Grace in the intricacies of – the game.'

'If you refer to chess, Sir Richard, I should tell you now that I am more than proficient.'

It was said with something of a snap. I tensed. Had he blown it?

No, of course he hadn't. He was in no way dismayed.

Holding her gaze, he said, in French, 'But no, Your Grace, I most definitely did not mean – chess.'

There was another long moment.

Suddenly, she stood. The court snapped to attention.

She cast him a long, enigmatic glance from under her lashes and swept from the room. Hastily, we all bowed. It was a magnificent exit, leaving as it did, so much unsaid. Her ladies followed her out. Their ladies followed them. Margaret sent me a swift smile over her shoulder.

People sighed and stretched and began to congregate around the glittering pile of fabrics in the room. Chamberlains appeared to supervise its removal. I was suddenly conscious of wobbly legs, a splitting headache, and an overwhelming desire to pee.

'Let's go home,' I said.

260

Chapter Nineteen

I let everyone have a drink that night. God knows, we'd earned it.

Weller lit every fire in the house, every lamp, every candle. We changed from our finery, locked the doors, shuttered the windows, and sat down in the kitchen. He'd even had the sense to order in from the inn round the corner. We dined very snugly on boiled fowl, a really good broth, roasted beef and frumenty. Look it up.

We discussed the events of the day, running through our own individual perceptions, speculating on what might happen next. The appearance of Clive Ronan, bold, brazen, and unconcerned was a shock to us all. We knew he was here somewhere, but this close to the queen …

And what of the queen herself?

'She'll send for us,' I said, confidently.

'She might not send for all of us,' grinned Peterson. 'She certainly preferred some of us over others.'

'And rightly so,' said Farrell calmly, mopping up the last of his sauce with a piece of bread. 'At last, the technical section comes into its own.'

'About bloody time,' said Guthrie. 'I think all of us have wondered, at one time or another, just what exactly you do all day down in Hawking.'

'The mysteries of the technical section are not for lesser minds. Suffice to say we have, once more, saved the day.'

'Depressing, isn't it?' said Schiller. 'That we should live to be grateful to the technical section. Who'd have thought?'

'She will send for us,' I said, dragging them back on track. 'It's just a case of when.'

'First thing tomorrow morning?' suggested Randall. 'She did seem a bit – keen.'

Schiller shook her head.

'It's a game,' she said. 'She'll make us wait.'

I nodded. We had only just over two weeks. If she decided to play hard to get, we could have a problem.

Farrell looked at Peterson. 'We might be called to discuss business. Maybe an opening will present itself. Something will happen.'

It didn't.

We stayed at home the next day, just in case. And the day after. We used the time to discuss our biggest problem – what to do with Ronan.

Typically, the security team were still all for executing him on sight. We had some difficulty explaining why this would be A Bad Thing.

'We'd be wrecking our own past,' said Schiller again. 'If we kill him now, he won't go on to attack us in his future. Changing his future means we wouldn't be here today to kill him. Paradox.'

'So what *do* we do with him?'

I was at a bit of a loss. We couldn't leave him here, free to screw up the timeline. And we couldn't kill him.

Farrell pushed his plate away.

'Once again, and not for the first time, the technical section will save the day. We have enough on our plate. We must unite the queen and Bothwell. If we don't do that then everything else is immaterial. I suggest we concentrate on that. If the opportunity presents itself and it well might, we follow Ronan, wait until he's alone, render him helpless in an efficient but painful manner, and get him back to St Mary's for Dr Bairstow to decide. Removing him from this time will solve our immediate problems. He's done – or will do – so much damage to the timeline that I think dealing with him ourselves is a bit above our pay grades. This should be decided at Director level,

I think. And maybe by more than one Director.'

Round the table, heads nodded in agreement.

He caught my eye. It would give Dr Bairstow the opportunity and satisfaction of dealing personally with the man who had caused the death of his Annie, crippled him, and murdered members of St Mary's past, present, and future. An admirable solution, not least because it left us free to concentrate on the queen up the road and wait for the summons.

Which didn't come.

After four days, I was stressed and even Farrell was looking tense.

'Relax,' I said, trying to ignore my own jiggling left knee. 'You weren't that bad. She's just playing hard to get.'

He sighed. 'If she plays much harder, we'll miss her completely.'

I wasn't anywhere near as confident as I sounded. Time wasn't just ticking on – it was flying by. The silence from the palace was deafening. Had it really been just an afternoon's flirtation for her? Why wasn't she impressed by our show? Did the proposed trade deal not tempt her at all? Had we overestimated her desire to put one over on Elizabeth? What was going on up there? Had she forgotten all about us? And the vitally important question – had Ronan, working through Castelnau, persuaded her to send Bothwell away? Or worse, execute him? Guthrie and his security team were scouring the streets daily, looking for Ronan but there was no sign of him anywhere. We suspected he spent his time with de Castlenau and we couldn't get to him there.

Typically, when it did come, the summons gave us only one hour's warning. We scrambled to be ready in time. More mind games. Randall couldn't remember where he'd put the chess set for safekeeping. Schiller fumbled getting me laced into my dress. Neither of us could get our hair right. Markham fell down the stairs. Sometimes, the word 'shambles' just doesn't even begin to describe us ...

Never mind opening with 'It was a dark and stormy night ...' it was a dark and stormy day. Early summer time in Scotland. It wasn't raining yet, but it would soon – the clouds were so low that even I was nearly banging my head on them.

We were dressed to kill. I wore the heavy black and gold dress, which weighed a ton, and stupid little jewelled slippers that weren't going to keep my feet warm at all. Farrell, Guthrie, and Peterson wore boots. In this century, as in any other, men wore the comfortable, practical stuff, and the women wandered round expiring underneath over-decorated tea-cosies and with inadequate footwear. I was wearing only the bare minimum of undergarments necessary and it had still taken Schiller nearly an hour to get me into them. Consequently, I was not in a good mood.

We checked each other over.

'Have you got it?' I asked. Peterson flourished the jade chess set we were presenting to the queen.

She'd sent a closed coach. We were conveyed in style if not comfort as we jolted and bounced our way to the palace. It would have been quicker to walk. We sat in silence except for the odd curse as Peterson or Guthrie, both tall men, banged their heads on the roof. Which put me in a much better mood.

Our second visit was low-key, but we got in much more quickly this time. We stood tightly together in a stiff little group, facing outwards. I had my back to the doors but felt Peterson stiffen.

'Carefully. Look over towards the fireplace. On my right.'

We turned our heads casually. Talking to the French Ambassador and a group of other men and slowly moving towards the doors was Ronan. Where was he off to?

I felt a strange tingle in the air.

Something was happening.

Again.

Words came out of my mouth.

'Right, change of plan. Major, you, Chief Farrell, and Markham – go after Ronan. That's your priority. We must get him back to St Mary's so the Boss can decide what to do with him.

'Peterson and Schiller, you get back to the house. Lock all the doors. Get everything ready for emergency extraction. If we do get Ronan, we may have to leave quickly. Go back to the pods and wait there.'

'What about you?' said Peterson.

'I'll concentrate on our original plan and try to see the queen. I doubt it on my own, but you never know your luck and we still have to point her at Bothwell. I'll make Sir Richard's apologies – sudden   indisposition – whatever – and   try   to smooth over any difficulties, Maybe, since we're actually trying to put things right, History will cut us a break for once. Give me the chess set and I'll see what I can do.'

'She'll be furious.'

'Can't help that. It's more important to get Ronan out of here before he does any serious damage and, since we've been summoned, we can't all disappear.'

Farrell said, 'I think I should be the one to stay.'

'Excellent idea,' I said, 'and I'll get out on the streets after Ronan.'

There was a thoughtful pause.

They weren't happy, but as far as I could see, I was in the safest place here. And I would be out of the rain. And I was the boss. And seriously, no one, least of all me, anticipated what was coming. They quietly disappeared and I stayed put.

There is a huge advantage to living in a masculine world. It is very, very easy to make yourself inconspicuous, if not almost completely invisible. Without a gaggle of men around me to give me status, I practically disappeared into the woodwork. I drifted around the room, paused vaguely at the head of a passageway, took a step backwards, then again, ostensibly admiring a small tapestry. Another step backwards and the hum of voices behind me grew fainter.

It couldn't be that easy, of course. There were guards everywhere. I took off my cloak, folded it over my arm and carried the chess set carefully before me. Now I was an indoor lady, carrying something precious, maybe at the queen's behest. Palaces are very much like hives. Both have a queen and both assume that if you're inside then you're meant to be there. That someone, somewhere, has run the checks and you've passed muster. Confidence is the key.

I swept up and down corridors, passageways, and the occasional staircase with measured steps, bearing my precious burden carefully before me. It seemed to work. One guard actually opened a door for me. I nodded and gave him a small smile. Nothing too effusive, but acknowledging his courtesy. Always smile at the man with the big gun/spear/sword/tank/clipboard/whatever. If this afternoon went badly, he could be the one arresting me later on and I'd need a friendly face.

From what I could remember of the building plans we'd studied, and given the increase in guards, the decrease in foot traffic, and the general air of hushed reverence and luxury, I was near the queen's private apartments on the second floor. She was here somewhere, anticipating the arrival of the charming Sir Richard, but making him wait, nonetheless.

I tried to breathe slowly, swallowing down my heart-hammering fear. My hindbrain was telling me to be careful – it was all far too easy so far.

Which just goes to show we should all listen to our hindbrains far more often, because, at that moment, I turned a corner and walked smash into the other person surreptitiously prowling the building that afternoon. That man-shaped collection of testosterone – sex-on-legs himself – James Hepburn, 4th Earl of Bothwell.

There was no mistaking him. Even if I hadn't spent the last weeks studying his portrait, I would have guessed instantly from his behaviour. Whom else but the opportunist Bothwell would be wandering, unescorted, around the Queen's private quarters?

Speaking of opportunist … Instead of pushing me away, or even just steadying me, he gripped my arms tightly, and boldly and openly scrutinised me from top to toe. I was suddenly thankful for the truly enormous number of clothes I was wearing. Obviously, he liked what he saw – female and with a pulse – because he pulled me close and crushed himself against me. I could feel his mounting excitement. I don't think he could help himself. It was just instinct. He moved on anything wearing a dress. He backed me against a door. I could feel the handle hard in the small of my back.

'Ouch!' I said, indignantly.

He stopped and looked down, actually seeing me for the first time. Brown-green eyes, thickly fringed with black lashes laughed down at me and a rakishly broken nose only added to the charm. I could certainly see what all the fuss was about, and I was pretty sure that Mary Stuart could, as well. No wonder she kept him at arm's length. Lady Caroline Lamb once described Lord Byron as, 'Mad, bad, and dangerous to know,' but Bothwell was the prototype; the original. If he was ever in the same room as the queen …

'Ouch?' he said, laughing.

I resisted the urge to fan myself violently.

Obviously feeling he had wasted enough time on foreplay, he started fishing down my bosom again. I took a deep breath, which on reflection probably wasn't my best move. He buried his head down there and began to tug at my clothing.

'No,' I said firmly, pulling things back into place. 'No.'

He ignored me. I had a brainwave, ground myself against him and blew down his ear.

Now I had his attention. He raised his head.

'In here.'

I groped behind me for the latch. The door opened and we both fell in. My faint hope that the room might be occupied died away.

He lay on the floor, laughing, while I hung on to my cloak and chess set as if they were my lifelines – which they were. Because I'd had an idea. A really, really, bad idea, but also a really, really, good idea. If it worked. I felt a sudden deep conviction. It would work. It was opportunity seized. It was inspiration. History had nodded. It was up to me now.

I had Bothwell. Now I needed to keep him here.

He was grabbing for my ankles. I stepped back, smartly.

'Wine!' I said.

'What?'

I was right. He was already well away. Wine was definitely the way to go. I swerved towards the door.

'I'll fetch some wine.'

'We have no need of wine.'

He moved more quickly than I expected, pulled my feet out from underneath me, and down I went. He caught me neatly. Obviously, he'd had a lot of practice. It was probably one of his best moves. Sadly marred only by the chess box falling on his head.

He cursed. 'Are you trying to murder me, woman?'

I pulled away to a safe distance and said again, 'Wine.'

He smiled up at me from the floor. He was easily the most sexually attractive man I'd ever met. Women must fall for him by the shedload.

I opened the door, peered cautiously out into the passageway and carefully pulled out the key, concealing it in my hand. He got up and, to my huge relief, threw himself on the bed, linking his hands behind his head. Then he sat up suddenly.

'I'll come with you.'

'No! I mean, you stay here and – prepare yourself.'

God knows what I meant by that. Sometimes words just fall out of my mouth, but he took this for encouragement and began to unlace himself.

I fled.

I'm not proud of what I did that day, but up to that moment, I was reasonably OK. I'd had a wild idea and I never really thought it would come to anything, but it did. I can blame History all I want, but it was me. I did it. And if it means anything, I'm sorry.

I'd managed to drag my cloak out with me, but the chess set was gone for good. There was no way I was ever going back in there again. The next woman who walked through that door wouldn't stand a chance …

Shoving my cloak into a nearby chest, I smoothed my hair, straightened myself as best I could, and keeping the key tight in my hand, set off again.

Straight into Mary Stuart, Queen of Scotland, Dowager Queen of France and self-styled Queen of England. Only a single lady-in-waiting, the very young girl, Margaret, accompanied her.

Oh yes, History was with me that day.

'Mistress Hampton. They told me you were in the outer chamber.' She looked over my shoulder for the charming Sir Richard.

I backed against the wall and sank to a deep curtsey. 'Your Grace, we have been given a room, whilst we awaited your pleasure.'

'You have been well attended to?'

'Oh, yes, Your Grace. We have been playing chess to pass the time.'

She smiled. 'I have eagerly awaited the chance to pit my skills against your brother.'

I smiled back.

'I wish you would, Your Grace. Three straight games have I lost to him. You can imagine how he crows.'

She laughed. 'Indeed I can.'

'We have a snug room along here, Your Grace, and a good fire to await your pleasure.'

I could see the idea pleased her. An intimate evening with a personable man. A peaceful interlude with fire and wine. A little gentle flirting. A chance to display her talents. She had only one lady with her. She'd planned for this ... It all hung in the balance. If she dismissed her woman then I would go for it. If she didn't ... I don't know. I'd think of something. Some other opportunity would present itself. No it wouldn't. It was this or nothing. I could feel History at my shoulder.

She was speaking to her lady-in-waiting, sending her away. I was passing the point of no return. My heart-rate picked up and my palms were clammy. I could hardly believe my luck. Bothwell, alone, in a room nearby. The Queen, unattended. What were the odds? This was what happened when History was with you. I gripped the key until it hurt and worked hard at keeping my face neutral.

She walked slowly before me, chattering gaily, excited and happy. I never heard a word. There was still so much that could go wrong. I half hoped it would. That someone could come along and see us, that a door would open somewhere, that guards would suddenly appear. Nothing irrevocable had yet happened. I could still walk away from this. A pulse was beating hard in my throat. I swallowed, but there was no relief.

Because once she was inside that room, her life would never be the same again.

Ten paces to go.

Then six.

Then three.

I murmured, 'Just here, Your Grace,' took a painful breath – and opened the door.

I stood back to let her go in first.

She paused on the threshold and peered into the dimly lit room. Second thoughts? A premonition of danger? We will never know. I put my hand in the small of her back and pushed as hard as I could. She was a tall woman and I was worried I might not be strong enough but – whether she was off-balance or I found the strength from somewhere – I don't know. I only know that I pushed her into that room and everything that happened to her subsequently was my fault.

No time for that now. I pulled the door shut, fumbled for desperate seconds trying to get the key in the lock and eventually it turned.

I knelt on trembling legs and pushed the key under the door. So much for any protestations of innocence. They – the world – would say the door had been locked on the inside and the key had simply fallen out of the lock. I leaned my forehead against the cold, hard door and tried not to think about what I had just done.

From inside the room came a very faint sound.

Then silence.

I had taken a woman, a decent, intelligent woman who had never done me any harm and betrayed her in the worst possible way one woman could do to another. I had deliberately pushed her into a room containing a man who was, under his superficial charm, an unstable, violent rapist. And then I had locked the door and walked away. There was no way she would get out of that room unscathed. I had ruined her life. The events of tonight would alienate her court, her nobles, everyone. Her reputation would be in shreds and not in any way redeemed by her subsequent marriage to Bothwell. All her years of careful, patient work undone in one single night. By me. She was only twenty-five. Younger than me. Her life was over. This was not something of which to be proud.

But now I had to get out. I had no idea how long I would have before someone raised the alarm. I had to move. Retrieving my cloak, I called up Peterson.

Anxiety sharpened his voice. 'What's happening?'

'The queen is with Bothwell,' I said, suddenly very tired. 'And we need to go. Now.'

'We have a problem.'

I stopped. 'What?'

'We still don't have Ronan. They all split up when they went after him and Guthrie's not back yet.'

'Can you raise him?'

'No, he said he'd call us. He was very definite.' He would be. If he was stalking Ronan through the dark alleyways of Edinburgh, he wouldn't want us yammering away in his ear.

I said, 'Major, this is Max. Abort. Get back to the pod or the house. We're in trouble and we have to go now. Abort Ronan. Confirm please.'

Nothing.

Shit. This is what happens if you try to combine two missions. But we weren't finished yet.

'Tim, get everyone away. Non-essential personnel to go now. Strip the house and get to the pods. Don't wait for me. That's an order.

'Chief, keep trying Guthrie. Find him. I'm not kidding, guys. If we're still alive in half an hour, it'll only be by some miracle. Get out now. I'm on my way back, but don't wait for me.

Maxwell out.'

Right, that was them sorted. Now to get myself out safely. I paused at the head of the stairs and looked back over my shoulder. Silence. Not a sound. What was going on in there? Did she still think she was with Sir Richard Hampton? Had Bothwell knocked her unconscious before raping her? Were they going at it like mink? Was she struggling for her life and the screaming could start any minute now? How long before she was missed? How long before she was discovered?

I can't tell you how it felt to walk slowly and carefully down the stairs. I had folded my cloak again and carried it carefully in front of me across my arms like some precious relic. Everyone had seen me presented to the queen. I hoped to God they would think I was conveying her garment somewhere with all the care and reverence such a task warranted. They had to. It was going to be my way out.

But not if I ran. Not if I gave way to the all-consuming urge to run. To run like hell. To pick up my skirts and bolt along corridors and down stairways, past groups of chattering courtiers, past stony-faced guards, to erupt into the cool evening air and run for my life to Canongate, friends, and safety.

I made myself walk even more slowly, my face calm and pleasant, telling myself that each step took me further away from that chamber and nearer to escape. Every passageway seemed endless. Every dark corner held some nameless danger. Every shadow concealed a threat. The afternoon had darkened as the weather worsened. To me, the palace had taken on an air of menace and I was wandering an enormous labyrinth. Ariadne without her thread.

A door slammed behind me and a voice was raised in reproof. I stopped dead and waited for my heart to catch up with me. It had leapt from my chest and was over by the wall somewhere.

I took a precious moment to slow my breathing, lifted my chin and continued the slow, self-important walk of a lady carrying out an important task for the queen. I threaded my way carefully through the groups of people. I looked down my nose, careful not to catch anyone's eye but not avoiding eye contact either. It was taking a long time to get out. In fact, it seemed to be taking for ever, but I'd taken the long route, through more private areas of the palace, and hoped to come out somewhere quiet, from where I could easily slip away.

It seemed to be working. I could feel cool, damp air in my face. I was nearly there. I shook out the cloak, swung it around my shoulders and walked slowly towards the open doors.

At last, I was outside. Where my luck immediately ran out. The storm was upon us. It was hurling down rain; great sheets of it plummeting out of the darkness, slanting through weak beams of light and bouncing off the cobbles to knee height. The noise was deafening. I looked around the packed and heaving courtyard. Steaming horses were being led away. Anxious, drenched, impatient messengers ran back and forth, shouting as they went. It seemed chaotic but there was order when you observed closely. Bad weather notwithstanding, enormous numbers of people were being shunted to where they needed to be.

Trying to be as inconspicuous as possible, I stood back, swallowed down my anxiety and considered. I was almost the only woman there and certainly the only one not a maidservant. Soon, I would be drawing attention and even if I managed to get away, people would remember me. I needed to be gone as soon as possible and every instinct I possessed was shrieking to get out of there, but it was vital I did not draw attention to myself. There were whole platoons of guards around the place whose sole responsibility was the safety of the queen and one false move from me would set them off.

I was looking out at the courtyard, but all my attention was behind me. I couldn't believe the screaming hadn't started yet. At every second, I expected to hear voices raised in urgent command, clattering feet, slamming doors. I had to go. Rain or no rain, I had to go now. Running would attract attention. Even going out in this downpour would attract attention, but I had no choice. The alarm could be raised any minute now and I must not be trapped here.

Pulling my hood over my head, I eased my way through the waiting crowds in the doorway and stepped outside. I kept to the shelter of the walls and picked my way across slippery paving and around piles of horse dung. Keeping a horse between me and the only guard I could see, I hurried away.

The first thing that happened was that I went blind. Even in Whitechapel they had streetlights. Obviously here they didn't, but there were usually flaming torches or lanterns outside the more important houses, or light spilling from windows and open doorways. Or failing any of that, moonlight. But not tonight. Tonight, because I needed to move quickly and quietly, the universe had decreed absolute bloody darkness. If I'd been able to get my hand out from under my cloak, I wouldn't have been able to see it in front of my face.

The second thing that happened was that I fell over. I didn't trip – I slid. My stupid little indoor slippers had no grip whatsoever, and I went down with a crash, straight down on my left knee. Hot pain jolted through my leg as I somehow pulled myself upright, getting yards of wet velvet twisted around me and threatening to trip me up again.

So, there I was, two minutes outside the palace, and I'd travelled about six feet. At this rate, it was going to take me about two and a half years to get to Canongate.

And I was deaf. I couldn't hear a thing over the sound of rain drumming on my hood, splashing off the rooftops and gurgling its way down the street. A whole army could come up behind me at any time and I wouldn't know a thing about it. And if I turned my head to check behind me, the hood stayed pointing forwards and all I got was a face full of cloth. With regret, I pushed it back on my shoulders. The rain streamed down my face and stung my eyes. I could drown any minute.

More carefully now, I began to inch my way forwards. Inching was all I could do. My heavy skirts were soaking up the rainfall running down the street. My feet in their stupid, sodden, well-named slippers were frozen, and I could feel every single rough stone through their thin soles. I stretched one hand in front of me, both to avoid walking into walls and to break my fall if I went down again. I could deal with a sprained wrist but a damaged ankle would be fatal. I took half a dozen steps forward, checked over my shoulder, half a dozen more and check again. Don't panic. Keep calm and carry on. Just keep going. Don't stop. Don't think about what's going on behind you. Don't waste time imagining the worst. Keep moving.

I used my free hand to bunch up my skirts, which were heavy and wet and wanted nothing more than to wrap themselves around my legs. Every few steps I had to let go, wipe the water from my eyes, push my hair back, pick up my skirts again, take another half dozen steps, check behind me, and just keep bloody going.

I had no idea how far I'd gone. I suspected about twenty feet. And all my attention, which should have been on finding my way forwards was behind me, waiting for the inevitable hand on my shoulder. I pictured being dragged back before a queen who would want every last ounce of revenge. Who could blame her?

And what of the others? If they left me here, they stood a fair chance of getting out of the city and away. They needed to get out before the gates, or Ports as they were known, were closed. And the pods were outside the city gates.

I was lifting my com to tell them to get away, that I'd join them later when I slipped again. Same bloody knee, obviously. I was sitting in the rain, tangled in skirts, cloak, petticoats and cursing buckets when I saw the light coming up behind me. Coming fast.

Shit, shit, shit.

I scrambled up and took two long steps to the left, bumping into something hard. A wall. I pulled my hood over my face and crouched painfully, hoping if I was below their eye-line they'd miss me.

They did. They weren't soldiers, but three young nobles, come from God knows where, on their way to God knows where, and concerned only to get themselves there as quickly as possible. Two of them held lanterns in the shelter of their cloaks, and alternately laughing and cursing, they splashed their way down the middle of the street.

As soon as they passed me, I stood up and began to follow them. The light was dim and mostly ahead of them, but, after the pitch-blackness I'd been groping my way through, it seemed like a sound and light show to me. Best of all, I thought I knew where I was. If I carried on down here, then I would come out near Canongate and there were any number of alleys and snickets I could hide in when the alarm was raised. As it would be. I couldn't believe I'd come this far without hearing the sounds of pursuit behind me. Maybe I would make it after all. Maybe History would nod again and get me home, safe and sound.

Fat chance! The young men, suitably attired for the prevailing weather conditions, moved much more quickly than I ever could. They reached a corner and disappeared. I was back in the dark. And still the rain came down.

A soft voice spoke in my ear. Farrell.

'Where are you?'

'Never mind that for the moment. Did you get Ronan? Are you all out of the house?

'No. And yes. Markham, Schiller, Weller, and Randall have already jumped. Peterson's with Number Five, waiting for me. I'm waiting for you. Where are you?'

'What about Guthrie?'

A pause.

I said more urgently, 'What about Guthrie?'

'He hasn't come back and I can't raise him.'

My heart slid sideways. He was dead. And that bastard Ronan was still out there.

I could hear the strain in his voice.

'Where the hell are you? Tell me.'

'Not sure. Somewhere between the palace and the house.'

'I'm coming.'

'No. You can't see your hand in front of your face here. There are soldiers after me and I've hurt my knee again.'

'No, *you* can't see your hand in front of your face. I've got a Maglite.'

Well, he just bloody would have, wouldn't he?

'Get under cover and wait for me, Max.'

'I'm not leaving without Guthrie.'

'Neither am I, but we'll get you first. Just stay there. Don't move. I'm on my way. Two minutes.'

It was considerably longer than two minutes, but eventually I saw a gleam of light. With huge relief, I stepped out of a sheltering doorway and walked straight into the arms of Clive Ronan.

I swear – if I bumped into one more person that day, I would have screamed.

Both of us were taken aback, but I had the advantage. I knew who he was and, in the dark, he didn't have a clue about me.

We'd done it! We'd got the queen and Bothwell together, and now, here was Ronan. Right in front of me. Mission accomplished.

If I could just hold on to him for a minute or so – that's all it would take. Leon was on his way. I hoped.

I threw myself at him. He slipped on the wet cobbles and we both went down hard. He cursed and thrashed around. He was on the bottom, smothered in wet velvet and brocade. His lantern had smashed as he fell and we were grappling in the darkness. I struggled to get an arm free and pull out a hairpin. Still my weapon of choice in any century.

We rolled around blindly in the dark. At any moment, I expected to feel the bright, sharp pain of his dagger between my ribs, but I wasn't going to let go.

He tore himself away and scrambled to his feet. Desperate, I grabbed a leg, hung on with both arms, and bit the inside of his thigh as hard as I could. He yelled – a sound abruptly cut off when Farrell clouted him with his Maglite.

He reeled away. Still on the ground, I lunged for him and Leon, attempting something similar, fell over me. We both went down again and Ronan disappeared into the rain and dark.

'Don't let him get away,' I shouted, flailing wildly amongst yards of sodden velvet.

He pulled me to my feet. Somewhere behind us, I could hear

bolts being pulled back as a concerned citizen grappled to get his door open and discover what all the noise was about.

He pulled me away. 'Come on, before someone sticks their head out and sees us. Did you see which direction he came from?'

'Yes, down here.' I pointed to a patch of even deeper darkness. He shone his torch down a narrow alley.

'Which knee?'

'The left one again,' I said with resignation.

He stood on my left side, put his arm around my waist and took some of my weight on his hip. Now that I was safe – relatively – my concerns were all for Ian Guthrie, who had gone alone into this maze of dark alleyways. Not a wise move. I feared for him.

At this range, we could use the tag reader. Even so, it seemed to take for ever to find him. There were any number of dark places where he could be and we searched them all. Eventually, we found him in an alley, propped limply against a barrel. My heart lurched with fear. Farrell bent over him. Blood ran from a seriously bad gash above his eye, mixing with the rain streaming down his face. I exhaled with huge relief. Dead people don't bleed. His eyelids flickered in the torchlight. He was conscious. Dazed but conscious.

We liberated a handcart we found backed against a wall and bundled him into it. Farrell pulled and I pushed, casting anxious glances over my shoulder. By my reckoning, about an hour had passed. More than enough time for soldiers to be combing the streets and alleyways, weather or no weather. They would surely have gone straight to the house in Canongate and have sealed off the Ports – the gates – as well.

We saw no one.

The torrent had ceased and the rain was now merely heavy. There was no sound apart from the ceaseless drumming and splashing of water. No sound of running, no shouting, no lights, no commotion as a peaceful city was roused in the search for someone with whom the queen would surely want a very nasty word. I limped along and thought through the possibilities.

278

The first was that the alarm had been raised, but the queen had ordered no further action. Bothwell might or might not have been arrested, but no other culprit had been identified.

The second was that the alarm had been raised, but members of her court, scenting an opportunity, had ordered a cover-up. To safeguard the reputation of the queen they would say, but this night power would pass from her to them and henceforth she would be queen in name only. Again, Bothwell might or might not have been arrested.

The third was that the alarm had been raised and a methodical search was taking place for our party and would descend on us at any minute. A possibility that seemed less likely with every passing minute.

The fourth was that no alarm had been raised at all. She hadn't done so in the original timeline – whether from shame or because he'd been monumentally a good shag was unclear. Dr Bairstow had once said to me, '*History is lazy. History suffers from inertia.*' Suppose History now was influencing events to restore the timeline to as close to its original course as possible. Mary would not denounce him, but go on to marry him, lose her kingdom, and then her life just as she was supposed to do. As Darth Vader would have said, '*It is her destiny.*'

Which could mean we were hurtling to hell in a handcart with unnecessary haste.

'Slow down,' I said to Leon. 'I don't think they're coming.'

He stopped and got his breath back.

Guthrie sat up and was spectacularly sick.

We trudged on in silence.

Unexpectedly, Farrell said, 'Did you … *bite* him?'

I grinned in the dark. I might not have been allowed to do him any serious injury, but he'd carry that mark with him to the end of his days.

Guthrie heaved again and Farrell said, 'Over the other side this time, Ian. The last lot went all over my boots.'

We approached the Port with caution. Not surprisingly, given the amount of rain falling, no one was in sight. That didn't mean there was no one there.

'Hold on,' said Farrell. 'Guard ahead.'

I tensed. Maybe the palace had sent out messengers who had somehow slipped past us in the night and were, even now, waiting for us in the dark shadows.

Wrong. A stout guard met us, wiping foam from his beard. I thought of Falstaff.

He was suspicious. Of course he was. He lived in his own small world and knew nothing of courtiers and queens and palaces, but he knew a suspicious bunch of reprobates when he saw them. Richly dressed nobles would never be out on a night like this. A woman doubly so. Richly dressed nobles, soaked to the skin, dishevelled, dirty, bleeding, one of them in a handcart – this was well above his pay grade and there was no chance he was going to let us through. And for us any delay could be fatal.

He shifted his weight, prior to turning his head and shouting for reinforcements. This was very, very bad.

We're really not supposed to injure contemporaries. It's a kind of prime directive. Whatever the risk to ourselves – we're supposed to get by on cunning, running, and balls of steel. For me, it's more of a prime suggestion. So far this year, I'd beheaded Jack the Ripper, killed Isabella Barclay, presided over an execution, and stood by while Guthrie and Markham took out four of Nineveh's finest. And I'd bitten Clive Ronan, as well. I'd bloody well had enough.

I reached over, seized Guthrie's stun gun from under his cloak and zapped the fat bastard.

Sorted.

No one said a word.

We were out of the gate and away.

I heard Peterson's voice in my ear; his restraint only emphasised his anxiety.

'What is going on? Where the hell are you?'

'On our way,' puffed Farrell.

We were heading uphill, the ground was wet and slippery,

and my feet were numb with cold.

'Can you show a light?'

We stared into the darkness. Above us and to the right, a light flashed three times and then shone a steady beam through the rain.

'It'll be quicker now without the cart,' he said. 'Guthrie, can you walk?'

'No idea.'

'Lean on me. Max, can you walk?'

'Probably. Can I lean on you, too?'

He sighed. 'Once again, the technical section is the last man standing.'

Guthrie said groggily, 'Doesn't the technical section just piss you off?'

'Tell me about it.'

Leon took Guthrie and I took the torch. We stumbled through the dark, tripping and cursing. I made us stop occasionally to listen, but there was nothing and no one behind us. No one had raised the alarm. If they'd found the gate guard they'd assume he'd drunk too much or he'd had a funny turn. I suspected he'd come round, picked himself up, and gone inside for something to calm his nerves.

The tension eased. Even the rain was slowing.

'So,' said Leon, 'tell me what happened. How did you manage it in the end?'

I told him what I'd done. It was easier in the dark where I couldn't see his face. I tried to keep it detached and business-like, but he must have heard something in my voice.

We trudged on a few paces and then he said, 'You're cold and wet. It's been a tough assignment. But, for us, it all happened hundreds of years ago. What you did was meant to happen. She could have screamed for help. She could have denounced him. She didn't. Not originally and not on this night, either. I understand how you feel – she might have gone on to be a remarkable woman. But she made bad decisions and she had to live with them. And remember – she was no innocent.

She was almost certainly implicated in the murder of her husband. And the poor wretches who died with him.'

I couldn't see his face, but he'd flirted with her, charmed her, and gazed into her eyes …

'What about you? If you'd played your cards right, we could have been calling you King Leon by now.'

'I've found my queen.'

He waited for me to say, 'Hey, you're not talking to some daft Scottish bint now, you know,' but, for some reason, I didn't. I was tired, depressed, and not very proud of myself. I just wanted to sit somewhere and think about what I'd done.

We trudged a little further.

'I was wondering,' he said slowly, 'if perhaps you would like to go somewhere for dinner. Tomorrow night. Like normal people do.'

I was roused from my little pit of self-pity. 'You're asking me out on a date? Now?'

'No, of course not now. Tomorrow night. If you're free, of course.'

Of course I was free. I was always bloody free.

I leaned around Guthrie. 'I'll have to check, but I think I am.'

'Good. I'll ring Joe Nelson and book a table.'

'The Falconberg Arms? In the village?'

'Well, no choice, really.'

'What?'

'No car,' he said briefly.

I stopped dead.

They carried on for two or three steps before he realised he'd left me behind. Guthrie stared blearily from me to him and back again.

I was all set to have it out there and then and sod all the queen's horses and all the queen's men.

'I don't believe you. We're fleeing for our lives in the rain-swept gloom of 16th-century Scotland and you're still banging on about your bloody stupid bloody car?'

'Seriously?' he said. 'You think I'm not going to be

referring to it at regular intervals for the rest of your life? That I'm not going to drag it into every argument we ever have? That I'm ever going to let you forget? There will be 'Driving The Car Into The Lake' anniversaries. I shall commission a special card from Hallmark. There will be celebration cakes. We may even get a telegram from the King.'

He paused. 'Well?'

'Seriously? I said. 'You think where the car leads the owner can't follow? Let's see Dieter winch *you* out of the lake every Friday.'

'OK. Better now?'

'I think so.'

'Come on, then.'

I thought I could hear Guthrie laughing.

We headed for the light, finally tumbling soaked, cold, and exhausted into the pod.

Peterson was waiting for us. I could tell by the way he was complaining about the mess we were making that he had been anxious. Guthrie and I sank to the floor. Pools of water gathered around us.

I said, 'Report.'

'Everyone else has jumped. I've done the FOD plod. Rigorously, before you ask.'

The FOD plod – Foreign Object Drop – was our check we hadn't inadvertently brought anything contemporary into the pod.

He passed me a towel. 'What about Ronan?'

I groaned with frustration. 'We had him and he got away. Again. Every time. Bastard!'

'What happened about the queen? I gather you saw her?'

'I left her and Bothwell together.' No need to say any more. 'Let's go home.'

The world went white and there was a slight bump. That's Peterson. He always bumps on landing.

He activated the decon lamp and we waited for the blue glow.

'Leave your stuff,' he said. 'We can collect it later.'

I said, anxiously, 'Can you see Number Five?'

'Yes, I can see it from here. They're waiting for us. We're all back safe and sound.'

We always wait for each other. I insist on it. We always finish a mission together.

We stepped outside to cheers and applause. We were home. I could smell dust, hot electrics, and pods. Something warmed inside me. I looked up at Dr Bairstow, waiting alone on the gantry, smiled and nodded. He nodded slightly, twitched something that might have been a congratulatory smile – or not – and limped away.

I turned my attention to the rest of my team.

'So,' said Schiller, impatiently. 'Were we successful?'

'Are you kidding?' I said. 'We were bloody amazing!'

Helen and her team appeared, impatient and irritable at our non-arrival in Sick Bay.

Nurse Hunter expertly intercepted Markham, who was trying to slope off to the bar.

'Why?' he was saying, plaintively. 'Do you know how awful 16th-century beer is? I need something to take the taste away.'

She put her hands on her hips in mock horror.

'You've been drinking the beer?'

'Well … yes.'

'You idiot!'

'What?' He was dumfounded. 'Why?'

'Have you any idea what lived in 16th-century water?'

'None at all,' he said proudly. 'But a couple of modern beers will soon see it off.'

'You wish! You've almost certainly picked up a dose of worms and 16th-century tapeworms are the worst. Left untreated, they lodge in your intestines, where it's warm and wet – and I should imagine yours are warmer and wetter than most – and they just grow and grow. Finally, when they're so big there's no more room, they start to work their way up your gullet. Not overnight, obviously, but, one day, you'll be talking to someone and you'll feel the worm's head, nodding away at

284

the back of your throat.

Markham paled.

'And by then it's far, far too late,' she continued, remorselessly, 'because anything strong enough to kill a thirty-foot worm isn't going to do you any good, either.'

Everyone else stepped back from him.

'What about the other end?' Dieter asked the question to which no one else wanted to know the answer. 'The tail. Where does that appear?'

'Well, guess.'

'I need a drink,' said Markham, desperately.

'Sorry. Beer is the very worst thing you can drink when you've got a tapeworm. They just love the yeast. Doubles their size overnight. Definitely no beer for at least six months.'

She grinned; blonde, fluffy, and evil. 'You've gone a really funny colour.'

'I feel terrible,' he said plaintively.

'You poor, poor boy. Would you like to lean on me?'

'If that's all right with you,' he said, bravely.

'Well, it's not. Get your arse up those stairs. Now.'

Guthrie uncrossed his eyes and focused on Helen.

'Would it be possible to dissolve Mr Markham and keep the worm?'

She snorted and he was whisked away. The others trailed off behind them.

Which left Leon and me.

'So,' he said, brightly, as I limped down the hangar. 'When would you like to tell me about you and the Earl of Bothwell?'

Epilogue

I got over it, of course. We always do. But sometimes the shadows linger on.

I spent a day in the library, following the history of events after our intervention. Mary Stuart went on to marry Bothwell and spent the rest of her life in tears and regret, exiled from her own land and imprisoned in England. I never called her The Tartan Trollop again.

Bothwell fled to Denmark and spent ten years chained to a pillar, unable to stand upright. He died insane. I try not to think of his green eyes and careless charm.

Elizabeth Tudor was saved and went on to have the entire age named after her.

James VI became James I.

Everything was exactly as it should be.

And at the end of the day, Leon was right. It all happened hundreds of years ago.

I nagged and scolded until I had everyone's reports, wrote my own, signed and initialled everything in sight, and took it all off to the Boss, who congratulated me on a job well done. I thanked him politely.

We sat in silence for a while and then he said, 'It had to be done. And you were the one to do it.'

'I know.'

'No one said it would be easy.'

'I know.' I tried to smile. 'It's been a rough year.'

'And it's not going to get any better. I'm sorry if you and

your department were expecting an easy time for a while because that's not going to happen.' He passed me a file. 'Read through this please, and talk to your people. I'd like a preliminary mission plan by next Wednesday.'

I was a little hurt. He was tough, but it wasn't like him to be insensitive. A few days to let events settle in our heads would not have been unreasonable. I took the file, sat back, and glanced at the first page. I read the brief and looked at his expressionless face.

'Well, can you do it? Or shall I give it to someone else?'

'Over your dead body, sir.'

He's not big on facial expressions, but at that moment he looked like a cat who had not only got at the cream, but knew how to open the fridge. And who had possibly just invested in his first dairy herd as well.

'You'd better get on with it, then.'

I got up quietly, left his office, smiled politely at Mrs Partridge, strolled slowly along the corridor, round the gallery and down the stairs to the half-landing. Down in the hall, a bunch of tea-sodden disaster-magnets shouted, argued, and gesticulated. The History Department at work.

Eventually, they noticed me and silence fell. I kept my face quite expressionless.

'OK, you lot. Strike the Mary Stuart material and start packing it away. I want this room cleared and ready for our next assignment by the end of today, please. Get the Archive staff in here to advise on what to keep.

'Miss Lee, please set up a meeting for two o'clock this afternoon, in my office with all senior history personnel, together with Chief Farrell and Major Guthrie, if they're free.

'Dr Dowson, here's a list of information I need from you as soon as possible, please.

'All of you to clear your diaries for at least the next fortnight.

'Dr Peterson, could I see you in my office at your earliest convenience?

'Miss Lee, please telephone Dr Black at Thirsk and ask her

to contact me when she has a moment.

'Tomorrow morning, first thing, we start our new assignment. Thank you, everyone.'

I never thought they'd let me get away with it, but it was worth a try.

'We have a new assignment? Already? That was quick. I thought we'd get a bit of time off, at least.'

There was muttering. I let them mutter. I knew what our new assignment was. Gradually, silence fell. I let it settle. Tim got it first, but he knew me very well.

'You're kidding!'

'Nope!'

'How did you wangle that?'

'Wangle what?' demanded Van Owen. 'What's going on?'

I grinned at her.

'Come along, Miss Van Owen, think for a minute.'

They all just stared at me. It was a wonderful moment.

I held up the file. As I once said to Dr Bairstow – deep down, very deep down, I was having a shit-hot party.

'Ladies and gentlemen, we're going to Troy.'

THE END

The story goes on in *A Second Chance ...*

The Chronicles of St Mary's
by
Jodi Taylor

St Mary's is back and nothing is going right for Max.

Once again, it's just one damned thing after another.

The action jumps from an encounter with a mirror-stealing Isaac Newton to the bloody battlefield at Agincourt.
Discover how a simple fact-finding assignment to witness the ancient and murderous cheese-rolling ceremony in Gloucester can result in CBC – concussion by cheese. The long awaited jump to Bronze Age Troy ends in personal catastrophe for Max and just when it seems things couldn't get any worse – it's back to the Cretaceous Period again to confront an old enemy who has nothing to lose.
So, make the tea, grab the chocolate biscuits, settle back and discover exactly why the entire history department has painted itself blue ...

A seasonal short story

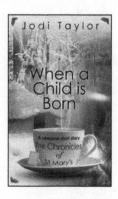

It's Christmas Day 1066 and a team from St Mary's is going to witness the coronation of William the Conqueror.

Or so they think.

However, History seems to have different plans for them and when Max finds herself delivering a child in a peasant's hut, she can't help wondering what History is up to.

The Chronicles of St. Mary's Series
by Jodi Taylor

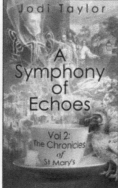

For more information about **Jodi Taylor**
and other **Accent Press** titles
please visit

www.accentpress.co.uk